DREAM FEVER

"I feel very odd."

"Odd?" He swallowed. "How so?"

"Breathless. M'skin burns. M'heart is poundin' double-time." She searched for his hand and placed it just beneath her breast so that his thumb brushed the soft, firm fullness. "Oh, Nicholas." She sighed. "I like that."

"Do you?" His voice sounded tight and dry to his own ears.

"I've been trying to sleep, and all I can think about was how I felt when y'touched me."

"And how was that, Irish?"

"Like butter in the sun." Her face neared his, her lips but a breath from his. If she kissed him he would shatter. "I want to be yer wife in every way."

"Katherine Sutcliffe is one of the most powerful voices in the romance genre."

Kathe Robin,
Romantic Times

Katherine Sutcliffe

Dream Fever

AVON BOOKS ◆ NEW YORK

AVON BOOKS
A division of
The Hearst Corporation
1350 Avenue of the Americas
New York, New York 10019

Copyright © 1991 by Katherine Sutcliffe
Cover illustration by Victor Gadino
Inside cover author photograph by Debra Shore
Published by arrangement with the author

This book is dedicated to

Nashville, Tennessee
The home of hospitality

And to several special friends there:

Joyce Jackson

Ruby Taylor

Lloyd Lindroth
(Whose harp music is heavenly!)

Bob "Robbi" Robison

And to my friend:

Guy Davis
(Who opened the door and let the rabbit out)

A special thank you to:

Tom Drum, Tom Thurman, Carol Bryan of
Handleman Books

When I was a little boy, they called me a liar, but now that I'm grown up, they call me a writer.

—*Isaac Bashevis Singer*

I Do Not Love Thee

I do not love thee!—no! I do not love thee!
And yet when thou art absent I am sad:
And envy even the bright blue sky above thee,
Whose quiet stars may see thee and be glad.

I do not love thee!—yet, I know not why,
Whate'er thou doest seems still well done, to me;
And often in my solitude I sigh
That those I do love are not more like thee!

I do not love thee!—yet, when thou art gone,
I hate the sound (though those who speak be dear)
Which breaks the lingering echo of the tone
Thy voice of music leaves upon my ear.

I do not love thee!—yet thy speaking eyes,
With their deep, bright, and most expressive blue,
Between me and the midnight heaven arise,
Oftener than any eyes I ever knew.

I know I do not love thee! yet, alas!
Others will scarcely trust my candid heart;
And oft I catch them smiling as they pass,
Because they see me gazing where thou art.

—Caroline Norton

Prologue

London, England
October 1861

"Dueling is a hanging offense. For the love of God, Nicholas, what can you be thinking?"

"Get out of my way." Nicholas Sabre snarled at his older brother. "Why don't you run home to Papa and tattle? I'm sure you're fairly champing at the bit to do so."

Christopher Sabre shook his head, yet stood toe to toe with Nick, refusing to budge. "She's not worth it, I tell you. The girl was using you—"

Nick twisted his hands into Christopher's coat. "I'll kill you too if you say one more disparaging word about her."

"My God." Christopher peeled Nick's fingers from his jacket. "I can't help you any longer, Nick. I've done all I can. Father and I both have. He's continued to look the other way while you seduced half the women in Europe, and he's paid your gambling debts to the point of bankruptcy. But he cannot sanction this murder. He's ordered me to tell you that if you go through with this fiasco he'll wash his hands of you. You'll be disinherited."

"How many times have I heard that?"

"He means it this time."

"He meant it last time, and the time before that." Nick glanced toward the cluster of men in the distance. Fog swirled around them as they awaited the song of the lark that would herald the morning. Their faces looked white and serious.

Christopher moved up behind him. "Listen to me. I understand why you're doing this, Nick, and it has nothing to do with the feelings you may or may not have for Jocelyn Laraine. When in hell are you going to stop trying to make the world pay for its ridiculous injustices?"

"You sound more like the noble Earl of Chesterfield every day."

"He hasn't been a bad father, Nick."

Nick threw back his dark head and laughed, a bitter, ugly sound that rang like eerie bells in the silence.

Christopher stepped before him again, blocking his view of the man he would duel in the next moments. "Why are you doing this?" he demanded of his brother. "Tell me, damn you. What makes this girl any worthier than any of the others you've used then thumbed your nose at the last years?"

"She's not like those others."

"She's bewitched you! Why can't you see that? Beneath those innocent eyes and that guileless smile she has the heart of a viper. A stunningly beautiful viper, but a viper nevertheless. She's used you to make Lord Price jealous, and nothing more."

"You're a goddamn liar," he said coldly.

"I wish I were. I wish to our heavenly God that I could stand here and applaud your chivalry, Nick;

I would if I thought you were right about the girl; by gosh, I would defend you to the end in court. Father and I would like nothing more than to see you settled and happy for the first time in your life. I know what it's been like for you, watching our parents' disgraceful philanderings when you were young, then having Mama desert us the way she did by running off to India with that damned naval officer."

Nick's mouth curved in a chilling smile. "Yes, well. She got what she deserved, didn't she?"

Stunned, Christopher drew back. "How can you say that? She was massacred—"

"Along with her lover."

"Did it ever occur to you that she might have loved the admiral?"

"Lady Chesterfield loved no one but herself, and whoever happened to be her paramour at the time . . . of which there were many, as I recall."

Christopher shook his head. "Papa and I forgave her. Why can't you?"

"Papa didn't just forgive her, Chris. Papa was glad to be rid of her. He had his own liaisons to keep him occupied."

"So to get revenge, you damn and defy the world, make Father's life hell any way you can, drag the Sabre name and reputation through the mire."

"What I do with my life is my business."

"You won't have a life if Price kills you. And believe me, if you're found guilty of murder, you'll hang." As Nick turned away, Christopher put a hand out to stop him. "You were young, Nick, and they hurt you. Mama deserted you when you were impressionable and so you've spent your last years lashing out, hurting others like you were hurt, using women and money and drink to fill the emptiness she left here." He touched his heart. "Don't you think I've felt the anger, the betrayal a thousand times? But what's done is done and it can't be changed. Once I realized that, I could, at last, put the hurt to rest and get on with making a decent, upstanding life for myself."

"Which is exactly what I'm attempting to do now."

"By killing a man because he said he slept with Jocelyn?"

"It's a slanderous lie and I intend to challenge it." Nick yanked his arm free and motioned for his second. The dark of the sky was blurring to gray, and across the clearing Lord Price, eldest son of the Earl of Almsbury, had removed his jacket.

"Nick, are you certain—"

"Yes!" he shouted, whirling to face his brother. "Yes, damn you, I know she's telling me the truth."

"Have you slept with her yourself?"

"Of course not. She's too much the innocent—"

"Then how the hell can you be sure?"

"She swore—"

"Oh, Jesus, Nick." Chris closed his eyes.

"Now who's the cynic?" He shook his head as if to dispell his anger. Placing a hand on Chris's shoulder, he said more softly, "I have to believe. Can't you see that? I've been desperate to find something, someone worth fighting for, and now at last I have. Jocelyn is the only one who can save me from myself, Chris. I need her. I need someone to need me and love me, and—"

"Mr. Sabre!" called a voice. "We're ready to begin the count."

"Nick, I beg you. There's still time to withdraw your challenge!"

Nicholas moved through the mist to stand face to face with Lord Price, who regarded him with a smirk. Once, they had been friends, but that had been years ago, before Nick had turned his back on everyone who had ever meant anything to him and set out to "take vengeance on society," as his father had once described it. Now, as they watched each other's eyes, they remained silent while the seconds and attending physician looked on from a safe distance. After the weapons were offered, then chosen, Price said quietly, "For all your cynicism and callousness, Sabre, you're a fool for an innocent face."

"Backs together, gentlemen."

"It's a shame that either of us has to die over a whore, Nick."

He closed his eyes and felt the sweat roll down his temples.

"Why can't you see that she's used you? She wanted me back, is all."

"On the count of five, gentlemen, turn and fire your weapons."

"Nick, she thought to make me jealous. She thought I'd come running back. But I don't want her. By God, I wasn't even the first to have her."

The count rang out and Nick stepped away, blinking sweat from his eyes. The past twenty-one years of his life tumbled before him, all the years of anger toward his parents who had found more satisfaction in someone's else's bed than in their own—all the lying, cheating, philandering . . . Was it any surprise that he'd become the sort of man he was? How could he have known about love? Trust? Faithfulness? Such things had meant nothing to him, until recently. Until he'd met the demure little creature whose eyes had so enchanted him, whose sweet smiles had melted the ice of his heart and, for the first time, made him believe that "happily ever after" could truly exist. Then the man his peers had nicknamed "Notorious" had walked away from his gaming tables, turned his back on his mistresses, gone down on his knee to a woman and asked for her hand in marriage—because he knew without reserve that he could trust her.

"Five!"

He spun on his heel and fired.

The girl came from nowhere, her white face twisted with despair as she threw herself on Price's prostrate form, her hands trying desperately to stem the flow of blood from his chest. Throwing back her head, she pierced Nick with her eyes as he slowly approached her. "Bastard!" she cried. "You've killed him. You've killed the only man I've ever loved. You should put that gun to my head and pull the trigger. Go on and kill me too, I beg of you!"

He stopped.

"I'm pregnant," she wailed. "Pregnant and you've killed my baby's father!" She leapt to her feet, her bloodied fists raised, and flung herself against him, pummeling his chest while the smell of the perfume he'd given her the night before washed over him in a sickening wave. He didn't move, but stood with his long legs planted firmly apart as she continued to beat him and rake his face and throat with her nails. "How could you think I could really love you? You who reeks of whores, who squanders his father's money on gambling . . . your own mother could find so little to love in you that she fled into the arms of another man!"

He stared down at the broken body on the ground, and cocked the trigger of the gun a second time.

Her voice faded as he raised his sights to take in the stunned and silent spectators who looked comically frozen where they still huddled around the stiffening corpse, their moonlike faces gaping at him.

"Nick!"

He raised the gun.

"Nick! Oh, my God, Nick . . . !"

"Bastard! I hate you. I hate you. How can you think anyone could love you . . ."

He put the gun against his temple.

A weight hit him from behind with a horrible force, pitching him forward so he stumbled and fell, slowly, slowly, as if time had ground to a stop. He sprawled heavily over the earth, groaning, the gun exploding near his head and the bullet hissing and biting the flesh of his ear. He felt pain, and heat Then his brother was wrenching the gun from his hand and flinging it into the bushes, shouting for someone, anyone, to take the "hysterical bitch" away before he was driven to murder as well.

"The police!" someone shouted. "The police are coming!"

The thud of running footsteps reverberated against the ground where Nick lay with his good ear—the one that didn't feel as if it had been ripped from his head—pressed against the cool wet dirt. Then came the shriek of police whistles, and he heard his brother weep, saying, "Damn. Oh, damn."

Lyttleton, New Zealand
February 1866

The Lyttleton pothouse was cramped and murky, the dark made gloomier by the dense fog of tobacco smoke. The air was hotter than a North Island sulfur spring. If a single burning ash from any of the two dozen cigars in the room fell to the sawdust floor, the place would go up like a keg of dynamite.

Jamie MacFarland, captain and part owner of the sailing vessel *Tasmanian Devil*, raised his pewter tankard of ale. "To all hale and hardy men of Canterbury!"

"Here, here!" the men responded.

"And to our wives—God bless 'em—wherever, *whoever*, they are!"

A deafening cheer rose from the crowd, each man's face radiating his enthusiasm as he quaffed his drink and contemplated the amelioration of his lonely existence on this island, thousands of miles from the nearest civilized country.

"May yer journey be a safe one, Jamie!" a voice called out.

"And productive," another echoed.

"And may yer cargo have tits out to here and fornicate like bloody rabbits!" someone shouted. The men roared their approval; their laughter shook the walls of the smoky hospice, as did the crescendo of foot-stamping and back-slapping that caused many of them to slosh ale over the floor and on their thick-soled boots.

Jamie grinned as he regarded the men standing shoulder to shoulder, big healthy bodies pressing closer to the bar in their eagerness to down one last drink before the proprietor of the Harbor Pothouse ushered them out for the night. These were ordinary farm laborers, carpenters, mechanics, navvies, bush hands, and shepherds. All had fled to New Zealand with the Queen's promise ringing in their ears:

An unending supply of food, land, sunshine—everything a man could ever want, and more.

Aye, there was that, Jamie supposed as he studied the weatherworn faces of his friends. Here in New Zealand, there was the cleanest air, the sweetest honey, the bluest skies, and the lushest grasses he'd ever seen. It was heaven for certain. Only God had forgotten to supply the one essential element men needed to survive: women.

Any woman would do. Fat. Thin. Ugly. Lovely. As long as she spoke—not necessarily English—and had no aversion to a lusty tumble two or three times a day, she'd do. Not that there weren't *any* women on the South Island. But those few were married. If they weren't already wed when they'd arrived, they were soon after. Even the scurviest females from London were snatched up in New Zealand faster than they could set foot on the fertile soil. It was a sorry state of affairs when a man couldn't get himself serviced by some buxom wench with a mind toward copping an extra penny by a poke out back of the pub.

A true shame...

But Jamie MacFarland was about to change all that, along with making enough profit to see himself settled once and for all on a section of the Canterbury Plains. In a few months he'd be making his last journey to England, during which he intended to arrange for mail-order brides for himself and the room full of lonesome men. Then he was selling his half of the *Tasmanian Devil* to his partner, buying himself a sheep station, and retiring to the good life.

He threw back his head of coarse red hair and downed the ale. Then his gaze locked on the form near the rear of the room, and his eyebrows went up. "I'll be a ring-tailed wombat," he muttered to himself. "If it ain't the Devil Lord himself."

The Devil Lord, or so the good folk of Christchurch and Lyttleton had nicknamed Nicholas Sabre, sat in the only chair in the tavern, his shaggy, dark head face-down on the table. Jamie wondered how he'd missed seeing him all night, then reconsidered. Sabre had an uncanny way of coming and going so inconspicuously that one rarely noticed. He avoided the company of his peers as one might the plague. Then again, one could hardly call the room full of boisterous roughhousers Sabre's peers. They weren't. Not one man among them could boast of an earl for a father or a lineage that could be traced all the way back to King William of Orange.

Not that Sabre did much boasting himself. Since his arrival in New Zealand five years ago, Nick had made but two friends on the South Island, one a mangy old shepherd named Frank Wells, and the other Ben Beaconsfield, the sheep farmer who had hired Sabre soon after his arrival in Christchurch.

It had been Jamie's own *Tasmanian Devil* that had transported Sabre to England's colony. Jamie himself had inspected the papers accompanying his handcuffed passenger, and had watched solemnly as the police had escorted Sabre to his cabin where he had stayed until the ship was at sea. Now, not for the first time Jamie wondered: If Sabre could choose his punishment all over again, would he opt for deportation to this lonely edge of the world, or would he gladly accept the sentence of ten years in Newgate Prison?

Jamie and the other inhabitants of Christchurch and Lyttleton had often conjectured on the nature of Sabre's crime, drawing only one conclusion. For a man of Sabre's importance to be chained and escorted out of the country with no more fanfare than a hardened criminal would receive meant only one thing. Murder. It had to be. No doubt it was his illustrious station in life that had kept the noose from his neck.

By God, but Sabre was a dislikable sort: haughty beyond belief, arrogant despite his sorry circumstances, and recklessly handsome. He had the look of the devil about him for sure, and the temper of Satan himself. Those deep black eyes could chill the marrow of your bones. Jamie had felt the coldness himself those years ago, as he and Sabre had stood face to face on the deck of the rocking ship. The set of Sabre's shoulders and jaw, the curve of his mouth, but most of all his eyes had bespoken a pride and sorrow as impenetrable as an iron barricade. Those eyes had held Jamie spellbound. Immense intelligence, colossal fear, monstrous anger had all been swimming in their depths. Few things had so affected Jamie during his life. Even after these many years, the image still haunted him, and he had to wonder how a man's soul could die and his body survive, to walk and talk like a human being while inside he was incinerated by hate.

The men and women of the South Island gave Sabre a wide berth . . . which wasn't difficult. Since purchasing his own sheep station in Malvern Hills two years ago, he rarely showed himself in town. He made a point of avoiding all public functions, and generally sent his old shepherd, Frank, into Christchurch to purchase supplies. His only other companion was his dog—a black-and-white mutt named Betsy who never left Sabre's side.

Jamie strained to see through the smoke. Sure enough, there was the dog, its spotted muzzle resting faithfully on the Devil Lord's black-clad knee.

Jamie elbowed his neighbor and motioned toward the shadowed figure. Little by little the din quieted as each man turned and noted Sabre's presence.

Unlike the others, who wore traditional crimean shirts and brown trousers, Sabre was dressed in the tailored suit coat and pristine white shirt and cravat that attested to his aristocratic background.

"Bloody hell," Jamie said. "You'd think he was on his way to tea with the Queen by the looks of 'im."

Johnnie Goddard—nicknamed "the Weka" because he could warble just like the large, wingless weka bird that roamed over the island—squinted his one good eye and peered through the smoke. "Foxed again by the looks of 'im. Never did know a high-stockin' who could hold 'is ale."

"'Omesick, he is," said Tucker Broombaker, then smirked at Jamie and added, "While yer about fetchin' us wives, Jamie boy, ye ought to pick one up fer 'is lordship there."

"Wot?" The Weka guffawed as his sightless eye rolled up in his head. Swiping a dribble of brew from his chin, he said, "Ain't no woman born dumb or desperate enough to marry the likes o' him. Why, he'd strangle 'er in a fortnight." He affected a shudder, hacked twice, and spat toward a brass cuspidor at his feet.

Jamie narrowed his eyes as Sabre slowly raised his head from the table, spilling hair as dark and thick as Australian coal dust over his suited shoulders. Sabre reached for his tankard and raised it to his mouth, yet his black gaze was locked straight ahead, giving the appearance that he wasn't aware of, or just didn't give a damn that everyone was gaping at him as if he were a rampaging warthog.

Jamie pushed away from the bar and sauntered toward Sabre, his gaze shifting occasionally toward the dog. Everyone had heard the story of how Sabre had sicced the mutt on Sean O'Connell six months back, just because Sean had been stupid enough to butt-kick one of Sabre's ewes that had strayed onto O'Connell land. But it wasn't the dog that made the hair on the back of Jamie's neck stand at attention as he closed the space between himself and Sabre, the surrounding crowd parting like the Red Sea to let him pass. It was the uncanny way the man had of staring into a group of people without seeing them. It was the fists that lay pacifically on the tabletop. There was something about an aristocrat's hands—long-fingered, big but not meaty, as if meant for a life of leisure.

Yet those hands had seen their share of hard work during the last five years. Browned and weathered by the sun, calloused by sheep shears, and scarred from accidents, they contradicted Sabre's heritage. Jamie remembered well that Sabre hadn't filled out his clothes when he'd first met him on board the *Tasmanian Devil*. Now the seams of his coat sleeves were strained to their limit, and the starched collar of his shirt barely met around his neck. The whiteness of his cravat made his face appear all the darker; his hair—worn as long as a Maori's—blew the last illusion of his aristocracy to hell.

One could have heard a twig snap all the way from the Malvern forest, so quiet had the room become by the time Jamie stopped at Sabre's table. "Mr. Sabre." Jamie spoke loudly enough so the onlookers could hear.

The dog raised its head, and Sabre calmly dropped his hand to stroke her, scratching just behind her white ear. Sabre's face was expressionless as he lifted his eyes to Jamie's.

"Might we buy you a drink, sir?" Jamie asked, raising his hand in silent communication to the bartender, who jumped to fill another tankard with ale and hurried it to the table.

There was no response as Sabre finished the last of his drink, nor as the tankard was plunked on the tabletop before him. Everyone pinned their sights on Sabre as they waited, holding their breath, for him to make a move.

He reached for the full tankard, and everyone relaxed, mumbled among themselves, and shuffled in relief, only to fall silent again as Jamie leaned across the table.

"We are sayin', sir, that what you need is a wife."

Sabre closed his eyes and drank again.

Johnnie, having elbowed his way through the on-lookers, goosed Jamie in the ribs. " 'E don't know wot the blazes yer sayin', Jamie, me boy. 'E's soused."

"Gets that way ever' time he comes in," someone added.

"He don't come in often," declared a man with big lips and protuberant eyes.

Frowning, Jamie waved his hand before Sabre's face, his eyebrows going up as the man did little more than blink and then drink again.

"Anyhow," Jamie began with some caution, at the same time reaching into his coat and withdrawing his last proxy contract, "we're all suspectin' that you must get mighty lonely out in them hills." He eased the paper onto the table. A pencil appeared from over his shoulder. Jamie took it and placed it beside the proxy marriage contract before bending nearer Sabre's ear. "If you'll just scribble yer signature on that line, sir, yer troubles will be forever over. Just imagine ... there'll be a lovely little woman waitin' for you ever' evenin' when you come home from the hills ... "

Sabre's dark eyebrows drew together as he stared hard into the tankard at his fingertips. Jamie couldn't surmise whether the Devil Lord was truly hearing anything that he was saying or not, though there was little doubt that something was churning behind those black eyes—something besides anger, for a change.

Jamie pointed one big, roughened finger at the paper, and said, "Right there, guv. Won't cost you a pence for a lifetime of happiness. Yes, sir, this one's on me."

A moment passed. At last, Sabre drew his eyes up to Jamie's. He fixed him with a look that made

Jamie wince as guilt nagged at his conscience and a voice in his head shamed him for the prank. Then he told himself again that he was doing Sabre a favor. Too much solitude wore on a man. This past month a Kutarere schoolteacher had killed himself out of loneliness; that was the main reason why these men, crowding around the table, were more than eager to purchase whatever companionship they could, by whatever means.

"Mr. Sabre," Jamie said, "if you'll just sign there, I'll be leavin' ya to yer ale and yer dog."

Sabre's mouth curled at one end. "Promise?" He slurred it.

There came a murmur in the room. Few men had ever heard Sabre speak. They shuffled back slightly, as if anticipating some physical impact from the deep utterance.

"Aye," Jamie replied, nodding.

At last Sabre clumsily reached for the pencil, swiped at it, missed, then recovered with a haughty lift of one heavy eyebrow and the righting of his shoulders within his worn suit coat. More carefully, he plucked it from the tabletop to regard it with some scorn before putting its crudely sharpened point to the paper. He wrote his name in a flourish, bringing a mutter of approval from the crowd, then he shoved it away and reached for his tankard as Jamie retrieved the marriage contract and studied the signature with a smile.

"Nicholas Winston Sabre, Esquire," he read aloud. Smiling, he folded the document carefully and slid it into his pocket.

Chapter 1

Kenilworth, England
March 1866

"I'm tellin' ya," the stranger, a plump woman with small round eyes was saying, "I worked for the Radcliffes and they was friends with his lordship Pimbersham. That tart who was livin' with Pimbersham these past years weren't 'is wife. She was 'is mistress, no matter wot anyone says to the contrary." The woman sniffed and puffed out her chest in importance. "As if anyone of Lord Pimbersham's station would marry a woman like Glorvina O'Neile. Why, all of London knew her as that *Irish whore*."

As Summer O'Neile stood in the threshold of the merchant's doorway, teeth chattering, body shaking, the cold drove like a lance into her back.

"Poor, lovely Summer," came the words of the village woman near the display case. "Abandoned by her mother."

"Kindhearted Summer... forced to endure the abuse of that awful Martha Haggard all these years

while she waited for her mummy to come back,"
said the grocer's wife. "The delightful child has no
idea that her mother is really Lord Pimbersham's
mistress, and *not* his wife. That whore Glorvina
O'Neile is undeserving of such a loving daughter."

Summer backed out the door, into the bleak evening, her ears still burning with the horrible truths
she had suspected the last years but refused to believe.

Whore!

The implication rocked her—yet, as she stood
there shuddering, anger filled her up so she could
no longer swallow or speak, she knew the gossip
mongers were right. She could continue to deny the
nagging suspicions from now until doomsday, but
the evidence was there. Had always been there, but
she'd been too proud and stubborn to admit it.

Forgetting the cabbage that Martha, her guardian,
had sent her to purchase, she let the coins drop from
her hand and fled into the night, the words still
ringing in her ears.

Once, Summer and her mother had been together
in Ireland. Summer had grown up there, and Glorvina had never kept from her the fact that her father
had been a wonderfully handsome, but footloose
Irish soldier who'd passed through Dublin when
Glorvina was only seventeen. Glorvina had called
Summer her *love child*, making it sound, in those
long ago days, like something special and good. But
when she'd turned eight, her mother had brought
her to Kenilworth and gone on to London alone.

Now Summer could see that there was no other
explanation for Glorvina's absence in Summer's life.
All the excuses her beautiful Irish mother had written over the years seemed lame in light of the harsh
truth. Glorvina had said that she'd married a stern
aristocrat who would be shocked to learn that his

wife had an illegitimate daughter tucked away in the countryside, so she was waiting for just the right moment to tell him.

For Summer, the waiting had been interminable. At first Glorvina's letters had been full of detailed descriptions of her life with the well-respected Lord Pimbersham. Her mother wrote of travels to Europe, and teas with royalty. Summer would sit by her window, and as Martha read her the words, Summer would gaze out on the green countryside and imagine that her auburn-haired, violet-eyed mother must be the grandest lady in all of London; certainly, the most beautiful.

Glorvina had visited on occasion, but not often; their good-byes had become too painful. Eventually, Glorvina stopped coming altogether, and the letters had dwindled. Hope of joining her mother died as the weeks turned to months, the months to years, but still Summer clung to her mother's explanations. When anyone in the village asked about Glorvina, she always managed to regale them with tales of her mother's life, claiming Glorvina was certain to show up at any moment in her grand coach and sweep Summer away to London. How those people must have pitied her!

She stumbled on, disoriented by the dark and the whirling snowflakes. The road dipped downward and was sheltered by an outcropping of limestone that muffled the roar and hiss of the gale so that it sounded like little more than a crooning of the wind in the distant trees. She didn't see the horseman until he was virtually upon her. The great beast loomed at her from the dark, forcing her to throw herself aside, into the mud, or be trampled. The horse whinnied and reared, nearly upsetting its rider. The cloaked man, doing his best to restrain the unnerved animal, turned his hooded head and glared at Summer before bringing his riding crop down with a snap across her face.

"Idiot!" he roared. "What are you trying to do? Kill me?"

Summer scrambled up, numb fingers curled into fists as she glared at the stranger. Then her eye caught the glimmer of the crest on the saddle pouch, and the realization struck her. He was a courier from London. There was only one reason why he would be riding this way, away from Martha Haggard's place. He had delivered a letter from her mother! She ran.

Lights glowed from the windows of Martha's cottage, which stood at the end of a long avenue of elm trees rising out of a garden of dead bracken and rotting flowers. A faint gleam of light showed through the parlor window, and there was Martha, appearing and disappearing behind the parted curtains, occasionally stopping to press her nose to the frosty pane in anticipation of Summer's return. As usual, Summer's stomach twisted with dread at the thought of facing Martha. Suddenly everything came clear to her now. Martha had known the truth all along. The woman had never even tried to conceal her disapproval of Glorvina and Summer; she'd always been full of snide remarks and castigating looks. But apparently, the money Glorvina had paid her had been good—far better than the pittance she received from her midwifery duties, some of it earned by Summer, who'd begun serving as her apprentice when she was twelve. Summer recalled that the last twelve months had seen the cottage re-thatched and the larders supplied to overflowing. Recently Martha had even purchased a new milk cow. All with her mother's blackmail money. Dear God, how much had Glorvina had to pay for Martha's silence?

Anger and pity toward her mother warred in Summer as she trudged forward, her ankles sinking in freezing mud. She shoved open the gate and marched to the house. All the frustration, anger—nay, *fury*—she'd swallowed back over the last years boiled up inside her as she threw open the door and came face to face with her dour guardian.

"There you are," Martha said. "What in God's good graces took you so long, gel?"

" 'Tis a long walk t' the village, ma'am, and in case y' haven't noticed, it's snowin' and sleetin'—"

"Don't get sass-mouthed with me," Martha interrupted, shaking her finger at Summer from her place by the hearth. "And close that door before we freeze."

Summer slammed it, making Martha's eyebrows shoot up.

"Y've heard from m' mother," Summer said, setting her chin and allowing her voice to lapse into its heaviest Irish lilt, knowing how it grated on Martha's nerves. Martha had made no secret of her disdain for the Irish, referring to them as heathens and barbarians, and refused to allow Summer to walk the five miles to the nearest Catholic church.

Martha began to pace, her shoes thumping against the fine Persian rug—another recent purchase, shipped from London. She studied the letter in her hand, occasionally looking up at Summer, her small beady eyes disregarding the muddy mess Summer was dripping on her spotless floor. That alone should have warned Summer that something was amiss.

"Aye, we've received a letter from London," Martha finally replied.

"And has m' mother sent y' more money?" Summer demanded. "Or perhaps she hasn't sent enough? Is that why yer in such a pique?"

Stopping, Martha glared at Summer with all the vehemence she had tried halfheartedly to mask. She raised the letter for Summer to see, knowing full well that Summer couldn't read it, not with any ease at least. Martha had made certain of that; Summer understood now why Martha had refused her all but the most remedial education. The realization that her mother's letters might have divulged more than Martha had ever allowed Summer to know hit her with force.

She grabbed the letter anyway and swiped at the rain on her face, focusing hard to see through the water clinging to her long dark lashes. Her eyes, as violet as her mother's, stared hard at the words before looking back at Martha.

"What does she say this time?" she demanded angrily. "Don't tell me the great Lord Pimbersham has finally married her?"

Martha's dark eyes widened momentarily. Summer couldn't help but note the gleam of spiteful pleasure in them.

"So. You know." Martha smirked and turned back toward the hearth. She stood before it with her palms toward the flames. At last, her head tilted toward Summer, and the eyes that had been full of wicked amusement seconds before, now pierced her with malevolence. "I hadn't received my stipend for keeping you in over two months, so I wrote your mother to impress on her the importance of timely payment. I'm not a wealthy woman, as you are well aware. My midwifery duties don't pay enough to feed one, much less two."

"What's yer point?" Summer demanded.

"She's dead."

Summer didn't breathe as the air trapped inside her swelled to a throbbing pressure in her chest.

"She's dead," Martha repeated, her voice clear

and incisive in the still room, her eyes unblinking. "She killed herself. Apparently her lover—Lord Pimbersham—grew tired of her and tossed her out on the streets. Humph. It was just the place for her, if you ask me. A whore is a whore whether she's working the streets or being kept like a queen by the aristocracy. Your mother got what was coming to her. She blew her brains out."

Summer turned away from Martha and stared at the door, vaguely hearing the tap of ice against the window as the sleet fell harder from the night sky. She couldn't think. Her mind felt numb. Martha's voice droned on behind her . . .

Her mother was dead.

Images of Glorvina as Summer last remembered her rose up in her mind's eye. It had been two long years ago, on Summer's fifteenth birthday. How beautiful, yet sad Glorvina had seemed. Gazing into her mother's face had been like peering into a reflecting glass. Glorvina's lush red hair had been the same as hers, curling naturally, riotously around her pale, oval face—only her mother's tresses had been swept up and fixed in a coil with many pearl hairpins, while Summer's had spilled gloriously to her hips. Later she had heard her mother chastising Martha for allowing Summer to wear it in such a fashion. "Summer's a young lady now," Glorvina had told her.

"There's naught of a lady about her," Martha had retorted. "She's wild as the wind, is that one. Besides, if you're so worried of what's to become of her, take her with you back to London, and good riddance."

Summer had prayed—oh, how she'd prayed—for her mummy to do just that. She hadn't, of course. Glorvina had kissed her good-bye, boarded her lover's fancy coach, and returned to London without her.

Now she was dead, and all hope was gone.

Summer understood how her mother must have felt, clinging to the hope that Pimbersham would marry her; it must have been the greatest desire of her life. No doubt the lusty old bastard had strung Glorvina along, making false promises while having no intention of marrying her. He had humiliated her mother. Crushed her. Tossed her out like refuse. *Damned aristocrat.*

Summer went in silence to her room, lying stiffly across the bed and gazing blankly at the ceiling. She was vaguely aware that Martha came and went at her door, her voice fading in and out, like a bad dream. "Orphan . . . Whore's girl . . . Can't expect me to keep you now that there's no money."

Tears leaked from the corners of Summer's eyes.

Only when silence had fallen as softly as shadows in the house did Summer sit up. Perched on the edge of the bed, her feet not quite touching the floor, she stared into the silvered glass over the dresser, touched the angry stripe of the courier's lash on her cheek, then her mouth, red and full, slightly pouting now and without the usual impish upward curl at the corners that belied the sorrow she kept buried in her heart. Sometime during the last months, she had attained womanhood. She had a young woman's height and grace, yet the last vestiges of childhood still showed in the roundness of her high cheeks and the sprinkling of freckles across her nose. She'd hated her freckles when she was younger, yet her mother had only laughed when Summer had tried to scrub them off. "They're fairy kisses," Glorvina had described them in a whisper. "Y've been blessed, me dearest darlin' daughter, by the *daoine sidhe.*"

Blessed by the fairy people? The idea had made Summer laugh.

"Oh, aye," her mummy had insisted, squeezing Summer tightly, their laughter tinkling like music through the flower gardens. They'd stooped beside a bed of foxglove and Glorvina had pretended to search through the fragrant flowers. "The fairies are only a few inches high and have airy, almost transparent bodies so delicately wrought they can dance on a dewdrop without breakin' it," she had explained. "Their garments are as white as snow and shine like silver. Their hats are selected each mornin' from the red flowers of the foxglove."

On her hands and knees, Summer had poked her nose deep into the fragrant tubular blooms on their lofty stalks, certain she had seen one of the gentle people waving up at her from under a silken petal. Her nose dusted with pollen, she had smiled adoringly up at her mother as Glorvina laughed and blew the golden sprinkles away. "Mother Mary and Saint Francis," she'd said, "they've done it again. Kissed ya on the nose!"

"Another freckle?" Summer had squealed in delight, all of a sudden in love with her freckles.

"Two!" Glorvina had informed her. "Imagine bein' kissed by two fairies in one day. Why, it's unheard of. Summer Shannon O'Neile, y'll dance and sing with the *daoine sidhe* for sure now."

"And drink dew ever' mornin' and night?"

"For the rest of yer life, little one. They'll sing y' fairy tunes while y' sleep, and they'll dance on yer bedstead as y' dream. Oh, Summer, if I were only so incredibly lucky..."

The memory faded.

Summer stared down at her shoes, the sudden pain inside her paralyzing in its enormity. Her mother was gone. Forever and ever and ... Without any last good-byes she'd gone away, left her for always; there was no hope now of Glorvina ever coming back. No more strolls through the gardens looking for fairies. No one to hold her and soothe her and make her believe in the *daoine sidhe*. The excruciating agony of it made her eyes fill and her throat constrict in sobs that she tried to silence by covering her mouth with her hands.

At last Summer slid from the bed and retrieved her valise from the wardrobe. There was little to pack: a dress; a pair of mended stockings; a comb and brush; a tintype of her mother in a silver oval frame that she kept on the dresser near the bed, where she was certain to see it every morning when she awakened. Summer touched her finger to Glorvina's likeness, took a shaky breath, then tucked it into the valise. She reached for her cloak.

Martha had turned in for the night. The house was dark and cold and silent as Summer moved down the corridor and out the front door. She didn't look back until the gate swung closed behind her. Shivering, clutching her wrap around her as best she could, she stared briefly at the cottage, vaguely reminiscing on all the wasted years she'd spent there, futilely praying for a reprieve from her unhappiness and isolation. But it was over now. All over.

Richmond, England
August 1866

Summer took the stairs two at a time in her haste to reach the second floor of the manor house. Panic seized her as the clock struck resoundingly four times. Pimbersham would be expecting his tea.

This charade could not continue much longer. She'd taken the position of scullery maid working for Pimbersham out of necessity; it had been the only way to get inside the rambling, musty old house. The only way to get at *him*.

And catching Pimbersham's attention had been incredibly easy. He'd noticed her almost immediately. By the end of her first week he'd cornered her twice, making his snide innuendoes, fondling her: a pinch here, a grope there. She'd smiled her way through each mauling and coyly played the part of loose-moraled dimwit, all the while feeling dirtied and disgusted that her mother had tolerated his touch. Much more than his mere touch.

Why had Glorvina endured it? No riches were worth the price of someone's soul, nor their pride and dignity. But then, that was the way of the damned aristocracy, buying hearts as easily as trinkets, and discarding them when someone better came along. She'd seen it all in the last six months, had watched Pimbersham and his friends playing at being human, but falling far short of the mark.

Thoughts of revenge had rioted in her mind since her arrival at Pimbsbury Hall, the need growing stronger when she learned that Pimbersham had buried her mother in a pauper's grave, without so much as a headstone.

She reached the top of the stairs and caught her breath as she smoothed her starched white apron over her black muslin uniform skirt. Biting her lower lip, she did her best to tuck her burnished curls up under her cap, all the while listening to the silence.

She'd grown wary of the silence. Where there was noise, there were people. Other servants. Some of them friends. They knew Pimbersham and his ways and had recognized, even before Summer had, that the old man had taken a shine to his newest employee. They had also warned her of the dangers of finding herself alone with him, unless, of course, she was agreeable to his advances—which she wasn't.

Fortunately, she'd struck up a friendship with Sophie Fairburn, who, ironically, had been her mother's lady's maid. Sophie was a buxom blonde with a heart as big as all of England. She craved the good life, and was willing to do whatever was necessary to grab her share of it. That meant satisfying Pimbersham when he was so inclined, which was three or four times a week. He was a "randy ol' bugger," as Sophie said.

"But how can y' do it?" Summer had demanded of her friend, knowing full well that the need to understand Sophie's motives was the only way she had of comprehending her mother's reasons for remaining here despite her unhappiness. "Nothin' is worth a person's dignity. No amount o' money, nor a roof over yer head can make up for a woman sellin' her body and soul t' get it. I'd rather rot in a sewer and starve than give an ounce of m' flesh to some . . . *aristocrat!*" She spat the word as if it were something vile on her tongue. "Sophie, how can y' let that old bastard use y' in such a way?"

"Why not?" Sophie had answered, her chin lifted a little too much and her mouth fixed a little too firmly to resemble a real smile. "What else have I got? Besides, it's better'n walkin' the street. If you don't believe me, luvie, take a trot down to the East End o' London. Not that I'm sayin' you should give in to the old buzzard. Fact is, you should stay as far away from him as you can. You're a good girl, and that's a fact; you'll stay that way if I have any say-so about it."

The girl's words had touched Summer, and before she knew it, she'd found herself opening up to Sophie, telling her she was Glorvina's daughter.

The admission had made Sophie laugh gently.

She'd known the truth all along, even though Summer had given her name as Cynthia Riley when she'd first appeared at Pimbsbury Hall. Summer's endless curiosity about her mother had given her away. She learned from Sophie that Glorvina had been snubbed by Pimberton's friends, who'd wanted nothing to do with her. But she'd still been kind and considerate to everyone, even the help, and had devoted many hours to charity work. "She was the best mistress I ever had," Sophie had claimed, reaching out to put a comforting arm around Summer's shoulders.

But now Sophie was leaving. She'd told Summer so three weeks ago, when she'd rushed up the back stairs toward Summer, waving a paper in her hand and dancing on her tiptoes, drawing other servants from their quarters.

"I'm leavin'!" Sophie had cried, then burst into gales of laughter.

Her gaze fixed on Sophie's flushed face, her arms locked around a chamber pot, Summer had demanded, "What are y' sayin'? Yer goin' where? With who?"

"I'm married," she'd whispered for Summer's ears alone. "Can you believe it?"

"T' who?" Summer demanded again, doing her best to keep the rising panic from her voice. "When?"

"An hour ago." Lifting the paper for her to see, Sophie pointed to the impressive-looking signature scrawled over the bottom of the page. "You're lookin' at a sheep farmer's wife. I married me a farmer, sight unseen. A proxy marriage. I'm off to New Zealand in little more'n a fortnight."

"I'm lookin' at a lunatic!" Summer had gasped. "Y' can't go and marry some man y've never even seen. New Zealand! Where the blazin'—"

"Watch your mouth," Sophie scolded.

"He could be a pervert," Summer argued, her eyes round.

"A pervert?" Winking, Sophie had flashed her friend a wicked smile and teased, "Then I'll know just how to handle 'im, won't I, luv?"

"Worse than a pervert," Summer pressed on, following her friend into the nearest room. "There's gotta be somethin' wrong with him. Why else would a farmer from New . . ."

"Zealand. It's somewhere near Australia, I think."

"Why can't he find his own wife?"

"Women are few and far between in New Zealand." Smiling, her blue eyes sparkling, Sophie patted Summer on the cheek. "It's all right, luvie. So what if he is a pervert?"

"It doesn't seem right," Summer insisted. "Marryin' some man and y' don't even know his name."

"Sure I do." Sophie held up the paper. "It says here. I'm Mrs. . . ." She glanced at it again, just to make certain. "Nicholas Winston Sabre, Esquire. Damn me, but that name sounds familiar. Oh, well, never you mind, lass. Pervert or no, I've got me a husband and a home at last. What more could a girl want, I ask you?"

"Married."

"Shhh! I ain't told the old sot yet. Don't intend to till I go. The bloody bastard'll be holdin' back my wage if I ain't careful."

"She's leavin'," Summer had said to herself. She'd followed Sophie down the stairs and out through the kitchen, feeling the future press in on her as the silence drew out between them. She'd looked up to find Sophie smiling at her.

"If you'll take my advice, sweet cheeks, you'll get shut of this rat hole before I go. Don't rightly know if there's anyone else here who'll be willin' to take my place in the old codger's bed. He'll be scratchin' and sniffin' after you once I'm gone, mark my words."

"I—I can't go," Summer had replied with a determined shake of her head. Then Sophie had fixed her with a look so intense and motherly Summer had felt ten years old.

"Look," Sophie had begun. "I don't know why you've come here. Maybe I don't want to know. But I do know one thing." She placed one hand beneath Summer's chin, tipping up her face. "There's no undoin' the past, lass. What's done is done."

Now, as Summer fetched the tea tray and carried it to the salon where, thankfully, Pimbersham was occupied with a visitor, she couldn't help thinking of the great unhappiness her mother had experienced within these forbidding walls. Summer frowned and went back down the corridor, to the servants' quarters near the rear of the house. Her mind was in a quandary. If she was intending to take revenge on Pimbersham, she would be forced to do it soon. Yet even as she paused at the threshold of Sophie's room, she knew that murder wasn't in her.

How could she even have imagined it? Such thoughts had simply been angry, childish fantasies spawned of pain and disappointment. Of disillusionment, and abandonment. Sophie was right. She couldn't bring her mother back. Nor could she right the wrongs Pimbersham had inflicted on a woman who'd desired wealth and the respect of the aristocracy even more than she'd yearned to hold her own child in her arms.

Summer found Sophie huddled over her partially packed valise, weeping softly and dabbing at her eyes with a kerchief. She hurried to her friend, eased onto the bed, and searched the girl's face for the cause of her obvious misery.

"Oh, lud." Sophie wept, shaking her head while her fingers wrung the cloth in her lap. "I've gone and ruined it, lass. I've made a right muck of my life now."

"What's happened?" Summer asked. "Is it Pimbersham? Is he angry b'cause yer leavin'?"

Sophie blew her nose. "I ain't told him yet."

"Then what's—"

"I'm pregnant." Sophie slid from the bed. With her back to Summer, she said, "I just found out. I'm two months along. Oh, lud. Two months gone and I ain't even met my husband."

"What'll y' do?" Summer asked.

Sophie blew her nose again, and, looking at Summer, replied, "I'm gonna make that son of a whore pay for doin' this to me. I swear to God, I'm gonna make him regret the day he was born."

That afternoon Summer was in the upstairs hallway when the sound of raised voices came to her. She concentrated on the rising and falling argument emanating from an open doorway down the corridor. The realization that it was Sophie and Pimbersham made her heart skip a beat.

"Of course it's yours," Sophie cried. "I ain't some trollop, you know. I don't sleep around."

"What do you expect from me?" responded the furious booming voice.

"Money, that's what. If you think I'm gonna raise this kid on Beggar's Street—"

"Preposterous! I have no intention of supporting some illegitimate—"

Summer closed her eyes, the impact of Pimbersham's words a cruel blow, an acid sting that brought hot tears to her eyes. The words blurred together as she imagined her mother standing before the irate lord of the manor admitting that she had an illegitimate child tucked away in some small village far enough from London so as not to cause him any embarrassment.

"You'll support us all right," Sophie declared. "Or you'll regret it. We'll just see what your grand society friends think of what you like to do to young girls—"

The shouting grew louder, then a cry rang out. Her heart pounding, Summer started down the corridor, only to be brought up short as Pimbersham ran from the room to the top of the stairs, where he hesitated, wiping his hand with a bloodstained kerchief. He didn't see her there, frozen in the shadows, thank God. No telling what he might have done.

Then he was down the stairs and Summer was running to find Sophie, terror squeezing her breathless. Why was it so quiet? Where were the other servants?

"Oh!" She sobbed. "Oh, Sophie . . ."

Sophie lay with her head near the fireplace, the bloodied poker thrown to one side. Summer fell on her knees beside her and took her in her arms. The girl's face was pale, but she was alive. She opened her eyes, and, seeing Summer, managed to smile. "The bastard's killed me," she said.

"I'll fetch a doctor—"

"Don't bother, pet. I'm done for. You'd best get shut of this place now, if you know what's good for you. Forget what's happened here—what he did to your poor mummy, and me."

"Don't die," Summer pleaded, holding Sophie tightly. She tried to control her emotions and keep her voice and expression gentle. "Please don't die. Yer all I've got. My only friend in the world."

"Poor Summer," Sophie whispered. "Your mummy loved you so. She did, you know. She told me every day." With great effort, she pressed the paper she held into Summer's hand. "Take it. It's your only way out, lass. Run as fast as you can—to the other side of the world, if you have to. Maybe there you'll find what you're after."

The words spun around and around in Summer's head, grief and confusion dulling them to a low roar. Sophie's eyes were closed now, her face cold. Summer lowered her to the floor, then raised her eyes toward the door.

Pimbersham stood there, filling the threshold with his massive, fleshy body draped in a gold silk dressing gown over a starched white shirt and a pair of black trousers. The absurd idea occurred to her that once, a very long time ago, he might have been handsome. A life of overindulgence had wiped all traces of it from his features.

"Y've killed her," she said with a strange calmness. She didn't feel calm. She wanted to scream and cry. She wanted to run, but her legs felt rusted in place. Still, slowly, she forced herself to stand. Her eyes never left his face. He was smiling. Actually smiling. A knowing smile that turned her blood to ice water.

"Did you think I wouldn't know you?" he asked, his voice a husky whisper. "My God, you are just like your mother. The moment I set eyes on you I knew. That lovely hair. Those soft red lips, made for passion. Made to arouse a man with thoughts of what they could do to him, for him. And that luscious body. My God. So young. So supple. You look just like Glorvina did when I first met her. She was innocent and naive then too. I didn't know about you, but I soon learned. She was stupid enough to think that I wouldn't have her followed when she traveled to Kenilworth. Once, I ventured there myself. I watched you as you played in the garden." His wide mouth turned up in a smile that made her heart stop, and the idea occurred to Summer that he wasn't in the least moved by the fact that he had just killed a woman. "I like young girls," his voice rasped.

Summer backed away. There was blood on Pimbersham's shirtfront. Sophie's blood. Oh, God . . .

"Your mother was once very beautiful. Before her lovely curves went to fat and her sweet disposition turned into a virago's. Before she became a whining shrew, making demands she had no right to make."

Summer glanced toward the door behind him, wondering again where the other servants were.

"You thought to take revenge on me, didn't you?" he continued, coming closer. "You blamed me for your mother's death. She simply didn't understand that a woman like her would never fit in with my circle. They would have made her a laughingstock. I did her a favor by not marrying her, dear Summer."

He came at her so suddenly she had little time to react. She turned and tried to leap away, horrified when she tripped on Sophie's foot. Before she could right herself completely, Pimbersham was barreling toward her again. She managed to slide around him and dive toward the door, only to be brought up abruptly as his fingers clamped around her arm. She cried out, more from alarm than pain, then did her best to squirm from his grasp while her cap tumbled from her head and her hair spilled like dark fire over her shoulders.

He smelled of sweat and sherry. Perspiration beaded over his upper lip and ran in transparent pearls down the sides of his face.

"L-let me go," she cried, clawing at his hands.

"But I can't do that, Summer. Can I? Hold still now. By God, you're fiery. I like that. Yes, oh, yes..."

She struggled again. All the infantile illusions of avenging her mother's misery rose up before her in a bright red cloud of fear. Lunging backward, she broke his hold and ran for the stairs. His footsteps rolled like drums behind her; his breathing resounded in the silent hall like rushes of wind.

Then his hands were twisting into her hair, dragging her back. "Help me!" she screamed, knowing there were servants with their ears pressed against the doors, silenced by their own terror. She drove her hands into his chest. "Bastard!" she hissed. "Pig. Get yer filthy hands *off... of... me!*"

The blood was roaring so deafeningly in her ears she failed to hear someone's shout of warning until it was too late. She threw herself against Pimbersham with all of her strength. His flaccid face resembled pale marble as fear swept through him. His arms flapped ineffectually at his sides, making him look like a great bird that had somehow forgotten how to fly. Then he was gone, tumbling down the immense curving staircase, ungainly limbs cracking and banging against the wall, stairs, and gracefully shaped balusters that did nothing to stop his fall.

He landed in a mangled heap at the bottom. A servant dashed from her hiding place, inspected the shattered body of her employer, then looked up the stairwell, where Summer stood, riveted, her hand pressed to her mouth to staunch the scream she could feel worming its way up her throat.

"Ye've killed 'im," the woman said, her voice an urgent whisper that nonetheless crashed like cymbals against Summer's ears.

"It—it was an accident." The words were dust in her throat.

"It don't matter, lass. Ye've killed him, sure as if ye held a gun to 'is head."

"He killed Sophie. See for yerself!"

"Think the courts are gonna give a rat's ass?" another voice from the shadows said.

"They'll hang you for certain!" still another called out.

As she descended the steps, her eyes fixed on the body sprawled at the bottom, an awful thought came to her. She tried to force it from her mind, certain the observers could read every terrible, shocking emotion on her face: Pimbersham had deserved to die for what he'd done to Glorvina and Sophie and God only knew how many others. At the bottom, she hesitated, her eyes searching for some safe harbor. Then, slowly, she backed toward the door.

She hit the front steps running and didn't stop until she reached the end of the drive, not daring to look back, only scanning the muddied roadway for something, *anything*, to sweep her away from this madness.

A steady drizzle had been falling for the last two days. It clung to her heated flesh and hair and clothes. *Mummy. Oh, Mummy*, she thought. *What do I do now? Where do I go?*

But her mother was gone; she couldn't help her . . .

A coach lumbered out of the mist and fog. Six pounding beasts bore down on her where she stood, shivering with fear and lost in the middle of the road, clutching something to her breast like a lifeline. She couldn't move, just stared at the horses and the man who drove them, whip hissing and cracking the air like lightning. Perhaps, if she closed her eyes and stood very still, they would run her over, put an end to this dreadful misery, this life of certain loneliness. She had never asked to be brought into this hellish world. Why must she endure it?

The driver of the conveyance yanked back on the reins to avoid hitting the misty shape in the roadway, managing to bring the team to a halt just paces away from Summer.

It was the London-bound mail coach. She could see that now.

Blinking rain from her eyes, she called out, "Are y' goin' t' London?"

The driver nodded, spilling runnels of water from the brim of his hat.

She slogged her way to the door of the coach that was opened from the inside by a portly middle-aged man who gazed at her inquisitively as she fell into the seat. As the coach got underway, he smiled and offered his overcoat to warm her.

"Thank y'," she said as he tucked it around her. "Yer very kind, sir."

"Not at all," he replied. "What will you do when you reach London, dear girl? You seem so very sad and . . . lost."

Staring out the window, watching the hills and valleys roll by behind their curtain of rain, Summer thought on her answer. Then her eyes were drawn to her lap, and the paper she clutched in her hand— Sophie's last hope for happiness.

Summer stared a moment at the document with its official-looking seal. Her eyes were drawn to the signatures—two of them—one penned with flourishing swirls and aggressive slashes, the other a scrawl: S. Fairburn. Profession, domestic.

Dare she grab this opportunity to flee the mistakes of her mother's past, and her own? She hadn't any choice in the matter. She'd just murdered an aristocrat. And although she'd been justified, Pimbersham's peers would not see it that way. She would surely hang, or go to prison.

Forcing herself to meet her companion's eyes, Summer relaxed in her seat. "I'm goin' t' New Zealand," she told him softly. "To meet m' husband."

"Indeed. And who might that be, my dear child? You look so very young."

"Sabre." She whispered the name to herself, feeling both thrilled and frightened by the sound of it. "I'm Mrs. Nicholas . . . Winston . . . Sabre. Esquire," she hastened to add, then looked out the window again, repeating the name over and over to herself. "Nicholas Winston Sabre . . . Esquire."

Whoever he is.

Chapter 2

*Lyttleton, New Zealand
January 1867*

Summer sat on a pile of rope that reeked of seaweed and fish, and cursed her stupidity. The clothes she'd purchased in Melbourne were hot and made her skin itch. She swatted at sand flies and watched the other "brides" leave with their new husbands to a chorus of timid giggles and enthusiastic whoops of delight. At last, the entire ship had unloaded its passengers and crew, and still she sat, staring up and down the rickety wooden pier in search of the man called Sabre.

For the last excruciating three and a half months, each time she retched into a bucket as the ship pitched beneath her, she'd tried to picture what Sabre might look like, hoping to all the saints in heaven that life as a sheep farmer's wife would prove to be worth the torture of languishing these many weeks on a rolling ship. The images of Sabre that her dizzy mind had conjured had ranged from tall and blond to squat and bald. Undoubtedly, he smelled of sheep.

Summer sighed, left her perch, and paced, her discomfiture mounting as she studied her surroundings. Lyttleton wasn't much to look at, but the scenery was nice. The lush green of the flatlands was rimmed with snow-topped peaks set against a sky so blue that Summer had to blink before she could take in the vibrancy of it. She'd learned during her journey that ten miles beyond the port town of Lyttleton lay Christchurch, and that colonization of the area had begun but thirty years before. There had been savages living here then, called Maoris. Skirmishes between them and the settlers had resulted in the loss of many lives. The ship's crew had hurried to explain that the Maori were peaceful now and content with the settlers' presence, but Summer didn't like the idea that somewhere out there, among those hills and valleys, was a group of people who had once been angry enough over the violation of their land rights to murder folks with lances.

She stopped at the edge of the pier and gazed out at the bay. "Where the blazes are y', Sabre?" she asked angrily.

The only response came in the squawk of a gull as it streaked toward the water, skimmed the white-tipped waves, and soared again with a thin silver fish gripped in its beak. Several children appeared in the distance, running with baskets in their hands along the surf where the water broke and foamed around their bare ankles and dashed away their footprints. Occasionally, they stopped and plucked shells from the spray. Then, meeting with their heads together, sun dancing off their silken hair, they made a game of comparing their treasures. Soon they were off again, racing with the waves.

Summer watched with envy and appreciation.

She loved children. She worshiped their innocence, their naiveté. She'd begun to lose both at an early age, soon after her mother had left her in Martha Haggard's care.

She turned and discovered a man walking toward her down the pier, a wide-brimmed hat in his hand. His hair was very dark, his strides long. A flush suffused her body, and she wondered if anyone as young as she had ever died of a heart attack, because she was absolutely certain that she was having one now.

He wasn't handsome, exactly. But he wasn't ugly either. A long way from it. The closer he got, the better-looking he became, *and* he was smiling. She was glad now that she'd taken the money that the captain, Jamie MacFarland, had left Sophie in her cabin to purchase a few new clothes. Summer hadn't met the man himself, however. He'd taken a tumble off the mainmast and had broken both legs before her arrival at the ship. So he'd been recuperating in a London hospital when the *Tasmanian Devil* set sail.

She hoped she didn't look too young. Having taken every measure to appear a woman who knew exactly what she was doing, which she didn't, she had purchased a rather drab-colored skirt and a white blouse in Melbourne. She'd also bought a pair of leather shoes with inch-high heels that made her feel far older and more mature. The porkpie hat fixed to her head lent a certain sophistication, the shop owner had assured her.

"Hello!" the man called, waving.

Her stomach tightened, and nervously, she raised her hand. "Hello!"

"Missus Fairburn Sabre?"

She swallowed and cursed the blush that rose in her cheeks. Her heart thumped with expectation and guilt as the circumstances pressed in on her.

"Y-yes," she replied, positive she could feel the word *liar* branded across her forehead.

At last the man reached her and extended his hand, his smile growing as his dark green eyes assessed her. "Faith and begolin'," his deep voice boomed. " 'Tis a true pleasure t' be makin' yer acquaintance."

"Yer Irish!" She blurted it, making his black eyebrows rise as he detected her accent. Then before he could mutter another word, she cried, "Just imagine! I've traveled halfway 'round the world, anticipatin' marriage t' some awful ogre, but instead o' some ogre who's squat and bald, m' husband is Irish. *Irish!* Merciful heavens, but the *daoine sidhe* must surely be dancin' on m' shoulders this very moment. They've brought me good luck for certain—"

"Lass. Lass!" he interrupted as Summer stepped back and inspected him thoroughly, shaking her head in disbelief.

" 'Tis a true miracle, Mr. Sabre. That it is. Y' can't deny it. A match made in—"

"I'm not Sabre," he said, his voice raised to be heard.

Summer froze. Her heart sank like a stone to the bottom of her stomach. "N-not Sabre?" she asked in a dry voice.

He looked somewhat chagrined, and definitely embarrassed as he shook his head no.

"Oh."

"The name's O'Connell. Sean O'Connell. I just learned from the other passengers that you were stranded here."

Summer straightened up her spine, her eyes never leaving O'Connell's.

"I doubt that Sabre will be here," he admitted.

"Why?"

He looked perplexed as he considered his response. At last, he slapped his hat on his head.

"He's not dead . . . ?" Summer demanded. What would that make her, exactly? A widow? Not even that, she decided. They weren't married, she reminded herself. Not really.

"We should be so fortunate," Sean replied, more to himself than to her. Then, taking a breath, he said, "He lives out in the hills." He pointed his thumb over his shoulder. "He won't know about y'. What I mean is . . . he wouldn't have heard that the *Devil* is anchored. Sabre doesn't come t' the plains often, y' see, and no one ventures t' his station more'n necessary . . . I wouldn't be here m'self, y' understand, but I was on m' way for supplies when I noticed the ship."

Disheartened, Summer stared out toward the hills flanked by mountains and wondered how she was supposed to get from here to Nicholas Sabre's sheep station. Then, as if reading her thoughts, Sean said with a strange gleam in his eye, "I'd be more than happy t' ride y' up if y' don't mind sharin' a wagon with the supplies."

Smiling, Summer nodded, dislodging her hat and setting it akilter. "I'd be much obliged, Mr. O'Connell."

"Sean," he corrected, then reached for her valise.

If the short, hard journey to Christchurch was any indication of the difficulty of the longer trip to Malvern Hills where Sabre resided, Summer suspected she wouldn't be venturing to town often.

Upon leaving Lyttleton, they had rumbled over a rudimentary road to the top of the Port Hills where Sean was forced to use a powerful double brake before descending the steep, winding, and bumpy wagon path. Occasionally the road ran by a cliff, and Summer was able to look straight down to the ocean a hundred feet below. They took the route much too swiftly for her liking, but she kept quiet, listening politely as he fanned her consternation with tales of the tragic accidents that had befallen the hapless travelers who hadn't taken the care they should have along the way.

Soon they were rolling along the Summer Road that stretched along the seashore, every now and again moving under monstrous overhanging crags that blotted out the sky.

Christchurch was surprisingly civilized and pretty. Extremely English, yet primitive enough to remind Summer that the colony was yet new, and a very, very long way from home. While Sean bought supplies, Summer wandered, enjoying the feel of solid ground beneath her feet while her eyes feasted on the hardy people milling about the well-paved streets. There were gas lamps on every corner and a lovely pillared post office surrounded by gardens of brilliant blooming flowers. Shops of every sort sold china, building supplies, farming equipment, foodstuffs, and clothes. Summer stood for a long while admiring a splendid party dress on a mannequin in a shop window.

Once, during those years when she'd believed that her mother was married to Pimbersham, she had daydreamed of donning such a beautiful dress. Now she could only gaze at it in wonder and imagine herself wearing it to meet Nicholas Sabre. She'd impress him for certain in that. He'd regret not having met her at the ship, his arms full of flowers and presents like the other men who had greeted their new wives.

As she focused harder on the window, she realized that a group of men was forming behind her, their wide-eyed faces reflected in the glass. She turned slowly to face them. One in particular caught her eye. Slightly hunchbacked and wiry-thin, he stared at her with one good eye, the other wandering in all directions.

She smiled and his eyebrows shot up. The muted whispers of his companions stopped as they gaped, mouths open and eyes unblinking. They were all dressed alike, in blue shirts, brown trousers, and thick-soled boots, giving Summer the idea that perhaps their clothing was some sort of uniform. When she opened her mouth to speak, they scattered like frightened guinea hens in every direction.

The realization struck her that, although there were many people around, few of them were women. There were lots of children, however, scrambling around the lamp poles and dodging in and out of the alleys between the stone and white-washed businesses lining the streets. Their faces were browned by the sun and glowing with good health, as were those of the adults. Not one person among them seemed to be either a pauper or a beggar. Each appeared robust and content.

Her mind drifted to the dreams she'd spun during the voyage, when she'd spent long hours holed up in her tiny cabin curled on her berth, doing her best to ignore her seasickness. She'd imagined that Nicholas Sabre was the kindest and most generous man in New Zealand. He'd love her at first sight. He'd give her the home she'd always dreamed of, and in the years to come there would be children, so many happy children who would know beyond any shadow of a doubt that their parents loved them.

But here she stood. Alone again.

She stared up at the taffeta-and-crinoline creation in the window, disappointment blurring the ribbons and ruching and ruffles of pale lavender, feeling abandoned. Her throat constricted and her eyes stung.

Who was she to dream such dreams? What right did she have to experience such a keen letdown when Sabre, Esquire, hadn't appeared to sweep her off to his home in the hills? They weren't even married, after all. Jamie MacFarland had married Sabre to good, kindhearted S. Fairburn, not Summer O'Neile . . . murderess, daughter of a whore. For a while she'd allowed her imagination to get the better of her.

"Ah, well. That's what y' get for bein' a silly dreamer," she told herself aloud, hating the knot in her throat that made the words little more than a hoarse whisper. She wiped her nose, blinked one last time at the dress in the window, and walked off down the street in search of Sean.

Sean told Summer that Sabre's station was located some forty miles from Christchurch. They traveled as far as the village of Leathfield before the sun set. They acquired rooms in a very nice inn for the night, enjoyed a fine meal, then retired to their separate rooms. It seemed she had barely closed her eyes when Sean was pounding on her door again, rousing her from sleep. The sun had not yet risen, and she found, upon rolling out of bed, that the air was extremely cold.

"Y'll get used t' it," Sean assured her when she met him for breakfast, teeth chattering as she rubbed her arms to warm them. "The weather's mild generally," he continued. "Cool at night and pleasant durin' the day."

It was true. Once the sun broke the surface of the sea, the air warmed considerably. For the next hours, Summer gazed over the treeless Canterbury Plains, transfixed. Sean pointed out the titi palms, more commonly known as cabbage trees, and the large prickly bushes which, he informed her with a smile, were known as "wild Irishmen."

Cocking a smile at him, Summer replied, "I wonder why."

He laughed, a full-chested sound that made Summer giggle. Then he shook his head and regarded her with that gleam in his eye again. "'Tis a pity a lass as bonnie as you will be wasted on a man like Sabre."

The remark brought back her trepidation. She had purposefully avoided discussing Sabre, afraid the topic would bring up questions about herself and her reasons for coming to New Zealand. But the regretful tone of his voice was enough to stir her curiosity.

"What, exactly, are y' sayin'?" she said.

"Y' might as well know; Sabre's temper is the blackest in all the South Island."

"Meanin'?"

Sean peered down at her from beneath the lowered brim of his hat. "I'm meanin' just that. No one on the South Island can get on with him."

"Oh." Her shoulders sank as she gazed out over the undulating downs of yellow tussock, the tall native grass of the island, shimmering under the sun like oceans of rippling hay. "I knew this was a mad idea," she finally said in exasperation. "Truly mad." Tipping her head, her brows drawing together, she said, "Y' might as well spill it all, Mr. O'Connell. I won't be bangin' on his door unprepared for the worst."

His green eyes were dark, his lips pressed around a tussock stem as his big hands manipulated the reins with gentle tugs. "Maybe I shouldn't," he said. "What point would there be in m' scarin' y' out o' yer wits before y' even set eyes on the man?"

Her shoulders sank a little more as she waited.

"Well . . ." He looked off toward the mountains. "There are two groups o' settlers in New Zealand. First there's the farmers, like me. We're allowed only so much land from the government, and that's fair enough. But when yer raisin' sheep or cattle, y' got t' be movin' them around a lot, t' wherever the grass is greenest. There are areas called runs that border our property, land owned by the government. For a price, the government allows us t' graze our sheep or cattle there . . . until someone comes along and buys it. That's the Cockatoos, who are a lot o' damn squatters who save up enough money t' buy themselves a plot o' land, which are generally much smaller than the farmers' sections. They build themselves a shanty, turn their animals loose, and before y' know it the grass is no longer fit t' graze. Then they move on t' another run, then another. Sabre is a Cockatoo. He's settled on a section that was once m' run. Some o' m' best grazin' meadows are now feedin' his damned sheep. I raise cattle, y' see, and once his woolly beasts have grazed, there's naught left for m' animals. Not that he cares. Not that any one o' the bloody Cockatoos care what they do t' the decent landowners o' this good island.

"Sabre's past is murky. Rumor is he was banished from England for high crime—possibly murder . . ." He looked down at Summer to gage her reaction. She stared straight ahead and said nothing. "He's a recluse and rarely has anythin' t' do with anyone. So, me darlin', I'd watch that lovely neck, if y' know what's good for y'. Send for me, if y' need me . . . and y' will, that's a fact. He's a brute, for certain."

If all that wasn't enough to make her consider turning around and returning to Christchurch immediately, the next tidbit of information almost did it. Sean informed her that Nicholas Winston Sabre, Esquire, was an aristocrat.

An *aristocrat!* One of the loathsome creatures who had brought all this heartache on her in the first place. No doubt she'd find herself misused and neglected just like her mother had.

They were in the hills now, winding past dark green meadows dotted with sheep that lifted their newly shorn heads and peered at them from doleful brown eyes. "These'll be Sabre's sheep," Sean explained, and for some inexplicable reason Summer was awash with excitement.

Why, she couldn't figure. She'd just been informed that her husband-to-be was the worst sort of man. More than that, he was an aristocrat, maybe even a murderer.

But then, so was she, so it wasn't as if she deserved anything better. She didn't, however, deserve an aristocrat.

She considered asking Sean what her Nicholas Sabre looked like. Might as well be prepared for that too. But she couldn't bring herself to do it. The news he'd just imparted was enough to leave her lightheaded with dread. If she learned he looked like an ogre, she'd surely demand to go back to Christchurch that very instant. But, not for the first time, she was assaulted with a yearning that had driven her since the moment her mother had plunked her down on Martha Haggard's doorstep those many years ago. She wanted a home of her own and a family, and the sad truth was, a woman of her character couldn't afford to be particular.

So she said nothing, just sat on the wagon bench, hands gripping its splintered edge as they jostled through a shallow, sluggish stream choked by watercress, then up the other side. Occasionally, she caught herself closing her eyes and breathing in the foreign scents. She'd already learned the smell of hot dust rising from under the wagon wheels. Now that they'd left the flatlands behind them, the trees were growing thicker along the road. There were tall gaunt totara pines that smelled pungent in the warm air. Honeysuckle climbed their trunks and coiled through their needles to drape toward the ground, brushing Sean and Summer's faces with huge heady-scented yellow blooms. There were hedges of flax crowding the sandy shoal of the shallow rivers, their tall, spiky red blossoms attracting bees.

Birds fluttered about their shoulders: the kaka, a species of parrot; the parroquet with bright green feathers; and the bellbird, whose song resembled the peal of silver bells. Summer could hardly believe the majesty of it all.

Then they topped a rise. Far down in the flat, as Sean termed the valley, stood a small dilapidated house constructed of rough-hewn, unpainted lumber. Several metal smokestacks jutted up through the lopsided roof. Thin trails of dark blue smoke curled from two of them.

"Well," Sean said. "There it is."

Flooded with apprehension, Summer closed her eyes and forced back her terror while Sean encouraged the stubborn horses down the steep track, soothing them with words and occasionally applying the brake when the gradient became too steep. She couldn't make herself look until he had brought the wagon to a complete stop. Opening one eye slowly, then the other, she gazed with disappointment at the pitiful hovel.

"Blazes," she uttered under her breath.

Sean jumped from the wagon and made haste to the rear, dragged down her valise, then hurried to help her alight. Noting her obvious nervousness as she continued to regard the place, he gave her a sympathetic smile.

"It's not much t' look at, but he's only got himself t' blame. Most folk lend a hand when a friend builds a house, but Sabre's got no friends." He caught her arm and tugged her toward the porch that looked as if it might drop off the house at any moment, never once taking his eyes from the door. Finally, he dropped her valise on the step, gave her hand a perfunctory wag, and turned back for the wagon.

Spinning on her heel and catching her porkpie hat as it sailed off her head, she watched him jump onto his wagon seat. "Y' aren't stayin'?" she cried.

"Sorry, darlin', but I'm not up t' a confrontation today," he replied. "And there would definitely be one if he caught me on his property. I only gave y' the ride because yer much too pretty t' leave languishin' on the pier."

From somewhere in the house, a dog barked.

"But what am I supposed t' do now?" she demanded.

He appeared contemplative, then shrugged. "Knock, I guess."

"Just like that?"

He shrugged once more and reached for the reins. When his gaze came back to Summer, an odd look of melancholy came to his eyes. Almost reluctantly, he added, "If y' keep walkin' down this road five miles y'll come t' my place. Yer always welcome, lass."

Then, he gave the lines a twitch and the horses lurched into motion. Summer, her ostrich-feathered hat crushed against her chest, watched until Sean and his wagon disappeared over the next rise. There she stood, alone on a path interspersed with eroded patches of dirt and weeds, her gaze fixed on the lopsided shanty.

Home.

She closed her eyes, and though she'd never fainted in her life, she thought that she just might do it now.

There was a rusty plow leaning against a nearby tree. A cracked enamel pot had been tossed into what appeared to be a feeble excuse for a vegetable garden. The steps were sagging and from beneath them came the clucking of a hen. Summer saw its beady little eyes peer out at her as it sat on its shaded tussock nest.

She noted that the shingles on the roof were curling. Then, on second inspection, she decided that they looked more as if they had been uprooted on one end by a high wind. Tattered quilts hung inside the windows instead of curtains.

Taking a long, slow breath, Summer retrieved her valise and forced herself to mount the steps one at a time, making certain they would hold her weight before she gave them her all. At last she stood at the door, her heart in her throat. She wanted to cry. She wanted to wrap her fingers around Sophie Fairburn's throat and murder her all over again. Then she wondered what Sophie would have thought about all this. Knowing her, she would have slapped her work-worn hands together and whooped in pleasure. But then, Sophie had never aspired to be more than she was, nor had she ever expected more from life than she deserved, the way Summer had.

She rapped hard on the door, and was surprised that it felt so solid against her fist. What had she expected? That it would fall off its hinges at the first touch?

The dog barked again, and she could hear footsteps approaching from the opposite side.

Run! she screamed silently.

Where to? came her mind's equally silent reply.

Anyplace. Away from here. Away from a husband who wasn't her husband and who was a murderer to boot. Away from an aristocrat who resided in a hovel that any beggar in London would turn up his nose at.

The door began to open and she took two steps back, then, recalling the poor state of the porch, she froze, balanced on one foot like an acrobat on a wire as her gaze locked on the grizzled, white-haired old man filling up the doorway. Her heart sank to her feet.

"What's up?" came his voice, snapping her attention back to his face. He peered at her through a wreath of pipe smoke. His blue shirt and brown trousers were similar to the ones she'd seen on the men in town. *Oh, saints,* she thought, *he'll be dead of old age before our first child is born.*

"M-mister Sabre?"

"Who wants to know?"

"Summer." It came out a whisper. "Summer..."

"Who is it, Frank?"

The question had come from further inside the house, behind the man named Frank who watched her as he puffed on his pipe. Hope sprang anew. In truth, it nearly jumped up and smacked her in the face. She gripped her hat with both hands and had just started to speak when Frank moved aside and gave her an unobstructed view of his companion.

He moved slowly through the interior shadows so she could just make out his silhouette. Then he drew nearer. He was broad-shouldered enough to block out all else within her line of scrutiny. It seemed that he emerged from the darkness by degrees, the light inching up his long legs, narrow hips, and splendid torso like a new sun casting its brilliance upon the awakening earth. Summer realized that she had ceased breathing; her body tensed with such heightened anticipation that she might have shattered had someone touched her.

Then the light found his face.

Praise to all the saints in heaven; he was the most gloriously handsome man she'd ever seen! She found herself incapable of speaking, almost winded.

He said nothing, nor did he smile, just stood there with a look of such intense gravity that she began to feel giddy. His eyes were fringed with the longest, most luxurious eyelashes she had witnessed on a man. Then the dog whined, and her eyes were drawn to the mutt, wagging its tail at Sabre's knee.

"Who are you?" Sabre asked. "What are you doing here?" His voice was deep and very soft, but ... emotionless.

Gathering her courage about her, she stepped closer, only to be brought up short when the dog growled and took a threatening stance between her and Sabre. She gripped her hat a little tighter.

"M' name is Summer, sir. Summer ... Fairburn." Flashing him a smile, she thrust her hand toward him and added, "I'm yer wife."

Chapter 3

The girl who was trying so desperately to look like a woman, and failing miserably in her tiny heels, oversized skirt, and ugly hat, continued to smile up at him, her hand thrust out even though he ignored it. He hadn't moved and he hadn't spoken. He was still trying to make sense of her presence here on the threshold of his home. No one, aside from himself and Frank, and Ben and Clara Beaconsfield, had ever so much as put a boot on his front porch. Had anyone suggested to the good ladies of Christchurch that they should pay him a call, they would have swooned, and then rattled off a dozen reasons why it wouldn't be seemly to search out the Devil Lord.

But here was one who was bold enough, or perhaps just ignorant of his reputation. She seemed to fully expect him to throw open his door and invite her into his ramshackle palace for tea. Who the hell was she, anyway? And what was that she'd said about.... "I beg your pardon?"

She stared at him, owl-eyed, her smile a trifle less sincere. "Yer wife," she repeated.

Lifting one eyebrow, he frowned and shook his head very slowly. "You must have the wrong house."

Her hand lowered and clenched. "Yer Sabre, Esquire. Isn't that so?"

"Correct."

"Then I'm yer wife."

"I don't have a wife."

"Yes, sir, y' do." She swallowed and added, "Me."

He glanced at Frank, who was watching the violet-eyed girl with the white skin and fiery hair from across the room, his teeth clamped about his pipe stem and his mouth on the verge of a smile.

"M' name is Summer," she continued. This time he detected her accent. "Summer . . . Fairburn . . . Sabre. Yer wife." She stressed *wife* with a furrowing of her brow and a stubborn jutting of her jaw. Her hands were gripped around the bird feather on her hat in such a way that brown barbs sprouted between her knuckles.

"Where, exactly, did you come from?" he asked.

"London."

"How did you get here?"

"By boat." She rolled her eyes and mumbled, "Did y' think I flew?"

"What I mean is, how did you get *here?*"

"Oh." She cast a wary glance at Betsy. "Mr. Sean O'Connell brought me, seein' that y' weren't at the dock t' meet me and all . . . like the *other* husbands," she added with a degree of pique.

"O'Connell."

"Aye." Her gaze came back to his. "He's yer neighbor, I believe."

"I know who the son of a bitch is." Seeing her

eyes widen at his sudden display of irritation, he took a step toward her. She backed out the door and onto the porch, taking cautious glances over her shoulder until she reached the steps. At last she stopped, feet planted while she blinked in the harsh sunlight. "I understand perfectly now." He towered over her until she was forced to tip back her head to see him. Spots of color dusted her cheeks. There was a scattering of freckles over the bridge of her nose. Her lips were very pink, and parted; little breaths panted through them that made her bird feather quiver. "This is some sort of plot between you and O'Connell to run me off my land."

"Plot?" Her lips formed the words as if she didn't quite comprehend.

"Plot," he repeated in a softly menacing voice, his eyes never leaving hers, which were wide, round, and the color of English violets . . . and burning brighter by the minute. "You can tell O'Connell that this land is bought and almost paid for, and all the underhanded tricks he could pull from now until hell freezes over are not going to make me leave. And furthermore, let him know that if I catch his cows on my run again, I'll shoot every last one of them. Between the eyes."

"I'll tell him no such thing. He said y' were foul-tempered, but he didn't mention that y' were deaf and daft and obviously missin' a good portion o' yer memory." Bending, she yanked open her valise and dug through her belongings, few as they appeared to be. Filmy garments spilled out over the filthy porch: stockings, a chemise, a white cotton nightgown. Nick found himself staring at them, his body responding as if it was a snake coiling around his boot, not a pink satin ribbon.

"There. Maybe that'll help jar yer memory."

He forced his eyes away from the ribbon and

stockings, to the paper she unfurled and held before his eyes. Numbly, he noted her hands were trembling. Her face held an expression between agony and anger. He looked hard at the paper, noted the legal phraseology:... *do hereby grant one James MacFarland the absolute right to act in my behalf... the choice of a wife... and do hereby grant my permission to stand in my stead as legal proxy in taking the undersigned woman as my spouse...*

"Well?" She peered at him over the top of the paper. "Does this look familiar or what?"

Approved by Her Royal Majesty's most gracious and humble servant: George M. Billings, Registrar General, Christchurch, New Zealand. Signed before these witnesses on this day, Twenty-three February, in the year of our Lord, Eighteen and Sixty-Six... Nicholas Winston Sabre, Esquire.

"Obviously," he said, sliding his foot from under her nightgown, "it's a forgery."

"A forgery."

"Clearly."

"Are y' standin' there and tellin' me that y' didn't sign this?"

"I am."

They glared at each other, her eyes narrowed suspiciously, his squinted in malevolence.

"I say yer lyin'."

"And I say that you and O'Connell should try harder next time to come up with a more plausible plan to rob me of my station." With that, he buried his hands in her clothes, shoved them into the valise, then shut the bag with a snap, stood, and thrust it at her. She refused to take it, just fixed him with the most astonished, furious, obstinate stare he'd ever encountered. So he threw the satchel into the yard where it landed in a thatch of Cape broom. That elicited a gasp from her. Then, lowering his

head to within inches of hers, he said, "The last
thing I need or want is a wife."

"Then y' shouldn't have signed that proxy."

"I didn't."

She stuck the paper up between them. "Y' did."

"What the hell do I need or want with a wife?"
he demanded furiously.

Her small mouth curled up on one end. "If I have
t' explain that, Mr. Sabre, y've definitely been too
long without a woman."

"Get off my porch," he said in a dangerous voice.
"I couldn't afford a wife even if I wanted one, which
I don't. I'm doing well to feed myself and keep this
station functioning. I do not, I repeat, *do not* desire
some money-grabbing female who would ruin me
with her appetite for frivolity and fripperies."

"Fripperies!"

"Fripperies." He snatched the hat from her hand
and flung it. It hit the ground and rolled, looking
like a flightless brown bird wobbling in the weeds.

"*Oh!*" Summer cried, and as she turned to regard
it in outrage and disbelief, he planted the sole of his
boot upon her shapely derriere and shoved her
down the steps, where she stumbled and landed on
her backside with an *oomph!*, skirt hiked to her shins,
face blazing.

"My regards to Sean," he said. "And tell him that
if he wants my ass on a platter to come take it himself. And you might remind him that I'm not easily
seduced by other men's wives, fiancées, or whores
he's hired to do his dirty work, regardless of what
he thinks about me." Bestowing a nasty smile upon
her, he finished, "Good day, Miss Fairburn, or
whoever the hell you are." Then he offered her his
back.

An egg came sailing over his right shoulder and
splattered against the door frame. He slammed the

door just as a second egg hit it with a dull thud.

Frank stood at the window with one edge of the quilt pulled back. "Right spunky, ain't she?" he observed.

Nick moved to the window and looked out. The girl was dusting off her seat, shaking grass from her skirt hem, tugging furiously at the cuffs of her long sleeves. Then she shoved them up toward her elbows while hurling a string of scurrilous remarks at the house.

"Wonder where she got that marriage contract?" Frank ruminated, drawing on his pipe. He watched her as she grabbed her hat from where it had landed and plunked it on her head. It slid down over her brow.

"O'Connell," Nick replied. "Obviously."

"Sure as shootin' looked legal to me." Frank's eyes were heavy-lidded, giving him a perpetually sleepy look. He gazed up at Nick, waiting for a reply while his lips formed a lazy smile.

However, Nick's eyes were on the girl, who was plucking the valise from the Cape broom and giving it a hard enough shake to make her ridiculous-looking hat tumble all the way off her head; she caught it in midair and replaced it, cocked at an angle on the crown of her shining hair. Nick noticed that when her hair was full of sunlight the curls were like flames spilling down her slender back.

She was very young. The bone structure of her face had yet to develop fully beneath her youthful flesh. Her breasts, or what he had seen of them beneath the overlarge blouse, were small and round, and her hips were yet slim. Watching her move toward the road with angry strides, he was plagued by the idea that Frank was right; that signature had looked disturbingly authentic.

Reaching the track, she looked one way, then the

other, appearing more confused now than angry. A gust of wind whipped the hat off her head and stirred up enough sand that she disappeared momentarily behind a hazy cloud. When the dust settled, she still stood forlornly in the middle of the wagon path, small shoulders slumped and hat clutched to her chest. And she was still yelling at the house.

He returned to the front door and opened it cautiously.

". . . supposed t' do now, damn y'?" she was saying.

Leaning indifferently against the door frame, Nick crossed his arms over his chest and curved his mouth in a hard smile. "Walk!" he yelled back.

"All the way t' Christchurch?"

She was weeping now; he couldn't hear her, but he could see her shoulders shaking. Frowning, he stood upright and shoved his hands into his pockets. "O'Connell got you here," he replied angrily, disturbed by the pang of guilt tugging at his conscience. Then again, he didn't have anything to feel guilty about. None of this was *his* doing. "O'Connell can take you back to Christchurch," he shouted, and slammed the door against the sight of her white face and dark, frightened eyes.

Rejoining Frank at the window, Nick watched Summer tread up the hill, kicking at stones, stumbling occasionally, her valise in one hand, hat in the other. She looked back once, just at the top of the rise, and a vague memory materialized in his mind, an image of him sitting in the back of a sweltering pothouse while a group of men crowded around him, cutting off his air. He'd been drunk. So drunk. The long, lonely ride from the Hills to Lyttleton had given him too much time to dwell on his past mistakes. Then there had been the people, watching him from every shop, alley, wagon, and horse. Whispering behind their hands. Judging. Sitting there in that pothouse with his veins throbbing with ale, he might have done anything to make them leave him alone. *Anything*.

But agree to marry a mail-order bride? Especially one who was still wet behind the ears and filled out her clothes as if she were wearing a grain sack?

When it snowed in hell.

Five nights later, Nick lay in bed with his arms behind his head and stared at the ceiling. Soon dawn would creep through his window. Betsy slept on a pillow near his feet, snoring.

His body hurt deep in every muscle, joint, and bone. It was always that way during shearing season; exhaustion was a way of life during those torturous weeks. He tried to calculate the number of sheep he and Frank had already shorn, but his thoughts scattered too easily. There had been hundreds. There were hundreds more to come, filling his days and nights with the sound of their strident bleating. The stench of the sheep dip, made of hot water, tobacco, and sulfur, seemed to have permeated his skin so that no matter how often he scrubbed his hands with lye soap the smell never left him. Or perhaps it was simply the memory of the stink that had seared into his brain. The idea of never again smelling anything but sheep dip made him swear softly in the dark.

Nick tossed back the covers and threw his legs over the side of the bed. Elbows on his knees, he looked out at nothing, doing his best to focus his mind on the day's work ahead—and not on the memory of a chit with red hair, violet eyes, and a white nightgown adorned with pink satin ribbons. Recalling the feel of all that softness against his calloused palms made him shiver. Who the devil did she think she was to come sashaying up to his house with her ridiculous bird-feather hat, assuming he would fall for her and Sean's scheme to run him off his land?

How had they hoped to accomplish it?

No doubt she'd meant to insinuate herself into his life and convince him to move away. Or perhaps she'd had something more sinister in mind. Perhaps she and Sean had meant to kill him; she'd inherit everything and turn it all over to O'Connell. Sean would finally get what he'd spent the last three years wanting: Nick's land, and revenge. The idea almost made him laugh.

Leaving the bed, he eased on his pants before lighting a lantern and moving into "the library," as he termed the tiny room just off the kitchen. It was more like a niche in the wall, with just enough space to hold a crudely built pine desk. On the walls around the desk he'd constructed shelves, which he'd lined with volumes on numerous subjects, mostly having to do with sheep: Alderman's *Sheep Farming Annals*, Spencer's *Parasites and Sheep*, Wickersham's *Beginning Shepherd's Manual*, and Wolfe's *Castrating Your Rams*. It was there that he also kept his ledgers, stationery, a gray metal box containing his gun, and several ornate silver frames that displayed likenesses of his father, the distinguished Byron Sabre, Earl of Chesterfield, and of his older brother, Christopher.

He kept an orderly desk; Nicholas Sabre might have a great many faults, but he could say that much about himself.

Settling into the chair at the desk, he put his lantern aside and rubbed his eyes. A headache had centered at the base of his skull. His eyes felt like sandpaper and so did his face. He'd been too busy with the shearing for the last two days to shave. Frank hadn't felt well, so that had slowed down the clipping considerably. Most sheep farmers with a flock as large as his employed a dozen or more men working fourteen-hour days in order to get their wool to Lyttleton before the competition. The earliest farmers to market were paid the premium price for their bales. Those who followed were forced to take what they could get . . . which was pitifully little. Well, he couldn't afford anything but top price for his wool, not if he intended to hold onto his station.

Damn sheep. Damn *bloody* sheep and their stinking wool and their constant bleating and their razor-sharp hooves that could cut a man's flesh as keenly as a knife. Damn this place, this country, where a man couldn't hire a decent housekeeper or cook because all the servants thought themselves better than their employer.

Just like you did when you first went to work for Ben Beaconsfield, his conscience chided him.

He propped his elbows on the desk and cradled his forehead in his hands as he recalled those first turbulent months in New Zealand. Anger and humiliation had consumed him. He'd been forced to answer to someone who'd been little more than a dirt farmer back in England. And for a man of Nick's station in life, that had been a sore trial.

But, as the months had progressed, an acceptance of his circumstances had taken the edge off his fury. He could still remember the moment when he'd realized that the anger was no longer there, burning inside him. It was the same moment he'd put the sharp blades of a wool clipper all the way through his hand. There had been a great deal of blood, and Ben's wife, Clara, had screamed and fainted. But Nick had felt nothing. Neither fear nor pain. He'd stood there staring at the red rivulets running to the ground and all he'd thought was: *Maybe it will kill me.*

From then on it had been as if his entire emotional being had ceased to function. There was no exhilaration over success, or despair from defeat. There was only . . . existing. Day after day. Month after month. Trapped in this virulent ignominy, he had come to feel as imprisoned by his isolation as any man in Newgate Penitentiary. It had seemed a lifetime sentence. Then . . .

Five days ago a woman-child had shown up on his doorstep looking for all the world like she'd just stepped out of the *Delineator Journal of Fashion* . . . in someone else's clothes. A small red-haired child-woman with freckles who said she was his wife. Her nightclothes and underwear had stirred something inside him, like a spark in the night. The sensation had startled him. He'd stood there, staring down into her unusual eyes, feeling like a man waiting to be handed some judgment—Jesus, he knew *that* feeling—anticipation winding up inside him like a coiled spring. It was still wound so tightly he couldn't breathe at times.

"Mornin'," came Frank's jovial voice behind him. "Coffee's on. I reckon we'll be to the shearin' early today."

Nick left his chair to face Frank, a gnome of a man who watched from the door with his usual patience, dressed in a blue shirt and brown pants, his shearing garb. His pipe bowl peeped over the top of his breast pocket, and Nick knew that by the time he'd poured his first cup of brew Frank would have lit his ration of tobacco, filling the small house with its pungent-sweet odor.

Frank Wells, with his slow, bowlegged shuffle and Texas drawl, was content in his role as shepherd and manager of Nick's flock. He asked no questions of Nick, and like Nick, offered no explanations of his past, aside from an occasional colorful rumination concerning some incident he had barely survived . . . of which there seemed to be many.

Frank had been an outcast himself when Nick found him wandering around Christchurch in his moleskin trousers, crimean shirt, and battered hat. The good citizens of the town had labeled him loafer, swagger, go-silly, bush ratty—all names they bestowed upon crazy vagrants who had no permanent home or occupation.

Nick had always suspected that Frank was an escapee from an Australian prison, but he'd never broached the subject because it didn't matter to him. Likewise, Frank had never shown any real interest in Nick's past, which suited Nick just fine. But Frank did have a knack for seeing through a person's motives and wasted little time in offering his opinion on certain matters. Nick had threatened to fire him on numerous occasions, but he never had. And Frank kept on proffering his sentiments, whether Nick appreciated them or not.

Nick quit the library and headed for his bedroom. Sunlight filtered around the edges of the quilt covering the window, lending enough light so he didn't need his lantern. Throwing open the wardrobe door, he reached for a clean white shirt, his suit coat, and a cravat.

"Goin' somewhar?" Frank asked from the hallway.

"Christchurch."

Silence fell, then Frank said, "Well, I reckon we won't be shearin'."

"No. Take the day off, if you want. You look as if you could use the rest."

"I *have* been feelin' a mite poorly. It's that galdern lumbago, ya know. Been botherin' me since I was livin' in San Antone, Texas. Remind me to tell ya someday of the time back in '36 when the peaceful citizens of San Antone was swooped down upon by a lot of damn Comanches."

Nick put on his shirt and coat, leaving his cravat hanging, untied, around his throat, then went back to the kitchen. He poured himself a cup of coffee and stood at the window, looking out on the hills while he sipped it. He sensed Frank behind him.

"Compared to the Comanche, these Maori savages are a lot of gutless yellow-bellies. No respectable Comanche would've jest handed over his land to a bunch of palefaces the way they did . . . Any particular reason why yore goin' to Christchurch?"

"Supplies."

"I picked up supplies two weeks ago. Did I fergit somethin'?"

Nick put down his cup and proceeded to tie his cravat while continuing to gaze out the window.

"Come to thank about it, I did fergit to pick up some blue and white vitriol and linseed meal. We got a horse with the thrush, ya know."

Nick barely glanced at his shepherd before leaving the room.

Frank said, "It's been months since ya rode into Christchurch. I s'pose ya must have a good reason for goin'."

Stopping at a mirror hanging on the wall by the front door, Nick carefully retied his cravat, ignoring Frank's grizzled reflection peering over his shoulder.

"If yore intendin' to ride to Christchurch just to check out the girl . . ."

Nick's hands stopped their motion. He glared at his own image in the mirror, watching hot color creep up his dark cheeks. In his haste to set off for town, he hadn't thought to shave.

"She ain't in Christchurch," Frank continued. He pulled his pipe from his pocket and slid the teeth-marked stem into his mouth. He looked like an owl, all round eyes with tufts of thinning white hair standing out at all angles around his face.

"The girl?" Nick questioned.

"The one with all the hair who said she was yore wife."

"Ah," he replied, with a sardonic lift of his eyebrow. "I'd totally forgotten her."

Frank smiled knowingly. "She ain't in Christchurch."

"What makes you think I care where she is? And she's not my wife." Grimly, he forced himself to finish the intricate knot and tuck the cravat into his shirt. His dark eyes gleamed with an unattractive light as he said, "I can't conceive of O'Connell thinking that I would be stupid enough to fall for that asinine scheme. Imagine Nicholas Sabre sending away for a mail-order bride. And an *Irish* one at that. Marriage is for fools, Frank. So is love. Besides, monogamy isn't natural. I've never known one faithful married couple...including my parents." He turned to face his companion. "The girl isn't my wife."

Frank shrugged. "That ain't what the others say."

"Others? What others?"

"The ones who say they witnessed yore signin' that proxy contract. Scrawled yore name on it as big as Christchurch, they vowed. Yep. Right thar at the Harbor Pothouse at the table in the corner. Jamie MacFarland bought ya an ale and—"

The memory came flooding back of the hours he'd spent drinking in the disgusting little pothouse those many months ago.

Then the image of the girl—Summer—rose up before him again. Every stunning detail, and some he hadn't acknowledged until this very moment, though they had been there during the last few days, tapping him on the shoulder while he sweated over squirming sheep and tossed and turned in his sleep.

She'd been the first woman to look at him without suspicion in nearly six years. Of course, she hadn't known him; by now, she would have heard it all, or at least as much as the gossip mongers knew, which added up to a lot of conjecture and speculation.

"She ain't in Christchurch," came Frank's voice again.

"No?" Nick responded with his usual lack of emotion.

Frank took the pipe from his mouth and studied it. "Nope," he finally said.

"Then where is she?"

"O'Connell's."

Nick's body tensed.

'Workin' for him, I understand."

"*Working* for O'Connell?"

"As a maid."

"A—"

"Maid." Frank shook his head and scratched at his thatch of white hair as he watched Nick's face turn to cold stone. "No sir. Never thought I'd see the day when a wife of Nick Sabre's was scrubbin' floors for an O'Connell."

Summer stared up the black tunnel to the blue sky beyond. There came a twittering and fluttering from somewhere near the top of the flue, then a chorus of chirping baby birds. As soot trickled down to settle over her face, she huffed and fussed, and on her hands and knees, crawled out of the yawning hearth, into the light.

She swore aloud. "If I'd wanted to be a damned chimney sweep I'da been one in London." She flung her oily black cloth into a bucket of water while she contemplated the room. Sean lived respectably enough. The place wasn't without its creature comforts, but Summer had seen hogs that lived tidier. Not for the first time she wondered when he'd last had the place cleaned. For the past five days she'd scrubbed floors until her knuckles bled and dusted until she'd breathed in enough of the fine silt to make her lungs ache. If that wasn't enough, the cheeky bugger had made his desire for her "companionship" more than obvious. Oh, not in any overt way, like Pimbersham had. There had been no groping or pinching, no snide insinuations. But she'd found Sean watching her when she least expected it. And his eyes had spoken volumes.

Upon first arriving at Sean's station, she'd felt more than a little desperate, on top of being furious. Clearly, Sabre hadn't approved of her. Why else would he reject her so adamantly?

Frowning, Summer grabbed a cloth and began dusting the knickknacks that lined the mantel. There was a little seashell box and wax flowers under glass domes. "Typical aristocrat," she mumbled to herself as Sabre's image came to mind. On second thought, she shook her head. There was nothing "typical" about Nicholas Sabre. Neither his appearance nor his manners. With the flower case gripped to her stomach, she relived those first moments she'd seen him standing in the shadows, his wide shoulders and long lean legs bringing frightening new sensations to life inside her. Then the light had struck his face, leaving her winded.

That face... Saints, but the thought of it now

made her shake. As shockingly masculine as the rest of him was, it had left her speechless and wishing that she were prettier, or older, or more sophisticated. His countenance, burned a deep rich bronze by the sun, had seemed both evil and beautiful, somber and ... expectant. For an instant he had looked shocked, even pleased, before that wall of suspicion and anger had slammed down between them. She supposed she should be thankful that he wanted no part of her. His house looked like something out of the East End. His reputation was worse than anything she had imagined in her wildest nightmares. No doubt he'd beat her, or worse ...

She'd tried to look her best for him. Perhaps she could have held her temper better, but what was a girl to do when he'd made his disapproval of her so apparent? There had never been a coy or meek bone in her body, and she wasn't about to begin such nonsense now, just so she could live with the brute in his falling-down shanty. Who the blazes needed or wanted him anyway? So what if he was the most handsome man she'd ever put her eyes on?

He was only a man. An embittered, angry, distrustful, scurrilous *aristocrat*. New Zealand was full of men who would appreciate her for what she could offer. Then she reminded herself that she couldn't just dismiss this supposed marriage. To admit that she wasn't S. Fairburn would not only raise questions about her true identity; it would also establish that she had intended to go through with a fraudulent marriage—which would, no doubt, result in her being sent straight back to England ... and to jail.

She plunked down the glass dome, stared down at the cloth in her hand, and felt her stomach turn over. Besides, who was she kidding? She was a sorry housekeeper and an impossible cook. After she'd prepared her first and only meal for O'Connell, Sean had ordered her out of his kitchen and made her swear upon the Testament that she'd never return. She wasn't even a good conversationalist because she knew absolutely nothing about the world.

"Summer, me love," Sean had said with an amused smile, "what have y' been doin' all o' yer life?"

What indeed, aside from being cloistered in a harpy's house for the last ten years? Aside from wandering through flower gardens in search for the *daoine sidhe* and believing in fairy tales. Even her journey to New Zealand had been an extension of her ridiculous fantasies. She'd honestly believed that she'd find the pot o' gold at the end of her rainbow. What she'd discovered, however, was that she wasn't even good enough for a destitute convict—the arrogant swine.

Straightening her shoulders, she glared up at a picture of the Last Supper on the wall, feeling the old anger and determination rise inside her. *Yer as good as anyone, Summer O'Neile*, the voice in her head whispered, as it had whispered during those years she'd waited for her mother to claim her . . . each time she'd seen the pity in the villagers' eyes or overheard the boys' mothers whisper, *She's a bonnie lass, but keep your heart to yourself, lad. Summer's illegitimate, you know. Associating with a girl like that can only lead to trouble.*

Putting the memories from her mind, she continued to dust, stopping long enough to look at one of the many framed tintypes placed throughout the house. The pretty but somber face behind the glass belonged to Sean's wife, Colleen, who had died three years ago. Summer had experienced a spear of pity upon first witnessing his obvious grief when he spoke of Colleen...which wasn't often. He'd offered little background on the lovely Irish girl who had followed him to New Zealand. She'd arrived before he'd finished building their house and establishing his station, so she'd lived with Ben and Clara Beaconsfield until all was ready. Then Sean and Colleen had been married by a minister on their new front porch, with Ben and Clara as their witnesses. Six months later Colleen had died. Every evening Sean walked up the path to the top of a hill where she was buried, and placed a flower on her grave.

Summer might have considered it all romantic had she not recognized a thread of anger in Sean's voice when he spoke Colleen's name. She sensed that his bitterness stemmed from something more than the fact that she had died so young, and so soon after their marriage. When she'd asked him about it, his normally pleasant facade had changed into a menacing mask, and his gaze had been cold enough to frighten her. He'd gripped the tintype of his beloved so tightly that his knuckles had shone white, and he'd replied, "Love killed her, lass...as did her immense dislike for New Zealand."

Summer gently ran her cloth over the silver frame and placed it on the table. Voices came to her from the back of the house, but she only vaguely listened. Area sheep farmers, as few as there were, were always coming and going, sometimes late into the night. The only time Summer had attempted to eavesdrop on their meetings, Sean had slammed the door in her face with a warning scowl that told her to mind her own affairs. Still, she wondered what sort of business they could possibly have that would make them so secretive.

The sound of an approaching wagon brought her head up. Whoever was driving was in a big hurry. She went to the door and threw it open just as the driver bounded off the still-rolling dray and hit the front porch steps in one stride. It took a moment for Summer to realize she was staring into Nicholas Sabre's face.

He looked like a savage, his dark hair wind-blown. Then it struck her that he would have to be the most civilized savage in New Zealand. What Maori Indian would be driving a dray like a maniac about these hills ... dressed in a black suit and white silk cravat?

"Sabre?" she whispered, while every imaginable reason for his presence ran rampant through her mind. None of those reasons had anything to do with her.

As all six feet four inches of him topped the steps, his shirt a startling white against his skin, she jumped back in the house and attempted to slam the door. He caught it with his shoulder, shoving, while she did her best to dig in her heels and keep him out.

"Open this door."

"No."

"I said open this door."

"Y've got no right t' come bargin' in here—"

"The hell I don't." He almost growled it, making Summer's heart take an unexpected leap.

"If it's Sean yer wantin'—"

"Sean O'Connell can go to the devil."

"Then what in saints are y' doin' here?"

He was silent for a moment. Then he said, "You."

Catching a glimpse of her soot-covered reflection in the wall mirror, she blinked in horror. "Me?" she cried.

"You're my wife ... or so you say. No wife of mine works for Sean O'Connell."

"But y' denied—"

"I still do." He shoved again; her feet skidded on

the floor. "But until I can prove that I didn't sign that damned idiotic contract, I won't have you under the same roof as O'Connell."

"O'Connell didn't bloody turn me out t' fend for m'self! At least *he* gave me a job and a roof over m' head."

"And a bed to share?"

"Why, y' arrogant pig!" She stepped aside, allowing the door to slam back against the wall, then glared up at Sabre. He towered in the doorway, looking as sinister as she remembered, his black eyes boring into hers, his brown hands fisted at his sides. "Arrogant swine," she repeated, her hands on her hips. "I'll have y' know that Sean O'Connell is a hundred times more a gentleman than you are."

"Sean O'Connell is a sheep-murdering, land-stealing Irishman. Now collect your things. I'm taking you home."

"Indeed," she replied, crossing her arms over her breasts. "And just who the blazes gives y' the right—"

"You, apparently," he snapped, cutting her off. With an unpleasant smirk, his gaze raked over her, reminding her what a fright she must look with her hair piled atop her head and tied with a rag, her face coated with soot. As her cheeks began to burn with anger and embarrassment she was suddenly thanking the saints that he couldn't see them.

"*You* are the one who showed up on my doorstep waving that blasted marriage certificate," Sabre continued. "Unless, of course, I was right all along and it's a forgery."

"It's no such thing," she replied as calmly as possible, then added sarcastically and with a smile, "Believe me, Sabre, after meetin' y' I wish it was. No woman in her right mind would want t' live with such an insolent goat."

His mouth tightened at her brave words and his eyes narrowed. "A chit of a child who's desperate enough to marry a man she's never even met can't be too choosy, my love. Can she?"

The smile slid from her face. Before she could formulate an equally caustic reply, he had taken hold of her arm and was dragging her out of the house, down the porch steps to his wagon.

Neither was aware that Sean, having overheard the commotion, had exited the house behind them. As Nick turned to heft Summer up onto the wagon seat, Sean stepped between them, both startling Summer and knocking her aside. By the time she'd regained her footing, Sean and Nick were standing toe to toe, green eyes burning into black.

"I don't recall invitin' y' t' m' house, Sabre." Sean's voice sounded thick with hate.

Sabre stared at him hard, his sable hair rising and falling in a sudden breeze. "Get out of my way," he replied levelly.

"Make me. Come on, yer lordship. Mr. Sabre, Esquire." He slugged Nick on the shoulder, making Summer gasp. Nick, however, didn't move, just narrowed his eyes and clenched his fists. "Need I remind y' that I swore if I ever caught y' on m' property I'd kill y'?" Sean said.

Summer looked around then as a dozen men followed Sean down the steps, some of them Sean's employees, others farmers she'd met on their previous visits. She recognized Virgil McIlhenny and Howard Goetz. And the fat one with a wad of tobacco in his mouth was Roel Ormsbee, she recalled. She was on the verge of pleading for help, then realized that a number of the men carried weapons: clubs, knives, a gun.

"Get in the wagon, Summer," Sabre ordered, but

as she moved cautiously to board, Sean's hand shot out and grabbed her.

"The girl's not goin' anywhere unless she's willin'," Sean said.

Nick's eyes went to Sean's hand gripping her wrist. His face darkened even more.

"This bastard causin' trouble, Mr. O'Connell?" asked Sean's foreman, Hank Morley, slapping his cudgel against one big palm, his mouth curved in a nasty smile. "You want I should rearrange his haughty face?"

"Y'll do no such thing!" Summer cried frantically.

"Shut up," Nick snapped. "And keep out of this. This has nothing to do with you."

Sean grinned and stepped closer until he was only inches from Nick. "If I give the word, these men will have y' pulverized into the ground inside of a minute."

"So what's stopping you?"

"Well, it would be a real shame t' make the lass a widow so soon, wouldn't it? Besides, I have somethin' special in store for y', Sabre. One o' these days I'm gonna make y' regret the day y' were born, if y' don't already. I'm gonna ruin y', Nick. I'm gonna cut out yer heart like Colleen did to mine, and then I'm gonna watch y' slowly bleed t' death."

Spitting into the dirt, Sean stepped back and turned his attention to Summer, the anger melting from his countenance as he studied her. His voice was much kinder as he asked, "Do y' want t' go with him, lass?"

Trembling, she turned her eyes up to Sabre, who stared straight ahead, rigid as a rock, his stolidity in the face of Sean's terrible anger as shocking as it was confusing. It occurred to her that if she gave in to her pride and irritation over Sabre's previous treatment of her and decided to remain here, working for Sean, Sabre would turn on his heel and never look back. It struck her, too, that the idea of such a thing left her feeling distraught.

"I'll go with him," she replied softly. Sabre's eyes flashed her way briefly, whether in surprise or relief, she couldn't be certain . . . or perhaps it was simply disappointment.

"Yer positive?" Sean asked.

She nodded, her gaze still locked on Nicholas. She studied him keenly, the proud undaunted set of his shoulders, the fine lines around his eyes put there from years of squinting into the bright New Zealand sun. The prominence of his cheekbones underscored the fact that he was an aristocrat among commoners. His long hair tumbled over his shoulders, and though his expression bespoke a ruthlessness that testified to his questionable reputation, his aquiline nose and high, wide forehead lent a nobility to his profile and added to his dark allure.

Summer mounted the wagon, yet interminable seconds ticked by until Sean backed away, allowing Sabre to board. Without speaking, Nicholas reached for the reins and turned the dray toward home.

Chapter 4

For the first fifteen minutes they rode without speaking. Summer sat as far away from Sabre as possible and occasionally glanced at him from the corner of her eye. Every now and again she caught him appraising her, his eyes taking in her hair and face somewhat critically, she thought. Once, their eyes locked for a shocking instant and she realized with exasperation that there wasn't a solitary item about his appearance that she could find remotely unappealing. Unlike herself. Her own hair had partially fallen from its knot atop her head. Sweat had begun trickling from her temples, and each time she swiped at it she came away with black smears on her fingertips. She shuddered to imagine how her face must look.

Staring out over the lush grassland, her hands gripping the wagon seat, she did her best to make sense of her situation. He'd booted her out of his house; now he was dragging her back. Not, of course, due to repentance over his previous behavior, but simply because of his feud with Sean.

Sabre cleared his throat, making her stiffen in anticipation.

"So where in Ireland are you from?" he asked.

"Why?" she snapped. "So y' can put me on the next boat home?"

"A tempting thought, I suppose. But it hadn't occurred to me."

She raised her chin and stared harder at the countryside.

"I'm curious," he insisted.

"I can't imagine why."

"A man should know something about his *wife*."

"But I'm not yer wife. Remember?" She cocked him a smug smile.

He looked at her so hard that she felt her stomach do a somersault. "That remains to be seen," he finally replied. "I admit there could be a slight possibility that I signed that proxy."

That brought her head around. Her heart beat double-time while she waited for him to continue.

"What I mean is . . ." He appeared to choose his words carefully while his hands manipulated the wagon reins with ease. "*If* I signed it . . . I didn't intend to. I was drunk and that bastard Jamie MacFarland took advantage of the situation. It was a prank, pure and simple."

"In other words y' *really* didn't want a wife."

A gust of wind lifted the hair around his shoulders. "I believe I've already established that fact."

"Or maybe y' just don't want *me*," she countered angrily. "Maybe I'm not good enough t' meet yer aristocratic standards. So it's easy enough t' just bundle me up and send me sailin' back t' London."

"That's not what I said."

"But it's what yer thinkin'." Damned conceited high-stocking. "I know yer kind. Thinkin' yer too good for the likes o' me." The dray bounced over a rock and she grabbed the wagon seat again, forced her gaze from Sabre's emotionless features, and glared toward a shepherd's shack perched on the side of a hill. "A man with yer reputation can hardly be choosy," she added spitefully.

His brown hands clutched the reins more tightly. "Besides," she went on thoughtfully, "how can y' be so sure that I'm not a fittin' wife for an aristocrat?"

He remained silent and apparently blind to anything but the rolling countryside for so long that she began to wonder if he had heard her. Then she reconsidered. He had heard her all right. She could see it in the set of his shoulders, the uplifted black eyebrow that said more than words ever could. "The fact is . . . once m' mother and father were very well off," she began. " 'Tis only unfortunate circumstances that have brought me t' New Zealand."

Sabre was staring at her now. She didn't have to look to know it; she could feel it as she focused her attention on a half dozen lambs frolicking in the clover-blanketed meadows.

"Do tell," he said.

Searching the hills, her mind scrambled for a way out of the lie she was spinning. She felt fifteen again, doing her best to dissuade the curious villagers who pried into her personal affairs with their nosy questions and sly insinuations. Then she remembered a story that Martha had been reading, the general plot line of which she had told Summer in scandalized tones.

"M' mother traveled t' England from Ireland when she was my age. She took the position o' governess for the very distinguished Lord Rochester, who became m' father."

"Rochester? I thought your name was Fairburn."

"Oh. Well, it was. His name was Rochester Fairburn, y' see." *Think*. Was she remembering the story correctly? Never mind. Sabre was certain to be impressed by it. "He hired m' mother t' be governess t' his children—his wife was deceased, y' understand." She looked at him askance and discovered he was frowning. "Anyhow . . . they soon fell in love and planned t' marry. But strange things had been happenin' in the house; Mummy had heard screams in the night comin' from the attic!" She punctuated *attic* with a sharp nod of her head that sent the remaining tendrils of hair atop her head shimmering down her back and springing around her face.

Sabre pulled back on the reins, bringing the wagon to a halt before he swiveled on the bench. With elbows on his knees, he regarded her intently, as if he truly found the tale mesmerizing. "Go on," he encouraged.

Go on. But how did she do that when he sat there looking so distinguished in his black coat and white cravat?

Taking a breath, she ventured more slowly, "The day m' mother and Rochester were t' be wed, a stranger showed up and announced that Rochester was already married, and that . . . his crazy wife was hidden in the attic!"

"No!"

"Yes!" she exclaimed, leaning forward for emphasis. Her eyes grew wider as she explained, "M' mother was heartbroken and ran away. Then, weeks later, she heard that the lord's manor had burned down—his insane wife set the fire! She rushed back t' the house to discover m' father had been blinded and his wife killed in the blaze. They were married anyway, despite the fact that they were destitute. Finally, I was born. Soon after, m' father died and eventually m' mother died too . . . of a broken heart, o' course."

"Of course."

She sighed and gazed dolefully toward the horizon. "Alas, I was a destitute orphan and forced t' take a position as a house servant. Then I bumped into Jamie MacFarland. The rest y' know."

"Fascinating."

"I thought so." Shifting on the wagon seat, she primly smoothed her skirt and apron, cocking her head just enough to watch Sabre from behind her slightly lowered lashes. "So y' see, Mr. Sabre, Esquire, I'm as good as anyone on this island. Includin' yerself."

"So it would seem."

He continued to watch her with something akin to amusement on his tanned, unshaven face. He didn't blink and he didn't smile. Yet there was something in the way he looked at her that brought hot color to her cheeks, made her feel frightened and exhilarated at once. Suddenly she wished she could leap from the dray and run all the way back to O'Connell's, but she couldn't. Unable to do anything else, she sat with her hands clenched in her lap while he visually diced her into little pieces.

At last, she found voice enough to say, "Y' don't like me, do y', Mr. Sabre?"

"No," he replied. "I don't."

She blinked at him, all too aware that his matter-of-fact admission had stunned her into dumbfounded silence. She tried to swallow, but discovered she couldn't. She could only form the word *Oh*, with her lips. She wasn't aware that her eyes had filled with tears until Sabre very slowly withdrew a kerchief from his pocket and gently put it into her hand.

"But then," he went on in an even voice, "I don't like *anyone* . . . Mrs. Sabre. So you shouldn't take it personally. I'm sure that once you get to know me better you won't like me either."

He took up the lines again, and the wagon rolled forward.

For the remainder of the journey, Nick contemplated telling the lass just what she was getting herself into—that is, on the unlikely chance that he *allowed* her to stay. Obviously, she had already been advised of his ongoing feud with Sean. He doubted, however, that Sean had gone into detail about the *real* reason for his anger toward Nick . . . idiotic as it was.

The entire island knew Nick as an aloof, unfriendly sort who preferred the company of his dog, sheep, and shepherd to that of his peers. But although they had their suspicions, they didn't know he was a convicted murderer. Surely no one could have informed Summer of *that*. Otherwise she'd have marched right back on the *Tasmanian Devil* and refused to make the long voyage to Malvern Hills. If he told her now it would solve this dilemma. So why didn't he?

Betsy bounded off the porch the moment the dray topped the rise. A black-and-white blur, she streaked up the wagon path and sprang into Nick's lap with enough impact to knock him backwards. Allowing the reins to fall where they may, he wrapped his arms around the squirming dog and tussled playfully with her while she licked his face, throat, and hands. Then Frank came out of the house, and watched them with his arms crossed over his chest.

Nick leaped from his perch. He was climbing the porch steps with Betsy at his heels when Frank said, "Ain't ya fergittin' somethin'?"

Without looking back, he replied, "No," and entered the house.

Once inside, however, he paused in the shadows, vaguely realizing that Betsy, having grown frustrated by his lack of attention, had begun whining. Listening hard, he heard Frank say, "Let me help ya down from that blasted wagon. Whoa there, jest wait a galdern minute."

"I can do it m'self, thank y' very much—"

"Frank Wells. I'd be obliged if'n ya'd call me Frank. There now. Where's yore personals?"

"At Sean's." Her voice sounded closer. Nick looked to his left, into his bedroom, at the bed. Frank had made it, as usual. The sun pouring through the window quilt cast patches of color on the white cotton coverlet so that it looked like a painter's palette.

"He hauled me away so fast I didn't have time—"

"No need to worry. Hell, I'll ride over thar myself and fetch 'em after a while."

The porch rumbled with their footfalls, then Frank shoved the door open. Slowly, Nick turned to face them, his gaze sliding over Summer to Frank, who regarded him with expectation.

"Well?" the old man said when the silence had dragged on for some time. "Whar you gonna put her, boss?"

Finally, he looked at Summer who stood, hopping mad, just inside the threshold. With her face soot-smeared and her hair a wild mess, she looked more like a scarecrow than a woman. She was wearing a man's shirt—no doubt Sean's—and it hung from her small shoulders, sizes too large. Once, both sleeves had been rolled up to her elbows; now, one spilled over her hand by a good six inches. The other still exposed her thin forearm that was smut-streaked as well. Her fingers were fisted. Her purple eyes were narrowed and boring into his.

At last, she stepped further into the house, looked first to her right, into the cubicle he sarcastically called the drawing room, which was furnished with a frayed, discolored settee facing an unadorned fireplace—nothing else, not a rug or even a picture on the wall, took away from its starkness. She looked at the kitchen to the rear. It was little more than a stove, dry sink, and crude table he'd constructed out of the lumber remnants left over from when he'd built the house. Then her eyes shifted back to him, and to the room behind him. At last, she turned to Frank and said, "It ain't exactly a castle, is it?"

"You don't like it?" Nick demanded.

A gleam of mischief lit her eyes briefly as she shook her head. "No," she replied with a less than sincere smile on her pink lips. "I don't. I've seen bigger chicken coops. They looked better, too."

"Well, that's fine," he told her, his voice menacing. "In fact, that's bloody fantastic, because you won't be staying long anyway, if I can help it. My signing that damned idiotic contract was a mistake, an unfortunate error in judgment made while I was inebriated, so you'd better not expect anything more from me aside from temporary shelter . . . until I can decide how to rectify our unwholesome *and* unwelcome situation."

"Fine," she retorted, her eyes flashing with anger as she moved across the floor to stand before him, toe to toe, her hair a fiery halo as it reflected the sunlight through the open door at her back. "Send me home and see if I care. Yer no prize yerself, Sabre. Truth is, I—I'd rather be married t' *him*"— she nodded toward Frank, making Frank's bushy eyebrows shoot up in surprise—"than a black-hearted misfit with the personality and demeanor of a corpse."

"You don't say."

"And furthermore, if y' think I'm gonna share that bed with y'—"

"Good God, you flatter yourself, young woman."

That rocked her. For an instant she looked taken aback, and even through the black smudges on her cheeks, chin, forehead, and nose he could see her complexion fill with color. She wasn't just angry. She was absolutely furious.

She stood rigid as a board as he stepped around her and moved for the threshold. Frank didn't budge, though his eyes followed Nick to the door, where he hesitated only briefly before saying, "Ride over and pick up her things at O'Connell's."

"Right," Frank replied, then asked, "Whar'm I gonna put 'em once I git 'em?"

"As far away from me as possible."

"Oooh!" came Summer's enraged response. "Y' ill-tempered—"

"Whatever ya say, boss," Frank interjected. "Whar ya goin' now?"

"To see Ben and Clara."

"What about me?" Summer cried.

Nick spun on his heel to find her on the porch looking like a bantam with its feathers ruffled.

"What about you?"

"Yer just saunterin' off and leavin' me here?"

"Exactly." He headed for the wagon.

"When are y' comin' back?"

"That's none of your business."

"Well, maybe I'd like t' go!"

"You're joking." He leapt on the wagon and took up the reins. The next thing he knew Summer had planted herself in front of the horses, her purple eyes flashing.

"If y' didn't want me, Sabre, damn yer soul, why didn't y' just leave me t' Sean?"

"Get the hell out of my way."

"I'm not a piece o' meat, y' know. I'm not some blazin' sack o' potatoes y' can just throw over yer shoulder and haul from one place t' another, fling aside, then forget about. Y' brought me here, damn y'. Y' brought me t' this country for all that, and now y' don't want me. Well, I'm gettin' pretty tired o' people flingin' me aside, Mr. Sabre, Esquire. If y' don't want me for a wife, then let's go t' Christchurch this minute and get shut o' one another!"

He gave the lines a twitch and the horses tossed their heads and heaved forward, forcing Summer to jump out of the way or be trampled. Her voice drifted to him over the rattle of wagon wheels, but he refused to look back, just set his shoulders and stared straight ahead as the words came to him:

". . . last man on the face o' this earth I wouldn't want t' be married t' y'! I've known jackasses that weren't as stubborn as you . . . Yer a pig from hell, Sabre! Yer a boil on the butt o' humanity and I hope ever' Maori savage in New Zealand shoves his spear . . ."

Clara Beaconsfield gazed up from her reading, lowering her book slightly. "Nicky, are you listening?" she asked.

"Yes."

"What did I just read?"

"I believe Miss Anville has just been approached by Lord Orville, who, undoubtedly, finds the little red-haired twit somewhat attractive, if rather thickheaded." He shifted in his armchair and stretched his long legs before him. "Silly boy."

Clara shook her head, causing the fine blonde ringlets framing her piquant face to bob up and down. Closing the book, she placed it carefully on her lap and sighed. "That was two pages ago. Lord Orville has just professed his undying devotion to Miss Anville and beseeched her not to accompany Mrs. Selwyn on her journey. And there was no mention of Miss Anville having red hair."

"No?" He sat a little straighter and looked at Ben, who was leaning near a lamp with rose-painted globes and crystal prisms. Ben, a slightly older man than Nick, was studying a yellowing copy of the *London Times* over the top of his spectacles.

"Seems Lords Gladstone and Disraeli are at one another's throats again," Ben remarked. "Gladstone was overheard calling Disraeli unscrupulous and unprincipled. In turn, Disraeli publicly dismissed Gladstone as a humbug in the House of Commons." Removing his glasses, he folded the *Times* and held it out to Nick. "There's also talk of the Earl of Chesterfield, if you're interested."

Ignoring the proffered paper, Nick left his chair and paced toward the fireplace where he regarded the tall white Minton vase boasting a spray of vibrantly green fern fronds on the mantel.

"I take it you're not," Ben said, and the paper rustled again. "There seems to be some discussion of his taking Gladstone's place as Chancellor of the Exchequer when he retires."

Nick shoved his hands in his pockets before turning to face his hosts. Usually, news of his father would have piqued his interest, or at the least stirred an amiable debate on British political issues. Tonight, however, his mind kept straying to a wife he didn't want, whose own background was, undoubtedly, as questionable and unseemly as his own.

Ben sat back in his chair and crossed his legs while his wife, Clara, folded her small hands demurely in her lap and waited for Nick's response. Their faces were oddly anticipatory. Then the realization struck Nick that they had been observing him with an unusual intentness all evening.

"Do you wish to tell us anything?" Clara inquired, her eyes bright.

He leaned against the mantel. "I could use a drink."

Ben poured them each a sherry. Nick tossed his back, closing his eyes as it hit his stomach. At last, he managed to say, "I'm married."

"We know," Clara replied.

"We were wondering how long it would take you to admit it," Ben added. "I understand she's been working for Sean the last five days."

Nick slammed the glass down on the mantel and swore under his breath.

Ben glanced at Clara. "I must admit to being shocked when I heard."

"Horrified!" Clara exclaimed.

"It was a black joke, Nick, and the lot of buggers should be tarred and feathered."

"How long have you known?" Nick demanded.

"Since yesterday. I hasten to add that it's my understanding that Sean had nothing to do with the scheme. He only heard the others talking the morning she arrived. What do you intend to do now?"

"He'll annul the marriage, of course." Rising from her chair, her robin's-egg-blue crinoline rustling, Clara stood before Nick, frowning. "I understand she was a house servant in London."

"I hear she's very pretty," Ben countered.

"Oh, pooh." Clara wrinkled her nose. "Is that all you men can think about? The question is, is she respectable?"

"You, my dear wife, are prejudiced when it comes to Nick."

"Perhaps so, but I wouldn't want him any unhappier than he has been already."

Nick allowed a smile to touch his mouth, just briefly. Clara had always reminded him of a china doll, so pale and fragile. How easily she and Ben could have fit in with the aristocracy back home; there were times, such as now, when the sickening realization hit him that once he might have looked down his straight nose at them just because they were a product of a "lesser" class.

"Well?" Clara said. "What is she like?"

"Young and skinny and foul-tempered ... and obviously a close acquaintance of Charlotte Brontë." He went on to explain how Summer's illustrious ancestry so remarkably paralleled that of Jane Eyre. By the time he had finished, Clara and Ben were laughing uproariously, while Nick, having poured himself another drink, stared into his glass, remembering Summer's face as she related her absurd story.

Clara dabbed at her eyes with a hankie. "Oh, my, that's delightful, but it certainly leads one to question her background. What will you do, Nicky? Certainly the Registrar General shan't hold you to the contract, considering the circumstances. I mean ... if the marriage isn't ... how shall I say—"

"Consummated." Ben smiled at his wife, causing Clara's cheeks to stain a becoming pink. He moved to the open door where he gazed out at the night, the fingers of one hand casually tucked into the back pocket of his breeches. "That is certainly a thought to hold on to," he finally said to Nick. "I shouldn't think that you would want to rush into anything without first giving it a great deal of consideration."

Nick put down his sherry glass. "As I recall, that sort of hotheaded behavior is what got me into this mess in the first place . . . that and a woman." He frowned at the memory. "I don't expect I'll be too quick to repeat my mistakes." At last, he moved toward the door. "It's getting late," he said. "It's a long ride home."

"You're welcome to stay over," Ben replied.

"Of course he'll stay!" Clara joined in. "I'll have Renee prepare the extra bed—"

"I can't," Nick interrupted. "I should be there in the morning. We didn't get any shearing done today so we'll have to make up for it tomorrow."

Ben said, "Nick, you know that I'll be more than happy to send over some of my men—"

"No, thank you."

"But—"

"No." He shook his head. "No."

Nick pressed a brief kiss on Clara's hand, then followed Ben out of the house. They sauntered down the path in silence before Ben said, "I'd be lying if I claimed I wasn't distressed over this marriage. I suggest that you get shut of the girl—an annulment—before something happens to make that alternative impossible."

"In other words, before I bed her."

"Such a commitment—"

"Would be the final noose around my neck." Nick laughed shortly. "Not to worry. The girl's not even remotely appealing to me."

"Need I remind you that it's been a long time—"

"No," he replied dryly, "you don't need to remind me. To be honest, it's been so long since I last crawled between a woman's legs—in fact, it's been so long since I've even wanted to—I have to wonder if I could."

Ben laughed quietly in the dark. Nick mounted the dray before looking down at his friend, who smoothed one hand over one of the horses' withers and said, "I hesitated to bring up the subject in front of Clara, but I wonder if you heard about Jake Madison?"

Nick pictured the old man's face. One of the first Cockatoos to settle in the area, Jake had successfully established a station out near Mount Torlesse and the Kowai Bush over a decade ago. "What happened?"

"The Clan hit him last night."

"How badly?"

"He lost everything. They burned down his house and buildings and spent the night butchering every one of his animals. They roughed Jake up pretty badly as well. Damn it, Nick, these raids have got to stop."

"Did you really think it wouldn't eventually come to murder, Ben?"

"It hasn't yet."

"But it will. Each hit has gotten worse than the last. You and I know the Cockatoos are helpless against a pack of animals like that. Until you and the few other farmers on the South Island who stand behind the Cockatoos are willing to confront the bastards, the violence will only get worse."

"And then our farms will be burned down." Ben shoved his hands in his pockets and glanced toward his house.

"Roy Tennyson wouldn't burn you out," Nick said. "You're too well respected by the other farmers. Perhaps if you try and talk to Sean again . . ."

Ben regarded him angrily. "I'm still not convinced Sean is involved. We all know Roy Tennyson is, and has been, the troublemaker since the beginning."

"I saw the Clan for myself today at Sean's: Roel Ormsbee, Virgil McIlhenny, Howard Goetz, and Ralph Gilstrap. There wasn't one man among them who wouldn't have shoved a torch in my face or a gun to my head had O'Connell given them the nod." Shifting on the wagon seat, Nick watched Clara walk to the door and gaze out at them. Her hair shone pale in the twilight, and the realization struck him that there was a girl back at his station waiting for him to come home.

Christ, how many times had he bid Ben and Clara good night and wished that there would be someone besides an old shepherd and a dog waiting for him back home? Now there was. Or was she?

"I'll speak to Sean . . ." came Ben's voice, and when Nick refocused on his friend's face, Ben was extending him the *London Times*, rolled neatly into a cylinder. "In defense of O'Connell, I'll say that if he has become involved in this deplorable fracas, it's because he's up to his ears in debt to Tennyson. I happen to know Roy loaned him the money to rebuild his barn after it burned down."

"Did you ever think that it might have been Roy who burned it down, just so he could get Sean under his thumb?"

Ben shook his head. "I'll talk to Sean. You know how difficult it can be to reason with him. He's as stubborn and pigheaded as you are about certain things . . . women among them. Neither of you will listen to reason."

"One should never be so naive as to use 'reason' and 'women' in the same context."

Ben laughed. "I'll drop by soon. Give Frank my best."

Nick tucked the paper into his coat pocket and watched as Ben climbed the steps to his neat white frame house with its gingerbread porch rails and windows bordered with pale yellow shutters. He thought of calling Ben back and telling him not to bother becoming involved with the Cockatoo feud.

He had a great deal to lose, after all. Aside from Tennyson's, Ben's station was the largest and most successful on the South Island. His house, his half dozen shearing sheds, and his acres of breeding pens, not to mention fifty thousand head of the country's finest sheep, were bounties Nick could only lie in bed at night and dream about. Someday...

"Ben!" he shouted.

Ben paused on the threshold of his front door and looked back.

"Forget it," Nick told him. "I'll fight my own battles."

"You're sure?"

He nodded, then watched as Ben stepped into the house and closed the door behind him.

Chapter 5

Summer sat on the ledge of the dry sink, swinging her feet and watching as Frank shuffled in front of the stove, drinking coffee and pressing balls of thick dough into flat cakes that sizzled on the greased griddle. "What are those?" she asked.

"Hoecakes." He flipped them over with a spatula; the crisp unleavened bread steamed. "Closest thang we got around here to bread. Tasty, too. And they keep right well. I'll just wrap these sapsuckers up in a towel and tuck 'em in yonder basket. They'll be mighty good come mealtime tomorrow when we is up to our belly buttons in sheep hair. Here. Take one and smear it with that thar *korako* marmalade. I swear, it's so good it'll make yore jaws lock."

Summer smeared the hotcake with the sweet peach mixture, then sampled it. "Ummm."

"Hot damn, didn't I tell ya it was good?" Frank chuckled. "It's about time somebody around here appreciated my cookin'. I've been workin' my magic in this kitchen for pert near two years and ain't seen hide nor hair of a compliment yet."

Summer frowned. She could just imagine Sabre sitting at the table with his unsmiling face and contrary disposition, eating Frank's food and telling him exactly what was wrong with it. Then again, he probably said absolutely nothing at all. "Why have y' stayed? I can't imagine yer toleratin' his temper for so long."

Frank slid the cakes off the griddle and replaced them with another batch. "Oh, he ain't got much of a temper. Sometimes I wish he did. Might liven the place up some. Naw, if'n he gits mad he just glares down that aristocratic nose, or walks off someplace whar he thanks nobody kin see 'im and hits somethin' that can't hit back . . . like a tree or the side of a house."

"Sean suspects he killed a man. What do y' think?"

"Me? Aw, hell, Nick don't pay me to thank. Probably he did," he added a bit more solemnly. "He ain't ever talked about it and I ain't ever asked him. Fact is, most of us are runnin' away from a memory or a mistake. Maybe even prison." Frank shook his head. "But, while ya kin leave bars and chains behind, there ain't no escapin' the prison in yore mind. Them damn memories kin lock ya up tighter'n any gaoler ever could." He poured himself a fresh cup of coffee and gazed out the window, his lined face sobering as he noted the crimson and orange clouds massed along the horizon.

"What about this feud between Sean and Sabre?"

"Them boys is gotta lotta anger built up inside 'em, darlin', and that can be a mighty dangerous thang. Set a pot to simmerin' long enough and eventually it's either gonna burn itself dry or boil over. Problem is, Sean and Nick are two peas in a pod. Proud, stubborn, and furious at life. Only difference is, Nick keeps his feelin's bottled up, while Sean walks around spittin' like a lit fuse. I often wonder which is worse . . . Reckon he'll be here soon," he added thoughtfully, then turned back to Summer. "Remind me sometime to tell ya the story of the day I was cookin' up some grub fer my brother and his *compadres*, and—"

Frank abruptly turned back to the door, head cocked, eyebrows drawn together as he listened. Thinking Sabre had returned, Summer leaped from the dry sink and stood ready to make a quick exit, when Frank jabbed the spatula at her and said, "Flip them hoecakes when they's ready."

"Is somethin' wrong?"

His blue eyes narrowed. "Them sheep is lookin' a mite suspicious, I'd say."

Joining Frank at the door, Summer focused on the distant buildings: a barn, a chicken coop, the wool shed where the skillion was crowded with sheep to be sheared first thing in the morning. "What's wrong?" she asked nervously.

She sensed it now. Something wasn't right. The sheep were quiet and all of them were facing the northwest. The air was still, the silence almost painful.

Frank stepped from the house, his sights pinned on the distant mountains. Little by little the dull twilight was taking on a yellowish-green tinge, and the mountains were disappearing behind a haze of dust as impenetrable as any English fog. Cupping his hands around his mouth, he filled the air with an ear-splitting whistle, then waited. "Good dog," he muttered. "She's done drove 'em down to the holler."

"Frank," Summer whispered. "Will y' tell me what's wrong?"

"Nor'wester," he replied as softly. "That thar dust is bein' driven by wind and rain. I say we got five

minutes tops afore all hell breaks loose." He spun
back for the house, suddenly as lithe as a man half
his age. Summer ran after him. "Hoecakes," he
barked over his shoulder. "Them sapsuckers is
burnin'."

"Where are y' goin'?"

"Nick'll be on his way from Ben's place about
now. If'n he gets caught in this . . ."

She stared first at the door, then at the griddle,
where black smoke was beginning to stream up from
each cake. She scraped them off, tossed them in the
vicinity of Betsy's bowl, then dashed after Frank.
He had grabbed a macintosh from a peg on the wall
and was just mounting his horse as she ran onto
the front porch steps. In that instant, a howl of wind
slammed the shanty, hitting her between the shoulders like a fist. She cried aloud and grabbed her hair
and then her skirt as the gust blew both up over her
head.

"Git in and stay in!" Frank shouted. "It's gonna
be a mean one!"

"Where are y' goin'?" she cried.

"Rivers rise *rápido* in these rains! If'n a man gits
caught in one . . ." The wail of the wind drowned
out his voice; the dust drove like hailstones against
her exposed flesh, blinding her. When she managed
to see again, Frank was gone.

She stumbled back into the house and had just
managed to slam the door when the first drops of
rain smacked against the windows and roof. The
floor trembled. The walls shook. Something ripped
loose on the roof and clattered and banged from one
end to the other. Summer ran to the parlor where
she covered her head in fear that the ceiling would
collapse. She moved to the kitchen and banked the
fire in the stove, otherwise afraid the hovel of sticks
and stones would go up like a bonfire. With no place

else to hide, she hurried to the bedroom where Frank, after a great deal of heated debate between them, had earlier put her "personals."

Sitting cross-legged in the middle of the bed, she listened to the wind moan and the rain drive. Not for the first time that day, she asked herself what in heaven's name she was doing on a sheep station that felt like a million miles away from another civilized soul . . . married to a man who wanted nothing to do with her . . . who had so disliked her on sight that he'd kicked her out of his house.

Well . . . she should thank the ever-lovin' saints that she wouldn't be forced to go through with the awful obligations of marriage. The very idea made her shiver. So what if he wasn't so bad on the eyes? The ogre obviously had a heart of ice and a reputation far worse than anything she had imagined during that terrible sea voyage from England.

She punched his pillow. Once. Twice. She rolled it up, tucked it between her knees, and pummeled it with her fists until her arms quivered with the effort. "That's for kickin' me out." *Whack.* "That's for not likin' me." *Thump.* "And that's for not bein' short and bald and as old as Frank." *Whack-thump-boof!* She hurled the pillow onto the bed and buried her face in it.

It didn't smell like sheep. It smelled like . . . bay rum and soap, and suddenly she felt a queer little flutter in the pit of her stomach. Frowning, she rolled onto her back and stared at the ceiling while the rain and wind rolled over the house and moaned down the stovepipe.

Even the darn house was disappointing. The walls were raw wood—not painted, much less papered. The ceiling beams were exposed; not a picture decorated the walls. Nor was there a solitary trinket to attest to Nick's past. Sean's knickknacks, displayed in every nook and cranny, had been hell to dust, but . . .

If she were allowed, she'd buy carpets for Sabre's floors—perhaps Persians like Pimbersham had had—and dress the windows with lace curtains, with plenty of material to spread over the floor because she'd once heard that lots of material puddled around the baseboard indicated wealthy residents. The old place could do with some more furniture as well—especially the parlor. Once they started entertaining they would need chairs for their guests. Maybe an upholstered wing chair or two. And she certainly wouldn't say no to a new settee. This one had obviously been used when Sabre had bought it. And what parlor would be complete without new brass andirons for the hearth? She could just imagine them glistening with firelight this winter. Oh, and not to forget the canary-bird. No respectable family in London was without one!

Ah, she'd had such dreams about coming here.

She wandered to the parlor, then back to the kitchen, spotted a curtain hung over a doorway, and peeked inside, expecting a larder. Instead, there was a tiny room filled with a crudely made desk and lined with shelves. Her gaze swept over books, pens, ink, a certificate of diploma upon the wall, papers on the desk, a lantern, several leather-bound ledgers, and a gray metal box. Two tintypes caught her eye, one of a distinguished gentleman—his father, no doubt—the other a younger man whose resemblance to Sabre was so striking, it was like looking into Nicholas's intense eyes. The straight nose was identical, the cheekbones just as high, the mouth as insolent. Only this man was smiling, turning what might have been a sinister countenance into one of warm friendliness.

Voices came to her from a distance, first Frank's,

then Sabre's, sounding like low thunder and bringing a knot to her stomach.

"River'll be way up," Frank declared. "At first light I'll mosey on down and have a look. Could be Johnson'll be diggin' mud out of his house agin. I might give him a hand if'n ya don't mind."

"There's the shearing," Sabre reminded him.

"I'll be back by noon. I'll deal with the horses while ya git out of them clothes."

Summer plunked the photograph back on the shelf and ran to the bedroom.

The back door opened, the sound of rain momentarily filling up the silence, then closed. Her heart pounded.

She heard the clinking of pottery then the scraping of a chair. Closing her eyes, she breathed easier, though she continued to strain to catch every sound. Carefully, she tiptoed to the doorway and peeked toward the kitchen, castigating herself for creeping about in such a cowardly fashion. It wasn't her nature to be so intimidated; she'd always given Martha as good as the old hag gave ... but then, Martha hadn't been a black-eyed, snarling, strutting brute. Well, she wanted things straight between them, once and for all. Either she stayed, or she went. It was up to him.

With a righting of her shoulders and a lifting of her chin, she stepped into the doorway. Sabre was sitting at the table, his head resting on his forearms, his black hair glistening with water. His eyes were closed. Rain dripping off his drenched clothes made puddles on the floor. His fingers were curled around a steaming mug of coffee. He looked up.

He unfolded his big body from the table and sat back, fatigue shadowing his features as he stretched out his legs. Slowly, the coffee mug came up to his mouth as his perusal slid from the crown of her head, over her shoulders, hesitated at the overly large blouse, then proceeded down, down so slowly that she thought she might collapse.

He put his cup on the table and nudged it toward her. She refilled it with coffee and placed it back on the table. He drank without saying a word.

Finally, she said, "Yer welcome. While I'm at it, can I get y' anythin' else?" No response. She grabbed up the plate of cold hoecakes and plunked it on the table. *Choke on 'em*, she considered saying, then thought better of it.

He reached for one and broke it down the middle. Mesmerized, she caught herself staring at his hands. Much to her surprise, he offered her half of the cake. To her greater astonishment, she accepted it.

"Sit down," he said. His voice was deep, no more than a whisper. After a slight hesitation, she dragged back a chair and sat down.

"So," he said. "Here we are. Tell me what you think of my humble abode . . . I mean, aside from it not being a castle."

She lowered her eyes. "It's not so bad," she replied, meaning it.

"No?" He took a lingering look at the barren walls before his eyes settled on her again, unblinking and black, holding her immobile. "I must admit I'm surprised you're still here."

"Where else would I go?"

"Back to Sean."

"Do y' mean y' still think I'm involved with Sean in some sort o' scheme to ruin y'?"

"Obviously, if that proxy contract is legal, then so are you."

She regarded him hopefully. "Then yer admittin' that I'm yer wife?"

He studied her over the rim of his coffee cup. "The rivers are rising," he finally said. He broke off a piece of cake and slid it into his mouth. "What I mean is, a trip to Christchurch is out of the question until the waters subside."

"Christchurch?"

He swallowed his cake and drank his coffee.

"Oh," she said, when his meaning sank in. "Yer sendin' me back."

"You really wouldn't like it here. It's lonely. Too hot in the summer and too cold in the winter."

"You seem t' do all right," she argued before catching herself. Only then did she realize she'd disintegrated her own cake into a pile of crumbs.

Nick watched hot color creep up Summer's throat from beneath the prudish lace collar. Her delicate fingers moved the cake crumbs from one point on the table to another while silence dragged on between them. Finally, he said, "It's really not much of a life for a young woman. How old are you, anyway?"

"Eighteen."

"A young woman of your age should have friends. Besides, as you can see, I lead a plain life. I'm practically destitute."

"That doesn't mat—"

"There isn't any money for those things that women seem to require to make them happy. No doubt you've already been dreaming about filling this place with doilies and lace curtains and fine furniture shipped from England."

Summer lowered her eyes. He put his cup down. "I probably couldn't afford the clothes you wore on your back when you first arrived here, Irish. At least, not without sacrificing money for food or supplies. I—"

She stood up abruptly. Her hands clenched at her sides as she stared at some point over his head. "Y've made yer point, Mr. Sabre. There's no need t' compile a list of all the reasons why I'm not welcome here. Y've got yer sheep and yer dog and yer friend Frank t' keep y' company; therefore, y' got no room in yer life for me. Well, that suits me just fine. I—I don't need y' either. This was a silly idea anyhow, comin' t' New Zealand. I've got plenty o' friends back in England and . . ." She swallowed once, twice, turned on her heel, and left the room.

He rose from his chair so fast it tipped backwards. In two long strides he caught her and spun her around. He heard the swift, surprised breath she took. She stared up at him, furious and hurt, her eyes glistening with tears. For an instant he was swept with a need to crush his mouth onto hers.

"What the hell do you want from me?" he demanded, shaking her hard. "Commitment? Devotion? Security? Sorry, my dear, but I don't have them to give. I'm fighting too damn hard to survive. If Frank and I aren't cinching our belts a little tighter from hunger, we're pacing the floor throughout the night worrying that some renegades wearing hoods are going to swoop down on us in the dark and destroy everything we've built during the last three years."

She tried to squirm away. He yanked her back so fast her head snapped. "I was drunk when I signed that contract."

"I'm well aware o' that."

"I never had any intention of sending away for a wife."

"So y've said repeatedly."

His eyes roved over her face. His body tensed. Gripping her tighter, he said, "I don't want a wife, goddamn you, so stop looking at me like a kicked puppy."

"Yer hurtin' me."

He released his grip; she slipped away and hurried from the room.

Nick leaned against the dry sink, crossed his arms over his wet chest, and tried to calm his pounding heart. It was impossible. Her image remained emblazoned in his mind, right down to the nine tiny freckles scattered over the bridge of her nose.

Frank's footsteps paused outside long enough for him to stomp the mud from his boots, then he shoved open the door. "Wicked," he declared. "That's one mean nor'wester. Mark my words, there'll be sheep bobbin' on the rivers lookin' like a buncha galdern dumplins in a stew pot." Blinking rain from his eyes, he wrenched off his boots and placed them by the stove to dry. "So." He reached for the coffeepot. "What's eatin' ya? Aw, don't even bother to tell me. You and the little missus has been at it agin. Well, not to worry. You'll git used to each other soon enough." He glanced at Nick over his shoulder. "Want some coffee?"

"No."

Frank emptied the pot and shoved it aside.

"I'm sending her back."

The old man tipped the cup to his mouth and winced. "Man, that's hot and thick enough to grow hair on yore tongue."

Nick scowled. "I said—"

"I ain't deaf. Hell, go on and send her back. Nobody'll miss her when she's gone. 'Specially not you. You kin keep on wallerin' in yore solitude and hatin' the world just so's the world kin keep on hatin' you." He leaned back against the dry sink next to Nick and stared down at his damp socks. The pounding rain filled the momentary silence. "Ya like the sound of that?" he finally asked.

"What? The rain?"

"Nope. Beyond that."

He listened. "I don't hear anything."

"That's right. That's exactly what yore gonna be hearin' till you die of old age. That's the last thang yore gonna hear when yore layin' in that bed in that room and preparin' to meet yore maker. Silence." He shook his head. "Silence kin be a mighty frightenin' thang, boss. Thank about it." He put aside his cup, slid his feet back into his boots, and exited the house.

The rain drummed. The wind moaned. The stovepipe clattered. Turning to the window, Nick looked out at the dark. Minutes dragged by until, at last, a tiny speck of light flickered to life in the distance. He imagined Frank stepping into the one-room building that was his home, lighting the lantern, trading his work clothes for his shin-long nightshirt, then settling down on his mattress to sleep . . . a sixty-year-old man, alone.

A raindrop caught Nick on the bridge of his nose. He watched the water spot on the ceiling grow dark and heavy before dropping its burden on the front of his shirt. Wearily, he searched beneath the sink for a pan large enough to hold an entire night's worth of leakage, then dismissed the idea. Until the land feud between the farmers and the Cockatoos was settled, he'd be up and down throughout the night checking out any suspicious noises. He hadn't been hit by Tennyson's pack of marauders yet, but his day was coming.

Deciding the roaster would do, he positioned it beneath the drip. He'd put out the lantern and started for the bedroom when he remembered it was occupied. He moved on to the parlor, only to be brought up short by the sight of Summer sitting on the settee, small shoulders erect, hands folded in her lap, sights set on the fireplace. On the floor at her feet was her valise, beside it her bird-feather hat.

"What are you doing?" he demanded.

"I wouldn't think o' displacin' y' from yer bed, Mr. Sabre. I'm sleepin' here."

"Don't be stupid."

"Y've made yerself perfectly clear. My residin' here is temporary . . . and besides, considerin' the circumstances, it wouldn't be proper for us t' sleep together."

"I had no intention of sleeping with you."

Her chin came around. "Oh?"

"I'm sleeping here."

"On this?" She looked at the settee.

"Yes."

She shook her head. "I'm the one who is uninvited. I shan't put y' out any more than necessary. Just forget that I'm here."

"That'll be the day," he muttered to himself. Moving around the settee, he swept up her valise and hat. Before she could skewer him with her eyes again, he grabbed her arm and propelled her out of the parlor to the bedroom, where he tossed the case in the vicinity of the bed, plunked the hat on her head, spun on his boot heel, and returned to the parlor. There he stood with his hands on his hips and stared into the empty fireplace and listened to the rain drip into the pan. Minutes ticked by, then:

"Mr. Sabre?"

"What?" When she didn't respond, he looked over his shoulder. She stood in the doorway with her burnished hair falling softly over the white nightgown with its pink ribbons tied in a dainty bow at her throat. The gown pooled over her toes by a good three inches. She was clutching a quilt and his pillow to her stomach. "What?" he repeated.

"I thought y' might need these." She extended the pillow.

He turned to face the hearth again.

The pillow, then the quilt, landed with a muffled thud on the settee behind him. Then the bedroom door closed with a short squeak of its hinges.

He didn't bother to remove his clothes, just extinguished the lamp, punched the pillow into place on the settee arm, and laid down. He stared at the ceiling.

Plink . . . plink . . .

The bedroom door squeaked. The floor creaked somewhere near the kitchen.

"What the devil are you doing now?" he yelled.

"I can't sleep with this water drippin'. I'm gonna put a dish towel in the pot so I can't hear it. Is that all right with y'?" The query trilled with sarcasm.

"Fine." He punched his pillow.

In a moment, the door squeaked again. He shut his eyes.

The wind died. The rain settled into a constant drone on the roof that lulled him to the very threshold of sleep. Something, however, held him back, some invisible force that kept his mind teetering on the brink of oblivion. The creaks and groans of warping lumber had finally fallen silent; the smells of strong coffee and Frank's hoecakes lingered, mixed with the delicate scent of something else, something sweet and foreign yet familiar. He breathed it cautiously, allowing it to dance through his bloodstream like the finest aged brandy, stirring his lethargic body into a drowsy, humming wakefulness. In his mind, there were fleeting visions of swirling figures in Parisian costumes. Fluttering fans. Lilting laughter. Coy flirtations. Images of him placing his lips on the curve of a female's arched neck while his body flowed like a river into hers.

Turning his face into the pillow, he breathed in the scent of a woman.

Groaning, he sat up, raked his hands through his hair, and massaged his pounding temples. He left the settee and paced, his mind bouncing back and forth over the day's events: his confrontation with Sean, Summer, Ben. Then Jake Madison's face materialized in his mind's eye. Cursing he strode to his office, lifted the lid on the gray metal box, and drew out the pistol. He rolled it in his hand, felt rather than saw in the dark its cold gray shape. It was heavy. Much heavier than the last gun he'd held those six years ago . . .

Blinking the memory from his mind, he exited the house, settled himself on the top step of the back stoop, hunched his shoulders against the drizzle, and stared out into the darkness.

"Leave me alone," he said to the rain. "Just leave me the hell alone."

Chapter 6

Summer hurled the last shovel of muck out the door and threw down the spade. Behind her, Dora Johnson said, "Praise the Lord, we're finished. I don't know about you, ladies, but I'm ready for tea and tarts."

Turning back to her hostess, Summer smiled. "So am I."

"Me, too," Nan Sharkey replied, plunking a bucket of water on the floor and arching her back. She waddled toward a chair and dragged it back to the table before easing her very pregnant body into it. Nan could not have been over thirty-five. Her hair was coffee-brown and worn in a corona of braids; her face was thin, but not unattractively so. Her husband, Arnold, was robust and broad-shouldered, his jolly square face burned a permanent bronze from the sun and wind. He walked with a limp, a result of a confrontation with a wild pig on a hunting expedition two years before.

Summer glanced about the filthy room, wondering how Dora could so lightly accept the fact that her fine house had been practically destroyed by the rising river overflowing its banks after the storm last night.

"Another day's scrubbing and it'll be good as new," Dora continued, rattling china and a tin stacked high with thick-crusted pastries. She placed the tarts on a flower patterned platter and set it on the table in front of Summer and Nan. "Help yourself," Dora encouraged Summer. "Don't be shy. I'm not certain what it is about New Zealand, but we're all perpetually hungry."

Summer didn't hesitate. Just as she expected, the tart melted in her mouth.

Dora laughed, wiping her hands on her apron. She was a shapely woman in her mid-twenties; Summer thought her very pretty. Her hair was honey-blonde, her eyes a sparkling green. She was big-boned and big-bosomed, with a smile that could make the most timid stranger feel at ease in her presence.

"Without your help, I wouldn't have finished the job until this time tomorrow," Dora admitted. "It was right kind and considerate of you to ride out with Frank and lend us a hand."

"Does this sort o' thing happen often?" Summer asked as she continued to inspect her surroundings. On better days, the kitchen would have glowed with cheery warmth. There were red-and-white checked curtains tied back to expose four-paned windows. A golden oak sideboard dominated one wall, its shelves lined with jars of pickled onions, peaches, and cabbage.

"Once a year at the most," Dora replied.

Regarding the mud-stained floor and walls, Summer shook her head. "Why did y' build in the flood plain?"

"Didn't originally. Eight years ago the creek

curved off to the east about a half mile north of the house. Four years ago Roy Tennyson—he owns the station north of us where the creek commences—decided he didn't much care for a lot of Cockatoos roosting on his run. So he brought over some surveyors and engineers from Wellington and figured that by changing the outflow of the creek at its source they could alter its down-land course. He intended to run the creek right through our house, I suspect. Fortunately, the plan didn't quite work out, though it came near enough. Now, once a year, we get flooded. But Dan and the boys are working on that. Soon as they get that dike finished, our flooding days will be over."

Dora placed cups, saucers, and a teapot on the table, then dragged up a chair and fell into it. "Eat another tart," she said, her smile widening as Summer gladly obliged, catching a sliver of peach on her finger as it oozed from the sugar-sprinkled crust. "I'll give you the recipe," Dora told her. "Frank loves them."

Summer reached for the teapot and poured Dora and Nan cups, then one for herself. "It'll take more than a recipe for me t' turn out somethin' like this," she said. "I can't cook."

"You'll learn. We all have to start sometime."

"I couldn't boil water when Arnie and I first married," Nan admitted, rubbing her belly. "Now here I am expecting our tenth child and I can hardly wait."

In that moment three young boys, all with Dora's honey-blond hair and green eyes, exploded through the open doorway, skidding across the slimy floor like ice skaters. One boy's feet slid out from under him, landing him hard on his skinny backside, while the others sprawled on their mother, their fingers smearing mud on her hands, arms, and dress. She only laughed and hugged them tightly.

"Whoa! Just wait a minute. You boys go right back outside and wipe your feet before coming in here."

Three pairs of eyes looked at her in astonishment before the youngest, Wayne, began to snicker. "You is only bein' funny, huh?" he asked her.

"Certainly not." She tweaked his pug nose. "Can't you see that we've been toiling extremely hard to clean this floor?"

"She's bein' funny," the oldest of the trio, Jason, said with a cheeky smile and his eyes on the tarts. "Can I have one?" he asked.

"*May* I have one," she corrected.

"Shoot, I don't care." He glanced at Summer and wiggled his eyebrows, making her laugh.

Wayne, too short to reach the platter of tarts, began to scramble up on Summer's lap. She dragged him onto her knees and offered the plate, smiling as he plunged at the treats with both hands, then tried to cram two into his tiny mouth at once.

"Wayne, where are your manners?" Dora scolded.

"Ain't got none. Least dat's what Pa says."

"Pa's right," said Allen, the middle one. Crossing his arms over his chest in a mature fashion, he regarded Summer with a quirk of one thin blond eyebrow. "She don't look like no lunatic, does she, Ma?"

Dora gasped and Nan choked on her tea. Summer covered her mouth with her hand to hide her smile. "Well, I'm glad t' hear that."

Like a flustered hen, Dora jumped from her chair and, rounding up the children, hustled them toward the door, muttering under her breath.

"But, Ma," Allen cried, "you said yourself that anyone who'd marry the crazy Devil Lord would have to be a lunatic!"

The door slammed. Dora held her hands over her face to hide her embarrassment. "It's all right," Summer told her.

"No. No, it's not. I thought I'd taught those boys better manners."

"Y' can't stop them from bein' children."

"I suppose not." Dora shook her head. "I'm awfully sorry, Summer. Children and their big ears and mouths . . ."

Summer nodded in understanding.

Dora sat back in her chair, her work-worn fingers idly tracing the flower pattern on the china cup. "I must admit we've all been curious. Mr. Sabre has remained such an enigma for so long, when we heard he'd sent off to England for a wife we were all shocked."

"Then when you arrived and everyone in town saw you," Nan said, "there wasn't a man who didn't envy Sabre. We all thought that once you met him you might change your mind about staying."

"Oh? Why?"

"He's so . . . you know, unfriendly. Then there's the mystery of his past. Doesn't he frighten you?"

She thought about it and shook her head. "Not really, although he can be somewhat intimidatin'."

"Then you like him?" Dora asked.

Summer realized that whatever she said would no doubt be spread from one end of the South Island to the other in a matter of days, if not hours. What, exactly, did she feel toward the unlikable, despicable brute . . . aside from intense anger?

"I understand that some of the other women who came over on the *Tasmanian Devil* have already decided to go home—back to England. They're having their marriages annulled," Nan said.

Summer stared harder into her teacup.

"They didn't like their husbands or the fact that they would be so isolated."

Dora shook her head. "I truly don't know what they expected to find here. If there were great cities and companionship, the men wouldn't need to send off for wives, would they? More tea?"

Summer nodded.

"Grant you, it takes some getting used to. Sometimes the loneliness can be maddening. It's too much for some people. Oh, they start out with good intentions and high hopes, but when you're living out here, hearing nothing but the wind blow for weeks at a time, you eventually go crazy. You stay and lose your sanity, or you pack up and leave."

Dora sighed. "The thing is . . . it's such beautiful country, so full of promise and potential. But people need the companionship of others. That's why we stick so close—the Cockatoos I mean." She smiled at Nan. "We're like a family. We have to be. Even so, making deep, lasting friendships is difficult. More often than not, just about the time you truly get to know someone, they up and leave, or die. Then there are the down-landers—the townsfolk and larger station owners. They don't like us. They don't even want us in town, though they sure don't mind taking our money. They won't allow our children in their schools and they bar us from their churches."

"And the problem is only getting worse since they've organized that hideous Clan," Nan added. Noting Summer's concern, she asked, "Haven't you heard?" A look of fear passed between her and Dora. Dora explained:

"There's a group of some ten to twelve men—farmers—who've taken it on themselves to run the Cockatoos out of New Zealand. They ride down on our stations during the dead of night wearing horrible black hoods over their heads. At first they simply threatened the Cockatoos, did a lot of waving of torches and shouting. No actual destruction to property took place. Lately, however, their visits have been more dangerous."

"They've realized that we won't be run off no matter what," Nan added.

"Now they're taking more drastic measures. Houses and outbuildings have been burned. Sheep killed. Two nights ago Jake Madison was severely beaten."

"That's horrible," Summer replied. "Hasn't anyone gone t' the officials in Christchurch?"

"Of course. But what can they do? We're fifty miles from town and our farms are miles apart. There's simply no effective way to police the situation."

"Well, I don't know about the rest of you," Nan said, "but Arnie has vowed that if they come calling on us again they'll get bullets between the eyes. They terrified our children last time. Jimmy is still having nightmares."

"Is there anyone in particular behind the raids?" Summer asked.

"Roy Tennyson," Dora said. "No one can prove it, of course, since he doesn't actually participate. And no one can be absolutely certain which farmers are involved since they all wear those awful hoods."

Dora's shoulders sagged in her thin periwinkle-blue cotton dress. The dreary morning light spilling over her features exaggerated her sudden fatigue. "We thought of hiring a teacher not long ago to educate our young ones. Even went so far as to build a schoolhouse. We had dreams of maybe using the school as a church too, if we could find a preacher who was willing to settle way out here. The men worked hard on that school for two months, every morning before sheeping and every night before bed. And it was *grand*. Painted all white with a spiraled belfry that you could see a mile away. Jeff Mead—he's a carpenter and a genius with his hands—built desks and chairs for the children, and a right nice one for the teacher. We all pitched in a portion of our earnings and sent to Melbourne for a bell. It arrived the day after someone burned the building to the ground."

She shook her head. "The men—damn their pride—decided after that that the young ones didn't need education anyhow. All they need to know to survive in this world is sheep, and sheep don't care if a man can read or write."

Thinking of her own situation, how Martha had refused her all but the most minimal education, Summer said, "But children need those opportunities. They may decide they don't want t' raise sheep."

"Try telling that to a lot of shepherds," Nan said.

"Yer the children's mothers. Surely y' have some say-so in what happens t' them."

Dora shrugged. "Even if we convinced the men to give it another go, they'd never agree to rebuild the schoolhouse. Too much of their hearts and souls went up in flames with the last one."

Dora collected the cups and saucers from the oil-cloth-covered table and carried them to the sink pan. She gazed out the window, resting her weight on her weathered hands as she watched her children wade into the swollen creek to collect a packing case and several wooden planks that were floating on the murky surface. Dora's husband Dan, Nan's husband Arnold, and Frank stood on the shoal, their hands on their hips as they watched.

"Sometimes," Dora began in a soft voice, "I can understand why Mr. Sabre stays so shut up in that shanty way out in the middle of nowhere. He leaves the world alone; in turn, it leaves him alone. He avoids trouble by not inviting it." Turning to regard Summer thoughtfully, she added, "Maybe he's not so crazy after all."

It was nearly noon by the time Summer and Frank were ready to leave the Johnsons' station. Although the rain had let up during the morning, the sky had turned dark and threatening again.

Dora and Dan and Nan and Arnie walked Summer to the dray. Dora stood back as Dan loaded a crate of preserved fruits and vegetables onto the wagon bed, their token of appreciation for Summer and Frank's aid, then helped Summer board. Nan handed her a bundle of warm tarts that Summer nestled on her lap.

Dora clasped Summer's hand, a genuine smile lifting her mouth and radiating from her eyes. "It was a real pleasure," she told Summer. "New friends are always welcome out here, Summer. We're glad to have you. Aren't we, Frank?"

He winked and nodded as he reached for the reins.

"Will we see you again soon?" Dan asked, the wind stirring his curly blond hair as he looped a lanky arm around his wife's waist, pulling her close in an easy, affectionate gesture. Dora swayed against him and rested her head on his shoulder.

The realization that she probably *wouldn't* see the Johnsons or the Sharkeys again made Summer's throat feel tight. She tried hard to force the sting of despair from her eyes. "I'd certainly like that."

"Wonderful!" Dora clapped her hands in pleasure. "Once a month the Cockatoos meet out at Rockwood and picnic. It's a beautiful area near the government bush, with forests on one side and paddocks of lush emerald meadows on the other. It's our only opportunity to dress in our finest and, oh, do we ever!"

Nan said, "Our gentlemen escort us on meandering walks through woodland trails lined with wild roses and honeysuckle. We dine on elegant linen tablecloths and sip wine until we're tipsy. Then Vicesimus Sellers breaks out his violin, and we dance amid the golden tussock to a chorus of singing birds and the most romantic music you'll ever hear. You simply must come!"

"It sounds wonderful!" Caught up in the women's enthusiasm, Summer laughed.

"Well . . ." Dora's gaze shifted to Frank, her eyes full of questions she'd been too polite to ask Summer straight-out.

"Perhaps Dora and the kids'll drop by sometime and say hello," Dan offered.

"That would be very nice," Summer agreed.

"So will we," Nan added. "Once the baby is born, of course."

Frank yelled, "Giddap!" and the dray rolled down the rutted path. Clinging to the seat and peering over her shoulder, Summer watched the Johnsons and the Sharkeys wave and smile. Behind them, the three boys tore up the foot trail, leaping imaginary barricades and flapping their arms like clumsy fledgling birds. The white clapboard house stood out like a beacon beyond them, the picture of a family and a home surrounded by mountains and meadows the exact image of what she had always envisioned as heaven.

As Frank drove them home through the increasing rain, Summer hardly noticed the water trickling in runnels down the front of the macintosh he had loaned her. Her mind kept replaying the day's events, the sights she'd seen, the friends she'd

made. Never in her life had she had *real* friends.
They had actually treated her as a person, not an
object of curiosity, not as Glorvina's illegitimate
daughter. They had made her feel welcome.

She'd heard the loneliness in Dora's and Nan's
voices. How many times during those years with
Martha had Summer craved the company of another
girl her age?

But Nicholas Sabre was going to put her back on
that dreadful ship and send her away.

By the time they reached Sabre's station the
downpour had dwindled to little more than a
dreary, saturating mist. Frank let Summer off at the
front porch. She stood beneath the dripping eave
and watched the old man and his wagon lumber
out of sight behind the barn.

Inside the house, she was struck again by its plain-
ness, in stark contrast with the Johnsons' comfortably furnished home, every room of which reflected
Dora's domestic talents. Standing just inside the
threshold with water dripping off her macintosh,
Summer tried not to think of the fanciful dreams
she'd spun the night before, when she'd temporarily
lost her senses and imagined that she would remain
in New Zealand, living under Sabre's roof as his
wife for the rest of her life. The very thought of him
sitting at his pitiful table, slouched so indifferently
in his chair and announcing that he was sending
her back—just like that, with no more show of regret
than he might have felt over sweeping sheep manure out his door—made her shiver with frustration.
Then she heard the dog bark.

Summer stepped onto the back stoop and focused
on the distant livestock pens, where sheep stood
shoulder to shoulder, nudging one another for space
while Sabre's dog bounced about their hocks, letting
loose a high-pitched yap every time an agitated ram

kicked out with its sharp little hooves. Then Sabre was there.

She didn't recognize him at first. Gone was the stiff-collared white shirt, cravat, and black suit. In their place was the traditional shepherd's garb of blue cotton shirt, with the sleeves rolled up to expose his dark forearms, and brown trousers and mud-crusted boots to his knees. He'd tied his hair back at the nape. Around his forehead ran a wide bandana to catch the sweat.

He mopped his face with his shirtsleeve as he regarded the bleating sheep, then, with a simple hand signal, instructed Betsy to cut out another animal for shearing. The bleating ewe dashed past him, into the shed. As he turned to follow, he looked up toward the house.

Even from this distance, Summer clearly imagined his face: heavy eyebrows angling over pitch-black eyes that were as cold and mysterious as a deep well. Today she'd spoken with families who were as desperate for companionship as she was. What sort of man felt not even the remotest need to reach out to another human being? Frowning, she watched as he spun on his heel and reentered the shed.

Crotchety, cantankerous, disreputable *aristocrat*. Thought he was better than the whole country of New Zealand. Why, he'd probably forgotten *how* to smile.

"Be that way," she muttered aloud, curling her hands into fists within the too-long sleeves of Frank's raincoat. "I've got a good mind t' tell y' to yer face what I think about yer insolence and ill humor." She kicked at a bucket on the edge of the stoop. "Maybe I'll just do that, Mr. High and Mighty Sabre. While I'm at it I'll have y' know that I don't *want* t' sleep in yer stupid bed—it smells like y'!—

or live in yer fallin'-down hovel with its ugly front porch that's little more than a nestin' coop for chickens. That's exactly what I'll do," she said aloud. "I'll tell him that he'll be doin' me a great favor by puttin' me back on that ship and sendin' me home . . ." She paced up and down the stoop, working up her anger until she nearly vibrated with it, then she took to the path, her eyes on the shed in case he decided to leave the building unexpectedly and caught her off guard.

The bleating of the sheep made her hesitate as she reached the shed. The building's green lumber lent a tang to the air that was hardly sufficient to mask the odor of so many animals pressing together as they waited their turn to be shorn. The door opened with a creak, allowing the pale glow of lanterns spaced at equal intervals along the walls to spill over her face. Wet heat and the stench of dung and damp wool gave her second thoughts about entering the cramped quarters. But she'd come this far and wasn't about to back down now just because she suddenly felt queasy and breathless, angry and exhilarated. Her veins hummed.

Shoving the door further open, she stepped inside, pausing long enough to allow her eyes to adjust to the gloomy interior. A row of windows near the raw-beamed ceiling allowed in minimal daylight. The earthen floors were level and neatly raked. Near the back of the building was a long table piled high with mounds of fleece. Next to the table stood several bins divided into compartments.

How still and quiet it was compared to the chaos of bawling animals outside. Only the click of shears interrupted the silence, then the scrape of feet, a grunt, a groan, a muttered curse. Cautiously, she peered around a sturdy beam and caught partial sight of Sabre where he crouched in the center of a pen that was hardly large enough to fit both him and the sheep he was shearing. His blue shirt was stretched taut over his wide shoulders and tucked into the waistband of his breeches. There wasn't a single dry thread on either.

He wrestled with the squirming ewe before managing to support her firmly between his knees. As Summer moved forward to see him better, she was mesmerized by the firm yet gentle coercion of his hands on the frightened animal. The sheep let out a solitary *baa* of distress before settling down to her fate, allowing him to rest her foreleg against his left side in order to draw her skin tight across her belly. As he brought the shears over the animal's flesh and the fleece peeled back to expose pink skin, Summer watched the play of muscles in his arms and shoulders beneath his soaked shirt. Sweat rolled in rivulets from under his hair and dripped off his eyebrows and nose and chin, so that he was forced to stop momentarily to blot his eyes and take a breath. For an instant deep fatigue showed on his face, in the weary closing of his eyes and the slow shake of his head. He glanced down at the shears in his right hand, opened them, closed them, shifted his weight to better accommodate the animal before stooping over again.

Summer could only stare, aware that, as before, her anger had dissipated at the sight of Sabre and his self-imposed solitude. Her heart gave a little squeeze at the sight of him, alone, struggling patiently with an animal that clearly had no desire to be stripped clean of her woolly mantle.

As Sabre tried to sit her upright on her back haunches, she delivered a kick to his shin that made him double over and grasp his leg; the ewe took that opportunity to lunge for escape. Before Summer realized it, she'd leapt from her shadowy hiding place and dashed to help. She threw her arms around the animal's neck while Sabre continued to grab the ewe's scrambling back legs. They hit the ground in a heap of tangled limbs, the ewe's loud baaing and Summer's laughter causing Betsy outside to set up a loud barking that made the sheep bleat all the louder.

Laughter. The sound of it filled the shed like ringing bells. Nicholas contemplated Summer where she lay sprawled over the subdued sheep, her pale arms, peeking from the sleeves of Frank's macintosh, reminding him of a china doll's, her hair spilling over the ground like a liquid fire that he suddenly ached to touch. He had been thinking of her as he stood here, his back aching with the strain of stooping for so long over contrary sheep, and suddenly she had burst through the dark and poured over him like sunlight amidst a storm.

"Have y' got her?" came her voice near his ear. His *wife*. He didn't need or want a wife. What had gotten into him that day at the Lyttleton pothouse, aside from too much ale and too many dark memories? Now, because of some weakness in the chains of solitude he had constructed around himself, he was staring down at this child-woman with the face of an impish angel, inwardly trembling at the sound of her breathing.

She was gazing back at him with eyes large and full of emotion. She smelled faintly of peaches and rain, and he wanted to bury his mouth into hers and absorb the taste and texture and warmth of it. He wanted to take her small breasts in his hands and exhilarate in their weight and roundness; he wanted to mold them into high points of pleasure until she sobbed.

Kiss me! Kiss me! Her parted lips seemed to beckon. *Touch me!* Her eyes implored him.

With agonizing slowness she placed her hand against his face and said, "Hello."

"Hello," he heard himself reply.

"Don't y' ever smile, Mr. Sabre?"

"No."

"Why?"

"I've nothing to smile about."

"I'm sorry for y' then."

They didn't notice as the ewe squirmed loose and scurried to the corner of the pen. They lay facing each other as dust motes swirled lazily in the lamplight around their shoulders.

Then her eyes were sliding closed in an ageless invitation, and he was lowering his head over hers . . .

The shed door squeaked and Frank called, "Ya in thar, boss?"

Summer's eyes flew open. Nick stiffened, reality driving like a fist into his groin. Groaning, he rolled away and smashed the shears he was holding as hard as he could into the ground. Through his teeth he said, "Get the hell out of here."

He heard her scramble to her feet, then there was nothing but the sound of rain dripping from the eaves. Frank stood in the doorway, looking embarrassed.

"Reckon I'd best learn how to knock around here from now on," he said.

Closing his eyes, Nick breathed in Summer's lingering scent and drove his fist into the earth, again . . . and again.

Chapter 7

The man was tall and slender, with thinning brown hair and warm eyes behind the thick lenses of his spectacles. He stared at Summer in blatant surprise as she opened the door to his knock. An entire half minute passed before he remembered his manners and removed his hat. His smile, at first reluctant, broadened as Summer invited him in.

"I'm Ben Beaconsfield," he said.

"I'm Summer Sabre." She extended her hand, thrilled that her efforts to bathe, wash her hair, and don her best clothes would not go to waste after all.

Ben held her hand as he continued to study her features. "I must admit, you're not what I expected," he confessed.

"Oh? And what exactly was it that y' were anticipatin', Mr. Beaconsfield?"

Soft color touched his cheeks as he shrugged, allowing his gaze to wander down the length of her as inconspicuously as possible. "Skinnier maybe," he replied thoughtfully. "Perhaps a bit older and more . . . worldly. How old are you?"

Frowning, Summer took his hat. "There certainly seems t' be a great deal of interest in m' age. I can't think o' what difference it makes. I'm eighteen."

"Just barely, I'd say. You look more like fourteen."

"I'm not sure whether t' take that as a compliment or not, Mr. Beaconsfield."

"No insult intended, I assure you."

"Good." She beamed at him. "I'm assumin' that yer here t' see m' husband."

"Who?"

"Sabre."

"Oh." He looked chagrined. "My apologies. I'm just not used to . . . ah . . ."

"Nor am I, t' be frank, sir. I have to keep remindin' m'self just what it is I'm doin' here." Noting the amused lift of his eyebrow, she added, "I'm sure he's doin' the same."

Her frankness took him slightly aback, but she rushed on, "He's down at the shed with Frank. They'll be up for supper soon if y'd like t' wait. As a matter o' fact, I'd be pleased if y'd stay t' share the meal with us. It's the least we can do since y' had Sabre over t' yer place last evenin'."

"Oh, I wouldn't think of—"

"Imposin'? But yer not. I've prepared plenty. The truth is, this meal is gonna be a surprise. I had nothin' else t' do t' while away the afternoon alone, so I decided t' try m' hand at kitchen work. I mean, what's a wife for? And speakin' o' food . . ." She spun on her heel and ran for the kitchen while Ben remained just inside the parlor, unable to take his eyes off Sabre's . . . *wife?*

He'd heard from O'Connell that she was passably pretty, but then, Sean was one for understatement. In a few short years, once maturity had added a roundness to her figure and accentuated the fine-boned contours of her face, the girl would be a breathtaking beauty. He'd never seen hair that color, or as curly. She'd tied it back at the nape with a pink ribbon, but one stray coil spilled over her white brow to the bridge of her perfect nose with its pert little tilt and scattering of tawny freckles.

Obviously she had taken some care with her appearance. Although her clothes were sizes too large and the shoes were so roomy that the heels clunked when she walked, she wore them with pride.

"Just make yerself comfortable," came her voice from the kitchen. "Might I get y' some coffee?"

"Yes, thank you."

Something was different about the parlor, he realized. One side of the quilt window dressing had been pulled back, allowing hazy light to stream through recently cleaned glass panes. There was a curious object in front of the settee—a crate hidden beneath the finespun material of what had once been a woman's petticoat. In the middle of the table was a chipped enameled chamber pot boasting a lush green potted fern that spread out in all directions.

"Here's yer coffee," came her voice behind him, making him jump and spin to face her. "Is somethin' wrong?"

"I was just admiring your ingenuity. Your table and plant really brighten up the room."

"Thank y'. I thought the place could use a touch o' frill and color."

Ben sipped his coffee, his smile turning into a grimace as the thick, black, bitter brew coagulated on the back of his tongue. His first instinct was to spew it back into the cup, but when he noted Summer's wide purple eyes watching him for some sign of approval, he swallowed and hid his shudder.

"Is it all right?" she asked.

He nodded and stared into the cup.

"It's m' first attempt at coffee-makin'. Did I get it too weak?"

"No! What I mean is . . . it's plenty strong. And very good." He drank again to reassure her, closing his eyes briefly as it hit the back of his throat. The effort had its desired effect. Summer's face lit with appreciation.

"I hope Nicholas thinks so." She motioned to the settee as she hurried away. "Make yerself at home. Food'll be ready soon."

He watched her dash inside the bedroom, where she paused to peer at her reflection in the wardrobe mirror. She smoothed her skirt and made certain her plain white blouse was tucked neatly into the waistband. She gave the ribbon in her hair a gentle tug, pinched her cheeks, and chewed her lips, took a large enough breath so her small breasts were displayed prominently for a moment, then dashed again for the kitchen.

Ben turned back to the settee, stared at the chamber pot and fern on the petticoat-slippered crate, and grinned.

She'd found a sheet in the bottom of Sabre's wardrobe; it made a fine tablecloth. An old butter crock she'd discovered had been transformed into another flowerpot for a broad-leafed myrtle with a deep scarlet blossom. She'd positioned it center table. Ben's place setting was hurriedly added just before Sabre and Frank entered the house.

"Now ain't this a mighty pleasant surprise," Frank said, regarding the food she had spread out before them. "Here I was thankin' that I was gonna have to cook fer the next hour—and me bein' dead tired—and ya done gone and done it already."

Summer glanced nervously at Nick. He'd washed his face and hands before entering the kitchen. His hair was still damp around the temples. He hadn't so much as looked her way, giving her no hope that what had transpired between them in the shed had meant anything at all to him . . . as it had to her. He greeted his guest, Ben, with little more than a perfunctory nod and plunked himself down in his chair.

"This looks most appetizing," Ben told her.

"Well, go on," she said. "Help yerselves."

Frank reached for a bowl. "What's this?" he asked. "A roly-poly puddin'?"

"An omelette."

There was a brief silence, then Frank whacked some eggs onto his plate and passed the bowl to Ben, who whacked as well and passed it on to Nick. Next she offered each man a hoecake. They turned them in their hands, regarding them with curiosity. Frank accidentally dropped his and it bounced off the edge of his plate.

Next, she hurried to heap a platter full of boiled potatoes and offered one to each man, who found it next to impossible to spear them. As Frank sawed into his, it fell open to reveal its raw center still cool to the touch. He cut it up anyway and popped a piece into his mouth, crunching loudly. He reached for his coffee to wash it down. His eyebrows shot up and Ben coughed into his napkin.

"Is somethin' wrong?" Summer asked, looking from one to the other.

"No!" Frank replied.

"No." Ben shook his head.

She glared at Sabre, who continued to stare at his plate and prod his potato with his fork. "There's soup, too," she told them, her sights still set on Sabre, who, glancing up, looked as quickly away.

Ben and Frank's faces brightened. "Soup?" Frank asked eagerly.

"I found the smokehouse and took a hank o' mutton, if y' don't mind," she informed him.

"I like soup," Frank enthused. "Don't you boys like soup?"

Ben and Nick nodded and put down their forks, with more than a little relief, Summer thought. She ladled the rich broth swirling with onions into bowls and set them before the men, then anxiously stood back to watch. They reached for their spoons and dipped them into the fragrant liquid. They put it into their mouths. In unison they spewed it out on the table and jumped from their chairs.

"Holy criminies, what in galdern blazes did ya put in that, darlin'?" Frank sputtered.

"Water," Ben gasped. "I need water!"

Summer dashed for the water pail and filled three cups, on the verge of tears as the men gulped it down and demanded more. "I can't imagine what I did wrong," she cried, wringing her hands. "I only put in mutton and onions and a bit o' salt I found in the larder."

His eyes suddenly round, Frank said, "Salt? Show me."

She hurried to the tiny larder and pointed to the squat barrel in the far corner.

"Gawd almighty," he exclaimed. "Darlin', that ain't salt, it's washin' soda."

Nick and Ben headed for the door while Frank bent double in laughter.

"Well, I don't know what yer findin' so hilarious!" Summer sobbed. "I've been sweatin' over this stove all afternoon for nothin'! Y' can't even stomach my damn potatoes!"

"Well, they coulda been cooked fer another hour or so—" Frank began.

"Oooh! Yer all a lot of ungrateful brutes!" She ran from the room, threw herself across the bed, and wept into the mattress.

Damn, damn, damn! She beat the bed with her fists. It wasn't enough that Sabre hadn't even noticed that she'd dressed in her finest and gone to great lengths to look her very best for him. She'd practically poisoned them all with her pitiful attempt at cooking. And she'd humiliated herself in front of Sabre's best friend—his *only* friend—when all she'd wanted was to be the sort of wife the stubborn, arrogant, detestable aristocrat might find appealing.

Oh, what was the bloody use? He was going to send her away regardless. The momentary gleam of interest she'd seen in his eyes earlier that day had been nothing more than lust. How could she have been so stupid as to hope he might find her remotely acceptable? How could she imagine that she could impress him with her ridiculous clothes or her poor cooking? *Washing soda*. Oh, saints, she might have killed them all!

"Summer?"

Her breath caught at the sound of Sabre's voice. She squeezed her eyes shut and buried her face deeper into the mattress. Maybe she'd suffocate before she was forced to look at him again. "Go away!"

Silence followed. Gasping for air, she peeked through her fingers to discover him still towering in the doorway, as unsmiling, unyielding, and unaffected by her distress as always. "Go away," she managed again. "Y' don't have t' rub it in, damn yer hide. I made a fool o' m'self; are y' happy now? Y' can send me away with a clear conscience. No man in his right mind wants a wife who can't even cook." She jumped from the bed and stalked toward him, nose running and hair bouncing. "Just who would want t' be yer wife anyway? Who wants t' sit and stare at a man who can't even smile? I've seen *fence posts* with more personality, Mr. Sabre. Any woman who would willingly marry y' might as well assign herself t' Bedlam, because y'd drive her crazy in a fortnight with yer surly attitude."

"Are you finished?" He snarled it.

"One thing more. Maybe I might not be as pretty as some, or as well-bred, but I deserve at least as much respect as y' offer yer stupid dog. So until y' plunk me on that boat back t' England, I expect y' to have the decency t' treat me like a human bein', instead o' lookin' at me as if I were sheep shit y' just scraped off the sole o' yer boot." She blinked, thrust her chin at him, and added, "Now I'm finished."

"Good. When I first came in here it was to apologize. Now that I think about it, however, I don't think I owe you an apology after all. I didn't invite you into my kitchen, my house, or my life. And maybe if you behaved half as well as my dog, you might be treated with a little respect!"

She gasped. "Are y' comparin' me t' an animal now?"

"Sweetheart," he drawled, "you could never compare to my dog."

She slapped his face so hard her hand and arm stung all the way to her elbow. Sabre didn't move, his long legs planted firmly apart and one side of his face turning red. They glared at each other for what seemed an eternity, his features hardening, his fists clenched at his sides.

Finally, Summer righted her shoulders and said in a choked, but decisive voice, "I'll be glad when those damn rivers are passable."

"So will I."

Another heartbeat passed before he turned on his

heel and quit the room. Summer threw herself back on the bed.

The next night Nick sat at his desk and wearily focused on the ledger. The debits and credits told him nothing new. He was tottering on the edge of ruin. He'd already received two notices from the Christchurch Bank that his loan payments were overdue, the last embellished with threats that if he didn't pay up soon they would be forced to take "measures." He'd written them after the first reminder, explaining that as soon as he drayed in his wool he'd be able to pay his debts; obviously they weren't interested in excuses because they'd written back immediately, reiterating that his payment was late and they expected it within a fortnight. The following notice hadn't been so congenial.

If he and Frank were very frugal during the next year, and the lambing season went well, they could double their wool profits . . . *if* his sheep didn't develop a disease and all die . . . *if* he wasn't ransacked by Sean and his hooded thugs . . . *if* he didn't blow his brains out the way Jake Madison had last night.

"God," he whispered aloud, wearily closing his eyes. "Just let me survive until next year."

Forcing the thought from his mind, he reached for a needle and thread, took up the white dress shirt that had lost a button, and set to the task of sewing. It was hard to believe that once upon a time in his life there had been servants to tend to such menial tasks. He squinted to see each fine stitch he took, swearing under his breath as his fingers fumbled with the tiny silver needle.

A floorboard creaked.

He looked up to find Summer standing there, rubbing her eyes and blinking sleepily, her hair spilling to her hips. Frowning, he turned away from her and continued sewing.

She moved up behind him. "Would y' like help with that?" came her soft voice, husky with sleep.

He shook his head and squinted harder.

Her hand came over his shoulder and he tensed. Her body, brushing against his, made his flesh burn. Then her slim fingers were wrapping around his shirt and coaxing it from his reluctant hands. The next thing he knew she was sliding her little butt up on his desk, her bare feet with their toes curled under peeping at him from beneath the hem of her nightgown. She bent near the light and concentrated hard to the task.

"Don't y' ever sleep, Mr. Sabre?" she asked without looking up.

"No."

"Ghosts?"

"Ghosts?" He rubbed the back of his neck.

"Regrets," she amended.

"Too many to name," he replied.

"Well, I guess y' wouldn't be human otherwise."

How utterly splendid she looked, he thought, with her perfect skin, dewy with youth, and her thick hair falling over her shoulders. Her lashes were feathery crescents on her cheeks, her raised eyes violet pools.

"We've all done things we're not proud of," she told him. "The trick is t' move on, not dwell on the past but concentrate on not repeatin' yer mistakes."

His mouth curled in a humorless smile. "That would depend on the mistake. Some aren't so easily forgotten."

"That's true. We continue t' believe that if we could only do things differently we would do them right." Her soft mouth pursed in concentration. "I think, however, that we probably would do the same things again and again. People often act on feelins rather than logic. And a person's true feelins, what he experiences here"—she touched her heart—"can't always be changed by reason."

Several minutes of quiet ensued as he watched her push the needle in and out of his shirt. Not for the first time that evening he wondered what would have happened yesterday if Frank hadn't interrupted them in the shed. At last, he forced himself to ask, "Is that why you're here? Did you make a mistake?"

She pricked her finger and stared at the tiny bloom of blood on her fingertip before sliding it between her lips. Before he realized what he was doing he lifted her small chin so he could gaze deeply into her eyes.

"Are you running from a mistake, Irish? Perhaps there was a man who hurt you? Did you love him? Did he break your heart so irreparably that you were forced to put an entire world between you, thinking distance would assuage the pain and regret?"

"What do y' care, Mr. Sabre?"

He dropped his hand and turned his face away, scrambling to discern his confused emotions. "I don't," he responded carefully. "I'm just curious about what would bring a young woman like you to New Zealand."

"What do y' imagine?"

He closed his eyes briefly before focusing on her again. "I suspect you were either whoring and grew tired of the business . . . or you were carrying on an affair with the lord of the manor where you were a maid. Perhaps he chose to end the relationship. Perhaps you were deeply in love with him. In either case, you thought you could put those memories behind you by coming here."

"That's what y' think? That I'm a whore?"

"Yes."

An ironic expression passed over her features, then she said, "I think, Mr. Sabre, that y' believe that every woman is a whore." She completed her sewing, then bit the cotton in two with her teeth. Handing him the shirt, she smiled, but offered no further comment or explanation regarding her past.

He looked down at the shirt in his hands. The button was securely fastened. There was only one problem. She had sewed the front of the shirt to the back.

"Well," he said, noting her crestfallen expression as she realized her mistake, "one thing is for certain. You were neither a cook *nor* a seamstress before coming to New Zealand, were you, Irish?"

She slid off the desk and walked on silent feet to the door, where he finally stopped her by announcing, "We're having dinner with Ben and Clara tomorrow."

She turned. "We?" she asked, sounding oddly timid and slightly breathless.

"We. As in you and I."

"Yer takin' me t' dinner at the Beaconsfields'?"

He concentrated on plucking the cotton thread from the shirt.

She padded up beside him. The scent of her washed over him. Still, he might have managed to ignore her, but she placed her hand on his shoulder; his body turned rigid.

"Well?" she said.

"That's why Ben dropped by yesterday, to invite us to dinner . . . that and other reasons."

"And are y' absolutely sure that they're meanin' for me t' come too?"

At last he raised his gaze to hers. She stood smiling hopefully at him, the light from the lamp behind

her dancing on her hair. Her eyes shone like ame-
thysts.

"Well?" she repeated.

"Yes. Clara specifically mentioned that this dinner
will be in your honor."

With a squeal of pleasure, she threw her arms
around his neck with enough force to knock him
backwards. He grabbed for the desk with one hand,
the opposite arm going instinctively around her
waist, and held on tightly.

"Imagine their invitin' me t' dinner!" she declared, hopping up and down within his embrace,
her hair brushing his face and chest, her soft breasts
undulating beneath his chin. As quickly, she
bounded away, leaving him with a hauntingly familiar ache that turned his body hard as stone.
"Imagine our bein' invited t' dinner as husband and
wife! I can't believe it!" Then she sprang at him
again, planted a kiss on his cheek, and dashed out
the door.

He closed his eyes and touched his face where it
was still moist from her lips.

"I've nothin' t' wear," came her voice from the
other room. A drawer opened then slammed shut.
Summer flashed past the study; frowning, Nick
slowly left his chair. He found her heading out the
back door.

"What are you doing?" he yelled.

Her voice trailed back to him. "I have t' wash m'
only good clothes . . ."

"It's one o'clock in the morning."

"They won't be dry in time if I wait."

He stepped aside as she hurried back up the
stoop, carrying two pails of water that sloshed on
his boots as she passed.

Within minutes more water was being heated,
and Summer stood over the washboard rubbing her

blouse against the corrugated metal. Still feeling her kiss on his cheek, Nick wondered how, when, he was going to remind her that Clara and Ben's invitation in no way altered their circumstances. Just because he'd weakened yesterday afternoon and almost allowed himself to make a very big mistake didn't mean that he'd changed his mind about her. He didn't want a wife, and he didn't want her.

The roasted joint was mouth-watering, the vegetables splendid, the peach pudding out of this world. Summer eagerly polished hers off and gladly accepted a second serving offered to her by a plump maid named Renee who constantly hummed to herself and cast appreciative glances at Sabre every chance she got. And who could blame her? Summer experienced a tug of pride and longing each time her gaze took in his elegantly tailored clothes and the ruby stickpin nestled in the folds of his pristine cravat. His manners were impeccable and his face breathtakingly handsome, despite the sardonic curl to his lips.

"More wine, Mrs. Sabre?" Renee asked.

Summer nodded and focused on her hostess, who glanced toward Nicholas sitting on the opposite side of the table. Nick regarded Summer's wineglass speculatively as Renee filled it for the third time, but when the maid offered to replenish his, he dismissed her with a shake of his head.

Sitting back in his chair, Ben said, "Perhaps Summer would like to look around the station after dinner."

Clara frowned. "Oh, really, Ben, whyever for?"

"Obviously so she can see what a real sheep station is like." He flashed Sabre a smile, and when he got little more than a raised eyebrow in response, he grimaced. "Not up to sparring tonight, I see."

"I'd love t' see it," Summer said, reaching for her wineglass.

"It's noisy and smelly," Clara declared. "I want to weep for those pitiful little sheep every time I see them crowded into those awful pens."

"Those pitiful little sheep are what enables us to live in this less than pitiful little house, my dear. Besides, I'd like to show Nick our new equipment."

"Perhaps Summer would care to wait—"

"No," she interrupted, then drank down the entire glass of wine. "I'm ready when the three o' y' are."

Nick shoved back his chair. "I think Summer could use a breath of fresh air," he said, coming around the table. When she turned up her glass one last time to drain a final drop of liquid from it, he gently removed it from her hand and set it aside. "Allow me," he told her softly and with a hint of amusement. Catching her arm, he helped her from her chair, adding in a low, velvety voice, "How are we feeling, Irish?"

"I don't know about you, Mr. Sabre, but I'm feelin' right well."

"A trifle dizzy perhaps?"

Lowering her voice to a whisper, she asked, "How did y' know?"

"I can only assume that you're not accustomed to drinking wine."

"Never had a drop until tonight." She leaned against his arm and peered up into his heavy-lidded eyes. "I'm sorry I slapped y' the other day."

"The incident has been forgotten. Here. Watch yourself. We're going down steps now."

"I'm cursed with a terrible temper," she admitted, her eyes on his tanned face. "But then, I suppose y've already noticed."

"It had occurred to me, yes."

"But yers isn't any better."

"Quite right," he replied in an amused drawl.

Summer glanced at Ben and Clara, who were walking ahead of them down a paved path toward an impressive set of buildings. Laying her head on Nick's arm, Summer sighed. "Yer friends are very nice. Do y' think that they approve o' me? Did I do anythin' durin' dinner t' embarrass y'?"

"Yes, they like you, and I really don't think you could do anything to embarrass me, Irish."

She tried to focus on his ruggedly handsome, unsmiling features, feeling a sharp stab of emotion in the vicinity of her heart that was becoming ever more familiar each time she was near him. Speaking seemed to be getting more difficult, but finally she managed. "Do y' still dislike me, Mr. Sabre?"

His hands in his pockets, he stared out over the lush green panorama, a curious look of suppressed irony and humor in his surprisingly warm eyes. "Whatever gave you the idea that I didn't like you?"

"You did. Y' told me so when y' dragged me away from Sean's."

"Ah. I do recall that I was less than gallant that morning." His amused glance slid over her features. "My apologies."

"Apology accepted." Her brilliant smile made him turn suddenly serious before he refocused his attention on their surroundings.

Beds of flowers, top-heavy with blossoms of every imaginable color, and giving off sweet scents, lined both sides of the path. The huge sprawling wool shed they were approaching was a far cry from the tiny building Nick had erected on his station. Here twenty men, each with his own roomy section, were hard at the task of shearing the bleating rams and ewes. As soon as they had finished each animal, the men shoved them through trapdoors which led into a small pen outside where a manager inspected each one for nicks on their hides. Young boys lugged armfuls of rolled-up fleeces to the wool tables, where wool-sorters studied the laid-out pelts and announced to which bin they belonged. The boys then hurried to roll up the fleeces again and delivered them to divided compartments labeled according to quality and kind of wool.

Next, Summer was shown the men's huts, where an entire second shift of workers was sleeping in rows of bunks or crowded around long tables piled high with tin plates and pannikins. Through a far door was the kitchen where a cook constantly supplied food and tea to the good-natured laborers.

Throughout the tour, Summer kept a close regard on her husband. As always, Sabre said little, but his eyes, usually void of emotion, gave his feelings away. The envy burning in their dark depths as he viewed Ben's operation made her feel ashamedly resentful that he didn't crave her one tiny bit as much.

While Ben proceeded to show Nick the mechanical shears that had just arrived from Australia, Clara and Summer retired to a bench swing hanging from the limb of a willow tree. A breeze rustled the leaves overhead and cooled the perspiration on their faces.

"So tell me how you like New Zealand," Clara said.

Her attention still on Sabre, Summer replied, "I like it very much."

"What did you do back in England?"

She smiled, "Is that why y' invited me here, Mrs. Beaconsfield? Were y' just curious about me?"

Color touched Clara's cheeks. "I confess I *am* a bit curious."

Summer regarded the woman's pretty features and porcelain skin. Her dress was exceptionally

lovely, bringing to mind the beautiful lavender dress
Summer had admired in the Christchurch shop
upon first arriving in the country.

Clara sighed and shifted her gaze back to her husband. "They're obsessed with these silly sheep. I
grow so weary of discussing lambing and shearing
and profits. I get so hungry to enjoy other women's
company."

"There are other women around," Summer replied.

Clara chose her words carefully. "Because of the
recent troubles between the farmers and Cockatoos,
and Ben's desire to remain neutral in the conflict,
it's become increasingly difficult for me to socialize
with women on either side of the issue."

"Nicholas and I are Cockatoos," Summer pointed
out.

"It's understood that Nicky and Ben have been
friends for years. Nick worked for us when he first
arrived from England. Besides, Nick is different."

"How so?"

"His background for one."

"Just because he is, or was, an aristocrat doesn't
make him any better than anyone else," Summer
argued. "Not any more than yer ownin' this station
makes y' any better than the lot o' Cockatoos that
are strugglin' to survive out here."

Clara regarded her for a long moment. "You're
quite right. I'm sorry."

They went on to discuss England. Clara, becoming dreamy-eyed, explained that before coming to
New Zealand she had wanted to teach. "I love children," she explained. "I worked briefly as a governess, before I met Ben, and did so enjoy the
challenge of instructing the young ones. I miss it
very much."

"Why not teach here?" Summer asked.

"It isn't possible, of course. We live too far from Christchurch."

"There are children livin' in the hills who need an education. I'm certain their parents would be more than grateful for yer help."

"I considered it once, when the Cockatoos built their school. I discussed it with Ben, and he . . . we . . . decided that it would be unwise. It might appear as if we were taking sides."

"So the children are made t' suffer because their parents can't get along."

Clara's face colored with guilt. "It doesn't seem fair, does it?" She sighed. "I do so love children. Ben and I would like nothing more than to have our own. But so far . . ." Her voice grew sad. "Still, we keep hoping and praying. One never knows what tomorrow will bring."

They moved on to other topics, including Sean O'Connell.

"There certainly seems to be a great deal of animosity between him and Sabre," Summer said. "Sean is upset over Nicholas's settlin' on his run."

"There's more to it than that," Clara explained. "If Nicky hasn't informed you, then perhaps I should. Sean blames Nicky for the failure of his marriage and the death of his wife."

Summer was stunned. "Sabre was in love with Colleen O'Connell?"

"No. But Colleen was in love with Nicky. They met when Colleen was staying with us while Sean finished building his house. I'm afraid Colleen caught a bad case of puppy love, and found every reason and opportunity to corner Nick."

"And yer certain he didn't return her devotion?"

Clara smiled. "Does Nicky act like a man who would woo some young woman under the stars? He let her know in no uncertain terms that he wasn't interested. When she realized she didn't stand a chance with him, she went through with the marriage to Sean, but apparently she was more deeply in love than we all realized. She practically pined away for Nicky, then she caught a fever and died."

"How very sad for Sean."

"He continued to love Colleen to the very end, even though he knew she yearned for Nick. We've all tried to explain to Sean that Nicholas in no way invited Colleen's affection. But when a man is rejected by a woman he loves, it does irreparable damage to his self-esteem. So he strikes out at others—as Sean is at Nick. As Nick did to..."

Clara's voice trailed off. Sensing she was on the verge of divulging information of some importance concerning Sabre's past, Summer said, "As Nick did t'...?"

"He hasn't talked to you about it?"

Summer shook her head. Flustered, Clara reached for a hankie tucked beneath the cuff of her sleeve. "Then I shouldn't say any more."

"But I have the right t' know somethin' about the man I married. Is it true what Sean says? Did Nicholas murder a man?"

"No," Clara said firmly. "He fought a duel. Years ago, the law would have stood in his favor, but the courts don't see it that way any longer. In my opinion, Nicholas's only mistake came from trusting and lov—"

Ben and Nick joined them just then, abruptly ending Clara's revelation. They returned to the house, and the remainder of the afternoon passed pleasantly enough, though after two glasses of sherry, added to the wine she'd consumed earlier, Summer's temples began to pound and her stomach felt queasy. She felt so tired, which seemed odd considering it was the middle of the day, and her mind kept wandering. Once she even dozed. She opened her eyes to discover Nicholas gazing down at her, his suit coat trapped behind his hands on his hips. The sight of him made her feel all fluttery inside.

She tried to sit up and sloshed sherry on her skirt. "Sorry. I can't imagine what's got into me. I can't seem t' hold m' eyes open."

"I suspect doing laundry throughout the night might have something to do with it. And this"—he eased the sherry glass from her fingers—"isn't helping."

"Are we leavin' now?"

Bending a little at the waist, he whispered, "Would you like to go home now?"

She nodded, spilling red curls over her forehead.

"Very well. Do you think you can make it as far as the wagon without my carrying you?"

She huffed in amusement, but when she tried to stand, the world careened crazily around her. With a cry, she tipped straight into his arms. "Oh, my! I musta tripped," she slurred. Throwing back her head, she stared up into his dark face . . . and the slow, lazy smile curving his sensual lips. Her mouth fell open, and she laughed. "Saints and begolin', Mr. Sabre, Esquire. Yer smilin'! Yer actually smilin'! I didn't think I'd ever see the day . . ."

His big hands gripping her waist, he set her on her feet. She swayed against him again, this time with unabashed horror. "Oh, I . . . I'm suddenly not feelin' too well."

"Perhaps Summer would like to rest a few minutes before you go," came Ben's voice somewhere behind them.

"I think that would be wise," Nick replied.

Summer felt herself moving across the floor, and it took a moment before she realized that Nick was carrying her. Then a door opened and cool shadows kissed her feverish cheeks.

Nick eased her down on a bed. A cool cloth touched her cheeks, her mouth, her forehead. "Are you ill?" he asked gently.

She nodded, awash with helpless shame. She attempted to cover her face with her hands, but he tugged them aside.

"You'll feel better if you get rid of it." He put a chamber pot in her lap. "Would you like me to stay or go?"

She nodded again.

"Stay?"

"No."

"Go?"

"No."

He flashed her a smile. "Very well, then. I'll stand over by the window."

She watched him move away, and for the first time noticed that they occupied a very pretty bedroom with a four-poster bed and a pale blue carpet. White lace curtains hung at the windows.

Then Summer hunched over the chamber pot and threw up . . . again . . . and again, until her shoulders trembled and her entire body ached. Until tears streamed down her face and she was mentally preparing herself to die.

Somewhere behind her came the sound of water being poured into a basin. Then Nick returned, his cloth freshly dampened, and proceeded to bathe her face. He replaced the lid on the pot and put it aside. Then he removed her shoes and coaxed her down on the bed. When she thought he was leaving, she cried, "Don't go!"

"As you wish," came his reply. The bed gave way beneath her, and, forcing open her eyes, Summer found herself nestled against her husband, her head on his shoulder as he stroked her hair soothingly and stared at the ceiling.

"I'm sorry," she said.

"It was the wine and sherry. From now on, don't mix your drinks," he told her sternly.

"Are y' speakin' from experience?"

"A lifetime of mixing drinks, I confess."

Smiling, she nuzzled his shoulder again and sighed. "I wanted t' fit in with yer friends. I wanted them t' like me."

"They do."

"We'll have them over t' our house soon, I promise I won't indulge."

He took a deep breath. "Try to nap, love. It's a long ride home."

Chapter 8

Ｓhe awoke, alone, to find the room full of twilight shadows. Her stomach felt fine, but her head was pounding. She'd made a fool of herself by being sick, but somehow it didn't matter. She'd seen a side to Nicholas Sabre that she had only dreamed of. He'd held her, comforted her; he'd even smiled at her. Was it too much to hope that . . . possibly . . . he had truly begun to like her?

Carefully rolling from the bed, she cradled her head in her hands until the world righted, then moved to the door and opened it slightly.

"The shearing and baling will be finished soon," came Nick's soft-spoken voice. "I'll simply take her back to Christchurch when I dray in the wool."

"She seems very sweet," Clara said in a sad voice.

"I can't afford the responsibility even if I wanted it. I'm already two months behind on my loan obligations and—"

Clara touched his arm, and Nick turned. Summer was standing in the door, her face pale, her eyes like purple bruises as she looked at him with unrestrained pain on her young features.

Clara swept past him and approached her. "Summer, dear, how are you feeling?"

"Fine."

"Can I bring you anything—"

"No. I'd like t' go home now."

"Certainly." Clara hurried to fetch Summer's hat while Nick continued to watch Summer waver in the doorway, refusing to look at him. "Here's your hat." Summer placed it on her head, and Ben rushed to escort her out the door.

"Thank you for coming," he said. "It's been delightful getting to know you. I trust I'll always remember your mutton soup."

She tried to smile.

"Wait!" called Clara. She went into the kitchen, then reappeared with a basket loaded with foodstuffs. The aroma of freshly baked bread wafted over them. Smiling, Clara whispered conspiratorially, "I've slipped in the recipe for the bread. It's Nicky's favorite. And Summer . . ." Clara moved closer and gave her hand a reassuring squeeze. "God bless."

Nick moved around the wagon to help her board. She yanked her arm away, and without looking at him, climbed up on the wagon seat unassisted. In a moment he joined her, took up the reins, and headed the dray home through the dark. They rode for some time without speaking; at last, she said in a furious, shaking voice:

"How dare y' humiliate me that way?"

"I'm sorry. I didn't know you were listening."

"Why did y' even bother t' take me there? Why would y' want them t' meet me if y' never had any intention o' lettin' me stay?"

"I thought you might enjoy it."

"Enjoy it!" She grabbed her throbbing head and took a deep breath. "I'm supposed t' enjoy meetin' people one minute and tellin' them good-bye the next?"

"I hadn't thought of it that way."

"Just when did y' plan on informin' me that y' were gettin' shut o' me with the wool? Saints!" she cried angrily. "I'm as expendable as a blazin' clump o' sheep hair!"

"I've already explained to you why I can't keep a wife."

"Because y' don't like me."

He groaned and closed his eyes briefly while beside him Summer sat with her fists bunched in her lap and her wilted bird feather drooping over her nose. The memory of her radiant face smiling up at him that afternoon as they strolled arm in arm down the walk came back to remind him, as it had every five minutes during the last three hours, that, indeed, he was beginning to like Summer Fairburn Sabre . . . perhaps too much. If he was smart he wouldn't even stop by his station tonight. He'd keep on driving all the way to Christchurch.

They traveled the remainder of the journey in total silence. Upon reaching his station, Nick stopped long enough to allow Summer to scramble down from the dray and run for the house, slamming the door behind her, then he drove the dray to the barn.

The night air felt unusually oppressive, but then, so did his mood. He unharnessed the horse, grabbed up the basket of food Clara had packed them, and started for the house, noting that no lights burned in either the shearing shed or Frank's shack. Perhaps the old man had decided to turn in early. No doubt they'd be putting in plenty of late nights if they intended to get the wool to Lyttleton next week.

He took the back steps two at a time, shoved open the door, and stepped into the kitchen that was lit by a single burning lantern on the table. Summer was standing near the stove, her eyes fiercely bright and her face a startling white . . . then he realized that she wasn't looking at him, but at something . . .

He turned, no more than glimpsing a black hooded face before the world exploded in a red haze of pain. The impact across his jaw hurled him through the doorway and onto the stoop, where he slid down the steps on his back, groaning as he hit the ground and rolled. Suddenly there were hands coming at him from every direction, twisting into his hair, his clothes, dragging him to his knees and then his feet, locking his arms behind him with such force that for a desperate moment he thought they intended to snap them off at his shoulder blades. He gasped before someone yanked back his head, then a fist drove into his mouth like a battering ram. His legs buckled, and he swayed on his feet. Numbly, he tried to focus on the dozen hooded men encircling him, their eyes glittering in the torchlight.

"Careful, lads," came a voice. "We wouldn't want to damage his lordship's aristocratic features, would we?"

"No, sir, we wouldn't," was the response, then Nick was hit again, so hard his feet left the ground. He sank against his captor and slid halfway to his knees before he was forced to stand again. There was no pain now, just a roaring white light that centered behind his eyes and threatened to push them out of their sockets.

". . . Sabre, are you listening to me?"

He forced open his eyes. Breathing was an effort; his nose was bleeding profusely, as was his mouth.

". . . friendly warning, Mr. Sabre. We've asked you politely to leave the area. There is plenty of land elsewhere—"

"No," he gasped. "Go to . . . hell."

The fists came at him again, battering his face, ribs, and gut. He lost consciousness and they threw water over him, shocking him awake to a fresh tide of raw pain.

"You Cockatoos are all a lot of leeches," the voice was saying. "Latching on to our runs—"

"I paid for my goddamn station!" Nick shouted at the blurred form with glittering yellow eyes, then he choked on his blood, and his legs gave way. He hit the ground, face-down. For a moment he lay against the cool, solid earth, hoping the nightmare would end soon. Then he heard Summer's cry, and dragging himself to his elbows, he blinked the dirt and blood from his eyes to see her running off into the dark, pursued by a hooded monster who threw his bulky weight against her and toppled her to the ground.

Nick clawed his way to his feet, only to be hit from behind and driven to his hands and knees again as two men tried to subdue him. He flailed with his fists and thrashed with his feet, spurred on by Summer's cries and glimpses of her attacker ripping her blouse and slapping her across the face.

"I'll kill you!" Nick shouted through his bloody mouth. "I'll kill you if you—"

A hooded man on horseback appeared through the night shadows, and with one swift kick sent Summer's would-be rapist sprawling. He leapt from his animal, and before the first man could recover, planted a booted foot on his throat and snarled in a heavy voice, "Be thankful I stopped y' when I did, friend, else y' would have sorely regretted yer fool-ishness. I've told y' repeatedly that our war's not with women and children." He glanced at Summer, clutching her blouse closed and sitting up, then he turned back to Nick and motioned for those who were pinning him to the ground to move away.

Lying on his back, Nick stared at the black sky behind the haze of torchlight and fought for consciousness while his body throbbed and burned in a hundred places. The hooded figure stared down at him with malice and amusement in his eyes.

"O'Connell," Nick managed to say. "Someday I'm going to kill you for this."

"If I don't kill y' first." Sean stooped to one knee beside him. "Why don't y' just give it up, Nick? I've offered t' buy the property from y'. Y' can take yer profits and push inland—"

"I'm not leaving."

The eyes regarded him coldly. "Then perhaps I should kill y' now and be done with it."

Nick's lacerated mouth stretched into a smile. "Go on, O'Connell; do me a favor."

Nick closed his eyes briefly. When he looked at Sean again, he was studying Summer where she sat huddled in the shadows, her face tense with fear and shock. At last, Sean's gaze came back to Nick's; he stood, glanced about the circle of men, and nodded. Several broke free of the crowd and ran toward the wool shed, the barn, and Frank's shack, their torches casting off sparks. Other men came riding out of the night leading horses.

The realization of what would happen next spurred Nick into rolling to his knees and struggling to his feet—only to have Sean move up to him again, twist his fingers into Nick's bloodied coat and shirt, and whisper, "This is for Colleen." He drove his knee up into Nick's groin, and the crucifying pain sent his head back with an agonized howl.

A burst of light illuminated the sky as fire climbed up the walls of the outbuildings. Then the mounted riders rode off, their whoops and yells diminishing as they were swallowed up by the night.

The penned sheep were wailing in distress; the

horses in the nearby corral were whinnying and rearing, and the chickens were pouring from their nearby coop, cackling frantically. Nick managed to climb to his feet just as Summer ran to him. "Frank is tied up in his shack!" she cried.

Horrified, she watched Nick sprint toward the fiery building. She grabbed up a bucket, ran down the footpath and plunged it into a water trough, then dashed back toward the fire, crying out Nick's name as he stumbled through the flames, kicked in Frank's door, and disappeared inside. Almost immediately, Betsy came bounding out, tail tucked between her legs and black-and-white coat smoking. Summer flung the water over the dog, tossed the bucket aside, and followed Nick into the smoke and fire, shielding her face from the blistering heat with her hands.

Through the boiling conflagration, she saw Nick stooping over the unconscious old man lying sprawled on his bunk, mouth gagged and wrists and ankles tied. Then Nick heaved him up and over his shoulder, as if Frank's weight were nothing more than a child's. The roof let out a groan, and as Nick turned for the door, burning timbers rained down on him, driving him to one knee as he fought to keep Frank from sliding to the floor.

Summer dove for the smoldering blankets on the bed, and threw them over Nick's back and arms where embers were setting fire to his clothes. Grabbing his arm, she looped it around her shoulder and helped him to stand, offering her support as they stumbled out of the disintegrating building.

Once clear of the smoke, she slid from Nick's side, dashed for the bucket again and refilled it, then ran up the pathway, sloshing water to the right and left before she tossed it over the wool-shed walls. Again and again she repeated the effort, occasionally catching glimpses of Nick slapping the fire with a water-saturated blanket. "The sheep!" he yelled over the snap and pop of the flames. "Get the sheep!"

Dropping the bucket, she ran for the skillion, threw back the latch, and shoved open the gate. The terrified animals lunged at her like a white wave, leaping over and under each other in their frantic effort to escape, knocking her to one side into the muck and manure, where she curled into a ball and covered her head with her arms as several sharp hooves bludgeoned her hands and ribs and legs.

Then Nick was there, fighting his way through the bleating animals, his sweating face reflecting the fire as he pulled her up into his arms and held her against his pounding heart.

Fear and pain left her numb, gripping his torn, soot- and bloodstained shirt and thinking that if he released her now she would surely fall. Instead, he swept her up in his arms and carried her to where Frank lay groaning as he regained consciousness.

Closing her eyes, she tried to draw air into her smoke-filled lungs, coughing, gagging, vaguely hearing Betsy's sharp barks as the animal darted back and forth among the sheep, skillfully herding them together and toward the safer, open meadow some distance away. Then Summer's bleary gaze went to Nick.

They had saved the wool shed; the fire had failed to take hold on the green lumber. Frank's shack, however, lay in smoldering ruins. The blackened blanket Nick carried dragged across the ground like a monstrous weight as he kicked at the last flames dancing along the length of a charred beam. Even from where she lay, she could see the labored rise and fall of his chest, then he moved toward her like a drunk, staggering and coughing, his face black and bruised and sweat-streaked, his clothes tattered.

"Help me get him to the house," he rasped.

She pulled herself to her feet and helped Nick lift Frank, wielding her slight weight as best she could as they carried him up the pathway. She hurried to hold open the door as Nick hefted the old man over the threshold, grunting and cursing, then dropped him to his bed, where he collapsed himself, facedown on the mattress.

Crawling onto the bed beside him, Summer curled her arm around his broad shoulders. "There, there, Mr. Sabre," she whispered. "We saved yer sheep. It's all right now." She took a long, slow breath, allowing the closeness of his big body to calm the terror of the moment when she'd thought those hooded men were going to kill him.

"There, there," she said, weeping quietly. She placed her head on his unmoving shoulder, and closed her burning eyes.

The moon was full, its light spilling through the window near the settee where Summer lay with her head on a pillow and her legs curled up inside her nightgown. She wasn't asleep, but held a damp compress to the side of her face where her attacker had struck her. Her body ached with cuts and bruises caused by the sheep's sharp hooves. Several blisters and burns marred her fire-reddened skin.

Hearing a noise, she looked around, startled, to find Nick standing at the foot of the settee, wrapped in moonlight and shadows. "Mr. Sabre, I thought y' were sleepin'."

"Frank snores. Besides, I hurt all over."

Sliding her feet to the floor, she moved toward him. "Yer welcome t' share m' bed with me. Here. Let me help y'. Y' shouldn't be up." Taking his arm, she nudged him down on the sofa where he propped his elbows on his knees and buried his ravaged face in his hands. Summer sat next to him, twisting the cloth in her lap as she studied his profile.

"I'm tired," he confessed.

"Why don't y' lie down and—"

"I don't mean that." He sighed and stared into the black fireplace. "In my head . . . I get so weary of all the thoughts swirling around in my head. During the day I work myself into exhaustion, hoping I'll be too tired to think or dream or . . . remember, but as soon as I lie down all the thoughts come rushing back." He looked at her. "Have you ever known regret, Summer?"

She nodded.

"I tell you, conscience is a curse from God. I've long since determined that this existence on earth is hell. We have to struggle too damn hard to survive."

"If life was easy, then heaven would be no reward, would it?" She smiled, watching as a succession of emotions crossed his face, which the moonlight threw in stark relief against the settee behind his head.

"Do you think I have a chance at heaven?"

"Aye," she replied.

He released a deep breath slowly, wearily, then with no warning lay his heavy head in her lap. His black hair spread out over her white nightgown like a spray of India ink. He closed his eyes.

Motionless, Summer studied his face—his exquisite face—now swollen, cut, and bruised, and her eyes filled with tears. Gently, she touched his forehead with her damp cloth.

"What are you doing?" he asked faintly, without opening his eyes.

"Returnin' the favor," she replied.

Little by little his features relaxed. His left hand drifted up to entwine his fingers with hers. A moment passed, then he whispered sleepily, "It's been a very long time since anyone has held my hand."

Two days after the clan's attack, Summer's cuts and bruises were almost healed, and the rubble left by the fire had been cleared away. She stood on the front porch, searching the horizon for signs of Frank and Nicholas's return from rounding up stray sheep, though she couldn't imagine why she bothered. Since the Clan's assault, Nick had grown more withdrawn and ill-tempered than ever. He rarely slept, refused to eat, and spent his waking hours shearing bleating lambs or pacing through the night as if anticipating a repetition of the nightmare that had nearly destroyed everything he possessed.

Still, she kept reliving those hours when he had slept with his head in her lap. She'd remained awake all night, frightened that any movement might disturb him. She'd watched the first rays of pale sunlight spill onto his battered face, softening the features into those of a young man's. It had occurred to her then that Nicholas Sabre, Esquire, was much younger than she had thought. Perhaps no more than twenty-six or -seven. Once again she'd found herself wondering about the family, friends, and lovers he'd left behind in England. Suddenly she'd been struck by a realization of what this loss of his peers—indeed, of his heritage—had cost him. She remembered vividly the pain of separation from her mother, the heartbreak of believing that no one in the world loved her. Such anguish wasn't easily mended by time.

Summer was about to return to the house when

over the opposite rise a wagon appeared. Dora Johnson raised her hand and waved.

With a squeal of delight, Summer leapt from the porch and ran down the path as Dora and Dan and the three towheaded boys began spilling from the wagon. Throwing open her arms, she greeted each squirming lad with a ferocious hug. "Y' can't know how glad I am to see another soul!" She laughed as Wayne planted his jam-sticky mouth on her cheek.

"We came as soon as we heard about the attack. Are you all right?" Dora took Summer's face in her hands, studying the faint bruise on her cheek.

"I'm fine. Sabre's a mess, though, and Frank has a knot on his head the size of a blazin' goose egg."

"Thank God it wasn't more serious." Arm in arm, they returned to the house, stopping at the sagging porch steps. "It's right pitiful, isn't it?" Dora said.

"I'd call that an understatement," Dan replied. He kicked a porch step and the resident hen let out a squawk. "Might have been better if Sean *had* burned it down. You could've started over from scratch."

"I don't think he could manage any better," Summer told him. "He was an aristocrat, remember. What do they know about buildin'?"

"He could do what we did." Dora grabbed hold of Wayne's breeches and dragged him out from under the porch steps, where the hen had set up a hysterical cackle. "We had the house cut out to our specifications in Christchurch. Takes about a month or so—"

"Six weeks," Dan said.

"The boards are all sawed into the proper lengths by machinery, then they're moved to the building site on drays. Then you just nail it all together."

"It would take six men no more'n a week to construct a solid house," Dan said, peering inside, his hands in his back pockets.

"Aye," Summer replied, "but it must be expensive."

"It wasn't cheap," Dan remarked from inside, "but it was worth it."

While Dora looked around the house, Dan and the boys fetched a basket from the wagon, which they placed on the kitchen table. Then, leaving the ladies to their woman talk, Dan and the boys wandered over to the shearing shed and the rubble that remained of Frank's cabin.

Dora proceeded to unload the basket—an assortment of pickled fruits and vegetables, a tin of tarts— then delivered what she termed her "housewarming" presents: gifts from the Cockatoo wives in the area. There were hand-knitted doilies, needlepoint pictures, a potted plant, and a jar of pickled lambs' tongues. Even before Summer saw them all, she was imagining where each treasured gift would go.

Back outside, Summer found her friend stooped over the ruins of a vegetable bed, snatching weeds out by the handful and tossing them into a pile at her feet. Summer joined her, and within half an hour the weed-infested plot had turned into a neat but bare little garden that would prove most worthy of the selection of potted flowers and vegetables Dora had thinned from her own garden and brought with her.

By the end of the afternoon the boys had rounded up the last free hen and shooed it into the pen with the others, and were now perched on the porch steps, licking tarts crumbs off their fingers.

"Hey, Ma!" Jason yelled. "Will you tell Wayne to stop pickin' his nose? I'm tryin' to eat."

"I ain't pickin' my nose," the tot cried with his finger stuffed up his nostril.

"The potted palms were a nice touch," Summer said, admiring the healthy plants on either side of the porch steps. "I don't know how t' thank y'."

"Nonsense." Dora put her arm around Summer's shoulder and gave her a hug. "Has Mr. Sabre given thought to what he'll do now?"

"He won't leave."

"Good," Dora said. "I think I'll enjoy being neighbors, and friends, with you . . . Summer, what's wrong?"

Blinking and spilling tears down her cheeks, she averted her face from her concerned friends and plopped down next to the boys, then burst into tears. Wayne patted her arm consolingly with his pudgy hand. Allen offered her a piece of peach tart, and Jason's young face screwed into a frown.

She glanced at Dora and Dan, who stood holding hands, watching her solemnly. "He's annullin' the marriage and sendin' me back. He said he's happy with his sheep and his shepherd and his dog, and he doesn't have room in his life for me. He said his signin' that damned idiotic contract was a mistake; he was in . . . in—"

"Inebriated?" Dan suggested.

"Aye." She smoothed her hand over Wayne's brow. "I dress in my best, and he doesn't even notice. I cook and nearly kill him. If I can't even cook, what good am I?"

Dora caught her chin and forced Summer to meet her green eyes. "Dear girl, if you can't figure that one out you're a babe lost in the woods."

"What are y' meanin'?"

Dora glanced at Dan, who motioned for the boys to accompany him on a walk. Then she sat down beside Summer and with her elbows on her thighs stared out over the lush countryside. "I take it," she ventured cautiously, "that this marriage hasn't been consummated or there wouldn't be any talk of an annulment."

"I told y'." Summer sniffed. "He doesn't want any part o' me."

Sympathy flickered in Dora's eyes, then they brightened almost immediately. "Summer, have you ever . . . *been* with a man?"

She shook her head, feeling her cheeks color.

"I see. Then what I'm going to suggest may seem a little shocking perhaps. But before I do, you must tell me one thing. Are you certain beyond any shadow of a doubt that you wish to remain here with Mr. Sabre?"

"I want that more than anythin'," she replied.

Dora squeezed her hand. "Then it's really very simple. You must appeal to his male appetite—"

"I've tried!" she cried. "I've cooked potatoes—"

"Summer, there are other . . . appetites. What I mean is, there are more ways to a man's heart than through his stomach." Taking a deep breath, Dora said, "You must seduce him."

Summer swallowed convulsively. "I can't. I just . . . can't." Her words were an agonized whisper. She paced down the walk, then back again. "I can't prostitute m'self like that. I can't give over m' body just so I can have somethin' better than what I've already got. I'd be no better than m'—" She bit off the words, frowning.

"Summer, don't you care for Mr. Sabre just a little?"

"More than a little," she confessed. "Much more."

"Are you, perchance, in love with him?"

Summer's head came up with a snap. "In love?" She tried to laugh, and sounded far less gay than she had intended. Her shoulders slumped. "I don't know."

"I see."

Summer watched her friend amble over to the garden and pretend to study the seedlings they had transplanted. "Exactly how does one know if they're in love?" Summer questioned.

"Do you feel breathless when he's around?"

She nodded.

"Dizzy?"

"Yes."

"Queasy? Weak? As if your feet don't touch the ground and that at any moment this huge bubble in your chest is going to carry you right off into heaven?"

Summer covered her face with her hands. "Yes!"

"Then you're in love, silly goose. Or very close to it." Dora laughed and pulled Summer back to the porch, where they gazed out at the undulating hills. "You're not prostituting yourself by going to bed with your husband," Dora said. "Besides, what did you expect in your circumstances? You married Nicholas Sabre sight unseen because you wanted a home and family, both of which you felt you couldn't get in England. Obviously you had every intention of committing your mind, heart, and soul—not to mention your body—to a stranger in exchange for a bright new future."

"I thought it would be easier. I thought he would at least like me. But he never wanted a wife. It was all a malicious trick."

"I see." Dora leaned back, elbows propped on the porch behind her, legs crossed at the ankles. "Well then, get shut of him."

"What?" Summer gasped.

"You heard me. Get rid of him. There are a hundred other men in this country who would sell both of their . . . arms . . . to wed a young woman as lovely as you."

"But I couldn't. It wouldn't be right. Y' might as well just put me up on a stage and wager me t' the highest bidder, and besides ... *none* o' them would be Nicholas!"

"Well, you'd better do something soon because next week is just three days away, and in case you don't know, there is a ship leaving Lyttleton mid-week for England."

Before Summer could reply, the boys came scrambling up the path. Their pa trailed behind them, patient and grinning but obviously eager to load his charges into the wagon and begin their long ride home. Dora gave Summer a last fleeting smile before joining her husband.

"We'll see you at the picnic this Sunday?" Dora asked as she climbed aboard the wagon and settled beside Dan.

She shrugged. "I don't know."

"Frank always comes, or at least he does when Sabre'll give him the time off."

"I'll try."

"Good. And Summer ... remember what I said."

She waved her good-byes as the wagon rolled away, then sat down on the porch step and stared off at the horizon.

Chapter 9

Nick had been counting the hours until supper-time, repeatedly checking his watch and wondering if he and Frank should knock off work early and head for home. He just couldn't concentrate; besides, the stray sheep had been rounded up hours ago, and every time he tried to think of some small chore that needed to be done, Frank, the old coot, only shook his head and said, "I done took care of it, boss."

The sun had nearly set by the time they reached home to discover Summer waiting for them on the back steps, her hair swept back and tied with a ribbon. She'd tucked a tea towel into her skirt for an apron, and the sight of her petticoat peeking from beneath her skirt hem brought a sudden tension to Nick's shoulders that, even an hour later, as he stood in the doorway with his arms crossed, his gaze following her around the kitchen, he couldn't seem to shake.

There were potatoes and mutton soup for supper. This time the potatoes appeared to be soft and, hopefully, the soup was untainted by washing soda. The smell of it made Nick's stomach rumble. He couldn't recall when he'd last felt so hungry. It made him restless as he absently listened to Frank ramble on about the upcoming wool auction. His gaze continued to follow Summer as she ladled the soup into bowls and hurried to place them on the table. Steam from the hot broth made her face flush, intensifying the violet of her eyes and the redness of her lips. Each time she nervously flashed those eyes his way he felt a jolt in the pit of his stomach.

Once the food was in place, Summer clasped her hands behind her and regarded her handiwork with a pleased expression. "There y' have it," she announced. "Enjoy."

"I reckon I will," Frank declared as he dropped into his chair and grabbed a spoon.

As Summer turned her attention to Nick, a glossy tendril of hair spilled over her brow. He was tempted to brush it away, but it occurred to him that, considering the unsettling goings-on in his body in that moment, touching her wasn't the wisest thing to do. "Well?" she said. "Aren't y' hungry?"

He dragged out his chair. Summer's eyes widened at the sight of a tiny tin soldier, rifle and bayonet upthrust, left on the seat.

"Oops!" She stifled a giggle as she hurried to grab it and drop it into her skirt pocket.

Nick frowned and slid into his chair. "Where did that come from?"

"One o' the Johnson children must have left it." She flashed a look toward Frank, who regarded them from behind his coffee cup, his eyebrows raised. "Don't y' like children?" she asked Nick somewhat hesitantly.

Nick spread his napkin over his lap. "I find children tolerable . . . in moderation."

"And how many *would* y' find tolerable?" Summer asked.

Nick reached for his spoon. "I always imagined four would be nice."

"Four? Why four?" She sank into her chair, and with her chin propped upon her fist regarded him dreamily.

He cut into his potato. "A man of nobility, such as my father, would naturally want to have enough heirs to assure his lineage—"

"What was yer father's title?"

"He is an earl."

"An earl . . ." She sighed in amazement. "Imagine. Yer father's an earl. Y' must be very proud."

"Proud?" He curled his mouth into a mocking half-smile as he stared into his soup. "Proud doesn't describe, even remotely, how I have always felt about the noble Earl of Chesterfield."

"And yer mother . . ." Summer gazed wistfully out the window. "I'll bet she was beautiful, like a princess."

Nick shoved the bowl away and reached for his water glass. "She was exquisite."

"Is she still livin'?"

His eyes grew stormy. A nerve in his bruised cheek had begun to tick. Softly, and without any emotion, he said, "No, she is not. When I was fourteen years old, she decided that life with her current paramour was more to her liking than her staid existence as Lady Chesterfield. So she bundled up her pretty clothes and jewels and sailed off to India with a retired commander of Her Majesty's Royal Navy. They settled in Meerut, just north of Delhi. On May 10th of 1857, they were caught in the India uprising. The rebels massacred every European they found.

My mother was hacked to pieces by a Muslim butcher."

Summer stared at his cold face. The exhilaration she'd momentarily experienced over so foolishly believing she had somehow touched a nerve of tenderness in this man disintegrated with an onrush of shock.

"I understand she was pregnant," he said indifferently. "I always wished I could have asked her just what the hell she wanted with more children when she so obviously cared so little for the ones she already had. But I suppose that'll have to remain one of the great mysteries of life, won't it, Irish?" He tossed his napkin onto his plate, shoved back his chair, and left the house.

The moon shone through the parlor window in a pale white stream. Slouched on the settee, his long legs crossed, Nick drank sherry. He didn't allow himself to drink often. It had once been a detestable weakness of his; he simply couldn't hold it well. It made him mean and stupid and raw with pain and anger. It left him stripped of his manhood and pride and dignity. It laid open his soul.

But he needed company tonight.

He tossed back the drink, then poured another as he recalled his quandary throughout the day. He laughed softly in the dark. The truth behind his ridiculous desire to come home early hit him the moment he saw Summer standing atop those steps. Even now he could vividly recall the brightness of her violet eyes; her hair had been a lion's mane of silken wildfire. She'd stood like a cautious child before her stern parent, trembling with anticipation and trepidation. His resolve to harden his heart against her had disintegrated the moment those glowing, soulful eyes had met his.

Leaving the settee, he paced to the window and looked out on the moon-washed hills surrounding his station. Still that haunting image of Summer standing on his back steps awaiting his arrival home didn't leave him.

Damn her. Who did she think she was to sashay into his life with her ragtag clothes and bird-feather hat, and stir up all these idiotic dreams of home and family? She had no right to open up his heart and unleash all the old doubts and insecurities he had tried so hard to bury over the last years. How could she possibly expect him to be a husband to her? Hell, he didn't know the first thing about being a husband, or a father. Lord Chesterfield had been a poor example of both.

He drove his fingers through his hair and pressed the heels of his palms against his temples as the voice in his head whispered:

You thought you'd buried all the feelings that had once made you so angry and confused. But now she has entered your life and you won't admit to yourself that you're so damned hungry to feel alive again you could almost curl up and tuck yourself into her beautiful little hands.

"Go to hell," he hissed in the dark. "I don't want her. I don't need her. I—don't—want—to—feel— alive. *It hurts too goddamn much!*"

Back and forth, he paced in the night, in and out of the moonlight, while the silence howled in his ears and Frank's grizzled countenance kept smiling into his mind's eye and repeating, *Ya like the sound of that? The silence. That's exactly what yore gonna be hearin' till you die of old age. That's the last thang yore gonna hear when yore lyin' in that bed in that room and preparin' to meet yore maker.*

What the devil was he supposed to do now? He'd been rendered dumb by a pair of flashing violet eyes and a scattering of freckles. He heard her lilting accent and laughter over and over in his mind as he tried to sleep on the settee.

He moved to the bedroom door.

Go on in, the voice in his head whispered. *You want her . . . don't you? You can't deny it. Have you grown so numb that you won't even acknowledge what your body is feeling? You're hard with wanting her.*

He slid one hand over his erection.

It hurts, doesn't it? You feel as if you're going to explode. You're suddenly remembering what it felt like to be inside of a woman who is hot and slick and encasing you like a snug wet glove. Go on. Just look at her. What harm can come from looking at her as she sleeps? You've walked to this door many times, but you've been too much the coward to enter. You're drunk now and weakened by liquor. You always used that excuse before . . .

He blotted the sweat from his face with his shirt-sleeve. God, he was burning with fever . . .

Go on in. That's right. Quietly. Slide through the darkness like a thief. Who will know? Besides, you have every right. She's your wife. In a drunken fog you signed your name away to a mysterious little fairy creature who does magical things to you with her eyes. Just imagine what her body could do . . .

She lay on her back, her face lost in a cloud of hair and moonbeams. Her shimmering nightgown twisted around her body. He watched the shallow rise and fall of her breasts, noted the childlike innocence of her profile, and the way her arms curved up over her head and her hands were cupped, palm up, to the darkness.

Touch her.

He stroked her hair with his fingers.

Smell her.

Closing his eyes, he inhaled her fragrance, redolent of musky female. The bouquet buzzed through his bloodstream more sweetly than sherry, expanded his senses until his flesh shuddered at the very thought of embracing her.

Take her. It's what you want. She won't stop you. Be nice and she won't stop you, because once the act is done there will be no turning back. She'll be yours forever; that's what she wants. For better or worse. She'll obliterate your misery. Ah, that's what you're afraid of. You're afraid that maybe, just maybe, you'll be happy and you're bloody terrified of being happy. But it could be different with her. That's what you're thinking. That's what all this confusion is about. You're afraid of taking the chance. Go on, Sabre. This seduction was inevitable. How long can you go on lying to yourself?

He turned on his heel and walked from the room. Entering his study, he kicked back the chair and dropped into it, braced his elbows on the desk, and twisted his hands into his hair.

Whether you want to admit it or not, that little freckle-faced fairy has fanned to life a spark of hope inside you.

He swiped at the shelf of books, and they toppled like dominoes to the floor. He struck out at his father's and brother's portraits, hurling them against the wall. The chair landed with a crash beside the door as he kicked it away.

Then Summer was there, materializing out of the darkness, her hair a lovely tangled mass, her dark eyes wide and distressed. "What's wrong?" she asked with husky drowsiness. "What's happened?"

His legs slightly spread and his hands doubled into fists, he stared down at her through the black hair spilling over his eyes.

"Nicholas?" Her face looked white.

Go on! Go on! Take her, you idiot. You know you want her. Your body is hot and hard for her. What the hell are you waiting for?

He reached for her and, closing his hands around her shoulders, dragged her up against him. Like a stunned and frightened bird, her body trembled, her eyes grew round, whether·in distress or anticipation his cloudy mind couldn't reckon. His senses were overwhelmed with the smell and feel of her. Her body felt like a furnace burning into his.

"Summer," he heard himself mutter, only it sounded pained and inhuman.

Six years. God, it had been six years since he'd last touched a woman.

His fingers twisted into her nightgown. As she cried out in fear and surprise and flailed helplessly in an attempt to wrench away, he rent the delicate material easily down the front, exposing one white, rose-tipped breast.

Summer stumbled back, clutching the gown closed with one violently shaking hand. She stared at him as if he had been suddenly transformed into some hideous monster.

"Oh, Christ," he said, as he drew away. Then, recognizing the hurt, confusion, and disappointment on her features, he felt the old maelstrom rise up inside him again.

"Well, what the hell did you expect?" he shouted, moving toward her. "If you were expecting hugs and kisses and love words from the likes of me, sweetheart, you were sadly mistaken. I wouldn't even begin to know how to go about it. So why don't you just get the hell away and leave me alone before we both regret it!"

She fled back to his room and slammed the door between them. He stood in the darkness with his head thrown back and his body burning.

It was Frank's duty to ride out over Sabre's sections twice a week to make sure Betsy was doing her job of keeping the sheep from straying too far from the pens. He invited Summer along, and she gladly accepted, thankful to at last experience something other than the four walls of Nick's cramped house—and Nick himself. Not that she had seen him. Since their last confrontation he'd taken to sleeping in the barn, and he ate his meals on the back stoop.

For lack of anything else to do, she'd continued to try her hand at cooking. She was becoming quite proficient at boiling potatoes. They had potatoes for breakfast, lunch, and supper. She'd even wrapped boiled potatoes in a towel and brought them on her ride with Frank. Sitting now on a hill overlooking the green flat where two dozen sheared sheep were grazing, she watched Frank bite into his spud with relish.

"I declare, darlin', but ya boil one hell of a mean tater."

"Yer just sayin' that, Frank."

"No, I ain't."

"I saw yer face this mornin' when I gave y' potato cakes for breakfast."

"Jest 'cause I ain't ever et flapjacks made of taters. They was good, though."

"Nick gave his t' Betsy. She wouldn't eat them."

"Dogs ain't got the sense God gave to a goose. Neither does Sabre most of the time."

Sighing, she watched a ram cavort around a ewe, which regarded the strutting stud with a bored expression as she chewed her grass. "If I was Clara Beaconsfield," Summer said after some deliberation, "I could cook bread and peach puddin'."

The ram lifted a front leg against the side of the ewe, turned its muzzle toward the sky, and with its tongue hanging out, let loose a throaty, gargling sound in the ewe's ear. Frank stopped chewing and his eyes grew round. "Hot damn. Atta boy. Charm the little gal and ya got her."

"What's he doin'?" Summer asked.

"Courtin'."

The ram then mounted the ewe and proceeded to hump. Summer's face turned red. Turning her back to the scene, she stared over the next rise as Frank guffawed in pleasure.

"Boss is gonna be mighty pleased to hear about this. Lambin' season is gonna be here quick this year, and it's gonna be productive."

"Obviously."

"I 'spect we'll see an improvement in Nick's attitude once we get over this lambin'."

"Y'll see it. I won't. I won't be here."

He polished off his potato and wiped his fingers on his shirt. "Aw, hell, ya can never tell."

"He hates me."

"Has he said that?"

Recalling their turbulent confrontation two nights before, Summer shook her head. "He doesn't have t'. Besides, it's obvious that he would prefer someone like Clara Beaconsfield."

Frank scratched his neck. "I'm just tryin' to imagine Nick and Clara together . . ."

Tilting her chin slightly, Summer regarded Frank while wind blew her hair over her shoulder. "She's very pretty," she said.

"Maybe. But then, so are you."

She smiled.

His twinkling eyes met hers. "Funny thang about women. Ya can take two pretty women and put 'em side by side and try to compare 'em, but ya can't. They is each unique. Take you and Clara. She's like a snow flower, pale and delicate. Her petals bruise easy. Yore like . . ." His eyes searched the hills, then he pointed to a distant rise that shimmered with golden brilliance. "Yore like that thar gorse. Wild and free and full of sunlight. It's jest like each of those tiny, hardy petals has soaked up the heat and color of the sun and is radiatin' it back to man and God."

"That's me?" She regarded him hopefully.

"That's you. And don't for a minute believe the boss ain't recognized it. Truth is, he's probably recognized it a whole hell of a lot more than ya realize."

Her shoulders sank. "But he's sendin' me back."

"And ya don't want to go."

She gazed out over the rich valleys and blue sky and pinkish-white sheep freshly shorn. She thought of Dora and Dan Johnson, and Arnold and Nan Sharkey. She thought of what awaited her back in London. She recalled how her pulse raced every time Nick was nearby. Somehow she had to find a way of breaking through the wall of anger he had erected around himself . . . if she dared. If his behavior toward her those nights before was any indication of how he could act when pushed to his limit, then the task of reaching him might be harder than she had supposed . . . and far more risky.

She lifted her chin and set her shoulders obstinately. "No," she replied with firm conviction. "I don't want t' leave. And I won't, if I have any say in the matter."

Chapter 10

She made mutton chops and eggs for supper. As she had for the last two days, Nick claimed he wasn't hungry and disappeared into the barn. Exhausted and suffering from the heat, Summer sat staring at the platter of meat while Frank told another tall tale about a near-disaster that had befallen him and his brother near some place called Fort Worth. When he paused to take a breath, she said, "I hate mutton. I hate t' look at it. I hate t' eat it. I even hate t' smell it. Don't y' ever get tired of eatin' it?"

"Sometimes."

She sighed deeply and pushed her plate away.

"Somethin' wrong?" Frank asked.

"Everythin'."

"How's the bread comin'?"

"It's been cookin' for three hours and it isn't done yet."

"Well, the chops is mighty good." He bent his head over his plate and chewed noisily.

Looking toward the open back door, Summer

frowned. "I give up, Frank. I've tried everythin' t' win Nicholas over—I've cooked and I've cleaned his house until m' damn bones are weary. I've tried t' make m'self presentable—"

"Yore purty as a picture," he declared with a mouth full of mutton.

She blotted sweat from her forehead and sighed. "I'll be glad when it's over. I wish he'd just take me back and be done with it. I thought I could win him over, but I can't. I'm fed up with tryin'."

Summer moved to the door, her heart squeezing as she saw Nick walking up the path to the house. Betsy loped alongside, jumping up occasionally against his leg in an attempt to win his attention. Nick, his head down, appeared to be lost in thought. His hair flowed like shiny black satin over his shoulders.

Taking a deep breath, she moved down the steps to greet him. Looking up, he stopped suddenly, and his face went rigid.

Summer took a deep breath to steady her nerves. "I've not asked y' for anythin' since I've been here, so I'll trust that y' won't be too angry if I make a reasonable request."

He made no response.

She focused on the sheep shed and did her best to swallow back the disappointment welling up her throat. "Y' mentioned that y'll have yer wool ready t' ship t' Lyttleton next week. I'm askin' y' not to wait until then t' take me back. I'm askin' y' t' get shut o' me Sunday."

The silence grew long and strained as Nick continued to regard her, and she forced herself to stare out at the somnolent ewes that stood nose to nose and blissfully dumb in the whirring summer quiet. At last, she allowed her gaze to move back to his eyes, and was stunned to find their expression uncommonly soft, slightly startled, and more than a little confused.

"You're asking me to take you back?" he asked.

"Aye."

When he said nothing more, Summer turned and mounted the steps.

"But I thought you were going to the Rockwood picnic this Sunday."

Thinking of the friends she wouldn't be seeing again, her knees grew watery, as if she'd scaled a New Zealand mountain instead of Sabre's rickety stoop. Forced to stop to catch her breath and will away the preposterous weakness, she gazed into the shadows where Frank sat hunched over his coffee cup. "It doesn't matter. I really didn't have anythin' t' wear anyway since m' good clothes were ruined. And it probably wouldn't have been much fun, seein' how I'd be there alone. It really doesn't matter, Mr. Sabre. It really doesn't matter at all."

Nick watched Summer enter the house and close the door. Turning on his heel, he walked directly to the wool shed, where he kicked open the door, then stood for a moment in the cool shadows with his hands on his hips and his gaze locked on the table of wool waiting to be sorted and placed into bins. So, she was asking him to get rid of her.

He looked down at the single flower he held in one hand, its yellow petals wilted and bruised. In a moment of insanity he'd picked the long-stemmed bloom with the intention of giving it to Summer as a kind of peace offering. The last days she'd worked herself to a frazzle trying to please him, and he'd ignored her like the coldhearted bastard that he always was. Just last night he'd lain on the settee in the dark and listened to her weeping in bed. He'd almost talked himself into going to her and apologizing for making her so unhappy, but then her soft sobs had died away. When he'd walked to the door to peer in at her, he'd found her small face partially buried in the pillow as she slept. It was just as well. He didn't know how to say *I'm sorry*.

The door squeaked open behind him. Frank said, "Ready to git started, boss?"

Nick tossed the flower to the dirt floor and grabbed up the shears. "What the devil took you so long?"

"Gittin' old, I reckon."

Nick gave a whistle; outside the shed Betsy barked and the sheep bleated. A ewe dashed into the shearing pen. A second whistle brought another sheep. Bending over the animals, Nick and Frank sheared in silence for a long while, sweating, cursing, scrambling to contain the irritated animals if they happened to nip the sheeps' hide with the shears. An hour passed before Frank said:

"That little gal is plum tuckered out."

"What's your point?" Nick flung a woolly pelt over the fence into the pile and whistled for another sheep.

"No point. Jest an observation. She's come a long way in her cookin'."

"Right. She can actually boil potatoes now. We have them three times a day. God, I hate potatoes."

"Least she tries. I was talkin' to Clement Cranston who got him a wife. She don't cook or clean; she don't even try to. Jest sits around weepin' and wailin' about missin' home. Laments that she ever came to New Zealand, claims she was happier emptyin' chamber pots in London."

"So why doesn't he send her home?"

" 'Cause she's the horniest woman he ever met. Says beddin' her is the only way he can git her to shut up about how unhappy she is. I told him, I says, 'Clem, ya ain't exactly a young man, yore just three years my junior. If ya ain't careful yore gonna hump yoreself right into the grave.' He says, 'Frank, at least I'll die with a smile on my ugly face.'"

They continued to shear.

"Summer was shore countin' on that picnic Sunday. Can't rightly understand why she don't want to go. Then again, maybe I can."

Stooped over a sheep, Nick blinked sweat from his eyes as he watched his shepherd neatly peel the wool off a squirming ram. "Well?" he said.

"Well what?"

"Why doesn't she want to go to the picnic?"

"Tellin' folks good-bye is hard fer some people. I reckon it's especially hard fer a little gal like her, who had so many dreams and hopes for a new beginnin'. It's my understandin' that she don't have a family back there, or many friends. I reckon she's feelin' a little bit lost right about now." He shook his head and swiped sweat from his lined face. "She shore did want to go to that picnic though."

Nick went down on one knee and, starting at the top of the animal's tail, ran the blades smoothly up the backbone to the crest of the neck. The wool fell away before he said, "Then she should go."

"I agree, but convincin' her of that right now might be another matter. Besides, she don't have nothin' nice to wear. Shoot, you know women."

"No. I don't."

"Well, they got to feel good about themselves. A girl's got to feel like she's the purtiest woman at the function and that all the men there is watchin' her and wishin' she was his."

"That's stupid. Besides, Summer would be the prettiest woman there even if she was dressed in a gunny sack."

Frank's head came up and his shears stopped. He

grinned. "So ya *have* noticed that she's more than fair-to-middlin' purty."

"I never said she wasn't," he snapped.

"Never said she was either." After shoving his denuded ram through the trapdoor exit into the "sheared already" pen, Frank arched his back and winced. Then he shambled over to the sorting table and began to grade the wool, separating it by quality into divided bins.

"Do you think she'd go if she had something decent to wear?" Nick demanded with some anger.

"Maybe," Frank replied loudly. "And maybe not. Ain't no way to tell unless she has the clothes. I reckon I could ask Dora Johnson if she has somethin' Summer could borrow."

"The hell you say. My wife is not wearing hand-me-down clothes—my father is an earl, remember, which makes me somewhat higher in rank than a beggar."

"Aw, heck. I fergot. My apologies, yore lordship."

They worked deep into the night. Frank was forced to drag up a tree-stump stool and sit while separating the wool. Nick's hands were bleeding, and so sore he couldn't so much as curl his fingers into a fist. Frank wrapped them in cotton bindings, then they stooped over the table together. Straining to study the fine threads of each pelt, they tossed the pelts into bins that were overflowing and spilling wool onto the floor. After hours of silence, Nick said, "This is damn good wool, Frank. Should bring top dollar. This time next year we'll be able to hire maybe six or seven hands to help with the shearing."

"That'd be real nice," came the weary response. "I jest hope I'm still alive to see it."

Frank's face was creased with deep fatigue. Tugging his watch from his pocket, Nick noted the time. Nearly midnight. "Go to bed," he said. "I'll finish up here."

"Don't mind if'n I do." As Frank eased off his stool, his joints popped. "Ya gonna be sharin' my bed in the barn tonight?" he asked as he shuffled toward the door.

"I'll chance the settee, I think."

"Have a good one then." The door creaked open, then closed.

Tired and aching in every muscle, Nick leaned against the table and looked at his dog. Betsy lay curled near his feet, and, as if sensing his attention, rolled her soft brown eyes up at him and thumped the dirt with her tail. Nick went down on one knee, and immediately the dog sat up, placed her spotted muzzle on his thigh, and quivered with pleasure as he ruffled her white fur collar and scratched behind her ears. "Think she'll be in bed, old girl?" he asked. Betsy whined and nuzzled closer. "I suppose I've hidden in this stinking shed long enough to make sure she's asleep." Grimacing, he pushed himself up, blew out the lantern, and left the shed, locking it behind him. He allowed Betsy one last cuddle before directing her to the pens.

As was the norm, dim light poured through the kitchen window, illuminating the path to the house. Stopping at the steps, he removed his manure-crusted boots, tossed them aside, and mounted the stoop in his stocking feet. He shoved open the door.

A putrid smell assaulted him. So did the figure of Summer sitting at the table, her face buried in the crook of one elbow while her shoulders shook. Beside her were two loaf pans heaped high with something that resembled lava rock and smelled like sheep offal.

Her head came up, just barely, causing her hair

to spread like a fire pool over the table. The lantern glow kindled her teary dark eyes as she regarded him with anger and desperation. Her gaze rendered him incapable of moving, suddenly too over-whelmed by the unsettling emotions that surged inside him like a riptide.

"Well," she choked, "go on and say it."

"Say what?"

"That I botched it again. The damned bread won't cook! I've bloody baked it for hours and hours and—and look at it!" She grabbed up a knife and stabbed it into a big black heap, sending splinters of crust flying to the floor. Yanking the knife blade out, she held it up to reveal raw dough.

He looked away.

She flung the knife across the room, pushed out of her chair, and, swiping at her tears with the back of her hand, skewered him with her eyes. She moved toward him with her hands fisted at her sides. "I tried, Sabre. I wanted t' do good for y'. I thought, yer alone and I'm alone, and it just seems so silly for two people who have no one else in the world not t' try and make a go of it. But it's obvious that y' don't want t' make a go of it, and I was just too dumb to accept it. The plain fact o' the matter is, if I'd made this horrible bread t' perfection, y' still wouldn't have found me acceptable. Y' still wouldn't like me because yer so twisted up inside with hate for yerself that y' got no love t' give any-one!"

She drew a deep, ragged breath as fresh tears spilled down her cheeks. Then she reached for a bread loaf and hurled it at his feet. "I hope y' choke on Clara's bread the next time y' eat it!" she cried, then she fled to his room.

He continued to stand in the doorway, the night air sending shivers up his cooling body. Again and again, he looked toward his bedroom, then to the bread at his feet. At last, he picked up the bread, carried it to the table, and retrieved the knife. Perhaps if he found something nice to say about it . . . But the black crust was four inches thick and the rest was nothing but a foul-smelling dough.

He wandered to his room.

She continued to weep hard into her pillow as Nick watched her from the door. *Console her, Sabre, you coldhearted bastard. Surely you can find something nice to say. Coward. You won't do it, will you, because you're weakening. You know that if you touch her now you won't be able to stop. If she turns her big beautiful eyes on you, you'll shatter like fragile glass. Then there would be no turning back. Ever.*

Woodenly, he moved to the parlor and sat on the settee, the sound of her weeping filling up the silence until he was driven to cover his ears with his hands and squeeze close his eyes.

Who are you kidding, anyway? You've never offered another human being one moment's kindness or consideration. You wouldn't know how even if you wanted to.

He left his chair and paced to the window.

At last, the weeping grew softer . . . became a hiccough. She blew her nose.

Minutes passed and finally silence fell. Only then did he move to her door again and look in. She lay curled up on the bed. The light shining from the kitchen reflected off the tear streaks on her cheeks.

Leaning wearily against the door frame, he closed his eyes. An odd sense of responsibility stole over him, one he couldn't quite shake. It wasn't the sort of responsibility that he felt for his sheep or his dog, or even for Frank. There was a disturbing sense of wanting to kiss away her tears and soothe her heartache. He wanted to see the bright, unfettered smile

she'd bestowed on him when she'd first introduced
herself as his wife. He suddenly realized that it had
been a long, long time since she'd last smiled that
way.

Moving to his study, he sank into the desk chair
and pulled open a drawer, dug beneath stacks of
papers, and finally withdrew a small wooden box
engraved with a scrolled S. He flipped the solid
silver latch and eased back the lid. Several coins
winked in the lamplight as he removed the few mon-
etary notes and counted them out on the desk. There
was pitifully little, the final dregs of last year's wool
profits, not enough to buy food for a week. Obviously there was no help there... then his eye
caught the ruby stickpin tucked into the corner.

He held the extraordinary piece up to the light,
studying the gem's reflected facets as his mind's eye
recalled his father giving him the jewel on his nine-
teenth birthday. It had been the first and only time
his father, the noble Earl of Chesterfield, had even
hinted that he loved his youngest son.

Closing his fingers around the ruby, Nick stared
for a long time into the lantern flame, then he slid
the gem into his shirt pocket, returned the money
to the box, and buried the box in the drawer.

He was halfway to the barn before he realized
that his feet were bare. The building was black inside, and overly warm and humid. As the door
creaked closed behind him, he stared hard through
the dark and yelled, "Frank!"

There came a rustle of hay, then, "Hell, is it mornin' already?"

"I was just about to turn in when a tnought occurred to me."

Silence.

"Now that the shearing is finished we can start
rebuilding your quarters."

"Ya woke me up to tell me that?"

"I thought you'd be pleased."

"Well, I reckon I am. Thank you very much. But how are we gonna afford it?"

"We'll have to sacrifice."

"Sacrifice. Like robbin' Peter to pay Paul."

"Right."

The hay whispered again.

"What day is it today, Frank?"

"Day? Well now, let me thank. Seein' how it's after midnight and all, I guess that makes it Saturday."

"That'll give you plenty of time to get to Christchurch and home by Sunday noon."

"What am I goin' to Christchurch fer?"

"Lumber, of course, and building supplies. We can't construct a house out of nothing."

"Can't that wait till we freight out the wool next week?"

"No."

Silence. Finally, "Yore jest hell-bent on gittin' it here by Sunday, huh?"

"I'm just thinking of you."

"Well, that's most gratifyin'. Yes sir, it shore is. I suppose yer wantin' me to haul the girl off with me?"

"No."

"No?"

"She stays until we dray the wool to Lyttleton, whether she likes it or not."

"Humph."

"What's that supposed to mean?"

"Nothin'. I didn't say nothin'."

"You must have been thinking something or you wouldn't have grunted like that."

"Yore right prickly, ain't ya, considerin' it's well-nigh to one in the mornin'. What grass burr's crawled into yore breeches?"

"I would've thought you'd show a little appreciation that I give a damn over your sleeping in here with a lot of horses and sheep."

"I've slept with worse... remind me to tell ya sometime about the whore what took a shine to me in Salido, Mexico. Me and Sam—"

"You'll leave at dawn," Nick commanded sharply.

"Dawn. Whatever ya say, boss."

Nick turned for the door, hesitated, looked back into the dark, and added, "Frank."

"Yep?"

"There's one more thing..."

Chapter 11

Summer spent Sunday morning penning letters of good-bye to the Johnsons and the Sharkeys. She even wrote to Sean, begging him to renounce his support of the Clan and try to put his past behind him and start anew. When Frank returned from Christchurch, she'd turn them over to him, and he could pass them on when he got the chance.

A racket brought her head up. She peered through the window and saw Frank pulling the dray up before the house. The back was laden with lumber and miscellaneous building supplies. She ran for the door, forgetting the irritation she'd felt at her old friend upon first learning that he had left for Christchurch without her.

He climbed down from the dray, removed his hat, and wiped his forehead with his shirtsleeve. Seeing Summer smiling at him from the porch, he shook his head. "I declare, it does an old man's heart good to look up after a wearisome journey and discover the purtiest gal in the country smilin' at him."

"Am I smilin'?" she replied. "I should be frownin'."

"What's Sabre gone and done now?"

"Y' should've let me go t' Christchurch," she told him as he mounted the porch steps. "Now I'm stuck until midweek. T' top that off, I'll have t' go with *him*."

"A fate worse'n death fer shore."

She followed him into the house, watching fondly as he ambled toward the kitchen, his legs bowed and his sweat-stained hat cocked back on his head. "So whar is the ol' horny toad?"

"Who knows? Who cares? I haven't seen him since yesterday."

Frank dipped a cup of water from the pail. He drank deeply, then took a second helping before putting the cup down with a satisfied sigh. "Probably screw-pressin' them fleeces into bales. Reckon I'd better git that wagon unloaded. He'll need to start stackin' them bales on the dray soon as possible. Would ya mind runnin' down and lettin' him know that I'm alive and kickin'? I'll move this lumber on down the holler where we intend to rebuild. I'll see 'im down thar in a few minutes."

Frank's footfalls rumbled across the floor, then he was out the door, whistling in the crystal-clear air. Summer's entire body bristled at the thought of having to face Nick again. It didn't help her mood to remember how upset she'd been two nights ago over the bread.

With a sigh of resignation, she started for the shed. It was a glorious day. The sky was a dazzling blue, and the distant mountains stood out sharp and clear against the horizon. Since all of the sheep had been turned out to pasture, their stench no longer hung in the air. Instead, it smelled like sunbaked earth and the rich grain smell of the Cape broom. Wild honeysuckle crowded the well to her right, its huge yellow-and-white blossoms attracting bees, and further down at the outhouse, a garland of jasmine spilled like a waterfall from the eaves. Its blooms resembled a burst of sunlight, so vibrantly yellow they hurt the eyes.

At any other time Summer would have been exhilarated by the beauty around her, but the idea that this would be her last Sunday here, and that, very soon now, her friends would be meeting without her at some Edenlike paradise to picnic and frolic left her tight-chested with despair. "Don't think about it," she muttered to herself.

The shed was empty. Thank God. She wouldn't have to face him after all, it seemed. But as she started back up the trail to the house, the sound of swearing caught her ear. Moving around the side of the shed, she discovered Sabre straining with some massive, bulky contraption of gears and springs. He was naked to the waist. His skin was brown and slick with sweat, and each muscle from his neck to his hair-matted chest to his corded stomach was straining to the limit of its endurance.

She lost her breath; her mouth fell open.

That familiar hot and shocking spark took fire and exploded deep down in her nether regions. She wanted to run. She wanted to hide her face with her hands—saints, she'd never even *seen* a man's bare chest before!

"*Damn,*" he swore, leaning his weight into the lever, gritting his teeth and squeezing his eyes closed with the strain. His arms shook, his belly tensed, his breeches slid low on his hips, revealing a strip of white skin and a streak of black hair that formed an arrow from his navel down into his pants. He swore again, dug his boot toes into the ground, and, with a growl, lunged one last time against the machinery. There came a whir and a click as the lever locked into place, and with a groan of relief, his body relaxed. He slumped against the iron monstrosity and bent at the waist, hands on his thighs as he struggled for breath. Then his shaggy black head came up, and he saw her. He straightened slowly.

She wondered how a man could sweat so much; it seemed as if water was pouring from every pore on his body. It ran down his face and dripped off his arms. It glistened like rain on his black chest hair. With great relief, she watched him reach for his shirt, but he didn't put it on, just stared at her with his whisky-colored eyes and dragged the shirt across his chest to dry it off.

"Did you want something?" came his somewhat breathless words.

She opened her mouth to speak. Nothing came out. Frantically, she tried to recall just why she was there. Spying the pail of water nearby, she blurted, "Would y' like a drink?"

His eyes narrowed, then he nodded.

She went to the pail and dipped the cup into it, then hurried over to him.

"Thank you."

"Yer welcome."

He turned the cup up to his mouth and drank deeply, head back and eyes closed. His lashes were thick black crescents against his face, and though she tried—oh, how she tried—she couldn't help but stare at his chest. She was no taller than his chin, so how could she help it?

Then the cup was empty and he was handing it to her. "More?" she asked.

He shook his head and wrist-wiped his mouth.

"What's this?" She pointed to the machine, desperate for something to take her attention away from him.

"A wool baler." He pushed away from the machine and walked around it. "It forms the wool into dense cubes. This frame stretches canvas around it. Before I unload it, I'll sew it together with rawhide, then I'll release these four iron pins and the frame will fall away, leaving the bale."

"Let's hope y' sew better than I do," she replied with a smile.

His dark eyes came back to hers, briefly, and he laughed.

"That contraption there"—he pointed to a cumbersome heap of pulleys and axles—"is a crane. Because the wool is so dense, it would be impossible for two men to lift it. So we hoist it onto the dray with the crane." He came around the machine, easily sliding his arms into his damp shirtsleeves, contemplating the bales stacked to one side. Several more bins of wool stood prepared to be squeezed into the presses. "Was there some reason you wanted to see me?" he asked again, flipping his hair, tied in a queue, over his back collar.

"Frank is home. He wanted y' t' know that he'll be unloadin' the dray."

Nick glanced toward the house. "I guess if you hurry you might still make the Rockwood picnic."

She shook her head and turned back for the house, her mood suddenly cloudy as a realization of her circumstances tumbled in on her again. Putting distance between them, she ran toward the house, refusing to look back when he called her name. She met Frank coming out the back door. She didn't speak to him, just slipped over the threshold and headed for her room, slamming the door behind her.

Leaning against it, she closed her eyes, acknowl-

edging the sting behind her lids. "Y' won't cry,"
she told herself. "Y' promised yerself that y' weren't
gonna lose one more tear over the black-hearted
ne'er-do-well. He's not worth one minute o' misery.
He's not worth—"

She stared at the box on her bed. "What . . . ?"

She approached it cautiously. Where had it come
from? What was it? She shook it. It was heavy, for
sure. And it didn't make much noise. Suddenly she
felt like a child again, when her mother would bring
her a present from London and they would make a
game of guessing what it might be.

Should she open it? Dare she? Perhaps it wasn't
hers. But she wouldn't know unless she opened it.

Crawling onto the bed, she closed her hands carefully on the lid and eased it up. A little. A little
more. Saints, but the expectation was positively
painful. *Silly goose! Yer gonna feel like an idiot when y'
discover it's somethin' for Nick.* That was it! Frank had
brought Nick a gift from Christchurch, and she
shouldn't be touching it at all . . .

Just a peek? Who would know?

She placed the lid aside and stared down at the
mound of tissue. Slowly, her trembling hand peeled
back one thin layer of paper, then another. As color
materialized, her heart began to pound, and tears
collected in her throat and behind her nose, turning
the sunlight-dappled world into water.

"Oh," she mouthed. "Oh."

She covered her lips, her cheeks, her eyes with
her hands, unable to look. It wasn't real. She was
dreaming again, damn her soul, and . . . it wasn't
real. But she looked again anyway, and as tears
spilled down her cheeks, she carefully, so gently,
eased the lavender dress out of the box and held it
up before her eyes. Oh, it was *the* dress. The very
dress she'd stared at in the shop window and imag-

ined wearing to impress a stranger called Nicholas Sabre, hoping against hope that he would think she was the most beautiful creature on the face of the earth and would fall in love with her at first sight. Oh, it was *that* dress!

Leaping from the bed, the dress crushed against her, she spun around and around. Then Frank was peeking around the door, his hat in his hands and his eyes bright with pleasure. She flung herself at him, threw one arm around his neck, and kissed his unshaven cheek. As quickly, she danced away on her tiptoes, her laughter flowing through the house.

"I can't believe it! It's the most beautiful dress in the world!"

"Like it, do ya?" Frank beamed her a snaggle-toothed smile.

Stopping stock-still, her eyes wide, she asked, "Why? How? What have I done t' warrant such a wonderful gift?"

He shuffled his feet and looked chagrined. "Well now, as much as I'd like to take credit fer it, it was the boss who sprung fer most of the cost. I pitched in a penny or two, I reckon, but it was his idea to git it. He sold a ruby stickpin, an heirloom, to pay for it."

She gasped. "Sabre? It was Sabre?"

He nodded.

Frowning, she stated seriously, "Frank Wells, if yer fibbin' me y'll grow bumps on yer tongue."

"Shoot, I wouldn't lie about nothin' so important as a dress, darlin'."

She squeezed her eyes closed, unable to take it in all at once. "I—I have t' thank him."

"Yep, I reckon. Why don't ya put it on first so's he can see it on ya? I got a suspicion that yore gonna look more'n a tad fetchin' in it."

She nodded, jumped for the door, and slammed

it in his face. She tore off her clothes in record time, then carefully, carefully, stepped into the layers and layers of petticoats and skirts, eased the bodice up over her breasts, and wiggled it over her shoulders. It fit! Oh, saints, the dress couldn't fit her more perfectly if she had stood for hours for a seamstress. There was only one problem.

Flinging open the door, she plowed into Frank where he stood waiting. "Buttons," she told him. "Will y' help with the buttons?" Offering him her back, she swept her hair aside. "Please," she pressed.

"Heck on a stick," he muttered, tossing away his hat. "I reckon it's been a hell of a long time since I done this. You'll have to stop yer jitterin' up and down—"

"I can't help it!" She laughed and jittered some more.

"Why is it folk thank that they got to put these damn tiny buttons on a woman's clothes?"

Betsy barked, close to the house.

"Hurry!" she cried. "He's comin'! It has t' be perfect when he sees it!"

Dropping his hands and stepping away, Frank said, "Darlin', any man with eyeballs couldn't help but thank yore the purtiest lady this side of London."

The back door opened. Summer froze, her hands clutched against her racing heart, sudden fear and shyness leaving her weak and speechless. Suddenly, facing Nicholas Sabre seemed terrifying, and not because of their past stormy confrontations. A moment ago they'd had a pleasant conversation . . . and he'd laughed. He'd actually *laughed!*

Frank grinned at Nick where he stood just inside the door. *Does she like it?* Nick asked with his eyes. Then Frank stepped aside and there was Summer, floating toward him, a rustling soft cloud of lavender silk and taffeta, her hair a burst of sunset color haloing her face.

He felt gut-punched.

Very slowly, she stopped before him and pirouetted on her toes. He couldn't take his eyes off her face. Her own eyes were crystal prisms of violet light, her translucent skin a sheer dusting of pink color.

Hands gripped as if in prayer beneath her chin, she bestowed on him a glorious smile. "Do y' like it?"

"Yes."

"How did y' know this was the dress I wanted?"

"I—" He swallowed. "I just told Frank to purchase the prettiest dress they had."

She moved toward him. He backed away, until his spine was pressed against the dry sink and she was gazing up into his eyes, her small, soft mouth curving into a smile. "Thank y'," she whispered. "Y' can't know how happy y've made me, Nicholas."

Several heartbeats passed, then Frank said, "If yore plannin' on makin' that picnic, ya'd better hurry."

Her eyes widened and she brightened again. Spinning, she ran back to the bedroom, calling, "I'll be ready in ten minutes. I'll just touch up m' hair . . ." The door slammed.

Frank said, "I'll pack up some food in a basket. It'll be ready to go when she is."

Relaxing at last, Nick crossed his arms over his chest and watched Frank shamble around the room, grabbing jars and boiled potatoes, hoecakes and potato pancakes, peaches and baked potatoes. "Hot damn," Frank mumbled. "Seein' the look on her face was worth the trip to Christchurch and back."

"So how much did you get for the ruby?"

Frank shrugged. "Not near what it was worth, o' course. The dress and buildin' supplies took all ya got from the gem and some I had."

"I could've purchased a half dozen rams with that much money," he admitted tightly.

"I reckon." Frank looked at him and smiled. "But I don't suspect yore little wife would've looked nearly as purty wearin' a ram as she does that dress."

The door opened again. This time Summer exited more slowly, her head held high, her shoulders back, presenting the dress perfectly. She had swiftly braided her hair and curled it in a corona around her head.

"Well, looka thar," Frank declared. "Ain't ya a fetchin' sight, darlin'."

Flashing him an appreciative smile, she looked over the contents of the basket, then turned back to Nick and regarded his attire. "Are y' wearin' that?" she asked.

"This?" He looked down at himself, then the realization hit him. His eyes coming back to hers, he shook his head. "I'm not going, Summer."

Strained silence filled the room. The smile melted by degrees from her face. "Not goin'?" she asked. "But I thought—"

"Frank is taking you. I thought that was understood."

Frowning, he shot his shepherd a hard look. Frank, appearing nonplussed, eyed him with his usual calm. Then the old man bowed his head, dragged a chair over, and plunked himself into it. "Sorry, boss. I jest ain't up to it after that trip. That bumpin' and jarrin' played hell with my lumbago. I'll be doin' good to shovel sheep manure fer the

next three days. Can't no way ride to Rockwood.
Nope. No can do."

Hot color crept up Summer's face. She glared at
Nick. "Y' mean y' bought me this dress and I can't
even go t' the blasted picnic? Why the blazes did y'
bother?"

Hands on his hips, he stared first at Frank, who
avoided his gaze, then at Summer, who didn't. "I
suppose you can wear the bloody thing on the journey back to London," he stated matter-of-factly.

Color drained from her cheeks; her eyes were dark
pools as she moved like an automaton to her room,
closing the door behind her.

She stood there for a long while, braced against
the door. Frank's low voice buzzed. Sabre's snapped
a reply. Someone stomped out of the house, and
the kitchen door slammed shut with a force that
shook the walls.

"Summer," came *his* voice from the other side of
the door.

"Go away and leave me alone."

"Summer . . . you don't understand what you're
asking me to do."

"All I want is t' go t' a picnic and see m' friends
for the last time. Is that so much t' ask?"

"I . . . can't."

She started to cry.

"Ah . . . Summer . . . ? Don't do that. Don't cry.
Christ, I hate it when you cry."

Looking down over the ruches and ribbons of her
exquisite dress, she wept all the harder.

"Summer . . . they . . . I don't . . . they look at me
as if I'm some sort of . . ."

"Ogre?"

"Yes."

"Warlock?"

"Maybe."

"Monster?"

Silence.

"That's because y' are!" She wept harder.

"Yes," he said. "I am. But I don't need people constantly reminding me of it. Maybe I'd appreciate just a little less of their passing judgment and gawking at me as if I walk around with horns and a forked tail."

"Y' might try bein' a little nicer t' people!"

"I'm trying," came the quiet response. "I'm really ... trying. Just don't ask me to rush into anything until I'm ready."

Furious, she flung open the door and glowered up into his taut features. "In case y've forgotten, Mr. Sabre, yer sendin' me away any day now. I haven't got time t' wait until yer ready ... if yer *ever* ready." Then she slammed the door again.

Minutes of stillness ticked by, then came an angry knock. "What?" she snapped, wiping her nose with her hand.

"Will you let me in?"

"Go t' blazes in a hand basket."

"I can't change unless you let me in."

She sniffed and frowned. "What d' ya mean, change? Change into what?"

"My suit."

Turning her head slightly, she said, "I beg yer pardon?"

"*If you want to go to that damn picnic I'll have to change my clothes!*"

She opened the door slowly, making it squeak, and peered up into Sabre's furious eyes.

Summer felt intoxicated! She felt like a princess. No doubt about it, she would remember this day for the rest of her life.

Sighing, Dora regarded Summer's gown with

great admiration. "It's the most beautiful dress I've ever seen. You look radiant, Summer. Truly happy."

Nan Sharkey looked up from her cushioned seat beneath a tree, where she lovingly cradled her newest offspring. "What I'd give to own a dress as lovely as that."

Laughing, Summer skipped over to her and squatted beside her friend in a pool of lavender silk. Her eyes were on the babe, barely more than a week old. "I'd happily trade y' this dress for her, Nan."

Nan and Dora exchanged glances, then Nan carefully held out the bundle to Summer. She shook her head and fluttered her hands. "I couldn't. I've never held a wee babe before—"

"There's nothing to it. Just keep her head supported in the crook of your arm." Nan slid the swaddled child into her arms. "Keep her close to your breast. Your heartbeat will soothe her. There! That's it. Why, Dora, don't you think Summer makes a lovely little mother?"

"Stunning!" Dora laughed.

The child turned its head and nuzzled Summer's breast. Summer's heart turned over. A slow glowing heat radiated through her; it centered in her chest and pulsated into a yearning so intense that she suddenly felt dizzy. "She's beautiful," she whispered, aware that her eyes had grown misty with emotion. "And look at her wee hands. Aren't they perfect? And her tiny eyelashes and precious mouth. Why, it looks like a pale-pink rosebud."

Looking up, Summer searched the group of men and women gathered in the meadow. Couples promenaded along a well-beaten path near the trees, holding hands and smiling into one another's eyes. Others lounged about the grassy plain, sipping wine from tulip-shaped glasses that winked in the sunlight. Then she found Nick, standing alone on the cusp of a cliff overlooking the next valley, his back to the party, his hands in his pockets.

"Why don't you take Phoebe over and show her to Mr. Sabre?" Nan said.

"Oh, I couldn't."

"Certainly you could," said Dora.

"I might drop her."

"Balderdash." Nan scowled. "Just take your time. I'm sure Mr. Sabre could use the company. And there's nothing better to start a conversation than a baby. Everyone has an opinion on babies."

"Well..." Taking a deep breath and gripping her precious bundle firmly, Summer moved off down the path, her gaze riveted on the ground, only occasionally straying toward Sabre's dark figure silhouetted against the sapphire sky. "Nicholas?" she called as she neared him.

He glanced over his shoulder.

"I have someone who'd like t' meet y'."

No response.

She stared at his broad shoulders and black hair, which fluttered now and again in the wind. "Phoebe Sharkey, meet Mr. Nicholas Winston Sabre, Esquire. Nicholas, don't be rude."

His shoulders rose and fell with apparent agitation, then he turned to her, his stony countenance crumbling when he saw the child.

"Isn't she lovely?"

His eyebrows lowered over his nose. He shoved his hands deeper into his pockets.

"She's just over a week old. Look how tiny and perfect her hands are. Would y' like t' touch her?"

He shook his head.

"Go on. Feel how soft she is." She dragged his hand out of his pocket and led it to the child, her mind and heart noting how big and dark and strong

his fingers looked compared to this tiny pink creature sleeping so soundly in the sunlight.

Reluctant, Nick probed at the baby's hand. It fluttered like a butterfly, then closed around his finger.
Summer breathlessly watched the hard lines and
angles of his face melt into pleasure. "Nicholas,"
she whispered. His lashes lifted, revealing his eyes.
"Yer smilin'."

"What's not to smile at?"

"Y' told me once that y' didn't have anythin' t'
smile about."

"Even ogres appreciate babies. They don't ridicule
and they're too young to judge."

"Would y' like t' hold her?"

He shook his head, tugged his finger away, and
returned his hand to his pocket.

"Why won't y' come join the others? Y've stood
in this place long enough t' grow roots."

"I said I would bring you. I brought you. I never
said I intended to participate."

"I think they would like y' t'."

He laughed sharply and turned away. Frowning,
Summer snapped, "Well then, just be stubborn. If
yer miserable, y've only yerself t' blame."

In a huff, she stormed up the path and relin-
quished Phoebe into her mother's arms. "Stubborn
man," she fumed, glaring toward Sabre with her
hands on her hips. "He won't give a blazin' inch."

"Oh, I don't know." Dora handed her a glass of
chilled wine. "Not one of us would have ever believed you could have managed to coerce him here."

"He's never joined us before," Nan added.

At that moment Vicesimus Sellers took a seat on
a rock and struck up a lively tune with his violin.
Couples began to converge on the area, their faces
bright with anticipation, feet tapping out the rhythm
and hands clapping. Then, in unison, the men

turned to their wives, bowed gallantly at the waist, and spun them into a dance.

Summer watched from her place beside Nan and Arnold, who had returned from playing horseshoes with the children over the rise. She watched with envy as the men smiled into their wives' upturned faces and guided them effortlessly through the dance. Occasionally her eyes searched out Sabre. He had moved to an outcropping of rock overlooking the dancing couples—Jeff and Fanny Mead, the Johnsons, and Emma and Dick Thorndike; he sat with one long leg drawn up and his elbow resting on his knee. The longer Summer stood there feeling left out, the more frustrated she became. Unable to tolerate it a minute more, she walked over the hill to watch the children play.

There must have been two dozen children, ranging in age from toddlers to adolescents. They, too, had taken up the rhythm of the music that lilted clearly over the hilltop. Clasping hands and forming a ring, they leaped and skipped around and around, a rainbow of colors amidst a backdrop of rippling emerald grass and white flowers that resembled billowy snowdrifts.

"Summer!" called Jason Johnson's voice. "Come dance with us!"

She joined them, and danced until she was breathless and laughing. "I have to rest!" she cried at last when several tall, lanky boys in their midteens tried to persuade her to join them for one last dance.

Wandering away from the frivolity, she sat down amid the grass and flowers, glad to be off her feet. She kicked off her shoes, rearranged the tissue paper she had stuffed in the heels, then wiggled her toes in the cool grass. The rich, musty smell of the earth, and the sweet perfume of the flowers, brought back memories of her childhood. Her mother had been little more than a child herself then, barely older than Summer was now. They'd dashed through meadows sparkling with flowers. They'd crawled on their hands and knees in search of the *daoine sidhe*, certain the fairies' magic would make their every dream come true.

"I could use a little magic in m' life right now, thank y' very much," she mumbled aloud, peering at the flowers around her. "If yer there and in the mood t' sprinkle a little fairy dust, I'd be much obliged."

Someone tapped her on the shoulder. Jumping, she looked around into Rebecca Sharkey's wide brown eyes. The girl, no more than four years old and wearing a soft yellow cotton dress printed with diminutive Michaelmas daisies, blinked her long black lashes and whispered, "Who're you talking to?"

"Fairies."

The girl looked around, incredulous.

"And leprechauns."

"What's that?"

"Of all the fairy tribes, the leprechaun is the luckiest one t' meet. He's the keeper o' the gold, y' know."

"Show him to me."

"I think y've scared him off."

"Let's find him."

"It'll mean searchin' under every flower out here." Admiring the chain of violets encircling the child's head, Summer pointed to it and asked, "What's that?"

"A friendship garland."

"It's very pretty."

Rebecca removed the ring from her dark hair and placed it on Summer's, drooping it over her brow.

The bouquet filled her senses like heady perfume.

"Now will you help me find the leprechaun?" Rebecca asked.

"On one condition. Y' must promise that y'll never reveal his whereabouts t' anyone. That is, if we find him."

The child dropped to her knees, almost disappearing behind the shimmering veil of flowers. "While we look, tell me more about the fairies."

On their hands and knees, they moved cautiously through the flowers, gently nudging aside the delicate blooms. "Leprechauns are smart and prone t' trickery. The only way t' keep one from disappearin' before yer eyes is t' keep yer sights on him all the time."

"Perhaps we can make him show us his gold."

"Perhaps. Once, there was a man named Owen a-Kieran who caught one o' the little people and convinced him to reveal where he kept his treasure. It was buried beneath a *bouchaillin-buidhe*, a Benweed. Owen let him go and proceeded t' tie his red handkerchief on the *bouchaillin-buidhe* so he would be able t' distinguish it from the thousands of others that were growin' in the field. He rushed away t' fetch his friends and bring his shovel. But when he returned t' the field, he discovered that the leprechaun had tricked him again. All of the thousands o' *bouchaillin-buidhe* were sportin' red handkerchiefs."

"Naughty leprechaun!" Rebecca giggled.

They tiptoed through the flowers and grass, eyes on the ground, until they came upon a pair of spread legs encased in shiny Hessian boots. Her eyes growing wider, Rebecca rolled her gaze toward Summer and whispered, "Is that him, do you think?"

Slowly, Summer looked up and up Sabre's towering, black-clad body. "Nope," she replied.

Then Rebecca looked up and her pink mouth fell open. "Ooops!" came her urgent cry. "Don't look now, but it's the Devil Lord. Should we run?"

Summer watched his eyebrow lift. "I don't think that would be wise," she said.

He sank to one knee before them, his sharp gaze taking in the chaplet of white flowers and green leaves swagged over Summer's brow. "What are you doing?" he asked softly.

"Lookin' for leprechauns. They hide under the flowers, y' know."

His dark gaze moved to Rebecca. "Have you found any?"

"Not a blasted one," the little girl replied.

"Do you intend to spend the rest of the afternoon crawling about on your knees?" he asked Summer.

"I've got nothin' better t' do." In a huff she sat down, her back to him, and crossed her arms. Rebecca did the same.

"I thought," came his words in Summer's ear, "that you might like to dance."

She spun her head around so fast that the garland slid down to her nose. He caught it with one finger and nudged it back into place. "Are y' askin' me t' dance?" she demanded.

"On one condition."

"Anythin'."

His long black lashes lowered and he regarded her mouth with a look that sent warm excitement rippling up her spine. "I'm not certain that 'anything' is the wisest choice of words right now. Not the way you're looking."

She leaned near him. "And how am I lookin'?"

"To quote a much-favored author of mine, Charlotte Brontë: 'You look blooming, and smiling, and pretty . . . truly pretty this morning. Is this my pale little elf? Is this my mustard-seed? This little sunny-faced girl with the dimpled cheek and rosy lips...'"

"That's lovely." Her eyelids felt heavy; made drowsy by the soft, deep cadence of his voice, she slid her eyes closed and dreamed that he kissed her at last.

And then his lips touched her mouth, as soft as warm air, and she gasped and opened her eyes. Color had crept into his dark cheeks, and a pulse was throbbing against his temple.

"Anythin'," she repeated breathlessly.

"We'll dance here and not with the others."

She nodded, too breathless to speak.

Offering his hand, he helped her to stand, and as the music lilted on the breeze around them, he slid his arm around her waist, cupped her hand in his, and spun her in a circle. Again and again he twirled her, until she started to laugh and couldn't stop, laughing and crying too. The children formed a circle around them, hands joined as they leaped and hopped and sang, their faces radiant with sunshine and pleasure. Then suddenly there were others, and over the hill the entire group of Cockatoos came running, the women's colorful skirts skimming the flowers, and the men hurrying them along.

And the music never stopped. Vicesimus Sellers leaped atop a hillock and trilled his tune as sweet as honey into the air as the couples dipped and swayed and spun all around Summer and Nick. Then Dora and Dan were there, and Dora laughingly called, "If you won't come to the party, Mr. Sabre, the party will come to you!"

Summer laughed as she watched her friends sail away, then she turned her eyes back to Nick. Slowly, so slowly, they ceased their movements, bodies close and hands touching. Would he turn on his heel again and storm off in a black cloud of rage?

His look was both fierce and unsettled, then his hands came up and cradled her head; his eyes burned into hers as he whispered, "Oh, my God." And he dragged her up against him, and buried his face in her hair.

Chapter 12

The children made a game of flushing wekas from the bushes. The bold, wingless birds looked very much like hen pheasants, with long brown tail feathers and a small pinion with a claw nestled amid the feathers. Although they were very entertaining creatures, they were also the scourge of farmers, digging their way into the henhouses, robbing eggs from the nests and sucking them dry, then turning on the hens and killing them. The older boys were rewarded each time they clubbed a weka.

Summer watched the scattering of squealing, laughing children chase wekas throughout the flower- and flax-covered glade as she and Nicholas strolled along the path, he with his hands in his pockets and she with her arm looped through his. She imagined that they made a handsome pair. More often than not she found some curious couple regarding them with smiles on their faces, and that pleased her. Nicholas had been accepted by the Cockatoos. She had the Johnsons and the Sharkeys to thank for that.

Smiling up at her husband, she said, "Y've made a great many new friends today. I'm very proud o' y'."

He glanced down at her with one eyebrow raised and his mouth curved in a half-smile.

"I imagine y'll be here ever' month now," she continued. "Y'll have friends droppin' by t' see y' and invitin' y' around for a meal. Y' won't be so lonely from now on."

"I don't recall that I was particularly lonely," he replied.

"No?"

Nick frowned and looked away. They walked on in silence, into the shadows of the forest where the heavy scent of humus filled the air and the laughter of the children faded to occasional high-pitched trills of excitement. At last, Summer said, "Yer a wonderful dancer."

"Thank you. It comes from years of training."

Summer laughed, a lilting sound that made the birds singing in the trees seem oddly discordant. "I'm tryin' t' imagine y' as a lad learnin' how t' dance. Didn't y' have anythin' better t' do?"

"I thought so, but to try and convince my mother that climbing trees and fishing for trout in the stream bordering our property would develop my character in a better direction would have been useless. Especially since she was carrying on a rather passionate relationship with my instructor at the time."

Summer's step hesitated as she watched Nick's profile take on the hard lines of displeasure she had grown to recognize. She understood his anger. His hurt. His regret and confusion. She had experienced them herself the years she had spent with Martha.

"I'll never forget the day I found out about their affair," he went on with a derisive smile. "It was my eleventh birthday. I had finished my lesson, and as usual, dear Mama had instructed me to wait outside in the coach while she ... discussed ... my progress with my teacher. After a while I grew bored, as boys often do when left to entertain themselves. I returned to the ballroom and found them sprawled over the settee, he with his pants down around his ankles and she with her beautiful white legs wrapped around his waist. She never knew for certain that she'd been discovered, although I'm sure she suspected when I refused to continue my lessons, not just dancing, but all the other lessons that were deemed to be so important for one of my so-called status. It was my opinion that if she would carry on an affair with my dancing instructor, she was no doubt also indulging in relationships with my music, voice, fencing, and riding instructors, not to mention my regular tutors."

Summer placed her hand sympathetically on his arm, and as his eyes met hers, she replied softly, "I'm very sorry y' were so unhappy, Nicholas."

They came to a fork in the path, and hesitated. The sound of whispering turned their heads. A man and woman stood in the distance, mostly camouflaged by trees and sprays of broad-leafed ferns. The man was kissing his wife passionately, then they sank from view behind a cluster of manuka scrub.

Summer's face turned hot, as did her body, the way it had that afternoon when she had seen Sabre's naked torso behind the wool shed. She glanced at Nicholas, who continued to stare at the bushes where the couple had disappeared. As their moans and gasps grew louder, Nick's face grew darker, his shoulders more rigid. Unnerved, Summer turned to escape the way they had come—to allow the couple their privacy—but Nick stopped her with a hard hand on her wrist, and spun her around. Poised, her body pressed against his, she stared up into his intense face while the couple's frantic sighs and moans and whimpers made the touch of his skin against hers catch fire.

He took her face in his shaking hands. "Do you know what sort of havoc you've played with my life, Irish?" he asked in a tight voice. Then he lowered his head over Summer's, his breath warm on her mouth. She melted toward him as he slid one arm around her waist and drew her up against his body. All the strength had left her legs. She didn't reply. She couldn't.

"Do you know what it cost me to come here?" He slid his hand around the back of her head. "Every vestige of pride that I owned, little as it was."

"Then why did y' do it?" she asked breathlessly.

"To see you smile again the way you smiled at me the morning you showed up on my doorstep."

Her eyelids drifted closed; she felt too mesmerized to keep them open. If only he would kiss her . . .

Yet he didn't, and when she glanced at him again he looked angry, almost tortured. Easing up on her tiptoes, she brushed her lips against his, as he had kissed her an hour ago. She felt his body tense. The air became hot and too thick to breathe. And then he was dragging her up against him in a powerful, punishing hold and lowering his head over hers.

"Damn you," he said roughly. "Damn you to hell for this."

He crushed his mouth onto hers and plunged his tongue into her. It was shocking. Primitive. Blatantly sensual. The trust and withdrawal, and the slick, hot wetness of his tongue darting against her own sent all thought scattering.

Nick groaned as reality faded to a hot pinpoint of pulsating desire that streaked like lightning through him. He felt her hands twisted into his coat as she clung to him, whether in fear or passion he couldn't tell. He didn't care. In that moment he wanted nothing more than to punish Summer for turning his staid existence upside down. He wanted to hurt her for making him feel alive again, experiencing all the hope and dreams and pain that went with it. Damn her for filling him with the absurd notion that there could possibly be a future for him . . . and her. But most of all, damn her for arousing his body. For obliterating his control over it, a control he'd struggled to maintain for six long years. Now he felt it melting away like ice under a hot sun as this girl— this stranger, his *wife*—kissed him back with an innocence that was as enrapturing as the feel of her small body trembling against his.

He kissed her harder, and harder still until she whimpered and her hands fluttered helplessly in an attempt to push him away. The gasps and groans from the hidden lovers spurred him on, until he felt consumed by pain and fire, and he could no longer contain the overwhelming need to crush her to him, to run his hands over her breasts and to tear at the delicate material covering them.

"Nicholas!" he heard her cry softly. Through a fog he looked down into eyes that were round and frightened and confused. *You're hurting her*, the voice in his head taunted. *You're losing control, old man. You're frightening her.*

"This is what you wanted, isn't it?" he demanded harshly. Shaking her so sharply that her head snapped back, he said through his teeth, "If you're going to seduce a man, sweetheart, you'd better be grown-up enough to deal with the consequences."

Her face drained of color.

With one hand still buried in her hair, he dragged the décolletage of her gown down with the other, exposing one flushed and perfect breast. Futilely she tried to cover herself; he knocked her hand away.

"You're my wife, *Mrs.* Sabre. I have every right—"

"Please." She spoke steadily, though her body trembled as she righted her clothing. "Don't be this way, Nicholas. I—"

"You want flowers and promises of undying devotion. Yes, my love, I know what you want. What I don't know is why you would expect to get those things when you sold your body and soul to a complete stranger—some man who was only interested in attaining a house servant who could cook and clean and satisfy him sexually. Maybe you need the reassurance of my devotion to alleviate your guilt over prostituting yourself for a home and a man's last name."

For an instant she looked stunned. Then the hurt on her features was replaced by unbridled fury, and she slapped his face.

For a long moment Nicholas said nothing, just stared down into her wide hurt eyes while his cheek throbbed.

Little by little sounds from the glade intruded. The children's screams brought Sabre's head up slowly, as if he were struggling to ignore the sudden intrusion. Again came the children's cries, more frantic this time. Followed by a gunshot.

It slammed Nick and Summer back to reality.

Nick caught her hand. They ran through the forest shadows and burst into the sunlight just as a hooded horseman wielding a club came galloping down on a group of screaming, running children. At a glance there appeared to be a half dozen Clansmen on horseback, some driving their frothing mounts wildly through the scrambling Cockatoos, kicking over the tables and strewing food and pottery over the ground. Others bore their animals down on several screaming women who struggled to protect their children. Across the glade Arnold Sharkey ran for his wagon. Dan Johnson and Jeff Mead yelled to their wives to dive under their wagons, then ran as fast as they could toward their own children huddled together near the forest's edge.

Nick grabbed up a broken tree branch, and shoved Summer toward the forest. "What are y' doin'?" she cried.

"Hide, and don't come out until I tell you," he commanded, then he tore off across the clearing toward a rider who was threatening a dozen crying children.

Nick planted himself between the horseman and children, his legs braced as he gripped the sturdy branch with both hands and waited for the pounding, foaming animal to near him, its masked rider howling a bloodcurdling cry. Nick held firm until the horse was within a yard of running him into the ground. Then, with a fast sidestep, he swung his cudgel in a high arc, slamming into the rider's chest with enough impact to send him spiraling end over end off the back of his horse.

As the man hit the ground, Nick snatched off his hood. The face of Roel Ormsbee, also known as "Squealer" for his extreme fondness for hunting pigs, glared up at him with unbridled fury, just before Nick drove his fist into his mouth with such force that the man's teeth gave way.

He heard Summer's cry of warning a moment too late. Something hit him in the back with an impact that drove the wind from him and made all sight and sound momentarily fade to nothingness. He sprawled over the ground with a groan as a pain like splintered lightning streaked up his spine and down his legs. Gritting his teeth, he crawled to his knees and looked up as the man who had attacked him from behind heaved back on the horse's reins and spun the animal toward him again. The blade of a knife flashed.

Nick grabbed for the fallen tree branch as the Clansman dug his heels into the animal's flanks. The beast surged toward him, hooves shaking the ground while the rider leaned out of his saddle, knife glinting, bearing down on Nick.

In the distance, Arnold Sharkey raised his rifle. The air cracked with an explosion. The man tumbled off the animal in a heap of limp limbs and black clothing. He hit the ground and didn't move, while behind Nick, Roel Ormsbee managed to claw his way onto his horse and tear out across the hills, the others following at the realization that the Cockatoos had every intention of fighting back.

Then Nick heard Summer scream.

Virgil McIlhenny ripped the hood from his head and tossed it to the ground as he spurred his horse toward Summer. She fled into the woods, but the trees and bushes didn't stop him. Hunkered low in his saddle so that the limbs swooshed over his head, he reached for Summer's hair and yanked her from her feet. The horse whinnied and reared, and rolled onto its side. The impact sent Virgil tumbling and Summer flying into a thatch of broom. Stunned, Virgil looked up just as Nicholas came at him with a roar, closed his hands around his throat, and proceeded to drive his fist into Virgil's face with the ferocity of a madman.

"Help!" Virgil yelped. He did his best to duck and cover his head with his arms—to no avail. Again and again Nicholas pummeled his face, until the bones of Virgil's nose collapsed and blood poured down his throat, making him retch and choke for air.

Summer scrambled from the broom. As Nick drew back his arm to hit Virgil again, she threw herself against him. "Yer killin' him!" she cried. "Nicholas! Nicholas, please stop!"

Dan and Jeff Mead ran up. Jeff grabbed Nick's arms and dragged him away, while Dan did his best to pull Summer aside. As Virgil stumbled to his feet and ran for his horse, Dan helped Jeff restrain Nick.

"Let the bastard go, Mr. Sabre!" Jeff shouted.

His teeth clenched and his hair a black spray over his forehead, Nick tried to wrench free. "He would have killed my wife—"

Wedging herself between Jeff and Nicholas, Summer attempted to quiet her husband. "He didn't hurt me, Nicholas. I'm fine. Please . . . I'm fine."

Gradually, the fierce, uncontrollable anger drained from him, and Nicholas was able to focus on Summer's features, her eyes wide with shock, her face white.

"I'm fine," she assured him, then she threw herself into his arms. He gripped her tightly, his face buried in her hair as she cried, "I thought he was goin' t' kill y' with that horrible knife!"

He smoothed back her hair and tilted her face up to his. There were tears streaming from her eyes, and enough heartstopping emotion in them to make his chest squeeze. A realization staggered him: after six long years of keeping a tight leash on his anger, he had lost it—totally, undeniably—the moment he saw the bastard lift his hand to Summer.

Arnold Sharkey sat on the rear of his wagon. He refused to look at the body stretched out on the ground before him. "I've never killed a man before," he said in an anguished voice. "I feel sick about it."

The crowd glanced nervously at the corpse.

"Who is he?" someone asked.

"Haven't ever seen him before," a voice replied.

"Me either," echoed the others.

Dora Johnson stood with her back to the crowd and hugged herself as she gazed out over the flower-blanketed fields. "It's not fair what they're doing. We have little enough as it is. Now they would rob us of our few hours of pleasure. We won't ever feel safe here again."

Nick leaned against the dray, his hands in his pockets as he regarded the dead man's heavily bearded face. Summer wandered some distance away, occasionally glancing back at him.

Nan Sharkey took a place next to her husband on the wagon. "So what do we do now?" she asked, even as her eyes strayed to her nine children huddled in the nearby shade.

"We take matters into our own hands!" Jeff Mead shouted. His reddish-blond hair spilled over his brow. "We start fighting back. Let this dead bastard be an example of what they'll face each time they try to run us off our land."

"Agreed!" Dick Thorndike declared. He shook a big fist in the air, his face red beneath a scattering of freckles. "If it's a war they want, by God, a war we'll give 'em!"

"Here, here!"

"And how do you propose we do that?" Nick asked in a deep, calm voice, bringing the men and women's angry, perplexed faces back to him. "We live miles apart. We have no way of knowing where they'll strike next. While you men are out riding around in packs and looking for trouble, who will stay home and safeguard the women and children?"

"We all know Roy Tennyson and Sean O'Connell are behind the attacks," Thorndike argued. "We start there."

"Perhaps." Nick's gaze drifted to Summer, sitting in the shade with the children, Rebecca Sharkey on one knee, Wayne Johnson perched on the other. The remembered image of her being run down by Mcllhenny made shivers run up his spine like razors. He felt sickened by it . . . sickened even more by the thought of losing her. How very ironic, considering he had been about to put her on a ship and send her away. "But even if you stop O'Connell, there will be someone else to take his place."

"Why won't the government help us?" Fanny Mead, Jeff's wife, was a frail, pale-skinned woman whose features had been lined early in life from hardship. She covered her face with her hands and wept while her husband wrapped a comforting arm around her heaving shoulders.

Nick moved to the corpse. "I know why none of you recognizes him," he said. "He's a convict from Australia."

Vicesimus Sellers moved up beside him. "How can you tell?"

"The number tattooed on his inner wrist."

The group congregated in a circle around the dead man. Nan elbowed her way through the crowd, and with her baby clutched to her chest, said to Nick, "Roy Tennyson is hiring murderers to do his dirty work now. That's what you're saying, isn't it, Mr. Sabre?"

"Let's not rush to any conclusions," her husband told her.

Stooping beside the body, Nick lifted the weapon the man had been prepared to use on him before Arnold's bullet had burrowed into his back. "I really don't think you'd be jumping to conclusions in this case. This man is—was—a hired killer."

"So what you're implying," Nan said, "is that Roy Tennyson is no longer content with scaring us. We are now dealing with a very dangerous group of individuals who will do anything, even kill, to run us off our land."

"Yes," Nick replied.

By the time Summer and Nick arrived home, the sun was teetering on the horizon. Frank had left a note on the kitchen table; he'd gone fishing. Sabre changed back into his work clothes, and without a word to Summer, returned to his baling machine.

Alone, Summer slipped out of her dress and hung it in the wardrobe, but not before sitting on the bed in her chemise and drawers for half an hour admiring the gown. She'd believed that the lovely, lavish creation would somehow make all her dreams come true. And for a time it had looked as if fairy tales *could* come true.

She wandered into the parlor and back to the kitchen, where she stood in the open doorway and stared down the path toward the wool shed, knowing that behind it Sabre was laboring with his shirt off, sweating, swearing. She didn't have to be there to know what effect the sight of him would have on her. She felt it now, as she had that morning and again in the forest. Shamefully unsettled. Disturbingly restless. A stranger to her own body. There were things going on inside her that left her feeling on edge and at a loss, but with the vague idea that Nick could somehow help. Shaking her head and frowning, she sensed that she had come very close to breaking through to him that afternoon in the woods—before his mood had turned ugly. Had she been more experienced, she would have known how to deal with his aggressiveness. Slapping his face in a moment of pique hadn't been the wisest action to take. Then the Clan . . . the ordeal had driven him back into his shell. His mood on the ride home had been the darkest she'd ever seen it.

A sound sent Summer running to the front window. Ben Beaconsfield climbed down from his wagon and mounted the porch steps. He carried an envelope in his hand. Hurrying to the door, Summer opened it a little, hiding her partially clad body behind it.

Ben smiled, but his expression was weary. "Is Nick around?"

"He's down balin'."

Ben looked away. "I heard about the Clan attack during the picnic. I'm sorry." He handed her the letter, his features worried. "This is probably not the best time to bring this to Nick, but the postmaster asked me to drop it off. Getting this letter won't please Nick. He'll be in one of his moods again."

"He's in one of his moods all the time," she countered, and Ben chuckled in agreement. "I can handle him," she said. "And Frank will be home soon. Besides . . . I'm his wife, at least for the moment. It's a wife's place t' stand by her husband through thick and thin."

Ben regarded her a long moment, a smile of understanding curving his mouth.

Summer studied the letter, recognizing Nick's own handwriting scrawled over the well-handled, crimped-cornered envelope. Across the address was stamped a single word: REFUSED.

Lowering his voice to a whisper, Ben explained. "It's a letter Nick sent to his father. God only knows how many Nick's mailed, but they're always returned, unopened. When do you expect Frank back?"

She shook her head. "He went fishin'."

Ben appeared thoughtful. "He usually sinks his line at Lake Ida. It's on my way home. I'll drop by; if he's there I'll send him home."

Ben left the house. In minutes the clatter of his wagon dwindled to silence.

Saints, what a day. Since that morning Summer had experienced every emotion available to a human being, from her true happiness over receiving a gift from Sabre, to absolute horror during the Clan's attack. Hope had filled her with a sublime madness when she'd believed that she'd won Sabre's affections—and perhaps a chance to remain in New Zealand as his wife . . . only to have her heart shattered when he'd turned from a passionate lover to a cold stranger who had thrust her from his arms and walked away with little concern and less affection. He was going to send her away and she felt . . .

Desperate.

The sun had dropped behind the horizon when Summer left the house. The cool air nipped at her exposed skin as she moved down the path, but she hardly noticed. Her heart was racing too fast. Her mind was telling her over and over that she was a fool for doing this. She really should have more pride, after all . . .

Nick was in the process of loading the last bale onto the dray as Summer came around the wool shed and stopped. The white chemise and drawers she wore shimmered in the twilight, and her hair spilled in a fiery cloud around her face.

"I've somethin' for y'," she said.

Nick raised one eyebrow.

She moved toward him very slowly and stopped mere inches from him—so close that he caught the scent of violet water on her skin. Her hair looked slightly damp, as did her skin. Obviously, she'd just climbed out of a bath.

Summer handed the letter to him. "Ben just dropped it off. It's from yer father."

He stared down at his own handwriting.

"Ben tells me that y' keep writin' him. Why?"

His gaze went back to hers. The anger he'd tried to work out of his system all during the ride home was suddenly there again, drumming at his skull. "That's none of your business," he snapped.

"Why don't y' just admit that y' want his forgiveness, Nicholas?"

He crushed the letter in his hand.

"What is it about y' that won't admit that y' need people?"

He turned away.

She reached for him, but as her hand closed around his arm, he knocked it away and faced her again. "Get the hell out of my life," he said. "Just because I was drunk enough to sign that idiotic marriage contract doesn't mean I gave you the right to meddle in my business or my mind." His eyes raked her and he added, "And get the hell in the house and put some clothes on."

She raised her chin and smiled. "Are y' bothered by my appearance, Nicholas?"

He shoved his way past her and grabbed the lever on the hoist, pumped it several times as hard as he could and tried to ignore his anger over his father's dismissal, as well at the effect her scanty attire was having on him. The memory of her body pressed against his that afternoon in the woods didn't help.

"Well?" she prompted angrily behind him. "Most men would find their wife appealin' dressed this way."

"I'm not most men."

"But y' are a man . . . aren't y'?"

He slowly turned his head and stared at her. Her eyes reflected the rising moon. Her small hands were fisted at her sides. "Yes," he replied in a dangerously soft voice.

Pulling her slender shoulders back, she lifted her

chin and said, "Oh? I haven't seen any proof o' that."

She knew in a moment that she'd made a grave mistake. Nick's face went black, his body hard.

Summer spun and fled. "Summer!" he roared.

His weight hit her with full force and drove her to the ground, where she skidded over green grass and stones and close-cropped tussock. Her cheek jarred against the earth, and pain shot through her head. The impact knocked the breath from her, and she struggled to gasp it back as his hands closed in her hair and dragged her onto her back. His body filled up the sky above her, and his eyes were like fire as his hands brutally closed over her shoulders and his weight pressed her into the dirt.

"You want me to prove to you that I'm a man?" he shouted hoarsely.

"I—I just want t' be yer wife, Nicholas—"

"I don't want a wife!"

Tears came then, spilling down her cheeks. She tried to touch his face with her hand, but he batted it away. His eyes mocked her. They raked the abraded flesh of her breasts that were exposed through the tatters of her ruined chemise. His breath became ragged.

With a trembling hand, he twisted his fingers into the material and fumbled with the ribbons. Then with frustration and anger he ripped apart the cloth until she lay completely exposed to him. His eyes drank in the beauty of her—in his wildest imagination he'd never thought she could be so perfect. He closed one hand over a soft white breast and felt her tremble. In an instant the realization tumbled in on him that . . . perhaps she was right. Possibly he was no longer a man after all, and he couldn't make love to her. Maybe he no longer knew how.

Summer turned her face away, burying her cheek

into the cool grass. The smell of dirt filled her nostrils. She closed her eyes, trying to make sense of what was happening. It was odd, but she couldn't think. His hands were doing strange and wonderful things to her body, touching her breasts and forcing open her legs so that his fingers could invade her intimate self through the slit of her drawers. There wasn't pain. His exploration was not brutal; it was urgent. Hungry. She could hear his breathing, a ragged sound in the twilight stillness. Then he bent his head and took her nipple into his mouth while his fingers made thrusting motions in and out of her, and his hips mimicked the action against her thighs.

Her scent was an aphrodisiac that swept rational thought from his mind. He groaned deep inside his chest. His hands ran over her. His lips tasted her. It had been so long since he'd last held a woman. Lust was an unleashed, roaring demon inside him, brutal and savage. The sight of her white body bathed in pale moonlight amid the tall, cool grass made his body burn with a fierce and frightening fever. He couldn't control it. In that moment he didn't want to. He would absorb her, feed his starving mind and body with the arousing womanly taste and smell of her, quench the hunger of denied desire that had been tearing at him since the moment he'd first set eyes on her.

She thrashed beneath him. His hands pinned her down. He took her breast into his mouth. Dipped his tongue into her navel. Pressed his face into the downy moist curls at the slit of her drawers and inhaled the musky scent of her. Touched the center of her womanhood with his lips and tongue, and savored the flavor of her.

She gasped and cried aloud in shock, flailed with her arms and legs, her words unintelligible to his riotous mind. Deeper and deeper he probed, drinking in the wonder of her with every straining, pounding nerve, until his body trembled, dangerously close to exploding. Reason scattered like so many leaves before a gale-force wind, impossible to contain. He craved that long-forgotten momentary death—ached to feel the sublime touch of brief madness that came with his body's plunge into that pulsating ecstasy.

He rose up over her, and his knees pressed her legs wide. The world shimmered with black shadows and creamy moonbeams. Her eyes—oh, those eyes—were wide and round, and her soft mouth was parted as she watched his face. She spoke to him, but the words faded, incomprehensible whispers dashed upon the dark land and sky. He might be able to catch them if he tried. But he wasn't interested in words; had no time for empty phrases and melancholy murmurings. Lowering his head, he pressed his mouth over hers and slid his tongue into her, cupping her face with fingers that smelled of her—that were damp with her. Then he slid his hand down her trembling body and one by one flipped open the buttons on his breeches, gasping with the delicious freedom, the erotic anticipation of burying the straining length of himself inside her.

Her arms came up and wrapped around him. "Please," came the faint word through his thrumming consciousness.

He drove himself into the hot heart of her. She lay still beneath him, shaking, her eyes leaking tears, her small hands gripping him to her with a heartbreaking longing.

Closing his eyes, he sank against her, buried his face in the dark silk hair spread over the ground. Her heart pounded fiercely against his, yet she didn't move and she didn't speak. Only the soft and warm breaths she panted against his shoulder hinted that she was even alive.

"Summer," he whispered near her ear. He wanted her with a desperation that was all-consuming. He withdrew slightly, then slowly, more gently, thrust into her again, and again, until he felt the tension drain from her body.

At last he succumbed. Fell. It was anguish, this defeat: a bitter, sobering vanquishment.

Closing his eyes, he began to move inside her with a frantic loss of control, his hot wet body pressing her into the ground. He moaned. He gasped. He groaned. He muttered over and over, "Oh, God. Oh, my God. Summer. Summer. Summer. It's been so long..."

Holding him as tightly as she could, she whispered, "I love y'."

He groaned. "I don't love you. I—can't—love—you. *Please* don't make me love you."

Burying his hands in her hair, he covered her mouth with a deep and searching kiss even as his body pounded inside her. When he broke away again, his face twisted in anguish. "I don't..." he began, then his body froze, and as his blood surged like fire to his limbs, his head fell back. He cried out his passion, his completion, his despair in a long, haunting, hurting howl to the rising moon.

Chapter 13

His head rested on her shoulder. His fingers lay twisted but relaxed in her hair. Summer stared up at the round white moon, feeling each rise and fall of Nicholas's chest against hers and the less-ening pressure of his body inside her. She burned between her legs, but something other than pain left her uncomfortably aware of how deeply he'd penetrated her. Closing her arms around him, she refused to let him go as he shifted his weight to one side and eased his body to the ground.

He watched her intently for a long moment, his fingertips lightly brushing her cheek. Sweat trickled down his temple and dropped onto her shoulder. "I love y'," she confessed again, breathless with fear and anticipation. She had never felt so reckless, so desperate. "I love y' with all my heart, Mr. Sabre, Esquire, and I promise I'll do ever'thing humanly possible t' make y' happy."

His dark eyes narrowed. A myriad of emotions moved over his features as he lay against her, barely breathing, his long fingers not quite touching her now—hesitant, like one holding his hand toward a flame. Her admission had stunned him, she could tell. Truthfully, it had shocked her as well. It was odd, what intimacy could evoke. God help her, but if he was to admit that he loved her too, she would probably get up and skip and dance and laugh uproariously.

Slowly, his hands came up and gripped her wrists, forcing her arms from around him. Sitting up with his back to her, he adjusted his breeches, then remained where he was, one long leg drawn up, the other curled beneath him. Staring out over the paddocks, he ran one trembling hand over his face.

Summer tentatively placed her hand on his shoulder. She felt desperate to look him in the eye, to know his thoughts. Yet he knocked her hand away.

"Don't touch me," he told her.

"It's all right," she said. "I understand—"

His head came around, framed by his glorious moon-kissed hair. "No, you don't. You couldn't possibly. Don't even pretend that you do. Don't say that you forgive me or love me, because the idea is preposterous and I wouldn't believe you." He slapped at a weed. He staggered to his feet, appearing dazed, then turned on her again. "This doesn't change anything, you know. This momentary madness was simply lust. Nothing more. Certainly not..." His mouth tightened. His fists clenched. He finished in a low and hostile voice, "...love. Grow up, girl, and learn the difference. I did the very thing I'd been struggling not to do since you showed up on my doorstep. I lost control, Summer. I allowed my disgusting temper and lack of restraint to get the better of me—"

"But I wanted y' t' make love to me."

"I didn't make love to you," he stressed angrily. "I practically raped you."

The words came like a blow. Staring through the dark at Sabre's tortured face, Summer blinked tears from her eyes and said nothing as he turned on his heel and vanished into the shadows.

She lay there, her knees curled into her stomach as she wept. *Damn, stubborn, prideful aristocrat!* Why was he so *afraid* of loving her back?

At last, she managed to gather her strength enough to return to the house. Nicholas wasn't there. No doubt he was off brooding in his wool shed or walking the paddocks with his dog, trying to convince himself that what had taken place between them was the result of lust, or a fit of temper. Saints, if he could only have seen his own face as he entered her. Yes, she'd felt his anger, but there had been need too, a need to be held and kissed and stroked. Why couldn't he admit it?

She removed her clothing and kicked it aside. It was tattered beyond repair, and the drawers were bloodstained. Seeing the crimson smears brought hot color to her cheeks and fresh tears to her eyes. What now? The single burning question remained: Now that their marriage had been consummated, would he allow her to stay?

The water in which she had bathed earlier had grown tepid. As gently as possible she sponged her scraped elbows and breasts, and washed away all traces of her husband between her legs. Then she donned her nightgown, lay down across the bed, and wept in earnest. She wasn't aware that Frank had entered the house until he asked softly:

"Summer? Darlin', what'n tarnation has happened here?"

She wiped her nose on her sleeve. Frank stood with a fishing pole in one hand, a string of trout in the other. Both slid from his hands as his gaze shifted from her scratched and bruised face, down to her torn and stained garments on the floor. "Fer the love of . . ." He went to her and gently took hold of her shoulders. "Lord help me, sweetheart. That boy didn't . . . Here now, darlin', let's git that purty little face cleaned up."

Only then did Summer realize that the lacerations on her cheek had continued to bleed, the skin grown sore and puffy. Having grabbed up the damp cloth Summer had used earlier, Frank tenderly pressed it to her face.

"I can do it," she said, trying to smile.

"Well now, I know ya can, but shoot; old men like me don't git to act the gallant often. Just humor me, if'n ya don't mind."

When the last traces of blood and tears had been cleansed from Summer's face, Frank stepped back and regarded her gravely. Without speaking, he left the room.

Nick sat on a stool in the shearing shed. His head pounded. Memories roared up from the past with a force that left him shaking and sick to his stomach with disgust and confusion. He'd been duped once by an innocent smile—had killed a man because he'd refused to accept the possibility that the only woman he'd ever loved and trusted had turned out to be a lying, cheating whore . . . just like every other woman he'd known, including his mother.

Then came Summer . . .

He looked up to find Betsy sitting in the corner, panting softly, her soulful brown eyes watchful. He held out his hand to her, and she growled, tucked her tail between her legs, and slid out the sheep shoot into the dark.

Frank exploded through the door. Nick focused

briefly on his face, thinking that his shepherd looked as if he'd aged twenty years in the last few hours. Then Frank's old man's hands were curling into Nick's shirtfront and wrenching him to his feet.

"Ya son of a bitch," Frank said, just before he drove his fist into Nick's face with the force of a battering ram.

Nick half-spun and stumbled against the shearing-pen fence, his weight snapping the lumber like matchsticks. He hit the dirt floor on his back and lay in the dark, staring at the ceiling through blurring eyes as Frank moved up beside him. In his hand he held a leather strap, one end secured around his fist.

"Seems to me," Frank began in a shaky voice, "that it's past time somebody taught ya some manners, and I'm jest the *hombre* to do it."

The strap came down with a whoosh across Nick's chest. Again across his stomach and shoulders. Pain flared up like fire inside him, his body writhing and twisting with the awful agony, yet he did nothing to cover himself. Just closed his eyes and buried his face in the dirt.

"The last man I got my hands on who'd raped a woman got himself castrated by my Bowie knife," came Frank's voice.

"Stop!"

Blinking dirt from his eyes, Nick looked up just as Summer threw herself across him, shielding his body from Frank's blows. Her face looked white, her hair a wild halo. "Stop," she commanded again. "Don't y' dare lift that blazin' strop against him again, Frank. He didn't rape me—"

"Then whar did ya git that bruise on yore face?"

"I struck a rock when I fell."

"And the blood?"

"I . . . was a virgin."

"All the more reason why I should strop him. No man worth a pile of sheep manure would run his bride down and mount her whar she fell."

"He was upset and angry." Her eyes met Nick's. He stared at her incredulously. "It was partly my fault. I was feelin' desperate because he was goin' t' send me back. I came down to the shed with the intention o' seducin' him. I understand why he reacted like he did," she told Frank softly. "I'm sure that if he had the chance t' do it over again, he'd act differently."

For the love of God, Nick thought. Just like that, she was forgiving him.

Pushing her aside, he rolled to his knees and climbed unsteadily to his feet. He glared down at her, astonished by the emotions squeezing off his breath. They terrified him. They ripped a hole in the barrier of his distrust and disarmed his fury. He saw himself once again upon that fog-shrouded dueling field, manipulated into committing murder by a woman whose only motive for pretending to love him was to win back the affections of another man. So what was Summer's motive?

Why did this little red-haired Irish girl who was his wife sit there and stare at him with hurt eyes swimming with hope? Couldn't she understand that he could never again allow himself to promise, to trust, to . . . God forbid that he should actually fall in love . . .

He turned for the door and came face to face with Frank. The look on the old man's features stopped him cold. There were tears in Frank's eyes. Anger and pain. Distress and confusion. As any *decent* father's might who had been forced to whip his belligerent, foolish son for some transgression, though it had broken his heart to do it.

Stiffening his spine, Nick stepped around Frank and walked out the door.

Summer left her bed at just after midnight. She couldn't sleep. There was no point in lying there in the dark, allowing her mind the freedom to imagine, and remember, at will. The images were too sharp. Too painful. Too . . . arousing. She felt exhausted by it all, and unsettled.

The front door stood open. A brisk, cold wind whipped over the floor, nipping her bare toes as she moved to the doorway and stared down at her husband's back. Nicholas sat on the top porch step, elbows on his knees. "Nicholas?" she asked, bringing his head up briefly. "Aren't y' comin' t' bed?"

The question rang in the silence, surprising even her.

When he didn't reply, she stepped onto the porch, pausing momentarily as the cold wrapped around her, making her shiver. Then she moved to the steps and eased down beside him.

"Y'll catch yer death o' cold out here " she told him.

The wind fluttered his hair as he turned to regard her in what felt like an eternal silence. "So will you," he said at last, and this time she saw his dark eyes lower to her breasts, covered in soft folds of thin cotton. Her heart responded with a thud. Her blood warmed, stirred. The sudden image of him burying his face between her legs made her dizzy with desire and discomfiture.

Taking a deep breath, she slid her clasped hands between her knees to warm them. "I thought y' might like t' talk."

"You think too much, Irish. Furthermore, you imagine that everyone else cares to know what you think. Me in particular." He looked away.

"What about Frank?"

"What about him?"

"I hope y' won't dismiss him. He misunderstood the situation, is all."

He glanced at her sideways, one eyebrow lifted in a show of mild contempt. "Did he?" he asked in an amused tone.

A star streaked briefly across the black sky. Summer watched the brilliant arc and pulsating white glow before it sputtered into oblivion. Her heart ached. She wanted to slink back to bed and pull the covers over her head. The spark of hope she'd harbored in her breast the last hours felt as ethereal as that flash of night fire that had come and gone so swiftly upon the horizon.

She rubbed her arms and started to stand. His hand came out to stop her.

"Sit down," he ordered.

"I was given the impression y' weren't in the mood for conversation."

"I'm not, but you're right. We need to talk. Go on." He motioned toward the step. "Sit down."

She did so slowly, cautiously, caught off balance by his sudden matter-of-fact tone, suspecting that she would regret having confronted him. He swiveled slightly and leaned back against the balustrade, regarded her from behind his heavy black lashes, his mouth curled in a half-smile. "I admit that I behaved badly tonight. I lost control of my frustration, anger, and long-denied sexual needs.

"But I refuse to take all the blame where you are concerned. You thrust yourself upon me when I had, at last, accepted my monkish state. After a lifetime of intense confusion and anger, I had managed to create for myself an existence that held some moments of contentment and peace. You, my dear little red-haired Irish wife, blew it all to hell with your wide violet eyes and childishly pouting lips and naive beliefs in leprechauns and fairies. No matter how hard I tried to ignore you, you were there, twenty-four hours a day, to remind me that every dream, hope, fantasy that I had convinced myself would never come true was suddenly possible.

"You just wouldn't give up, Summer. You won over my shepherd, Ben and Clara, and every Cockatoo in Malvern Hills. I couldn't look up from shearing sheep without seeing you standing there; I couldn't walk into my own house without breathing in air that smelled of you. Christ, I couldn't even eat because I imagined that everything you'd touch with your hands tasted of you. You'd invaded my home, my mind, my senses—you'd turned my body that hadn't experienced desire in five years into a cock-hard rutting beast."

He stared at her intensely, then his hand came up and his fingers lightly touched the bruise on her cheek. "I realize that's no excuse for how rough I was with you. I admit my recklessness. I apologize for frightening and hurting you. I don't know how I feel about you. Lust and anger and other feelings have become too confused inside me. I'm not certain I would recognize love right now if it hit me between the eyes."

Playing with a stray red curl that wound around the tip of his finger as he stroked Summer's hair, he said in a voice that sounded achingly sad, "I'm very flattered that you feel a great fondness for me. Few people have. I'm just not certain I'm capable of loving anyone, Irish. I *am* sure that if you'll only stop to examine your feelings, you'll discover that the emotion you call love for me is merely fondness. At the least infatuation."

He swallowed and took a deep breath. In that

instant he didn't even remotely resemble the menacing Devil Lord. He looked like a tousled-haired youth whose eyes were swimming with all the confusion he was feeling but couldn't voice.

"So what are y' sayin'? That y' don't intend t' come to bed with me? Ever?"

"I'm surprised you'd want me after that fiasco in the paddock."

"Sleepin' together doesn't always mean y' have t' partake in the unpleasant act, does it?"

The question brought a thinning to his mouth. Pulling one leg up, he slung an arm over his knee and continued to regard her with an intensity that made her stomach flutter. "Then I wasn't wrong," he muttered sourly. "You find the act unpleasant."

Her expression was faintly cynical. "Don't you?" Shrugging at his silence, she turned her face away, afraid the moonlight could somehow reveal the stain of embarrassment and discomfort coloring her cheeks. "Y' must," she responded for him. "Y' didn't appear t' like it at all. Yer face looked quite pained, then y' cried out. It must have been as excruciatin' for y' as it was for me. I truly can't imagine what this obsession for the sex act is all about."

"Good God, you *are* innocent." Nicholas rose with his hands in his pockets and stood with his back braced against the wind. Hair whipped about his shoulders, throat, and face. Standing spread-legged in the moonlight, as if balancing on the pitching deck of a ship, he resembled a barbarian. A pirate. All he needed to complete the breathtaking image was a ring on his ear.

"Why do y' consider yerself so unlovable?" she asked. "Is it because y' can find so little to like in yerself?"

There was no reply.

Slowly, Summer stood up, hugging herself

against the cold, and turned toward the house. Pausing, she looked back. "Are y' comin' t' bed or do y' intend t' stand out here the remainder of the night and catch yer death? Y' needn't worry, y' know. I have no intention of takin' advantage of y'."

He laughed abruptly and she thought, though she couldn't be certain, that she saw his shoulders relax. "Promise?" he asked.

Lightly descending the porch steps, she took hold of his arm, giving it a playful tug. As always he stared down at her, unsmiling, his eyes black and piercing. "Come on. I dare y', yer lordship. There's no reason t' be afraid o' me."

"I'm not afraid of you," he replied, so softly that the wind dashed it aside, the sound lost almost instantly.

She could not think what to say. It was just as well, because her voice had started to quiver at her childish challenge with an odd and nervous anticipation. The heat of his body warmed her through her fingertips, sending heated shivers all the way to her numb toes. Her heart made a queer little dance under her ribs. Then he tugged his arm away and stepped back, still not quite strong enough to hurdle the crumbling wall he'd erected between them.

Nicholas looked out over the black hills that merged with the star-studded indigo sky. How foolish he felt. And rotten. And bemused. His conscience pressed in on him like a weight.

He heard a noise and looked around. Summer had vanished into the house . . . and into his bed, no doubt. Christ, he was tired. And sore. His head was splitting. How long had it been since he'd slept peacefully? The very idea of laying his head on that goose-down pillow made him frown. But it would mean sleeping with her. His little red-haired wife who believed in fairies and leprechauns. Who, regardless of his despicable behavior, was willing to forgive him his trespasses.

"Yore up late," came Frank's voice through the dark.

The old man stood at the corner of the house. Betsy sat at his feet, ears flat against her head. *Traitor*, Nick thought.

Frank, wearing a coat lined with thick lamb's wool, puffed on his pipe and the ashes glowed orange in the darkness. He sauntered toward Nick in his typical unhurried fashion, and Betsy followed at his heels. "I was jest wonderin' about what's to happen tomorrow," Frank said.

"We go to Christchurch."

"And?" Stopping a yard shy of Nick, Frank regarded him from beneath his broad-brimmed hat. He looked old and tired.

"And we auction our wool."

"And?"

Nick shook his head, confused. "Make your point if you have one."

"Will I be lookin' fer a new employer?"

"No." He turned and mounted the steps.

"I reckon if ya ain't mad enough to fire me after what I done, I guess ya won't mind my sayin' this."

For a long moment Nick stared into the dark without answering. "Don't push your luck, old man," he replied at last. "I may have forgiven you for the lashing you gave me because I'm not above admitting that I needed it, but I don't wish to be verbally whipped for it."

Frank removed the pipe from his mouth. "I jest wanted to say that ya could do worse than have a wife who's as loyal as that little filly. I hope ya intend to keep her."

"And if I don't?"

"Then I reckon there's no hope for ya at all, son. I reckon I'm old and pert-near senile, but I still got brains enough to thank back on my misspent youth and all the mistakes I made. I hurt people along the way. Took advantage of many. There was a woman once who I took as a wife. Pretty as a peach, she was, and dainty as a flower. Cupid done drove his arrow straight as a dad-blamed Comanche's arrow through my heart the first minute I seen her.

"We lived together as husband and wife fer a while, then I got restless. Started dwellin' too much on the trails I hadn't rid yet and all the women I hadn't wooed. I left her. Didn't even say good-bye. Jest woke up one mornin' and told her I was ridin' to Fort Worth to do business. I did. Thang is, I didn't ride home agin."

Nick looked down in the old man's face. It was white and hollow-eyed. Haunted.

"Back then I had a cravin' fer liquor, and I guess it made me a little crazy—too crazy to thank what I was doin'. I woke up out of my stupor three years later and realized what I'd done. I rode home and learned she'd been killed by a band of renegade Injuns. She'd given birth to my son eight months after I'd left her. He was killed too."

"I'm sorry, Frank," Nick said, meaning it.

"I ain't askin' fer sympathy, boy. I'm only tellin' ya what my pa shoulda told me and my brother Sam as boys. Nothin' is gonna fill up those empty moments in yore life like Summer. No one is gonna make ya relish yore accomplishments like yore spouse. No one will stand as closely by yore side durin' the bad as well as the good times like yore little wife. It's Summer who'll bathe yore brow when yore sick and hold yore head when yore throwin' up yore guts. It's the wife who'll be holdin' yore hand when yore gray and feeble, while yore children—the ones who are grown and off livin' with their own families—are resentin' ya fer the mistakes ya made while raisin' 'em."

Nick's mouth curled in a cynical smile. "I see you must come from a home where such virtues between husbands and wives are the norm. I congratulate you. Where I come from, love has nothing to do with marriage. Men and women marry for money and position and heirs."

"Do ya feel in yore heart o' hearts that such behavior is preferable to the way the majority of the civilized world views marital commitment?" Frank shook his head. "I don't thank ya believe that at all or ya wouldn't be so bitter and angry at yore parents for how they acted. In fact, I don't believe fer a minute that all this upheaval over the last couple of days has anythin' at all to do with financial woes, or the threat of a lot of Clansmen. They exaggerated yore agitation and frustration, but it's that sweet thang in the house, and yore feelins for her, that has ya in an emotional quandary. I thank yore in love with her."

"Go to hell."

"She done floated into yore miserable life when ya least expected it and caught ya naked as a newborn babe. Ya didn't have time to put up yore guard against her and she punched ya right here." He jabbed a finger in the vicinity of his heart. "You thank I ain't seen the way ya watch her? Ya can't keep yore eyes off her. Yore fascinated by her, Sabre. A little red-haired girl with freckles who wears a porkpie hat with an ungodly brown feather has wrapped ya around her little finger, and yore furious at her because of it."

"I—don't—love—her." The words were a monotone.

"Keep on tellin' yoreself that enough times and ya might foolishly start to believe it, Nicky, my boy. O' course, I suspect it won't matter. I think ya just might have already smashed any chance of makin' this relationship work. Near broke my heart to see her tears after the disgustin' manner in which ya introduced her to one of the finer aspects o' married life. Yet she claimed ya didn't strike her—"

"I didn't hit Summer. I would *never* raise my hand to Summer."

"Aw, ya wouldn't bludgeon her with yore fist, but ya've beat her feelins black and blue, just like ya have the rest of the world for most of yore life."

"Is that what I've been doing?"

Frank nodded and took a draw on his pipe. "I only hope the little darlin' will give ya one more chance to right the wrongs ya've inflicted on her the last weeks."

Nick left Frank standing at the foot of the steps and made his way through the house to the bedroom door. Moonbeams splashed softly over the bed, faintly illuminating Summer's small form buried beneath the blankets. The air smelled of soap from her earlier bath; the tub remained where she'd left it near the wardrobe.

He moved to the foot of the bed and stopped. Her head came slightly off the pillow.

"Are y' comin' t' bed?" she asked.

"Yes," he replied, but didn't move.

"Well? What are y' waitin' for? A formal invitation?"

"I sleep on that side of the bed."

"Y' what?"

"You're on my side of the bed. I sleep on the right . . ."

There came a shuffling of bedclothes as she sat

up, spilling folds of sheets and blankets around her hips. "So do I."

Drawing in a deep breath, he did his best to calm his rush of frustration and . . . something else that had begun to hum in his veins. Perhaps if he ignored it it would go away. Then again, perhaps it wouldn't. "All right," he snapped. "Take it if you must. I don't have the energy to press the issue tonight. My bloody head is aching." Walking to the left of the bed, he removed his boots, flung back the covers, and dropped into them, clothes and all.

Summer sat like a statue, staring down at him.

"What?" he demanded harshly. "Don't tell me you sleep sitting up."

"Do y' always sleep with yer clothes on?"

"Recently, yes."

He stared at the ceiling, refusing to allow his gaze to drift toward Summer, whose profile was limned with pale white light. He couldn't move so much as an inch without touching her. He couldn't turn his head without smelling her. Her scent was fused into his skin and nostrils, and the taste of her lingered on his tongue.

Finally, she lay down, her head nestled on the pillow near his, her hair coiling over the snowy linen case and brushing his cheek.

"It's a small bed," she said softly.

"My apologies. I hadn't realized I'd be sharing it with anyone."

She tugged the blanket up to her chin, and then on second thought gently lay his half of the blanket over him, as if she were putting a child to bed for the night. "Y'll get cold if y' don't," she told him, then rolled to her side, offering him her back.

He stared at the ceiling for long minutes, until Summer's breathing became deep and her body had stopped its occasional fidgeting. Good. If she'd brushed against him one more time, he wasn't sure if he'd be able to control the disgusting need to bury his body in hers again.

Christ, what had he become? The need to roll his body over hers in that moment, to inch up that thin nightgown to the tops of her thighs and allow his eyes to feast on her beautiful white legs made him shake.

Go on. She won't stop you. She's forgiven you for being a bungling, depraved ass.

Summer shifted and rolled her small, warm body up against his, nuzzled her head against his shoulder, and sighed. He lay there tensed, body sweating, the skin burning where her soft curves pressed against him. Turning his head, he buried his face in her hair and inhaled, letting the fragrance flow through his aroused body like fine brandy—intoxicating. Delicious.

Take her. Go on and take her. Quench the fire. Satiate the hunger.

Easing his hand into the skein of long hair spilling over his pillow, he gently twisted it around his fingers, gripping it fiercely, little by little allowing the desire to rise until the throbbing, intense fire was an engulfing pain. How long had it been since he'd last allowed the passion to rush through his veins unguarded?

Summer shifted. Her head came up off his shoulder, and she blinked at him with wide, watchful eyes.

"I can't sleep," she whispered.

He brushed the hair away from her face with the tips of his fingers. Christ, they were shaking.

Lowering her head slightly, so that her lips barely brushed the tip of his chin, she said, "I feel very odd."

"Odd?" He swallowed. "How so?"

"Breathless. M' skin burns. M' heart is poundin' double-time. Here." She reached for his hand and placed it just beneath her breast so that his thumb brushed the soft, firm fullness; he felt her flinch, retreat with startlement, but just briefly before she closed her eyes and allowed her head to fall back, as if absorbing the heat of his hand. "Oh, Nicholas." She sighed. "I like that."

"Do you?" His voice sounded tight and dry to his own ears.

"Aye. Is that wrong? Does it disappoint y'?"

Brushing her nipple with his fingertip, he replied, "No."

"I don't understand this feelin'. The pain was awful, but . . ."

"But?"

"I've been tryin' t' sleep, and all I can think about was how I felt when y' touched me."

"And how was that, Irish?"

"Like butter in the sun." Her face neared his, her lips but a breath from his. If she kissed him, he would shatter. "I want to be yer wife in every way."

"The marriage was consummated. What more do you want? I can hardly send you packing on the next boat back to England now."

A look of excitement crossed her face. "Yer lettin' me stay?" With a squeal, she threw her arms around him. "Y' won't regret it, Nicholas. I'll learn t' cook somethin' other than potatoes, I swear it. I'll learn t' sew better. I'll even help y' shear yer sheep."

He laughed.

She smiled and touched his face. "I love y'," she said softly.

"No, you don't. You couldn't possibly. You don't even know me. Not really. Believe me, if you knew all my dark and dirty little secrets, you'd be running for the next ship back to London."

A hesitant smile turned up her lips. Her eyes narrowed. The next he knew she was sliding one leg over him, straddling his hips, making his already semi-hard body turn rock-rigid. Pushing herself up, her outrageous hair spilling over her shoulders, she peered down at him with an impish look and said, "I'm not lettin' y' up until y've told me every one o' yer dirty little secrets."

"No chance."

"Confession's good for the soul, y' know. And besides, a husband and wife shouldn't have secrets between 'em. Come on, Sabre. I dare y'. What are y' afraid of? That I'll be so disgusted that I'll pack up and leave y'?"

His mouth grew hard, his body harder. The possibility that she was right left him feeling disoriented, confused. He didn't give a damn if she left him. After all, her being here was only a black joke perpetrated by a lot of troublemaking farmers.

"Nicholas," she said, gazing down at him with dark eyes. "I'll tell y' all my secrets if y'll tell me all o' yers."

"Somehow I don't think yours could quite live up to mine, Irish."

"I might surprise y'."

"You'll be shocked."

"No doubt."

"Disgusted."

"I'll be the judge o' that."

A long moment passed as he gazed up into her pale face and tender smile, doing his best to imagine life without her, the long days spent shepherding his flock over the paddocks, having no excuse to return home except to sleep. Then there were the longer nights spent alone with only his dog for company and the sound of his own voice to disturb the silence.

"I'll never leave y'," she vowed.

"What makes you think I would even give a damn?"

"I'll never leave y'," she repeated.

Closing his hands on her arms, he gripped her tightly, drew her down against his chest so that her face hovered just above his, and demanded in an aching, urgent voice, "Swear it, Irish. Swear it on every one of your blessed Catholic saints in heaven—*swear you won't ever leave me!*"

Chapter 14

"**I** swear it," Summer told him.

The grip on her arms became painful. At an earlier time, when she knew him less well, she might have quaked in fear, but now the look on his ruggedly handsome face broke her heart. How young he appeared. And vulnerable. And afraid, though she knew he would never, ever admit those feelings aloud. Not Sabre, Esquire. He was too damn proud for his own good.

"I *swear* it!" she repeated fiercely.

At last, he eased his hold on her arms, though he didn't let her go. "From the time I was fifteen I lived a life of debauchery. I drank too much and spent my nights with whores. I rebelled against everything that was moral and decent. I cared nothing for power, influence, money, or society."

"Because y' didn't approve o' those things? Or because y' were jealous that yer father cared more for them than he did for y'?"

"Yes," he replied softly. "Because he cared more for them than he did for me."

"Then I can understand yer actions." She understood all too well.

His eyebrows drew together; his mouth turned under. The hold on her arms began to hurt again, but she didn't flinch.

"My favorite brothel in Paris specialized in orgies. For enough money a man could buy anything his fantasy desired, with discretion ensured."

She pursed her lips in thought, then asked, "What's an orgy?"

She caught him by surprise. "It's . . . well, it's . . . It's kind of like . . . It's when . . . You don't know what an orgy is?"

"Like a big meal or somethin'? I remember seein' a book once with paintins o' the Roman Empire. There were a lot o' fat men lazin' around wearin' sheets while beautiful women wearin' hardly anythin' were feedin' 'em grapes."

His hands ran lightly up and down her arms, cupped her face, and toyed with her hair. "Yes," he replied softly, a faint smile turning up his lips. "Very similar."

"Well, what's so wrong with that?"

"Nothing if grapes was all the young women fed them."

She narrowed her eyes in consideration. He dismissed the topic with a flip of his hand. "I was an intent but terrible gambler. I had a weakness for racehorses and cards and placing bets at White's— on everything from what the club would provide for food on a certain day to what color cravat a peer would wear at a particular hour of the day. Since I usually went through my stipend by the second day of having received it, I was constantly and deeply in debt. Had the clubs and my peers not begun to refuse my markers, I would have ruined my family.

"I overindulged in drink. I was buzzing by noon,

tipsy by three, and roaring, falling-down drunk by six. By nine I had moved on to opium or hashish, and by midnight I could usually be found unconscious in some woman's bed.

"Overall, I had a sorry opinion of life and of people. Specifically of women."

"Because o' yer mother?"

"Yes. When I was twenty-one I met a very pretty young woman and fell in love. I was prepared to put my hedonism behind me; I asked her to marry me. I went so far as to kill a peer in a duel because I trusted that everything she'd told me about herself and her feelings for me was the truth. Too late I learned that I was wrong."

Summer studied his eyes, then touched his lips with her fingertip and ran it along the full, sensual curve as if she were memorizing its shape. She couldn't think of what to say. Drinking, gambling, whoring: those things didn't concern her. The idea that he had loved another woman—perhaps still loved her in his heart of hearts—did.

Sliding his arms around her, Nicholas rolled, pinning her beneath him, pressing her into the down-stuffed mattress with his weight. The feel of his knees between her thighs felt intimate and made her breathless. Memories of those hours before, when he'd touched her, kissed her, plunged the heat and hardness of his body deeply—so deeply—into hers, brought that straining, aching sensation to life inside her again. How frightening, this desire. How shocking. How exhilarating.

"It's your turn," he reminded her.

"My turn?"

"I want to know your secrets. All of them." Lowering his head over hers, he breathed lightly against her temple. "Confess something startling, Irish, so I don't feel like such a libertine."

Her eyelids drifting closed, she smiled, drowsy with the warm, aroused thickening of her blood and the accelerated beating of her heart. "I stole a pie once off Helen Bostwick's windowsill."

He blinked at her lazily, a bemused grin tugging at his mouth. "You stole a pie."

"I did it on a bet."

"Really, Irish, there has to be something more shocking than that."

A hot flush raced through her, only partly caused by the fact that she could detect his passion rising high and hard at the juncture of her thighs. Merciful saints, how easily she had put her reasons for being here with Sabre, Esquire, out of her mind. She had killed a man and assumed a dead woman's identity to escape the fate of the courts. She wasn't even married to Nicholas—not legally! The realization hit her that just because this supposed union had been consummated and Nicholas Sabre was now willing to accept the circumstances of this arranged marriage, did not mean she wouldn't find herself kicked out of this house on her backside if he ever found out the truth.

"Summer?"

She focused hard on his features, on his eyes that regarded her with a sharpness that made her catch her breath. Forcing a smile to her lips, she wrapped her arms around him and hugged him close, succumbing to intense and desperate fear at the thought of his learning the truth and turning her away.

"I'd like to make love to you," he said softly, then he brushed the tip of her nose tenderly, tentatively, with a kiss that was as light as fairies' breath. Lifting her mouth toward his, opening it in eager invitation, she smiled and said:

"Yer askin' now instead o' takin'?"

"Would you prefer to be taken? Some women do. They like it hard and fast and frantic, any time and anywhere." He lightly touched her mouth with his own. "Then there are women who enjoy being seduced leisurely throughout the night. They like to be teased and titillated . . ." He hovered above her, weight braced on both elbows and eyes like black fire. His mouth curved in that satyr's smile that made him look every bit the Devil Lord. He was by far the most handsome man she had ever set eyes on. This sudden shift of mood, from an angry and belligerent rebel to a whispering, seductive lover, left little doubt in her swirling, whirling consciousness that Nicholas Winston Sabre, Esquire, could seduce Queen Victoria herself . . .

He tunneled his hands through her hair and gripped her head. She was helpless to do anything but submit. Even the memory of the earlier pain subsided with the frantic beating of her heart and the need that overwhelmed her. She would do *anything*, surrender her body and soul, if he would only learn to love her.

He kissed her again. She expected passion, but it was a gentle, slow, arousing glide of his tongue on hers, as if he were experiencing for the first time the sweet and succulent taste of forbidden fruit and finding it delicious.

He left her momentarily as he removed his clothes, and though her face burned with the realization of what would certainly follow, she could not look away as he peeled the breeches down his long, powerful thighs. The hard, muscular buttocks and legs were much paler in comparison to his back, and when he turned toward her again . . .

Saints, but he was magnificent! Perfection personified. She'd heard snickers and whispers, of course, from the village girls who'd peeked at their brothers or fathers; she'd truly expected to find her husband's masculine . . . part unappealing.

But perhaps there was more of Glorvina in her than she'd like to admit. She found this man's masculinity breathtakingly beautiful. As the blood rushed to her cheeks, to her fingertips and her toes, turning her body into a hot pool of sensations, the temptation to reach out and stroke the satin-and-steel length of him made her feel as wicked as Eve picking the apple.

He slid onto the bed, his weight bliss, the scent of his skin heavenly. Hair spilled over his shoulders like ribbons of water. She wanted to plunge her hands into it. Holding her breath, she slid her fingers into the heavy mane and luxuriated in its silken texture. The act brought a groan from him, a rich, full-bodied growl that was as primitive as it was sensual. *He likes that*, she thought, and more bravely she allowed her fingers to explore him, the noble ridge of his brow, the aristocratic arc of his high cheekbones, the sweep of his moist lips that once had been hard with anger but now were malleable with passionate promise.

His head fell back, and his eyes closed. A low moan of pleasure emanated from him, and when she would have withdrawn her hands from his face, he whispered urgently, "Don't stop. Please don't stop. It's been so long since anyone touched me . . ."

A shiver ran through him; his face tightened with the agony and ecstasy of her caress, filling her with a euphoria that made her heartbeat quicken. She allowed her hands the freedom to wander over the tight, firm flesh of his broad shoulders, marveling at the play of his muscles beneath her strokes. Down his back, she explored. He gasped. To his hips . . . He groaned. To the hard, round buttocks that flexed in reaction to being molded by her delicate hands.

He trembled. He buried his face in her hair and clutched her to him.

She held him tightly. "I love y'," she told him, and felt his body draw in on itself. "I love y'," she repeated, "and I don't care if y' like it or not."

"Despite the fact that I'm a 'boil on the butt of humanity'?" he said, quoting her words back at her, remembering the turbulent day he had stormed into Sean's house and dragged her home. "I'm sorry I hurt you," he said at last.

The admission brought the sting of tears to her eyes. This man had apologized very few times in his life; the realization made his confession all the more meaningful. "I trust y' won't do it again," she teased, and her voice was husky.

Their bodies pressed, touched, brushed, toes and calves and knees sliding, hands exploring the peaks and valleys while they studied each other's eyes in anticipation and hesitation—like two strangers discovering each other for the first time. Her fingertips detected the welts left on his skin by Frank's strop. He found the tiny mole at the crest of her right buttock.

"Is this where Master Leprechaun kissed y'?" he whispered in her ear, mimicking her own accent in such a delightfully wicked voice that she almost laughed.

"Aye," she said. "M' mummy used t' say that it was far luckier t' kiss me bum than it was t' kiss the Blarney stone."

"Is that so?"

"Aye, and—"

The next thing she knew she was sitting up in bed and he was sliding the nightgown off over her head, then tossing it to the floor and rolling her over onto her stomach. He touched his hot, moist lips to her backside and made her squeal with surprise and indignation. She kicked and squirmed, and gasped and giggled as his tongue played over the sensitive skin, dipping, flicking, and fluttering like a butterfly. His fingertips followed, stroking up and down her spine, her hips, the backs of her thighs to her knees, making her toes curl and her giddy laughter turn into a slow, low moan that seemed to emanate all the way up from that boiling point of arousal between her legs.

"You like that, don't you?" came his resonant voice.

Closing her eyes, allowing her head to fall back and her body to become pliant, she drifted with the gentle but commanding coercion of his hands. He lifted, caressed. Kneeling and swaying back against him, she pleasured in the shocking exploration of his hands over and around and up and down her body, skimming her breasts, her ribs, her waist, to her legs and in between.

Then his knees spread her legs and his body slid slowly, gently into her, filling her up by degrees, stretching and driving. She tensed. He eased. A hot, piercing ache shot through her, and for a moment the recollection of her earlier pain made her panic.

"Easy," he murmured in her ear, embracing her securely in his arms. Each tried to draw in deep breaths; the intimacy of their joined bodies made it nearly impossible. The air became quicksilver, the moonbeams sparks. In time he began to move again, and the pain was gone, replaced by pure, shining pleasure. Her sighs and gasps and moans seemed to belong to some other woman, some other body. The swiftness of the transformation startled her, yet he didn't falter. He rode her harder until she found herself matching the rhythm.

"My God, you're beautiful. So damn beautiful." His voice sounded tight. His breath brushed hot and

moist on the back of her neck where he'd swept her
hair aside. "And you feel so good."

Her head was thrown back against his shoulder,
her hands frantically gripping his moving hips. "M'
breasts are too small," was the only thing she could
think to say.

"Not to me." Closing both hands over the small
mounds, he caressed them so reverently that tears
rose to her eyes.

"Y've been with far more beautiful women than
me."

"Never."

"And smarter."

"Impossible."

"But all those others—"

"They weren't my wife."

She melted. He carried her, down into the folds
of the blankets, turning her until they were a confusion of arms and legs and kissing mouths and
tongues that thrust and withdrew with each long
plunge of his body into hers.

The heat began. A strange white sun buried in
the deepest depths of her being began to pulsate,
to radiate its hot fingers outward, taking control of
her body, her mind, her breathing. She lifted,
twisted, flailed while he, braced upon his out-
stretched arms and watching her face, continued to
roll his hips upon hers, his body into hers, while
his own features turned hard—his jaw clenched and
his brow sweating, the muscles in his body tensed
and quivering with the strain of holding back his
own relinquishing of control.

"Come on. Come on," he whispered, and although in her innocence she had no idea what he
was talking about, she closed her eyes and let her
body fly with the new sensations. The heat grew
stronger and hotter, taking her away where the

night shimmered with bright light and her cry became a litany of pleasure.

"Nicholas! Oh, Nicholas!" she called in that explosive instant. And the sun imploded, drawing her into its searing core, then hurling her outward until she became one with the night. How glorious. How delicious, this divine surcease. So this was the magic . . .

Slowly, slowly the blissful feeling subsided. She opened her eyes to find her husband regarding her with a look that filled her with happiness. His face was intense and beautiful, the ecstasy of the building momentum inside him etched in the tight line of his sensual mouth and in his heavy-lidded eyes. He rocked against her, harder and harder, more frantically with each tightening and thrusting of his buttocks. His breath came raggedly. His skin became slick. Twisting her fingers into the sheets beneath her, she matched his rhythm, as hungry and desperate for his surcease as he had been for hers.

Then it came, turning his body to stone, rumbling up from his chest in a primitive growl as his eyes squeezed closed and his throat arched and his muscles strained. Deep inside her she felt the throb like a heartbeat and the hot flood of semen that seemed to drain the very life and breath from him. Suddenly he was sinking onto her, depleted, body racked with tremors, hands twisted loosely in her hair and his breath panting softly against her face.

Sliding her arms around him, palms skimming over the sweat-slick ridges of his shoulders and spine, she smiled, hugged him close, and whispered, "Welcome home."

It was a tradition that when the Cockatoos were ready to transport their wool to auction, they formed a wagon train of vehicles and went into Lyttleton together. Nicholas and Frank had just finished loading their dray when the Johnsons' heavily loaded wagon topped the rise. Dora and Dan's boys were scattered among the wool bales, hanging on to ropes and whooping as they made a game of keeping their balance on top of the precarious cargo. Summer waved from the porch, laughing as Wayne threw both pudgy arms in the air and squealed with excitement.

Dora, first off the wagon, met Summer halfway up the path. They giggled and clung like schoolgirls.

"Summer, you look radiant," Dora exclaimed, her own eyes bright with curiosity. "I trust everything is going well?"

Summer's cheeks warmed as she cast a glance toward Nicholas; he walked over to meet Dan, who ambled toward him with his hands tucked in the back pockets of his pants. "It's goin' better than well," she replied.

"Meaning?"

"I won't be goin' back t' England after all."

"Summer, are you telling me that you and Sabre . . ."

She nodded.

With a cry, Dora threw her arms around Summer and spun her around so hard that her feet left the ground. Nicholas and Dan glanced at them. The boys stopped chasing chickens around the yard, and Frank, having removed his hat to mop the sweat from his brow, grinned and shook his head.

"Oh, Summer, that's wonderful! Just wonderful! Congratulations! Dan!" Dora cupped her hands around her mouth and called, "Dan! Summer is staying in New Zealand! Isn't that wonderful?"

The boys let out whoops. Dan flashed a smile. Frank chuckled and slapped his hat back on his head. Nick just leaned one narrow hip against the dray and proceeded to roll his shirtsleeves up to his elbows. The simple action so stirred the desire in Summer and so strongly revived the memory of their intimacies throughout the night that she suddenly wished they were alone in bed and tangled up in arms and legs, and in sheets that were wet through with their perspiration. It was hard to believe that at this time yesterday she had still been as innocent as a newborn babe.

"Congratulations!" Dan shouted her way, then Nicholas looked up, directly at her, and any thought she might have harbored of responding to Dan's comment evaporated. The memories were there for him too. She saw it in the slight narrowing of his eyes and the sensual curl of his mouth.

The door slammed behind her. Remembering her guest, Summer forced her gaze away from Sabre and turned toward the house.

Breakfast smells lingered in the kitchen, along with the faint hint of Frank's pipe tobacco. Dora headed straight for the coffeepot shoved to the back of the stove, gave it a shake, then reached for a cup turned upside down to drain on a cotton towel near the dry sink. "So tell me," she began in an amused voice. "How do you like the finer aspects of married life?"

Summer dropped into a chair and affected an exaggerated shrug. A betraying blush began to warm her cheeks, and though she did her best to hide her smile, she found the effort next to impossible.

Dora laughed, swept over to the table, and plopped down in a chair. "I suspected the moment the two of you showed up at the picnic that everything would work out between you. When he asked you to dance, I knew it. It was obvious to everyone there that the man was mad about you. You were an absolute dream in that dress."

"He sold an heirloom, a ruby stickpin, t' get the money t' buy the dress."

Dora's eyes grew round. "How romantic!"

"I feel just awful about it. I wish there was some way I could get it back."

"You could always speak with Mr. Goldsmith. He owns the jeweler's in Christchurch where Nick must have sold it. Perhaps you could buy it back and pay for it over a period of time." Dora sipped her coffee, then smiled. "Have you stopped to think how much Sabre's come to care for you, Summer? The fact that he would sell a family heirloom—"

"But he doesn't love me," Summer interrupted, bringing Dora's eyebrows up.

"No?"

She shook her head. Her earlier euphoria began to dissipate. "He told me so."

"I see." Dora regarded her thoughtfully. "Summer, pride sometimes speaks louder than actions. Besides, what is love? I vow very few couples are *truly* in love when they marry. More likely they're in love with the idea of being in love. Oh, no doubt there's sincere fondness. And certainly there's desire. The fairy-tale image of happily-ever-after is every dreamy maiden's fantasy. But real life isn't like that. True love takes time."

"But what if he never comes t' love me? I couldn't stand it, Dora, feelin' the way I do for him."

"Be patient." Dora gave Summer's hand a reassuring squeeze. "He's come a long way in the last few weeks. You've breathed life back into him, Summer."

"Dora!" Dan called from the front door. "Best get on out here or we won't make the wagon train in time."

Leaving her chair, Dora asked, "You and Nick and Frank will be joining the wagon train on the trip into Christchurch, won't you? In years past Sabre has chosen to dray his bales into town alone, but with all the trouble with the Clan, I don't know if that would be wise. There's safety in numbers these days..."

By the time they reached the porch, Dan and the kids had reboarded their wagon. Dan had brought the team around so that they were headed in the right direction. As Dora hurried away, Summer ran to Nick and Frank, who appeared to be in no hurry to join the Johnsons.

"We're goin' with them, aren't we?" she asked, slightly out of breath.

Nick checked the ropes securing the tarp across the bales on his wagon. "No."

"What do y' mean, no? Surely yer not thinkin' o' makin' that trip alone?"

His dark eyes turned down to hers made her shiver. "I've made this trip alone for the last two years. I didn't see anyone dropping by then to invite me to join in on their little caravan."

"They didn't know y' then."

"They don't know me now, Irish."

"But yer invitin' trouble if y' think t' drive t' Christchurch on yer own. The Clan would like nothin' better than to find y' solitary and defenseless out there."

"Little gal's right," Frank joined in. "One torch to that wagon and ya can kiss it all good-bye."

Her hands on her hips, Summer watched Nicholas turn his back on her and Frank, and proceed to check the horses. The look of stubborn determination on his features didn't bode well. "Y' know what yer problem is?" she demanded angrily, bringing his dark head around. "Yer too damn proud for yer own good, that's what!"

"Is that so?"

"Aye, that's so. They're tryin' t' do y' a good turn by invitin' y' t' join them—"

"It's not my welfare they're interested in, my darling wife. It's yours."

"Don't be daft."

Frank chuckled, thumbed back his hat, and took a seat on a porch step. "This is gonna git good," he mumbled, then snapped his fingers at Betsy as she came trotting around the corner of the house, ears perked and tail wagging.

Nick cast him a sarcastic grin, turned his back on Summer, and headed for the sheep shed. She ran to catch up, forced to take two steps to his every one.

"So what are y' goin' t' do if they come ridin' at y' out o' the hills?" she demanded.

"Shoot a few of them, I guess."

"Like y' did that night they jumped y' in yer own house?"

"I wasn't expecting them—"

"They'll attack after dark, y' know. If they don't kill y' outright, they'll burn yer wool."

"What makes you think they won't do the same thing to the Johnsons or Sharkeys or—"

"At least we'll all be together. We can stand side by side and fight off the bastards. We won't have a chance on our own."

Nick kicked open the shed door and stepped into the musty interior, Summer right behind him, her frustration mounting as she paced the dirt floor. "I don't think I've ever met a more stubborn individual," she declared. "Or one more unwillin' t' forgive people for misunderstandins. For the life o' me, I can't—"

The door clicked shut behind her. Whirling, straining to see through the dark, she focused on

Nicholas's grinning face where he leaned against the door. Her gaze dropped to his dark brown hands that were reaching for his breeches. "Blazes," she whispered, suddenly breathless. "What do y' think yer doin'?"

"What do you think?" He crooked a finger at her. "Come here, Mrs. Sabre."

She blinked in astonishment and backed away, but a smile toyed at her mouth.

"Come, come. Don't be coy." He moved toward her, flipping open the buttons one by one.

"But—but people don't make love in sheep sheds!"

"I'll make love to my wife wherever and whenever I want to."

"But Frank—"

"Isn't stupid. He won't interrupt."

Coming up against the sorting table, Summer tried to swallow the giddy laughter working its way up her throat as he moved toward her through the shadows. Her heart pounded. She was certain he could hear it. "But what about me?"

"What about you?"

"If the Clan attacked, they might shoot me."

"Are we still on that subject?"

He stopped so closely in front of her that she was forced to let her head fall back in order to look into his face. A flush of heat kissed his cheeks. Lifting her fingers to his face, she lightly touched his mouth, his chin, allowing her adoring gaze to convey her feelings.

"Tell you what," he murmured. "Perhaps you can convince me to join the train to Christchurch."

"Convince y'? Now, how can I do that?"

Wrapping his hands around her waist, he easily

lifted her onto the table, nudged her knees apart, and tugged up her skirt. His mouth curved into a wicked smile.

"I'll show you."

Chapter 15

They were six long hours into the journey and there had been no hint of mischief from the Clan. But now, night was falling—the setting sun reflected in shades of fire-gold and red from the snowcapped peaks of the Southern Alps behind them. If trouble came, it would come after dark.

Summer and Frank sat on the rear door of the wagon, lowered and suspended with chains. He was whittling on a piece of wood and whistling, every now and again lapsing into a monologue of life on the Texas prairie. Nick had heard all the stories before . . . several times. Summer, however, appeared transfixed by the old man's tales of Comanches and the wild Texans' battles for independence from Mexico.

"Yep. They all died. Ever' one of 'em. Mexicans butchered 'em. Their bodies was stacked high as the Alamo's walls when Santa Anna ordered 'em to be doused in kerosene and burned. The general didn't even give the heroes a Christian burial. Sam Houston got his own back, though, and then some."

Looking over his shoulder, Nick watched the sun dance off his wife's hair and recalled how it had felt sliding through his fingers.

Married. The very idea seemed ridiculous, and unnerving. But what was done was done. He'd learn to live with it if he must. Summer was young and inexperienced, but he could hardly deny that she was an eager and willing student in the art of lovemaking. Still . . . he found her adoration and vows of love more than a little disconcerting. He'd never been one to profess emotions he didn't feel, and the truth of the matter was, he wasn't certain how he felt about her. This need to be with her could not be mistaken for anything but lust. He might want her physically, but never, ever would he give his heart to her. Therein lay trouble, disappointment, heartbreak. He'd had enough of those to last him a lifetime.

They journeyed on for another hour before bringing the creaking, straining drays into a circle for the night. Campfires were started, dinner cooked. Children and dogs dashed about the vast flatlands while their parents scolded and cajoled them to remain within the safer confines of the wagon circle.

Vicesimus Sellers took out his violin and began to play. The Cockatoos danced, stomped their feet, brought out their treasured stores of homemade liquor, and passed the jugs around until many of the men were whooping and howling at the moon. Frank then entertained them by doing a complicated jig around the fire that he swore was a Comanche war dance. Arnold Sharkey good-naturedly hurled a fistful of horse dung at him and called him a liar. Frank then proceeded to ruminate about his days in Texas; most of the Cockatoos groaned and deserted the area . . . fast.

Nick kept a respectable distance from the carousing group. He made certain his rifle was in working order. He checked his tarp and bales for what must have been the hundredth time. Cloudbursts were notoriously frequent at this time of year. Then he sat in the firelight with his legs crossed. With a stick, he doodled numbers in the dirt as he attempted to calculate his possible profits. *Please, God, just let it be enough to see us through the next year.* After all, he had a wife to see after now.

"Nicholas?"

He looked up to find Summer watching him. She was stunningly beautiful.

"What are y' doin' sittin' here all alone?"

Shrugging, he forced his gaze away from her and went back to scribbling in the dirt.

She dropped to her knees beside him, hands planted firmly on her thighs. "Yer bein' unsociable again," she stated matter-of-factly.

"Would you like me to get up and dance with Frank?" He grinned, but just barely.

"I wouldn't mind it if y' danced with me," she replied, smiling sweetly, then she placed her hand on his knee and gave it a reassuring squeeze. "But I understand. Yer bashful."

That made him laugh. There had never been a bashful bone in his delinquent body.

"Some o' the people think that y' think yer too good for them."

"Is that what they say?"

She nodded. "*I* think yer overly worried about what they think. Y' should really try and relax around them. When they've come t' know y', like I have, they'll love y' too."

Sure they will, he considered saying, but then Nan Sharkey interrupted by calling, "Summer!"

Nan hurried toward them, smiling broadly, the baby Phoebe in her arms. "There you are," she said.

"Are you still willing to watch the baby for me and Arnie while we dance?"

"Certainly." Summer held out her arms. Nan slipped the child into them, made certain the bunting was tucked securely around Phoebe's arms and legs to prevent the night's chill from nipping her fingers and toes, then hurried back toward the distant firelight and music.

"Saints," Summer whispered as she gazed down on the sleeping baby. "Isn't she lovely, Nicholas?"

"Yes," he replied softly, never taking his eyes from Summer's face. "She is."

"There's somethin' about lookin' on a child that makes a person believe in miracles. Don't y' agree?"

He nodded.

A wide smile spread over her mouth. "Take her," she said.

"No, I—"

"Go on, Nicholas. Don't be a coward."

"I've never held a baby."

"Well, there's always a first time for everythin'."

Carefully, so carefully, she eased the babe into his arms, making certain his elbow was crooked just so and the child's head was near his heart. They sat there in the firelight, heads tipped over the sleeping infant, watching in fascination as the tiny rosebud lips puckered and suckled at an imaginary tit.

Summer laughed.

Nick laughed.

Nose to nose, they suddenly looked into each other's eyes, their breathing quickening.

"Just think," Summer said. "Someday, if we're lucky, we'll be holdin' our own child like this. Would that please y', Nicholas?"

He looked down at the baby again, a well of emotion rising up inside him as the truth of her words painted a canvas of bright pictures vividly upon his mind's eye. The realization that he would like nothing more than to have a house full of children with Summer left him speechless.

"Is somethin' wrong?" she asked.

Shaking his head, he slid the baby back into her arms, climbed to his feet, and slapped the dust from his seat and legs.

"There's one thing about children," Summer said. "They'll love y' no matter what sort o' mess y' make with yer life."

"True," he said, and walked off into the darkness.

It was just before ten when Dan Johnson climbed up on his wagon and called for everyone's attention. "I'll be needin' volunteers to take the first watch," he announced.

Several men stepped forward. After a moment's hesitation, Nick joined them. Then Dan called for others to take the second watch. They were all about to take their respective places when Allen Johnson scrambled up on his father's wagon seat and pointed off into the night. "A fire yonder, Pa!"

An expectant hush fell over the travelers as all heads turned toward the spot of flickering light on the horizon.

"What could it be?" a woman's voice whispered in the quiet.

Dick Thorndike, Royce Beckett, and Dan Johnson snatched up their guns. Nan and Dora and Fanny, along with the other Cockatoo wives, scurried about ushering the children to safety, while Jeff ran whistling for his dog, becoming panicked when the black-and-white shepherd failed to appear.

Grabbing up their rifles, the men ventured out toward the blaze on the horizon. Frank took up a position next to Nick, his shotgun cradled in his arms like a baby. "I smell trouble," he commented matter-of-factly. "Ya git a whiff of that stench?

That's flesh and hair burnin', I'd bet my left nut on
it. I smelled enough of it when I rode with the Rang-
ers. This here odor is animal. Sheep I'd say. Nothin'
smells worse than fried wool, 'ceptin' maybe human
hair."

"Shut up, Frank," someone called out from the
back of the group. "You're giving me the jitters."

It turned out that Frank was right. At least a dozen
sheep had been butchered, their bloated carcasses
piled atop one another and set afire. Then Jeff Mead
spotted the body of his beloved dog amid the conflagration. His face drained of blood. His eyes
turned glassy.

"My dog!" he wailed. "They've murdered Tippie!
Bastards! Murderin' bastards! Ah, God, they've
murdered my dog!"

By the time the men returned to the wagons, Jeff
had worked himself into a frenzy. It took six men
to stop him from riding out into the hills to confront
those who had set the fire, though there wasn't one
of the other Cockatoos who didn't sympathize. A
sheep farmer's most trusted friend and companion
was his wife first (if he had one) and his dog second.
It would take Jeff Mead years to train another animal
to replace Tippie.

Upon returning to the camp, Nick found it a hive
of activity. The women had rounded up the horses
and driven them inside the circle of wagons. They'd
constructed barricades from trunks and loaded any
extra rifles they had at hand.

But where was Summer?

A sense of disquietude ran through him as he
moved through the crowd, searching each face, asking the women and children if they had seen her
recently.

"Wayne! Wayne Johnson, you get back to that

wagon this minute!" Dora's panicked voice cried out.

Nick stopped Royce Beckett's wife. Startled, she stared at him as if he had suddenly sprung another head on his shoulders. The old resentment and self-consciousness rose inside him. "Have you seen my wife?" he asked in an even voice.

"No," she replied, and hurried away.

Clenching his fists, he watched her escape to the other side of the camp, then spun on his heel and returned to his wagon. He spied Frank standing off a few paces speaking quietly with Dan and Arnie. Nick thought of calling to them, letting them know that Summer was missing, but his voice had locked up in his throat. He hadn't felt this kind of fear since a half dozen Scotland Yard policemen had slapped cuffs on his wrists and informed him he was being arrested for the murder of Lord Price.

Then the tarp over the wool bales moved.

Catching a glimpse of coiling bronze hair trailing from beneath it, Nick reached out a hand and threw back the canvas. Summer blinked up at him, as did Betsy.

"What the hell are you doing under there?" Panic made his voice loud.

"Hidin'," she replied.

He shut his eyes briefly, then reached for her, closed his hands roughly around her shoulders and shook her as hard as he dared. "Damn you to hell, Summer, you scared the life out of me!"

"I did?"

"I thought those men had . . ." He shook her again, though less fiercely as his initial rush of fear and then anger disintegrated into relief.

Her cheeks suffused with color, Summer stared up at him, her soft mouth parted. She looked frail in the firelight, and so small. Her violet eyes were large with distress. Whether it was due to fear over the Cockatoos' circumstances, or alarm over his irritation, he couldn't tell. As it had the day before, after the Clan had attacked and he'd beaten Virgil McIlhenny's face in because he'd raised a hand to Summer, the realization of what losing her would mean to him hit him with full force. He wanted to bury his hands in her beautiful hair and force her to promise that she would never leave his sight again for as long as she lived.

"I'm sorry," she told him. "I only crawled in here t' hide while y' were gone. I didn't think y'd get worried—"

"There are madmen with murder on their minds out there. I came back to find my wife missing and you don't think I should have worried?"

"Aye," she replied, allowing the faintest smile to turn up her lips. "A man should worry over his wife. I just wasn't aware that y' truly cared, Nicholas . . . *Do* y' care?"

The directness of her words unnerved him. Releasing his grip on her, he lowered his hands and looked into her eyes. It seemed a thousand thoughts and emotions streaked through him. How could he confess to Summer that he cared when he wasn't certain he was ready to admit it to himself? "You're my wife," he finally said, choosing his words carefully. "Therefore, you're my responsibility. I wouldn't be much of a man if I shirked my responsibilities, would I?"

"That's all I am t' y'? A responsibility?" Her voice quavered, either in hurt or anger.

Closing his eyes briefly in frustration, Nick shook his head. "That's not what I meant."

"It's what y' said!"

"I only meant . . ." Summer turned away and he grabbed her. She glared up at him with flashing purple eyes. "Of course I care," he stated softly. "I care very much about what happens to you."

Summer tugged her arm away and rubbed it. The fierce anger that had momentarily touched her cheeks with hot color faded into melancholy. "Y' care what happens t' yer dog, Nicholas. And yer sheep. Carin' about what *happens* t' somebody, and carin' *for* somebody aren't the same."

Jumping down from the wagon, she stormed off to help Nan quiet her crying children.

Summer lay awake throughout the night, listening to the quiet murmurings of the men, the occasional whimperings of children. A dog barked now and again. Men kept watch. Women stuck their heads out of their hiding places and begged their husbands to be careful.

An hour before dawn, Nick joined Summer beneath the tarp. He fell heavily beside her, exhaustion sounding in his deep sigh.

"No sign o' them?" she asked.

"None," he replied wearily, then ruffled Betsy's fur where she lay nestled near Summer's thigh.

Summer waited for him to reach out to her, but he didn't. Finally, she wiggled over against him and lay her head on his shoulder. After several long moments of silence, she said, "I missed y'. I'm sorry I got so angry earlier. I know yer doin' the best y' can under the circumstances; it's not as if y' really want me here, after all. I'll just have t' learn t' be more patient."

He curled one arm around her and lightly stroked her hair.

Neither of them moved or spoke for the next hour, and it was with a sense of relief sometime later that they threw back the tarp to welcome the first light of day.

The remainder of the journey was uneventful, if not monotonous. The caravan reached the busy little town of Lyttleton at just before noon. The Cockatoos went directly to the shipping yards where the auction would be held. Summer nervously anticipated trouble, due to the great many farmers scattered around town. But she learned that, ironically enough, this was the one time of the year when the two factions got together with a minimal amount of trouble. The farmers and Cockatoos had one common goal in mind, and that was to get the highest price possible for their wool.

The bales were recorded by name and weight, then the Cockatoos and farmers put their heads together and debated on whose wool would go on the block first when the auction started at sunup tomorrow morning. The buyers would bid high for the finest wool, therefore raising the floor bids on all the wool that followed. The wool was studied with an eye toward quality: thickness, durability, length, and cleanliness; wool that was heavily stained, matted, or littered by thistles or fleas would bring minimal bids.

To Summer's delight and Nicholas's and Frank's surprise, they chose Nick's wool to be auctioned first. "Your wool is the best of the lot," Ben Beaconsfield declared, and slapped him on the back. "Of course this means you'll have to buy us all a round of ale at the pothouse tonight." Winking at Summer, Ben added, "It's a tradition that we all get a little crazy the night before the auction. Nick has never joined us before. This should be a real occasion."

The race back into Christchurch was wild and raucous. The town, already bustling with its permanent residents and those farmers who had drayed in their crops early, swelled with the inpouring of Cockatoos. Their wagons lined the dusty streets and the banks of the lovely Avon River, along which the town was built. Many families who could not afford rooms at the accommodation houses pitched tents along the river, while others hurried to secure bedding anywhere they could—including at the blacksmith's, who'd relocated his horses to an outside corral and rented out their straw-littered stalls to unmarried men. The public houses and churches had let space as well.

While Frank sauntered down to the blacksmith's, Nick managed to procure the last room at the hotel for him and Summer. As he paid for two nights' lodging, Summer gazed out the front window and watched the activity in the streets until she was forced to catch up with Nick as he climbed the stairs to their quarters.

The room offered little: a window that wouldn't open, a washstand with a peeling silver-backed mirror, and a bed that was barely big enough for one, much less two. Still, she supposed it was better than sleeping on the ground or in a hay barn.

Standing at the window and looking down on the festive street, she asked, "So what happens now?"

Nick moved up behind her and peered over the top of her head to the street below. "By the looks of those women running in wild packs, I'd say the women are supposed to shop."

She grinned up at him. "And where do the men go while we do that?"

"Drinking. Whoring. All that manly sort of stuff."

"But I thought there were no available women here."

"Frank tells me there's a ship in. That usually means there will be women about. Temporarily, anyway."

"Oh."

As he moved away, Summer turned to regard him. She leaned on the windowsill, watching as he dug a clean shirt out of his valise and tried to iron out the wrinkles with his hand. Giving up, he took his worn one off and replaced it with the clean one, added his cravat, neatly tied it about his throat, then slid on his suit coat.

"I take it yer goin' out," she said.

He nodded and buffed the dust from his boots.

With an edge to her voice, she said, "I hope yer not thinkin' o' whorin'."

He flashed her a dismissive smile just as a knock sounded on the door. It was Dora and Nan.

"Come shopping with us," Dora pleaded. "There's a ship just in from London, and its cargo was china, furniture, and clothing."

"Come on," Nan chimed in. "We save all year for this shopping spree. Arnie and Dan are watching the children for a couple of hours. You don't mind, do you, Mr. Sabre?"

He barely glanced their way. "Certainly not."

Summer frowned.

Dora grabbed her arm. "Hurry before the best things are picked over."

"Let me get m' hat," she replied. She placed it at a jaunty angle on her head and regarded its crumpled feather in the mirror, her eyes straying once again to her husband's reflection.

"Hurry!" her friends insisted.

"All right, all right," she muttered, moving to the door. Once there, however, she glanced back again and found Nicholas busily tying his hair back with a clean black satin ribbon. "I suppose," she said to Dora and Nan, "that if there's a ship in, that means the town is likely t' be overrun by a lot o' randy sailors . . . ?"

Nicholas's head came up and around. His eyes narrowed.

"No doubt," Dora replied.

"Good." Summer smiled and then, stepping from the room, slammed the door behind her. It opened as quickly, and Nick stared down at her.

"You'll need some money to shop," he said, offering her a number of coins and several pieces of paper currency.

"Thank y'," she told him.

"You're welcome."

She turned to rejoin Nan and Dora, who were waiting at the top of the stairs.

"And Summer . . ." Nick called behind her.

She looked around.

"Have fun," he said softly.

Dora bought a blue-and-white china tea service. Nan purchased booties for Phoebe and bolts of calico material for clothes. Summer stood at the shop window and gazed out at the street.

"Summer?" came Dora's voice behind her. "What's wrong?"

"Nothin'."

"Something is wrong," Nan said. "When a woman has no interest in spending her husband's money, there's definitely something amiss."

Summer couldn't help herself; she laughed. Turning to face her friends, she said, "He bought me that lovely dress. I wouldn't think of expectin' any more from him."

Lifting her eyebrows, Dora said to Nan, "You can tell she's newly wed."

"I just feel funny about spendin' his money," Summer argued.

"But surely there are things you need. Clothes, household goods . . . ?"

"We need foodstuffs and buildin' supplies."

Nan wrinkled her nose. "Heavens! That's no fun." She gestured toward the window. "Surely there is something in one of those shops that could tempt you into splurging on yourself."

Summer's gaze wandered over the row of neat, whitewashed buildings. There was a silversmith's shop whose bow window was stacked with shelves of decorated emus' eggs imported from Australia. Summer momentarily imagined what the elaborate fixtures would look like ornamenting the petticoat-slippered parlor table back home, then dismissed the idea with a shake of her head. Somehow Sabre, Esquire, didn't strike her as the sort of man who would appreciate such show pieces.

Then she spied the jeweler's. "Perhaps..." she murmured.

Dora and Nan pressed close.

Summer headed for the door. Her friends followed. She walked directly to Goldsmith's display window and peered inside. The shop was small, dark, and although not nearly as crowded as the others, was still occupied by several women. She glanced at Dora, then at Nan; taking a deep breath, she entered the shop, pausing as her eyes adjusted to the dim interior. Goldsmith himself was busy with a patron who was sitting in a chair, her back to the door; she appeared to be intent on her transaction.

Bending her head near Summer's, Dora said softly, "That's Blannie Tennyson."

"Roy Tennyson's daughter?" she whispered back.

"Wife!" Nan stressed. "Can you believe it? She's young enough to be his granddaughter."

Goldsmith looked up, adjusted his spectacles on

his broad nose, and smiled. "I'll be with you ladies momentarily."

"Sure you will," Nan muttered under her breath. "Just as soon as you're done paying homage to her highness."

Stifling her laughter, Summer moved to the long glass case running the length of the room and began searching the collection of pocket watches, stickpins, earrings, necklaces, and bracelets. The others trailed behind her.

"Some say that theirs was an arranged marriage," Dora continued in a low voice.

"It would have to be," Nan replied. "What woman in her right mind would marry the old goat?"

"I've heard she's miserable."

"Wouldn't you be?" Nan asked.

"Her father was Roy's business partner back in London. Some say that by marrying her he bought his way into society. Others say that the one thing Tennyson desires more than power and control is a son to pass it all on to."

"I can't think of a worse hell than being forced to live with someone you don't love," Nan said.

Summer stopped and looked around, her eyes meeting Dora's, flickering to Nan's, then dropping again to the merchandise spread out before her. Dora moved up against her.

"If you're applying what Nan just said to your own circumstances, then don't."

"Of course not," Nan said. "It's a completely different matter."

"Is it?" Summer demanded, hating the betraying blush she could feel creeping up her throat to her face. "Nicholas might disagree with y'. He's made it clear that he's accepted our situation because he has little choice, not because he's happy about it."

She turned away, tried to blink the sting from her eyes, and failed miserably as the room blurred.

"Are you looking for anything in particular?" Mr. Goldsmith asked.

Rubbing her hands on the skirt of her dress, Summer did her best to smile. "I was wonderin'—"

Her voice died as, peering over Blannie Tennyson's shoulder, Summer spotted Nicholas's ruby stickpin in the woman's gloved hand. Blannie's aristocratic voice was saying:

"This is really very extraordinary, Mr. Goldsmith. Stunning! I have a burgundy gown it will look smashing with. I'll take it."

"Y' can't!" Summer blurted.

Blannie looked around, her eyes wide with surprise. Goldsmith removed his glasses. "I beg your pardon?" he said.

"That ruby belongs to m' husband."

"My dear young woman, that ruby belongs to me," he replied. "I bought it several days ago from—"

"M' husband's shepherd. He sold it to y' in order t' get enough money t' buy me a dress."

"You are Nicholas Sabre's wife?"

She nodded, her eyes going back to the jewel in Blannie's hand. "I came here hopin' t' buy it back."

"I see." Spreading his hands, Goldsmith gave them all a discomfited smile. "As you can see, we have a problem. Mrs. Tennyson wishes to buy the pin, and—"

"But it's m' husband's. It's been in his family for generations."

"I can fully sympathize, Mrs. Sabre. If you had come in ten minutes earlier—"

She turned to Roy Tennyson's young wife. "Please, ma'am. I'd be eternally grateful if y'd reconsider purchasin' the pin. It's important that I have it."

Blannie regarded the jewel for a long moment before looking at Summer again. Her face seemed uncommonly pale, Summer noted.

Leaning on the countertop, Goldsmith frowned. "Mrs. Sabre, I must apologize for any discomfort this causes you, but were I to offer this ruby to you, have you the money to purchase it?"

"I'd hoped that perhaps some sort of arrangement could be made to pay it out—"

"Impossible." He shook his head. "Mrs. Tennyson has offered to pay cash. And even if she hadn't, I couldn't agree to your terms."

"Would y' mind tellin' me why not?" she demanded.

"Simply put, madam, Cockatoos are an unacceptable risk."

"M' money is just as good as anyone's!"

"Of course it is. When you have it."

Blannie pushed out of her chair and stood for a moment with her hands braced upon the glass counter before smoothing them over her gown. Only then did Summer realize that she was pregnant.

"Please wrap the pin securely," Blannie said to the jeweler. "I'll have my husband drop by later with your money."

Without looking at Summer again, Goldsmith took up the pin and disappeared behind a curtain. Blannie walked to the front door and stood with her back to them all until Goldsmith returned with her parcel. Thanking him politely, she exited the shop.

Dora took Summer's arm. Without speaking to Goldsmith again, the threesome left. For the next two hours Dora and Nan did their best to take Summer's mind off the incident. They visited linen and china shops, and enjoyed tea in the hotel's lobby. They promenaded the pathways running along the Avon River, stopping once to admire a vendor's collection of birds. His prize performer was an immense cockatoo, pristine white in color with an ugly-shaped head and bill, and large red rings around the eyes. The bird cocked its head at Summer, whistled, and croaked, "Oh, it ain't a bit of good! Come 'ere, luvie, and give us a drop of whisky, *do*."

Laughing, Summer declared, "I should buy him. And when Nicholas wants t' know why I did it, I can tell him that I have t' have *someone* t' keep me company while he walks about broodin'."

By the time they returned to the hotel, the afternoon had grown late. Arnie and Dan were looking more than a little frazzled from their afternoon spent tending thirteen children, and they were more than eager to join their friends at the pothouse. Having lined the young ones up along the hotel steps, Nan and Dora watched their husbands hurry toward the tavern.

"You'd think if they went another fifteen minutes without tipping a tankard they'd expire," Nan said as she bounced Phoebe in her arms.

A roar of laughter exploded from the pothouse. A pair of drunken, scuffling men stumbled through the door and into the street, followed by a couple of tawdrily dressed females with painted faces who shrieked and screamed and egged them on.

"I might've known," Dora said. "Offer a man a beer and a hussy, and they lose all common sense."

"Let them enjoy their drinking while they can," Nan replied. "It'll turn ugly soon enough. It always does. Cockatoos, whores, and farmers don't mix. If they don't kill one another tonight, they'll have a go at it tomorrow night once the men have their money in hand and the gambling starts."

Summer finally excused herself and returned to her room, though she regretted it the moment she opened the door. Sabre wasn't there. How silly of her to think he would be. As if he'd be lazing about the room mooning for her company, counting the seconds until her return.

She walked to the window and looked down on the pothouse. A growing number of men and women had converged around the fighters. But where was Nicholas?

Inside, no doubt. Drinking and whoring and doing all that manly stuff.

Sighing, she lay down on the bed. Saints, she was moping about like someone who'd lost her last friend. Why?

"Y' know why, Summer O'Neile Sabre," she said aloud. "Y' were hopin' for bonbons and flowers from yer husband once this relationship was consummated, and y' didn't get it. He acts as if nothin's changed between y'. He's off right now spendin' his time and what little money he has on ale and loose women, not even carin' that yer lyin' here in this dull room with yer heart breakin' because he doesn't love y'.

"Not only that, y' don't want t' admit that Nan's comment in Goldsmith's bothered y'. *I can't think of a worse hell than being forced t' live with someone y' don't love.*"

Was that what she was doing to Sabre? Making his life hell?

Footsteps sounded in the hallway. Heart suddenly racing, Summer sat up, smoothed down her hair and skirt, clasped her hands in her lap, and waited, each heavy thud upon the hardwood floor sounding like thunder in her ears.

The footsteps stopped. A doorknob rattled; a door

creaked open, then slammed. Then silence.

Summer sat immobile in the quiet.

She awoke later to the sound of gunshots. Except for the stream of dim light pouring through the window, the room was completely dark.

Sitting up in bed, rubbing her eyes, she tried hard to focus on her surroundings. The street noises had escalated, the racket of whooping men, of screeching women, of barking dogs.

Sliding from the bed, Summer moved to the window. Men on horseback galloped up and down the paved street, firing guns into the air. Many more lay sprawled, unconscious, over the sidewalks, empty tankards still in hand. There wasn't a woman in sight. Summer wasn't surprised. Any female, married or otherwise, who would risk venturing into that melee was taking her life in her hands.

A faint smell of food wafted to her. Her stomach rumbled. What was she supposed to do about dinner?

She paced. The longer she paced, the hungrier she became and the more tantalizing seemed the odors coming from the dining room below.

"Where the blazes are y', Sabre?" she asked aloud.

After another half hour, her patience came to an end. Throwing open the trunk, she extracted the lavender gown Nicholas had bought her, then set to the task of brushing, plaiting, and arranging her hair in a corona around her head. Donning the dress took a great deal of time as she struggled with the tiny buttons up the back. The effort made her arms ache, but she determinedly bent to the task.

She was just exiting the room when the door across the hallway opened. Sean O'Connell stepped out, his eyes brightening as he recognized Summer.

"Well now, fancy meetin' y' here," he said. "And aren't y' lookin' pretty as the proverbial picture?"

The thrill of seeing Sean dissipated the instant she remembered, somewhat sadly, that he was the enemy. Wrinkling her brow in displeasure, she slammed her door and made for the staircase.

"Whoa!" Sean sprang after her and took her arm. "Is that any way for a fetchin' young woman such as yerself t' be greetin' an old friend?"

"I don't see any friends here," she replied. "Only a traitor who would sacrifice his principles and peoples' lives t' get what he wants."

He affected a silent whistle and took a step back.

Hands on her hips, she glared at him. "Y' should be tarred and feathered and horsewhipped. Yer a troublemaker, Sean O'Connell, and I don't want t' be seen within a mile of y'. Any man who would purposefully set out t' ruin ever'thing another man's worked for is worse than any animal. A man who would intentionally set out t' harm babes frolickin' in a meadow—"

"Now, wait a minute. I had nothin' t' do with that," he replied hotly.

"Saints! Yer a liar as well!"

She spun on her heel to leave him. He grabbed her again, and bending his head over hers, repeated, "I'm tellin' y', lass, I had nothin' t' do with those riders last Sunday. In fact, I was here in Christchurch attendin' Mass. Y' can ask Father McClary yerself. It's not only me who's holdin' a grudge against the Cockatoos, y' know."

"Yer feud shouldn't be with the Cockatoos," she cried. "Yer feud should be with the government. The Cockatoos are simply buyin' land for sale by the government. They're breakin' no laws. But y' are. Y' come into a man's home and beat him and burn his dreams t' ashes. Y' say yer feud isn't with women and children, but who do y' think gets hurt?" She thumped him on the shoulder with her fist. "I thought we were friends, y' and I."

"We are," he responded softly.

"But y' brought those horrible men to m' home, Sean, and allowed them t' beat m' husband and nearly burn Frank alive."

"If y'll just let me explain—"

"No explanation will change things. Y' did what y' did."

"But I've done nothin' since that night the men visited yer spread. It might surprise y' t' know that there are more than a few of us who are growin' tired o' Tennyson's shenanigans."

Summer shook her head in disbelief, then turned again for the stairs. Sean followed.

The dining room was packed and people were waiting for tables—all couples or families. Summer viewed the scene with mounting frustration.

"I'd be most honored if y'd agree t' join me for dinner," Sean whispered over her shoulder. "I made reservations, y' see."

Whirling to face him, she said, "Sean O'Connell, if y' were the last man on the face o' this earth—"

"Yer hungry, aren't y'?" He raised one dark brow and grinned. "Well, aren't y'? By the looks o' this crowd, y'll be lucky t' get seated by midnight." The waiter walked up at that moment and called Sean's name. Without waiting for Summer's answer, Sean took hold of her arm and ushered her into the room to their table, smiling pleasantly as he gallantly drew back her chair. He sat down opposite her. How very handsome he looked in his suit, she thought. His clean-shaven face appeared smooth and lean.

Glancing about the room, catching more than a few heads turned her way, she muttered, "Blazes, I feel like Judas at the Last Supper."

The murmur of conversation droned on around them. Sean toyed with his knife and fork as he studied Summer's face.

"So, are we goin' t' sit here for the rest of the evenin' and refuse t' speak t' each other?"

"The only thing I'm interested in hearin' is how and why y' got mixed up with Roy Tennyson."

A fleeting, bitter smile turned up Sean's mouth. "There isn't one farmer in these hills t' whom he hasn't loaned money over the years. He holds the note on everythin' from sheep t' homes t' farmin' equipment. At any time, if he so chooses, he can demand repayment. Over the years, he set himself up as God t' these people, Summer. Then along came a group of independent men and women who were not about t' be manipulated by him. He tried subtly t' influence them, offerin' t' loan them money for their obvious needs, but they refused: they were very poor but extremely proud. Then came a few disgruntled farmers, m'self included, complaining about the Cockatoos buyin' up prime grazin' land along their runs, and suddenly Roy had an excuse for mischief. When a number of us voiced our concerns about his tactics, he came right back at us with the excuse that he was only helpin' his friends deal with an unpleasant matter that could eventually affect us all."

"If y' know all this, and it's true that y' don't approve, why won't y' help us go t' the authorities?"

"How do y' think the authorities got appointed t' their offices?" Relaxing in his chair, Sean regarded her closely. "I can't say that I'm not, t' some extent, t' blame for the trouble I've made for yer husband. But there's more t' our feud than meets the eye."

"I know about yer wife fallin' in love with Nicholas."

"Gossips have been at it again, eh?"

"Sean, I don't think for a minute that Nicholas was guilty of anythin' t' do with yer wife. I'm certain he didn't return her feelins in any way. I don't think he's capable o'. . ."

"O' what, lass?"

"Nothin'." She tried to dismiss her blunder with a shake of her head.

"He's not capable o' lovin' any woman? Is that what y' mean?" When she refused to respond, he gave her a faint smile. His green eyes grew slumberous, his face pensive. "If it's any consolation, darlin', I was a bit of a rouser before I met Colleen. I wasn't much for settlin' down and bouncin' bairns on m' knee. Then I met her and . . ." He shrugged. "I changed. But apparently not enough. I was so busy tryin' t' impress her with material things, I forgot—or never realized—that women should be made t' feel loved and needed and desired. I had all those emotions here"—he lightl; touched his heart—"but I was too damned proud t' say them. I'll be livin' the rest of m' life with that on m' conscience. And y' can bet that if I ever again meet a lass who I think I could come t' love as much as I loved Colleen, I won't hesitate in makin' her feel like the most cherished woman on the face o' this earth."

Summer gazed into his penetrating dark eyes and began to change her opinion of him. Then the waiter came for their order, and the subject was dropped.

Sean saw Summer to her room two hours later. He remained in the hallway until she stepped inside her dark room and shut the door. She leaned against it with her eyes closed as she waited to hear Sean's door close too. She opened her eyes, and was startled to discover her husband's dim form standing before the window, hands in pockets.

"Saints!" She pressed a hand to her heart. "Y' scared me out of m' wits. What are y' doin' standin' there in the dark?"

He did not respond, but turned slowly to face her.

Unable to see his features clearly, Summer asked, "Have y' been back long?"

"Long enough." His voice sounded deep, disturbed.

He'd removed his coat, which lay in a black heap on the floor. His cravat had been tossed near it. He stood facing her with his white shirt unbuttoned to the middle of his stomach, the right tail drooping beyond his hip while the left remained tucked into the waistband of his trousers.

"Where have you been?" he demanded, the query made all the more ominous by the dispassionate cadence of the words. Apprehension sent shivers down her spine, as did the image of him standing there in the shadows with the pale yellow light of the street gas lamps pouring over his broad shoulders.

He knew where she'd been. It occurred to her in that moment that he had no doubt gone looking for her when he found an empty room. He'd seen her with Sean and now he was going to try and catch her in a lie.

Raising her chin, she took a breath and replied, "I've been havin' dinner."

"Alone?"

"With Sean O'Connell."

He said nothing. He didn't move.

Summer walked toward the lantern with the intent of lighting it. She didn't like conversing with a shadow, especially one that was so seething with anger that she could feel the fury vibrating in the air around her. But Nicholas gracefully and swiftly blocked her path.

Towering over her, his hands still shoved deeply into his pockets, he said through his teeth, "Don't ever let me catch you with Sean O'Connell again, or—"

"Or what?" she demanded, fear, frustration, and her own vexation getting the better of her. "How dare y' come struttin' in here like some high and mighty god, dictatin' t' me what I can and can't do, especially in light o' what y've been up to. Will y' stand there and deny to me that y' weren't over at that pothouse drinkin' and whorin'?" Her clenched hands buried in the folds of her gown, she met his blazing look head-on. "Don't try and deny it, Mr. Esquire. Y' stink of ale and a whore's perfume, and by the looks of yer damned clothes, y've been in and out of 'em a time or two since y' left me in this hot, stinkin' room t' rot from hunger and boredom."

Her hurt and anger overwhelming her, she swung at his cheek with her hand. He caught it before she could strike him, and closed his fingers hard enough around her wrist that she gasped in pain. Then he jerked her up against his hard, sweating chest and twisted her arm behind her. His lips pulled back in a sneer.

"You're right, Irish. I went over to that alehouse with every intention of putting you out of my mind. I wanted to get drunk, and I wanted to get laid. I wanted to prove to myself that while you had bamboozled me into this marriage, I didn't give a damn about the vows I never took; I didn't give a damn about you." Burying his free hand in her hair and gripping her head fiercely so she couldn't turn away, he lowered his face over hers. "I could have had any one of those hussies. But something kept tapping me on the shoulder and whispering in my ear that you were out there waiting for me like a sweet, loyal little wife. And the drunker I got, the more clearly I realized that if I did that, I'd be no better than my parents."

He slowly backed her to the wall. His body pressed her against it as his long fingers closed firmly around her slender throat and gently squeezed. "Then do you know what happened?" he demanded in words that were little more than a husky whisper. "I began comparing the tarts to you. Everything about them disgusted me: the look of them, the smell of them, the taste of them. I kept telling myself that I'd prove to you that while I might be forced to go through with this charade of a marriage, I was never going to surrender my heart to you. Then I suddenly realized that it wasn't you I was trying to convince. It was me."

"What are y' tryin' t' say, Nicholas?"

"I came back to the hotel with all these confusing emotions clenched up in my gut like a fist. I felt ashamed that I'd left you shut up here. I wanted to make it up to you. And I found you wearing the dress I bought you, sitting down to dinner with the same man who beat my face in and tried to burn our station down.

"I wanted to kill you both. I stood here in the dark for two hours thinking how I could do it and get away with it. My mind kept rolling over these images of your returning to this room with your hair mussed and your mouth red from kissing him— your lovely face flushed the way it gets just after you've climaxed. Ah, God, I thought I'd go mad. If you had lied about being with him, I don't know what I might have done."

Slowly lowering one hand, he cupped it over her breast and squeezed, very gently, with trembling fingers. He brushed her temple with a kiss, lightly— so lightly—then touched his lips to her closed eyelids, her cheek, the corner of her mouth. She began to quiver. Not with fear or anger, or with the frustration that had driven her to want to slap his breathtaking face, but with an all-consuming desire that left her speechless.

"Then the moment you walked in, all thoughts of murder turned into this fever I get when I think of putting my body inside yours." His hand dragged up her skirt while his knees pressed her legs apart. She tried to shake her head. She really should refuse him. She'd been furious, after all, yet . . .

"I was a swine for leaving you here," he whispered. "I'm . . . sorry. I confess to not knowing the first thing about being a husband." He blew softly into her ear, and her knees weakened. "Perhaps it's time I tried harder, hmmm, Irish? Perhaps it's time I grew up and accepted my responsibilities. God, I don't want to hurt you . . . Please. Put your arms around me. I've wanted to make love to you all night."

How *could* she deny him? She now recognized the restlessness that had made her feel on edge throughout the day. She wanted him again. Badly.

Still, he didn't love her. He'd clearly admitted as much.

When he crushed his mouth to hers again, his face was wet and the heat of his chest was like a furnace burning into her breasts through her clothes. He dragged down her drawers, then fumbled with his breeches; they fell loosely down his hips, and his naked legs slid against her inner thighs, stretching them open even further.

Still he kept kissing her, as if he'd lost all control, his hands twisting into her hair, her clothes, running over her breasts and squeezing, releasing, then pushing down to her most intimate place and cupping her roughly in his palm. His fingers were doing startling things to her body that made her cry out.

She'd never imagined that being touched there by a man would feel so wicked and so wonderful.

He kissed her throat, her face, and pushed his tongue into her ear until she felt breathless and dizzy, until she swooned pliantly beneath his questing hands and urgent lips, turning as hot and fluid as that center of fierce wet heat between her legs that his fingers were exploring. "So lovely," came his murmured words, sounding drunk with passion as he buried his face in the curve of her throat. Then his hands were sliding under her buttocks and lifting her up, and suddenly he pushed deeply into her body in one swift, burning motion, slamming her against the wall while she flung her arms around his shoulders, her legs around his hips, and threw back her head, exalting in the rhythmic motion of his body moving against hers.

Again and again he drove into her, his breath coming in harsh gasps in her ear. "I like it hard and fast," he told her, driving and driving, until she began clawing at his back and whimpering his name as her body turned rigid and incapable of movement, and reality was a dwindling pinpoint of light flickering in her subconscious. She groaned with the spasmodic pleasure, then he tensed and threw back his head and squeezed closed his eyes, and deep inside she felt his body throb and burst and bathe her in a thick, wet heat.

They stood there, motionless, braced against the wall, their bodies cooling as they breathed heavily in the quiet. A door opened and closed somewhere down the corridor. A woman's light laughter sang out, and a baby wailed. Then silence descended again—an absence of sound so deep she thought for certain she could hear their hearts beating in the stillness.

When he slowly lowered her feet to the floor,

something primitive showed in his shadowed features, a possessiveness that burned like embers in his eyes.

"Y' do care for me. Why are y' so frightened of admittin' it?" she asked.

"Desiring someone and loving them aren't the same thing, Irish. Don't confuse the two."

Her eyes carefully searched his face, noted the strangely bleak tilt of his mouth that spoke more than words ever could. "Then if y' don't love me, let me go," she told him. "I'll find a man who will."

He laughed, and the sound was haunted.

"Over my dead body," he told her in a weary voice. "Over my dead body, Irish . . . and yours."

Chapter 16

The auction was over by noon. Nicholas's wool had brought two times the normal price, and it was with great pleasure and satisfaction that he, Frank, and Summer returned to Christchurch to purchase supplies for the next six months.

Summer assisted Nick and Frank in the purchase of kitchen staples: flour, sugar, salt, lard, salt beef, rice, and dried fruit. Frank selected fresh vegetables: radishes, turnips, cabbages. Summer pointed to a bin of earthy-smelling potatoes, and both Frank and Nick grabbed her by the arms and ushered her as far away from the spuds as they could get.

A large crate of English newspapers had just arrived in Christchurch. Nicholas laid down his coins for *Punch, The Field, Illustrateds,* and *Bailey's Sporting Magazine.* Frank shook his head. "Never could figure out why a man would want to read about what happened four months ago. Seems to me you'd only git homesick. 'Course, I never was one to read them sapsuckers. Seems they always want to dwell on the negative in life."

"And of course there is absolutely nothing negative in our lives," Nick replied sarcastically.

Grabbing up the pouch of fresh tobacco he'd just purchased, Frank grinned. "Not right this minute— not after makin' the profits we did on that wool this mornin'. I'm happier'n a—" His mouth snapped closed as the shop door opened and several burly men filled up the entryway. "Aw, heck," he mumbled. "Here comes trouble."

Having wandered to the far side of the plank-floored store, where she was admiring an array of freshly baked pork pies displayed beneath glass domes and imagining how wonderful they would taste with a bowl of peas, Summer looked around to discover Buzz Holland, the storekeeper, calmly but swiftly gathering up breakables from the countertops. Her gaze went to Nick, and saw his face go dark, his body tense.

The idle chatter of the shoppers fell to a dead silence as Roel Ormsbee and a half dozen of Tennyson's workers filed into the store. Nick glanced toward Frank, watched as he removed his pipe from his pocket and placed it on the countertop. The shoppers scattered, the women—all except Summer—scurrying for the exit. Tennyson's men positioned themselves throughout the room, legs spread and thumbs hooked over the waistbands of their trousers.

"Holland!" Roel yelled at the shopkeeper. "You must have something rotten in here. You done killed a hog and forgot to smoke it?"

"That ain't a rotting hog you smell, Roel," another joined in. "Can't you recognize the stench? That's a Cockatoo. Nothing stinks up a place worse than one of them worthless land-grabbers."

Nick, having turned his back to them, proceeded to slowly fill a burlap sack with coffee beans—his senses alert for any sound or movement, knowing even as he did his best to ignore the sons of bitches that they weren't going to leave this store without spilling blood. "Summer," he said quietly.

She hurried to him, her eyes wide and her face pale. "Leave the store," he told her.

"Not unless y' come with me."

"There are supplies to buy."

"But—"

"But nothing. We can't leave Christchurch without the supplies."

"Well now, what have we got here?" Roel said, moving toward them.

"Looks to me like one of them DeSmythes," another of the troublemakers replied.

Roel smirked as he stopped a mere three feet from Nick. The man's face was still bruised from the beating Nicholas had given him the afternoon of the picnic. His front two teeth were missing. "Looks like you're right. You do know what a DeSmythe is, don't you, Cockatoo? It's genteel people of feeble intellect—"

"Who prefer a crust and a thin claret in a drawing room to roast and a pot of ale in the kitchen," one of the others joined in, then they all burst into rowdy laughter.

Nick shoved the spade into the coffee beans; he set down the burlap sack. "Get out," he commanded Summer softly and sternly. Still, she didn't move, just stood there with her gaze locked on him in stubborn determination, her cheeks suffused with high color and her chin tipped with an obstinacy that made him want to shake her.

Ormsbee moved up against him so closely that Nick could feel his breath on the back of his neck. "What's wrong, DeSmythe? Can't handle the little woman? Maybe you ain't man enough. I reckon that's the case by looking at you. I bet you even crook your little finger when you drink your tea and eat your crumpets. Ain't that right, boys?"

The others agreed.

"And look at this." Roel grabbed up the stack of papers and magazines Nick had put aside. "He even reads. Just where did you learn such appreciation for fine literature?"

"Cambridge University," Nick replied with a cold smile.

Roel's eyebrows went up. "Cambridge University. Do you hear that, boys? We got us a well-educated piece of Cockatoo trash here. Bet it really galls his balls to have to live alongside the rest of these peasants. 'Course, it's my understanding that they don't care much for residing so close to a convicted murderer." Flashing a smile, he added, "I can understand now why he'd be desperate enough to buy himself a mail-order wife; no respectable woman would have him. Is it true what everybody says? That Jamie MacFarland found her in some whorehouse in the East End?"

Nick moved so swiftly that Ormsbee had little time to respond to the sudden attack. Twisting his hands into Roel's shirtfront, Nick drove him backwards, scattering crates of onions and pumpkins that rolled over the floor in every direction. He slammed Roel against the wall hard enough to shake the windows—slammed him a second time, and a third, before several hands closed over his shoulders, dragging him back.

Then a gun blast rocked the room, and everyone froze.

Ben Beaconsfield and Sean O'Connell stood in the doorway, Sean pointing the rifle toward the ceiling while Ben stepped over the scattering of vegetables and made his way toward Nick. Roel, having righted himself, his momentary shock giving way to fury at having been bested by Nick, glared at Beaconsfield and shouted, "Get the hell out of here, Ben."

"Let him go," Ben told the men holding Nick. When they didn't budge, he yelled, "Sean, you have another bullet in that gun?"

The men reluctantly backed away.

Standing toe to toe with Ormsbee, Ben regarded him without blinking. "It's come to my attention that you and these men are going out of your way to give the rest of us, those who don't wish to be associated with this sort of trouble, a bad name."

"If you got a problem with it, Beaconsfield, then take it to Tennyson. I got a job to do."

"Your job is seeing to it that Tennyson's farm is run smoothly and efficiently. It is not burning farms or murdering dogs or beating up law-abiding families. Your behavior reflects on all of us, even those who have no quarrel with the Cockatoos, and there are more than a few of us who have grown weary of it."

Roel's eyes cut to Sean, who remained by the door. "So it would seem," he said.

"Now get out of this store and allow these people to get on with their shopping."

Ormsbee adjusted his shirt and, nodding to his companions, moved toward the exit, pausing only long enough to look hard into Sean's face. "Mr. Tennyson is going to be real interested in hearing about this, O'Connell." Sean said nothing, and Roel glanced around, his swollen lips pulled back in a sneer as he addressed his companions one last time. "Seems Sabre has found something *new* to do with his sheep, boys."

"What's that, Squealer?" another of the trouble-makers replied.

"Raise 'em for wool instead of screwin'." Roel guffawed at the off-color joke, then left the store, followed by the others.

Ben looked at Nick. "Are you all right?" he asked.

Nick nodded. "I could've handled him, Ben."

Ben slid his hands in his pockets, glancing at Summer as she moved to Nick's side. "Of course you could have. I was only thinking about Frank." He flashed a smile toward the old man, who was busily packing his pipe and acting as if the last five minutes had never happened. Raising his voice slightly, Ben said, "I fear Wells is getting too old for a fracas."

"The day I'm too old fer a good fight," Frank responded, "is the day they lay me in a grave and shovel dirt on my face."

Ben laughed.

Nick didn't. He turned to Summer, who had begun to retrieve the vegetables from the floor. Taking her arm and forcing her to stand, he directed her toward the door. "Frank and I will take care of this, Irish. Why don't you find Dora and have a nice cup of tea."

"But—"

"For once in your life, just do as I say without an argument." He pushed her out the door and slammed it behind her. Then he turned back to Sean. "If I ever see you with my wife again, I'll kill you."

They spent their last night in Christchurch in pleasant companionship with the Johnsons and Sharkeys. They picnicked down by the river The men pitched horseshoes while the women chatted among themselves about marriage, children, and their dreams for the future.

Nick and Summer didn't return to their room until well after sundown. They spent the next hours in passionate lovemaking, until they fell into an exhausted sleep, only to be awakened what seemed to be just moments later by Frank banging on the door and announcing that it was time to rise and shine. The sun would be up at any moment, and the wagon train would be pulling out. Nick shoved on his pants and stumbled for the door. Shaggy-haired, bleary-eyed, and badly in need of a shave, he stared down at his shepherd's grinning face.

"Mornin'," Frank greeted him, teeth clamped on his pipe. "I was jest sayin'—"

"I know what the hell you were saying. So does half of Christchurch."

"I knocked fer five minutes. I reckon ya didn't hear me."

"I reckon not."

"Fast asleep, were ya?"

"So it would seem."

"Must've had a late night." Frank peered around Nick and chuckled as Summer sat up in bed and rubbed her eyes. Then he winked at Nick, turned on his heel, and sauntered down the hallway.

Within the hour, Nick, Summer, and Frank had boarded their dray and joined the wagon train as it lined up at the edge of town. Poised on the wagon seat, half-listening to Frank and Nick's conversation about the upcoming lambing season, Summer gazed about the street, her eyes returning again and again to the white-frame schoolhouse surrounded by a picket fence and flower beds. A group of children were congregating in the schoolyard, surrounding a poorly dressed boy and girl who were clearly brother and sister.

"Squawk! Squawk!" a boy with rusty red hair exclaimed as he flapped his arms and kicked dust at the pair of children in the center of the circle. "Squawk! The bloody Cockatoos are roosting again where they ain't wanted!" The onlookers began laughing and mimicking their peers.

The boy threw down his books and leaped at the troublemaker. They tumbled to the ground in a flailing heap while the others converged on the fighting pair, whistling and shrieking their encouragement.

Summer leapt from the wagon and ran toward them.

"Summer!" Nick shouted behind her.

She shoved open the gate and plunged into the crowd, elbowing her way through the kicking and screaming children until she reached the scuffling boys. At last, she managed to drag back the copper-haired boy long enough to allow the other boy to scramble to his feet, fists doubled as blood ran from his nose.

"What's going on here?" came a deep voice from the schoolhouse.

Summer spat dirt from her mouth as she rounded on the schoolmaster, who looked at her down his thin, hooked nose from the schoolhouse door. "I might ask y' the same thing," she replied hotly. "Didn't y' hear this young devil screamin' at these poor children at the top o' his lungs?"

With a haughty quirk of one thin eyebrow, he demanded, "Who, I might ask, are you? And what business is it of yours?"

"It doesn't matter who I am. Anyone with any conscience wouldn't allow this sort o' behavior."

"These children have no right to be here."

"This is a school, isn't it?"

"Indeed."

"And they're school age, aren't they?"

"They are *Cockatoos*." He sniffed in disapproval.

She shoved her hat back on her head. "Damn, but they look just like children t' me. Furthermore—" Her mouth snapped shut as another man moved up beside the discomfited schoolmaster. With his thumbs hooked in his waistcoat, he regarded her with a pleasant, albeit condescending smile.

"What have we here?" he said.

The schoolmaster squared his shoulders. "It seems the Cockatoos have found a champion, Mr. Tennyson."

Tennyson! Of course, Summer thought. She should have recognized him immediately. She'd seen that cold ruthlessness before . . . in Lord Pimbersham's eyes.

"Young woman," he said in an authoritarian voice that sent shivers up her spine, "offspring of landgrabbers are not welcome in the company of our more illustrious and refined progeny. You see what sort of disturbance they've caused."

Summer glanced at the bloody-nosed youth, her heart squeezing miserably as the lad's eyes welled with tears. "I'll be beggin' yer pardon," she replied hotly, "but it was the illustrious and refined progeny with the red hair who started the fight."

"The Cockatoo children have no right to be here, madam. If you wish for them to be educated, I propose that you do it yourself . . . in the hills where you, and they, belong."

"It's m' understandin' that the Cockatoos have attempted t' do so, sir. Y' burned down their school."

The schoolmaster's face flushed, and Tennyson's features turned dark. Only then did Summer realize that an audience of adult onlookers had gathered behind her. The group of townspeople, farmers, and Cockatoos was watchful and grave.

"I don't know what you're talking about," Tennyson replied in a smooth voice. "I gave no such orders to burn down your school."

"Just like y' had nothin' t' do with divertin' that river so it would flood the Johnsons' place ever' time it rains." She was halfway up the walk to confront Tennyson nose to nose when an arm came out of nowhere to latch around her waist and lift her off her feet. Squirming, her hat sliding down over her brow, she shouted, "Put me down! I've got a few more choice words I'd like to impart before—"

"Be quiet," came Nick's calm voice in her ear.

"But these people have no right to treat innocent children this way. Discrimination such as this is reprehensible! I protest! Do y' hear that?" she yelled to the spectators. "I protest yer bigoted attitudes and yer small minds and yer unfeelin' hearts toward these innocent children!"

Nick kicked open the school gate, his arm locked firmly around Summer's waist while she continued to struggle. "There's not one man or woman among y' who's any better than the other! Y' came t' this bloody country t' get away from class distinction and because y' wanted an opportunity to make a better life for yerselves, and here y' are lordin' over a group o' people who haven't been so fortunate. Yer all a lot o' blasted hypocrites!"

She was squirming furiously by the time Nick plunked her unceremoniously onto the sidewalk. Summer looked around to find herself surrounded by somber-faced men and women who lowered their gazes when she met their look directly. "Aye," she said more softly. "I'd hang m' head in shame, too. Tonight, when yer lyin' in yer beds, remember what y' just saw in that schoolyard. You and yer schools are teachin' yer children more than readin' and writin'. Yer teachin' them t' hate their fellow man, t' cast aspersions on the less fortunate, t' turn a blind eye t' the needy. Those children will be adults sooner than y' know. What sort o' kind, just, and gentle country can grow out of a foundation o' hate?"

There was no response. She didn't expect any. She might have been whispering into the wind for all the effect her words had on the spectators. The crowd parted. Tennyson approached, his eyes slits of anger as he regarded her and Nicholas.

"Something wrong here?" came a voice behind them. With a sense of relief, Summer looked around to find Dan Johnson and Arnold Sharkey. Behind them, the Cockatoos' familiar faces came into focus as they took a protective stance around her and Nicholas. Grinning, Arnold added, "I don't know about you, Dan, but I'm in the right frame of mind today for a fight, if it's necessary."

"It won't be necessary," Nick said calmly as he stood facing Tennyson, his eyes burning down into the shorter man's.

"If I were you, Mr. Sabre," Tennyson said, "I'd keep the pretty little lady under lock and key. She could prove to be very, very dangerous to you."

Nick's dark face reflected little of the anger Summer sensed seething inside him. In a steady, yet menacing voice, he asked, "Are you threatening me in front of all these witnesses, Mr. Tennyson?"

"Certainly not." He laughed and glanced around at the watchful crowd. "My, my, aren't we a bit hasty to jump to conclusions today? Me? Threaten? Why, sir, you judge me too harshly."

Nick stepped toward Tennyson. "If your hooded bullies set one foot on my land again, Tennyson, I will personally put a bullet between your eyes."

A cry of surprise reverberated through those lined up behind Tennyson, while the growing number of Cockatoos forming a protective semicircle around Summer and Nick pressed closer, as if daring any one of the others to make even the slightest move of aggression.

Nick took Summer's arm and, turning away, propelled her through the tense, silent crowd back to Main Street. Before she could say a word, he planted his hands around her waist and effortlessly hoisted her up onto the wagon seat. Standing below her, his white shirt grown dingy with dirt and sweat, his hands on his hips, he stared up at her.

Summer raised her chin and glared back at him.

Nick ran one hand through his hair. "I'll be lucky if we aren't torched to the ground by tomorrow night. Christ, Summer, what the blazes did you think you were doing?"

"How can y' stand there and say that? How can the lot o' y' allow that bastard t' refuse yer children a decent education?"

Hefting himself up on the driver's seat, Nick shook his head. "In case you haven't noticed, Irish, we're outnumbered and we're unprotected."

"But it isn't right. Y' can't make children suffer for their parents' problems. I know what it feels like t' be looked on with scorn and prejudice, what it's like t' be denied an education. Those children in that schoolyard can't help that their parents are Cockatoos. And if the truth were known, I think most o' those spectators didn't approve o' Tennyson's actions either."

"But they were smart, sweetheart. They kept their mouths shut."

"Keepin' our mouths shut is not gonna end the dilemma," she responded furiously, her eyes blazing. "It's about time somebody did somethin' about it."

He narrowed his eyes. "I don't much like the sound of that."

Her cheeks still flushed with anger, Summer

looked away, and Nick grinned. He caught her chin lightly with the tip of his finger and turned her face to his. "I'm proud of what you did back there, Irish."

Her eyes widened and her stance relaxed slightly. "Y' are?"

He nodded.

Taking his arm and searching his features, she said, "We could change things, Nicholas. If we all worked together, I know we could come t' some sort of peaceful understandin'."

Nick glanced down at her hand on his arm, then up at her mouth. It was smiling now, making his heart do strange things in his chest. Yes, he was feeling pride at her interest in the children's welfare, but there were other feelings, too, and they left him more than a little disconcerted.

Frank climbed up on the wagon and plunked down beside Summer. Wedged between the two men, she looked back and forth between them as they continued to regard her with expressions of bemusement and fondness.

"What?" she said.

"Nothin'," Frank replied, reaching for the pipe in his pocket.

Nick took up the reins, and as the wagon ahead of them rolled underway, he gave the horses a slap across the rump and yelled, "Giddup!"

Summer glanced toward the schoolhouse one last time. The crowd had dispersed. The children had returned to class. She thought again of the Cockatoo children who were forced to go without education for lack of a proper schoolhouse and a teacher. It wasn't fair. There had to be some solution to the problem, and she would find it. After all, there would be her and Nicholas's children to think about, and . . .

All they needed was a building where the children could meet . . .

There were plenty of empty shepherd's shacks scattered across the hills. Any number of them could be renovated and used until something more substantial could be built . . .

The wagon train rolled out of town in a cloud of dust. At the head of the line were the Sharkeys, then the Johnsons, followed by the Meads, then the Thorndikes. Next came Nick and Summer and Frank, discussing their profits and what they hoped to accomplish in the coming year.

"I'll sew curtains for the windows!" Summer announced.

"Maybe it's time we broke down and bought a cow," Frank said. Then, grinning around the stem of his pipe, he added, "I 'spect we're gonna be needin' that milk before long . . . what with all them little Sabres runnin' wild all over the place."

Summer looked at Nick and saw color creep into his cheeks.

Nick looked at Summer and saw her rosebud lips turn up in a smile.

"Remind me to tell you sometime about that Mexican family in Misantla I knew what had twenty-two children," Frank began, as Nick steered the wagon toward home.

Chapter 17

June, three months later

Summer had spotted the shepherd's shack as she, Nicholas, and Frank were returning home from Christchurch three months before. After several weeks of deliberation, she'd decided it would make a fine schoolhouse, once it was repaired. It perched, uninhabited, just off the track near Weka Pass. The roof had fallen in long ago. The thick walls were made of cob: blocks of wet clay with chopped tussocks stamped in. Once, those walls had offered some resident coolness in the summer and warmth in the winter. Now, however, after years of deterioration, the hot wind had dried the clay and sections of the walls had been pulverized into dust. Standing there with broom in hand, Summer watched despairingly as the fine silt blew in clouds about the room.

"Don't look so glum," Dora said behind her. "The place is shaping up nicely. It takes time, you know."

Summer gazed up through the hole in the roof.

"Have you told Nicholas about the school yet?" Dora asked.

She shook her head. "He thinks I've been spendin' my days visitin' at yer houses."

"You'll have to tell him eventually," Nan remarked.

"Aye."

"Are you still worried that he won't approve of what we're doing?"

"It's not that he won't approve . . . he'll feel that it's dangerous. If the Clan learns about it, they might retaliate."

A moment of silence passed as the women regarded each other's concerned expressions. Not one of them could deny the possibility—the probability—of trouble from Tennyson when he learned of their attempt to build a new school. But change had to begin somewhere . . .

"Jeff Mead will have the desks finished soon," Nan said. "Then he'll start on the roof. Everything's right on schedule. Another month and we can begin classes."

"Summer?" Dora asked. "Are you all right?"

"You look a little pale," Nan added.

Noting their concerned expressions, Summer did her best to smile. It wasn't easy. The nausea she'd experienced during the last weeks wouldn't leave her alone. All she wanted was to find a dark, quiet corner, curl up, and sleep. "I'm a bit peckish," she said.

"Again?"

Dora and Nan looked at each other, their eyebrows raised.

"Yes, again," Summer replied testily. "What the blazes is wrong with that? One day yer scoldin' me because I'm too thin. The next yer quippin' me about being tired and havin' a big appetite." Tossing back the kitchen towel covering the basket of food they had brought with them, she dug for the nearly empty jar of *korako* marmelade, grabbed up a spoon, and proceeded to eat. Dora sat down beside her.

"Summer, forgive us if we seem overly concerned. It's just that you haven't been yourself the last few weeks. You seem so preoccupied. Is everything all right at home?"

"O' course." She scraped the bottom of the jar and licked the spoon. Searching the basket, she discovered the last peach-jam tart. "I suppose if y' call livin' in utter solitude all right." Staring at the tart, she felt tears start to rise. "Damn," she muttered.

"Oh, my," Nan whispered, going to her knees before Summer. "Something *is* wrong. Tell us what it is, dear. Perhaps we can help."

"I don't know."

"Is it Nicholas?"

She nodded and wiped her nose with the back of her hand.

"He's not mistreating you—"

"No." She shook her head and then nibbled at the tart. "Sometimes I'd settle for his mistreatin' me just so I'd know he knew I was alive. Anythin' but his blazin' long silences. Saints, but sometimes I think I'll go insane if I don't hear another human voice. I wander about the house all day waitin' for him t' come home from the hills and his bloody sheep, but all he does when he gets there is sit himself down and bury himself in his stupid books. If it wasn't for Frank, I'd be a ravin' lunatic by now."

"We warned you there would be loneliness," Dora said.

Shaking her head, Summer left her chair and looked out the open door. Thinking back over the last three months, she sighed. She and Nicholas had grown much closer; she'd ceased pressing him for declarations of affection and he had been tolerable to live with, though he continued to remain too often aloof. To occupy the long, lonely daylight hours, she worked her fingers to the bone learning to do the domestic chores around the house, and even went so far as to help occasionally with the farm tasks.

At times, she felt overwhelmed and frustrated by her inability to accomplish anything easily. Her cooking was getting better, but her bread continued to be a miserable failure. Her attempts to sew usually ended in catastrophe, and her one attempt to pickle eggs had ended up with the walls splattered with vinegar and with eggs that were cooked hard as rocks. Frank had tried to bite into one and declared, "Hell, darlin', I could knock a grizzly bar out from twenty paces with one these . . . they's good, though," he'd hurried to add, seeing her crestfallen face.

And Nicholas . . . would he ever come to love her?

She turned back to her friends. "I had higher expectations o' marriage. I thought it would be the sharin' o' two lives. But Nicholas continues to seclude himself from me. If it wasn't for . . ." She bit her lip and finished hesitantly, ". . . sex, I doubt he'd speak t' me at all. And I'm gettin' damn tired o' that as well."

Smiling, Nan replied cheerfully, "I imagine he's making up for all the years he went without it."

Summer frowned and Nan ducked her head, hiding her grin behind her hand. "It's not that I mind it," Summer said. "I quite look forward t' it. There's nothin' I enjoy more than provin' t' Nicholas how much I love him."

"So what's the problem?" Dora asked.

"The problem is, I thought—hoped—that our time together would mean somethin' to him by now.

He's no closer t' lovin' me now than he was three months ago. And while I once believed I could come t' accept that he doesn't care for me that way, I'm findin' more and more every day that I can't."

Dora took her hands. "Summer, are you so certain that he doesn't love you?"

"Why don't you ask him?" Nan suggested.

"I can't. I couldn't stand t' see that closed expression come on his face again."

"Perhaps he's trying to convey his feelings to you in the only way he can," Dora said. "In bed."

There came the sound of an approaching wagon. Summer, Nan, and Dora walked to the door and looked out. A buggy lumbered down the hill with two passengers.

"It's Clara Beaconsfield," Nan said. "What is she doing out here? And who is that with her?"

"I asked her t' come," Summer replied, noting her friends' surprised expressions. "The gentleman with her is the new minister from Christchurch, Reverend Martin."

"But I thought we decided not to tell anyone outside the Cockatoos about the school."

"We can trust Clara."

"I can't imagine why. She *is* one of *them*."

"That line between *us* and *them* is becomin' less and less distinct every day," Summer observed, and Dora agreed.

"Paul Hunter's wife dropped by my place last week. He's the farmer who lives just north of Tennyson's place, near Lake Coleridge. I met her with a rifle. It took me a while before I was convinced she wasn't up to something."

"What did she want?" Nan asked.

"Just to say hello, or so she claimed. I pointed out that we'd lived there for eight years and she'd never bothered to speak to me before, much less visit."

"And what did she say to that?"

" 'I'm sorry.' "

Clara waved, and after Reverend Martin brought the wagon to a stop, he helped her to the ground. The two of them moved toward the building, Clara's eyes watchful as she recognized Dora and Nan.

"Why have they come here?" Nan questioned again.

Licking peach jam from her fingers, Summer glanced back at her friends. "We need a school and we need a church." Motioning toward the handsome young clergyman, she said, "There's yer preacher. And there"—she smiled toward Clara—"is yer teacher."

It had grown late by the time Nick and Frank finished helping Billy Malone, who delivered wood or coal to stations in the hills, unload his bullock-driven dray of dry wood near the back door of the house. Nick's arms ached. His hands were swollen and bloody from blisters and splinters. After hauling wood all day from the government bush, he wanted nothing more than a hot bath, a big meal, and a warm bed.

"I reckon we got this wood in in the nick of time," Frank commented. He heaved the last log onto the cord of wood and thumbed back his hat, shaking his head. "It's gittin' downright frigid at night, what with winter jest around the corner."

"You want I should stay and ax this wood for you?" Malone asked.

"You've already cost me thirty shillings," Nick said. "Not to mention the license I had to purchase just to cut the wood out of the bush. Why should I want to spend another fortune to have you do what I can do myself?"

Flashing Nick an amused, albeit sarcastic, smile,

Malone shrugged. "We all got to make a livin', guv. Know what I mean? Besides, I smell mutton stew. Mutton stew happens to be my favorite."

"Then go home to your wife and let her fix you some."

Malone laughed and headed for the dray, giving Frank a tip of his hat before scrambling up on the wagon seat and taking off.

"Right nice guy," Frank said.

"He's a leech," Nick drawled, moving toward the house. "It's highway robbery what he charged us to dray in that wood from the bush. He should don a mask and ride about the countryside holding us up at gunpoint. I'd respect him more."

Frank chuckled. "Wait till you see the bill fer that coal comin' tomorrow. You *will* spit a hissy."

"I can't wait."

Shoving open the kitchen door, Nick stopped in surprise. Nan and Dora were sitting at the table, their faces concerned. A clergyman stood near the stove, looking somber in his black suit and white collar. A thousand reasons why they were here in his house whirled through his mind, but they all came back to one.

"Ah, Christ," Nick barely managed to whisper. "It's Summer, isn't it? Something's happened to my—"

"Nicholas!" Clara entered the kitchen, wiping her hands on a towel. "You're home," she said with relief.

"Has something happened to Summer?"

"We were out at the school—"

"The school?"

Clara glanced at Dora, then Nan. They all stared back at him with wide eyes, and shrugged.

"What school?" Nick demanded.

Laughing a little nervously, Clara waved the

query aside. "That's not the issue really. We were there . . . all of us . . ."

"She hadn't been feeling well," Dora joined in.

"She was pale all day," Nan added.

"Anyway," Clara said, "we were all about to depart for home when she became dizzy. The next thing we knew, she had fainted right there on the floor."

Nick frowned. "Where is she?"

"She's lying down. She's awake now, but—"

He moved past her. She tried to stop him. "She's not feeling very well and her spirits aren't good. She's just a tad bit weepy. Perhaps you should—"

Shoving open the bedroom door, Nick found Summer curled up on the bed. Her face appeared white, her eyes glassy and sunken and ringed with dark shadows. Raising her head slightly, she blinked at him and said with a vehemence that took him aback, "Get the blazes out o' here."

"Are you ill?" he asked.

"What if I am? What do y' care, Mr. Sabre, Esquire? If I died dead as a bleedin' mackerel right now, y'd probably shout with joy."

Nick looked around at Clara, who stood slightly behind him. "She's just a wee bit testy," she said.

"I'd say that was a severe understatement, madam."

"I want t' be left alone," Summer demanded. "Get out and close the door. If I throw up again, I'll have m' damned privacy in doin' it, thank y' very much."

He stood there, speechless, searching for any possible reason for her fury toward him. They'd spent last night in the throes of passionate lovemaking. He'd been up and gone to the bush before daylight, careful not to wake her . . .

"I said t' get out!" she yelled.

He narrowed his eyes. "No."

She glared back him, her eyes like round purple saucers. Only then did he notice her disheveled appearance. Her face and dress were dirt-smudged, her hair tangled. "What the hell is wrong with you? What have you been doing?"

"Oh, so he's suddenly interested in how I spend m' bloody days." She swung her feet off the bed and stood up. "Well, maybe I don't want t' talk about it. How d' y' like them apples, sir?"

"I don't think I care for it a bit, Irish. You're my wife and I have every right to know what you've been up to and why you're acting this way."

Stopping before him, her hands buried in the folds of her skirt, she threw back her head and stared up at him. "Maybe I don't want t' talk. Maybe I just want t' close m' self in this blazin' room and be left alone. Maybe then y'll know what it feels like t' want the companionship o' the one y' love, but be met with little more than a perfunctory greetin' or occasional small talk about stupid, stinkin' sheep. Oh, but I do beg yer pardon, Mr. Esquire. How silly o' me to ferget. Y' don't love me, do y'? Y' don't care that I'm unhappy or unwell. If I was t' die right now, the only thing about me y'd miss would be our tumbles in that bed. Well, I'm tellin' y' here and now I'm puttin' an end t' that, Mr. Sabre, Esquire. I can learn t' *un*love y' as easily as I came t' love y', if it means preservin' my dignity and pride. So y' can take yer sheep and yer dog and yer self-imposed isolation, and y' can stick it where the sun don't shine. I'm leavin' y', Nicholas, and nothin' y' can say or do is goin' t' stop me."

Stepping around him, she headed for the front door. Nicholas remained where she'd left him, legs spread slightly as he stared at the floor between his feet, feeling his scraped and bruised hands throb, and his heart beat erratically in his chest. "Summer?" he called, gently at first. Then, hearing the door open, he pivoted on his boot heel and yelled more frantically, "Summer!"

She stopped, poised on the threshold, then turned slowly toward him. Her face white and her lips bloodless, she regarded him through glassy eyes, then slid silently to the floor.

"Summer!" Clara cried.

Nick leapt toward his wife and caught her up in his arms, breathing hard in fear as he hugged her close and hurried her back to the bed. What the *hell* was wrong with her?

Smoothing the hair back from her face, he lay her head on the pillow. "Summer," he beseeched her. "Summer, for the love of God, sweetheart, what's happened to you?"

Her eyelids fluttered. One big tear slid from the corner of her eye. "Seems I can't do anythin' right. Even leave y'."

"You wouldn't leave me," he said in a fierce voice, hoarse with feeling. "I wouldn't allow it."

Her throat constricted, and the anger melted from her eyes. Across the ridges and hollows of his face, she ran her hand, allowing her love for him to show in each tender caress. "I'm sorry I said those things. I . . . don't know what got into me. Y' can't help it if y' don't find me at all lovable."

"That's not true. I've never known another woman who was worthier of being loved."

"Then why can't y'?"

Clara joined them. She placed a damp cloth on Summer's forehead and offered her a drink of water.

"What's wrong with her?" he asked.

Smiling, Clara set the cup aside. "Oh, I don't think it's anything to be overly concerned about."

Moving up behind Clara, Nan peered over her shoulder, her dark eyes twinkling. Then came Dora, squeezing Summer's hand. "Congratulations, Mr. and Mrs. Sabre. I'm fairly certain you're going to be parents."

The words dropped, one by one, into the stunned silence of the room. His hand buried in Summer's hair seemed frozen. She gazed up at him, every muscle in her body tensed as she awaited his response. Bending nearer, Dora repeated:

"You're going to have a baby, Summer."

"A baby," she whispered aloud, and suddenly almost laughed at her failure to realize it before— she, who had helped Martha deliver scores of babies. Having babies was one thing she did know about, yet she'd misread all her own symptoms.

"Perhaps they would like to be alone," came Reverend Martin's voice from somewhere behind them, bringing Nicholas's mind out of his temporary shock. Little by little reality pressed in, and for the first time since he'd confronted Summer he wondered what these people were all doing in his home. And what was all this talk about a school?

"You're right," Dora replied. "I should be getting home or Dan will be worried. Summer, I suggest that you stay in bed for the next few days. You certainly don't need to be down at the . . . ." Her gaze went to Nick. "The nausea will pass soon, and you'll be right as rain. We'll talk more then."

Nan agreed, and joined Dora and the reverend as they filed out of the house. Leaving Summer momentarily, Nick caught Dora's arm as she hurried down the porch steps.

"I want to know what the hell is going on," he said.

Smiling nervously, Dora shrugged. "You're going to be a father. Congrat—"

"That's not what I mean and you know it."

"You should talk to Summer."

"Summer is in no shape to talk."

"It's nothing, Mr. Sabre. Really. Some of us decided to get together and rebuild the schoolhouse, that's all."

"Did Summer instigate this?"

Dora nodded. "Don't be angry with her. She wants very much to help the children. She's lonely, you know, and the school gives her something to occupy her time."

"It's dangerous."

"Three months ago I might have agreed with you. But we both know that there hasn't been any Clan trouble since the auction. More and more of the farmers are beginning to realize that Tennyson is in the wrong, and they're just as eager to establish some sort of regulated education for their own children. The old Yonkers place isn't much, but it'll suffice once Jeff Mead restores the roof. And Clara is going to teach. Ben Beaconsfield is one of the most powerful men on the South Island. I think even Tennyson would have second thoughts about causing him trouble."

Smiling, Dora placed a compassionate hand on Nick's arm. "Your concern for Summer's welfare is understandable, and, may I say, very touching. If you would only show her one fraction of the caring I see in your eyes right now, she'd have no doubts but that you love her."

He looked toward the horizon where the setting sun sent streaks of blood-red light into the mists veiling the mountain peaks.

As Dora headed toward her wagon, Clara's voice came from behind him. He turned to find her poised on the bottom step, her face serious.

"You *are* happy about the baby, aren't you, Nicholas?"

Roughly he combed back his hair with his fingers.

A baby. For God's sake, he was going to be a father. Why had the eventuality never occurred to him? If he'd stopped to consider that possibility, he might have acted more prudently—perhaps taken some precautions.

"My God, you're *not* pleased, are you?" Clara demanded, her tone wavering between anger and incredulity.

"I don't know what I feel at the moment," he replied honestly.

"Well, I do. I see it written all over that handsome, stubborn face. You're thinking that you don't need another responsibility, that it's enough to take care of yourself and this station without adding another burden."

"Perhaps you judge me a trifle too harshly," he replied mildly. "I never said I wasn't happy about it—or won't be happy once the shock has worn off."

"Well, make sure it wears off quickly!"

Clara left him standing there with his hands on his hips, and hurried to where Reverend Martin was waiting for her by the wagon. Only after she had boarded and the minister had directed the horses down the track did Nicholas turn back to the house.

Summer stood at the window peering out at him. He could tell by the look on her face that she had heard every word he'd just exchanged with Clara.

She dissolved back into the darkness of the house like a specter. Mounting the steps, Nick entered and closed the door behind him.

Frank moved about the kitchen, whistling some jaunty tune, rattling dishes, scraping utensils. "I declare," he said in a loud voice, "I thank Clara's outdone herself with this here stew. Y'all come on and git it while it's still pipin' hot."

Nick walked to the parlor door. Summer sat on the settee, her back to him, her small hands clenched in her lap. "Come to supper," he said.

She didn't move.

"I imagine you'll feel better if you eat something."

Her head snapped around. "So now yer the expert on pregnant women. Tell me, Mr. Sabre, have y' been through this before? Will this child be yer first, or are there other little dark-haired Sabres raisin' hell across England?"

A grin touched his lips, but just barely. Sliding his hands into his pockets, he shrugged. "None that I'm aware of."

"But yer not discountin' the possibility."

Frowning, he thought of admitting, *No, Irish, I'm not.* Truth was, sometimes he'd wondered if, somewhere out there, there had been a child, possibly a boy, born into this world with Nicholas Sabre's eyes and rakehell temperament.

"Well?" Summer demanded, bringing his mind back to the present, his gaze to her wide eyes. "Are y' discountin' the possibility or what?"

"There are no other children," he replied.

She stared at him as if she wanted desperately to believe him.

"I swear it," he said.

Frank appeared at the kitchen door, his face unusually animated, his faded eyes a-twinkle. "I said to come and eat. The stew's growin' cold."

At last, Summer left the settee, stood for a moment as if she were balancing on the pitching deck of a ship, then moved with her usual grace past Nicholas to the kitchen. It was reflex that made him reach out to stop her. With his fingers wrapped about her arm, he gazed down on the top of her head. "Look at me," he demanded.

She did, with hurt eyes.

"Just give me a while to get used to the idea," he told her. "After all, I was just getting accustomed to spending the rest of my life with you."

"Didn't it ever occur t' y' that this would happen eventually?"

"I suppose I didn't think about it one way or another." He watched the familiar anger wash over her features. She was wounded beyond measure, he could tell. "What I mean is, I hadn't considered it happening this soon."

With a small sigh, Summer moved to where Frank was still waiting. Taking her arm gently, he led her to the table.

"Hot damn, if this ain't the best news I've heard in a coon's age."

She smiled at him wanly.

Hurrying to fetch her a bowl of stew, he chuckled. "I always did have a soft spot in my heart for young'uns. Never figured I'd see any of 'em pidder-paddin' 'round here, though. Here, darlin', let me git ya a glass of water. How about a chunk of this here bread? Once ya git some of this stick-to-the-ribs food in yore belly, yore gonna feel fine. Ya got to remember that yore eatin' fer two now, so don't be shy about askin' for another bowl. Hell, I'll git that cow squeezed after supper and ya can enjoy yoreself a nice big glass o' milk. I understand expectin' women is suppose to drink lots of it."

Nick took a chair and Frank plunked the steaming stew down in front him before taking his own seat. "This is a momentous occasion," Frank declared, his weathered face beaming. "I thank we should take a moment out to thank our heavenly father for blessin' our lives with this wonderful event. The two of ya bow yore heads. I said to bow yore heads! No need lookin' at me as if I was a two-headed sidewinder. I may look like a saddle tramp, but I'm a God-fearin' man who ain't too big fer his britches to stop on occasion and offer a word or two of praise and appreciation, 'specially when He's gone out of His way to do a man or woman a good turn. I said to bow yore heads.

"Good. Our Father who art in heaven, thank Ya fer blessin' these two people with a baby. After all, there are other couples out there who would like nothin' more than to experience the thrill of bringin' a child into this world. Clara and Ben Beaconsfield, fer one. I'm sure that right now, sweet little Clara is wishin' that she could change places with Summer and wonderin' why she was destined to be barren. She might even weep a tear or two over it. But it ain't our place to question Yore motives, Lord. No sir. I reckon Ya've got yore reasons fer blessing Summer and Nick with this greatest gift Ya can give a man and woman, and if'n they don't seem right grateful now, just give 'em a minute or two. They may be pigheaded, but they ain't stupid, and once they git used to the idea, they're gonna be goin' to their knees and praisin' Ya too. Once they realize that bringin' a new life into this world will give 'em a chance to rectify old mistakes—wash 'em clean and begin anew—they're gonna be more than eager to build on the future instead of wastin' time dwellin' on the past, which can't be changed anyhow.

"Thank you agin, Lord. And amen."

Chapter 18

Nick immediately began constructing the nursery. Within a month he had drawn up the
plans, had sent Frank into Christchurch for the building materials, and had started building the small
room. Within a few days more, he and Frank had
most of the walls erected and were laying the floor.

The hammering awakened Summer for the fifth
morning in a row. Lying in bed and staring at the
ceiling, she allowed a smile to tug up her mouth.
She wanted to hug herself. She wanted to dance on
her tiptoes and kiss the stars. Saints, but never
would she have imagined that Nicholas would find
such pleasure in the prospect of becoming a parent.
He talked for hours about his dreams for their children: how his sons would one day own the grandest
sheep farm in New Zealand. Perhaps he and Summer would send the boys back to England for their
education—of course they would attend Cambridge, although Oxford wasn't out of the question.

Once, she discovered him writing out a long list

of names and they debated throughout the afternoon over which ones might be acceptable. There was Michael, Philip, Neil, Bradley, and William. When they couldn't decide on one, he shrugged, and with a roguish grin suggested that they have as many sons as they had names. Laughing, Summer reminded him that he'd once told her children should be produced in moderation.

"What if we have nothin' but girls?" she'd asked.

After a long moment's consideration he'd pinned her with his black eyes and said, "As long as they're as beautiful as their mother, I'll be pleased." Her heart had soared.

This transformation of Sabre's character seemed a miracle, although the changes hadn't taken place overnight. She was certain he wasn't even totally aware of them himself, and she was cautious in bringing them to his attention. Instead, she noted the changes with quiet glee, occasionally sharing a smile or wink with Frank when they each acknowledged the subtle differences in Nick's behavior.

Tossing back the bedcovers, Summer slid her feet to the cold floor and walked to the window. Nick and Frank, bundled warmly in their fleece-lined coats, were discussing the new addition to the house. It was little more than a ten-by-ten cubicle with walls that were, at present, nothing more than a skeletal configuration of timbers rising up from foundation joists. The joists rested on rough-hewn stones placed on the ground six or eight feet apart to keep the flooring from touching the ground.

Nick saw her at the window. Summer waved. He grinned, tossed down his hammer, and headed for the kitchen door.

She ran to meet him, stopping short as he filled up the threshold, all long legs, broad shoulders, and riotous black hair that made him look savage. There was no savagery in his dark eyes, however—not anymore.

"What are you doing running around without shoes?" he demanded as he slid out of his cumbersome coat. "You'll catch cold."

She glanced down at her toes, barely visible beneath the hem of her gown.

"How are you feeling?" he asked, dragging back a chair from the table and motioning for her to sit down. She stubbornly refused.

"I'm fine. I've been fine for some time."

"Frank's prepared you a pot of porridge."

She wrinkled her nose. "I'll have a cold potato instead."

"If you keep eating those damn things, our baby is going to be born with two dozen eyes scattered all over his body." He plunked the bowl of porridge in front of her. "Eat."

He poured himself a cup of coffee while, outside, the sound of hammering commenced again.

"So how is the buildin' comin' along?" she asked, nudging the bowl away.

He nudged it back. "Fine."

"At this rate y'll be finished before long . . . and just in the nick of time, I'd say. After all, it's only another five months before the babe is born."

Offering her a smile, Nick relaxed in his chair and wrapped his long fingers around his coffee cup. "It pays to be prepared. Besides, we're headed into deepest winter. Eventually the weather may prohibit us from working."

Summer glanced toward the window where the pale morning sun was just beginning to creep through the curtains. "Winters back in England were never like this."

"We'll feel it most in July." Finishing his coffee, Nick shoved his cup away and stood, reaching for his coat. Summer followed him into their bedroom, where she looked out the window and watched Frank hammer two lengths of wood together. Nicholas studied the wall.

"We'll cut the door out here," he told her.

"That's a good place for a door," she assured him in all seriousness, causing him to raise one eyebrow and regard her with feigned aggravation. He moved up behind her and wrapped his arms around her. His big hands caressed her rounding belly.

"When the walls are finished, I'm going to paint pictures on them."

"Pictures o' what?" she asked.

"Sheep."

Summer groaned, and, tipping back her head, she saw that he was smiling.

"I saw a tapestry in Christchurch that would look very nice in the nursery," he said. "I thought we could hang it on the north wall. I recall that my boyhood room had a great many tapestries on the wall."

"I imagine yer boyhood room was somewhat bigger than this."

"You could have put our entire house in my room. The ceilings were fifteen feet high and there were fireplaces at each end. The room was never cold . . . not like the rest of the house. The dining room was always the coldest. The table was large enough to seat twenty-six comfortably, so you can imagine what it was like when only four of us sat down to eat. My father sat at one end, my mother at the other. Christopher and I sat at the middle, on opposite sides, facing each other. We weren't allowed to speak during the meal unless it was on some topic of utmost importance. I hated mealtime because I always got a stomachache. I suppose because I detested seeing my mother and father ignore the other's existence . . . and ours. Chris and I devised silent codes and signals so that we could communicate . . ." His voice drifted off; his eyes were distant, his expression pensive.

"Chris is five years older than me," he said quietly. "So naturally, he left home long before I did. We each went to boarding school, although I wasn't so compliant about being sent away. By the time I was ten I had been expelled from three different schools. Eventually, my parents kept me home and hired tutors. I lived for the days when Chris came home, and dreaded the days when he left again. When he came home from university, which wasn't often, I begged him to take me with him when he returned to school. I became angrier and angrier each time he left me. Then my mother left too and . . .

"Anyway, the last I heard of my brother, which was just before I was shipped here, he was traveling to America to invest in some property near Boston. Seems he wasn't happy about the way my father washed his hands of me so completely."

His arms closed more tightly around her. Closing his eyes, he kissed the top of her head. "The idea of failing as a father frightens me."

"Y' won't," she said. "I know it in m' heart. Y' won't make the mistakes that he did."

He smiled into her hair. "I'm happy about the baby. He'll be the foundation on which we can both build our future and bury our pasts. God, I get euphoric just thinking about it."

They each laughed and clung to each other as sunlight spilled through the window onto their shoulders. Finally, reluctantly, Nick eased her away and turned for the door, announcing, "Frank and I are driving over to Windwhistle Bluff to check on the sheep. We should be back by mid-afternoon."

"I'll hurry and dress."

He paused at the doorway. "Why?"

"Y' can drop me off at the school." Watching his face go dark, Summer said, "I'm not stayin' away today."

"What the devil is so special about today?"

"We have three new students startin'. The Rinehold triplets. That makes an even half dozen pupils attendin' now who aren't Cockatoos. Before y' know it, the whole o' Malvern Hills will be traipsin' t' our school. I think it's a very encouragin' sign that problems are on the mend between the Cockatoos and farmers. Don't y'?"

"It's three miles to the school. I don't think it's a good idea for you to be riding that distance."

Summer smoothed her gown down over her rounding tummy. It felt especially warm, and she thought, though she couldn't be certain, that she had experienced a first flutter of movement inside the night before. A familiar and potent emotion stole through her as she thought of sharing the news with her husband tonight as she lay in his arms. "He's safe and snug as a bedbug," she assured him.

"He?" he asked softly.

"Aye," she replied, watching that little-boy's smile steal over Nick's features. "I'm hopin' for a boy who looks just like his father."

"And I had in mind a girl who looks just like her mother."

"Perhaps it'll be twins."

Nick flashed her a smile. "Good God, perhaps I should add on *another* room."

Laughing, Summer ran to him. He slid his arms around her waist and pulled her up against him so that the soft curves of her body molded against his.

"I'll miss you today," he confessed.

Filled with longing, she surrounded him with her

arms and held him, closing her eyes while she absorbed his presence and delighted in this fragile new intimacy between them. The immensity of her hope made her tremble, made her want to bury her face against his chest and weep out her adoration for him and his child growing inside her. Slowly but surely she was winning Sabre, Esquire, over by allowing him to come to grips with his circumstances and his emotions in his own way.

She would continue to be patient.

"Children! Children, please! Jason Johnson, sit at your desk immediately or I shall be forced to report your behavior to your mother. Class, come to order this moment!"

Clara threw a forlorn look toward Summer, who sat at the rear of the room, a slate balanced on her knees as she narrowed her eyes in silent reproach at the Johnson boys, who were pulling the girls' pigtails then diving beneath their desks to a chorus of angry squeals and foot-stomping. The children were obviously in no mood for school, and despite Clara's pleas for order in the class, showed no signs of letting up in their attempts to disrupt the proceedings.

"I give up," Clara cried. Throwing down her lesson book, she dropped into a chair and shook her head at the rowdy children.

Summer set her slate and chalk aside, and moved to the door. Her shoulders felt tense. It wasn't easy to concentrate on her lessons while trying to help Clara keep the children in line. The effort was giving her a headache.

Opening the door a fraction of an inch, she studied the hills surrounding the school. A sharp wind kissed her face, but though frost had blanketed the hills just hours before, the sun had shone so brightly that the film of ice glistening on the yellowing grass had disappeared completely. The sky was a dazzling blue.

Looking back at Clara, Summer nodded and opened the door. With a look of relief, Clara clapped her hands and said, "You are dismissed for recess, children."

With whoops of delight, the dozen girls and boys leapt from their chairs and stormed the door.

"They seem to be a little high-strung today," Clara said.

"They're not accustomed t' sittin' still for so long." Summer rubbed her own backside. "We'll get used t' it."

Clara stood in the doorway and watched the children scatter across the flat in a game of tag. "I certainly hope I'm doing the right thing, Summer. You know how Ben feels about not getting involved in this farmer-Cockatoo feud."

"Yer not involved in the feud. Yer teachin' innocent children how t' read and write. Besides, it's been months since there's been any trouble."

Her arms crossed over her breasts, Clara glanced at Summer and smiled. "I must admit, you've helped these people enormously. Ben and I are most impressed."

"I've not done so much."

"Poppycock. You organized the families—convinced them to allow their children to come here each day. You opened your own home for church services once a month, even convincing the new reverend to include Malvern Hills in his baptizing circuit. Aside from all that, you convinced me to get involved."

"Only by pointin' out that y' wouldn't want yer own children t' be discriminated against."

"What does Nicky think about all this?"

Summer frowned and focused harder on the playing children. "He'd rather that I wasn't involved.
He's become so protective since we learned about
the baby."

"He's thrilled about the child," Clara assured her.

"Yes, he is. I only wish..." Summer glanced
wistfully at her friend. "I wish it was his love for
me that had brought about this change in him. I
have an awful fear that once the baby is born, I'm
gonna have t' get in line behind him or her, Nick's
dog, his sheep, and his farm." Attempting to change
the subject, Summer reached into her pocket and
withdrew a folded piece of paper. She handed it to
Clara, who read it silently to herself, and nodded.

"Your penmanship is improving every day, Summer. Your spelling is perfect. When do you intend
to mail the letter?"

"When I feel the time is right."

"And you still don't intend to tell Nick?"

"No."

"Because you fear he'll be upset or refuse to allow
you to do it?"

"We don't discuss his father. Besides, there's Nicholas's pride t' deal with."

"But you believe that Chesterfield will read the
letter if it comes from someone other than Nick."

"I hope so."

"You must care a great deal for Nicky's happiness.
I wonder if he realizes what a treasure he's found
in you. And when will you mail it?"

"I'm not certain." Summer carefully folded the
letter and slid it back into her pocket. "Maybe never.
Maybe tomorrow. It depends on Nicholas, I suppose."

"Personally I think it's a wonderful idea, Summer.
Nicky is hurting deeply over his father's refusal to
forgive him. If your letter could somehow bring the

two of them together again, I'm certain Nicholas would at last be able to bury his past completely." Clara flashed her an encouraging smile, then, stepping from the schoolhouse, called for the children, who let out a collective groan as they fell in line and trooped back to the weathered shack for another hour of lessons before their parents showed up to take them home. Normally, the parents wouldn't take the time from their chores to cart the children to and from school. But no one was willing to risk the chance that the Clan would attack them; Roel Ormsbee and Virgil McIlhenny had already proven that they had no qualms about riding down helpless children.

School ended by three o'clock. By three-thirty all the children had departed, leaving Clara and Summer alone to tidy up the room. "Why don't y' go on home before it gets dark?" Summer suggested. "I have to wait for Nicholas t' come for me."

Clara looked reluctant. "I'll stay. I don't think it's wise for you to be here alone."

"I'll be fine. Besides, I have the gun in case there's trouble."

Clara finally agreed, and by four o'clock Summer was alone in the small house, righting the desks Jeffrey Mead had provided, picking up chalk bits and sweeping fine white dust from the floor with a tussock broom. Nick was late, and as the hour progressed, she found herself walking repeatedly to the door and staring out at the horizon. It wasn't like him to be this tardy. Usually he arrived at the school to pick her up before the last child had left for the day.

Saints, where was he? Surely he hadn't forgotten her . . .

Don't be absurd, she told herself. Nicholas had become fanatical about her welfare during the last months. He wouldn't allow her to go so far as to fetch a bucket of water for fear she would somehow strain herself and hurt the baby. The day she'd driven to Dora's and arrived home half an hour late, he'd been on the verge of panic. For the next hour she'd been forced to sit on the settee while he pointed out the dangers of roaming the Malvern Hills alone in the country's present state of unrest, and reminded her that in her condition she shouldn't take any unnecessary risks that might harm the baby.

She checked the coal in the hob to make certain there would be plenty for the next morning. Then she peeked inside the basket in which she had brought her lunch to school. There were several stale pieces of bread and part of a tart left. If Nicholas didn't show up soon, she'd be forced to eat the scraps for supper. She was starving and—

The door opened behind her.

Summer spun around, her smile of relief dying the instant the hooded figure filled the threshold. She stared at him dumbly before a stomach-churning fear swept over her.

Her mouth dry and her heart racing, she stumbled back against the desk as the man moved through the shadows, stopping at the verge of the lamp's glow. His eyes were mere slits in the black mask as he regarded her in silence.

Summer glanced toward the door, and the rifle resting there against the wall. Soft, menacing laughter sounded from within the shoulder-length hood. Then the man whispered, "You're a foolish young woman, Mrs. Sabre. You should know by now that your sort of meddling isn't appreciated here."

She pressed back against the desk. "Y' can murder me in cold blood," she managed, "but these children will be educated whether Roy Tennyson likes it or not."

"Murder isn't our way, Mrs. Sabre. You should know that by now. I'm here only to warn you that there are those of us who feel you should keep your nose out of our business . . . or else pay the consequences. You wouldn't want to see your husband's station burned again . . . or your husband hurt in any way."

Raising her chin with a determination she didn't feel, she replied, "Well, I must be makin' progress if Mr. Tennyson feels he has t' send his bullies out t' threaten a woman. I suppose ridin' down children playin' in a meadow didn't bring him enough satisfaction."

His hand lashed out so quickly, she had no time to respond. The impact across her cheek sent her spiraling backward onto the desk. She lay stunned for a moment, pain like a spear in her temple. There was a taste of blood on her tongue. Still, the pain brought her little terror compared to what she felt as she focused on the black-hooded figure. He reached for her with his big, black-gloved hands, twisted his fingers into her blouse, and pulled her roughly to her feet.

She flailed at him as he dragged her out of the schoolhouse. She clawed at his hood, his chest, and beat at his shoulders. He hurled her to the ground, where she lay sprawled on her back, her gaze locked on his mask as he stood over her, legs spread, shoulders shaking with laughter.

Suddenly there was movement all around her. At least a half dozen men, all wearing hoods, materialized out of the darkness, one carrying a can of kerosene, another a burning torch.

"Stop!" she cried, as the man began splashing the liquid over the walls of the school, then disappeared inside where he doused the floors and furniture. Summer scrambled to her feet, only to find her way blocked by the man who had dragged from the school. Desperate to save the schoolhouse, she fought the giant as best she could, knowing, even as the flames licked high into the night sky, that there was no way to stop the destruction. Furious, she struck the Clansman and dug her fingernails into the side of his neck. With a howl of rage, he brought his fist down across her jaw, and the world exploded in pain. Again he struck her, and again. As she felt herself drifting into unconsciousness, she heard someone yell:

"Let's get the hell out of here!"

Then there was blackness.

In frustration, Nick released the mare's forefoot and watched as the animal timidly touched it to the ground. One look at the pus leaking from the cleft of the hoof confirmed what he'd most feared.

"Thrush," came Frank's voice. "She ain't helpin' to pull this dad-blamed wagon no further tonight."

Nick cursed under his breath. The day had been fraught with difficulties: first they'd had problems with a wheel, then they'd become stuck in the mud down at Waimakiriri River. They'd discovered five sheep had tumbled over the precipice of Windwhistle Bluff, and now this . . . Bitter cold had set in, and another half a mile down the track Summer was waiting.

As always, she'd been on his mind throughout the day. The last weeks he'd found himself studying her closely for changes as they went about their daily routines. After those first weeks of nausea, there had been no more sickness, and few signs of weight gain, aside from the gentle rounding of her lower belly and the slight swelling of her breasts. During the long nights, he would lie in bed, feeling her soft curves pressed against him as she slept, and imagine what she would look like with her body swollen with his child. The rush of pride always made him breathless. Then, as swiftly, the fears would rush over him with fiery discomfort. She was so small, a child herself really—dear God, what if she died in childbirth? There had been moments in those early weeks when, out of fear, he had prayed hard that she wasn't pregnant after all; he would much rather spend the rest of his life childless than risk losing her altogether.

Perhaps he'd become a trifle too protective of her. She became cross with him, though he attributed her moodiness to her condition. Sometimes he found her weeping quietly into her pillow. Without her knowing, he would stand there with his hands clenched, denying the need to wrap her in his arms and ask what was wrong. Part of him believed the tears stemmed from the same old problem: his inability to admit his feelings for her. But there was another fear, a deeper dread that was only now beginning to worm its way to the surface: maybe she was unhappy with him and her circumstances. Maybe the idea of bringing a child into their poverty-stricken lives didn't appeal to her.

She'd made no bones about the fact that she found the solitude difficult to tolerate. Not that she was the only "mail-order" bride who experienced those feelings. Word reached them every now and again about some of the other brides up and leaving their husbands because they couldn't stand the isolation and hardship.

Christ, but he couldn't begin to consider what his life would be like without her.

"I reckon we're gonna have to unhitch these horses," Frank commented. "This old mare has hobbled jest about as fer as she can on that foot."

Nick nodded and Frank commenced unfettering the tired horses. That was when Nick glanced toward the horizon and saw the red-orange glow against the night sky.

Fire!

A moment passed before confusion and realization turned to gut-cold fear. He struggled for composure—his thoughts scrambling for some logical reason why the black of the sky should be obliterated by firelight.

He walked calmly to the horses and proceeded to help Frank unharness them. His fingers, numb with cold, grabbed ineffectually at the straps and buckles; he became incensed as the cold leather responded stubbornly to his yanks and tugs.

"Dammit!" he swore, bringing Frank's head up and his gaze toward the horizon. Frank said nothing as his eyes met Nick's and locked there in mutual fear and understanding.

At last, the harnesses peeled away. Nick grabbed the rifle from the wagon, swiftly checked the weapon to make certain it was loaded, then threw his leg up and over the uninjured animal's back. Digging his heels into the horse's flanks, he spurred the surprised beast up the track as the frigid wind blistered his face and brought the first telltale hint of smoke to his nostrils. Brighter and brighter the fiery light grew, until the stars were washed away by the gyrating, frenzied glare of flames stretching high into the night.

Reaching the top of the rise, the horse shied, reared and whinnied as the wind-whipped ashes scattered like tiny torches over the dry grass. Here and there over the hillside small blazes had caught hold, the conflagration spreading like fingers over the land. Amid it all the flaming ruins of the schoolhouse leaned precariously close to complete collapse.

"Summer!" Nick shouted, then drove his boots into the skittish horse again, forcing the animal down the hillside, into the smoke and around the flames licking at the animal's fetlocks.

He found Summer lying near a patch of yellowed tussock that was only just beginning to smolder. Nick hit the ground running and skidded to his knees beside her. She lay face-down in the dirt. It took all of his restraint not to grab her. As gently as possible he rolled her over and into his arms.

He closed his eyes as fear and pain drove like battering rams into his chest.

"She's dead," he cried hoarsely. "Oh, my God, she's dead!"

He couldn't move, just rocked on his knees and clutched her to his chest, his hands buried in her hair. Then Frank appeared through the smoke, panting from his sprint over the hill, his old face tense but his manner composed, as if he had faced similar disasters many times in his life. He calmly went to one knee and pressed his fingertips to Summer's neck.

"She ain't dead," he said breathlessly. "She's got a strong pulse. I reckon she's jest unconscious and in shock."

At that moment Ben drove his wagon through the smoke and flames. Several of his workmen leapt from the back and began working frantically to put out the fire. Ben jumped to the ground and ran for Nick and Summer.

"We were on our way home from Sean's place when we saw the fire," he shouted. "What—"

"They've killed her," Nick yelled. "Those bastards have killed my wife!"

Frank glanced at Ben, whose face had turned

white at Nick's words. "She ain't dead, Ben, but she's hurt bad. We got to git her home quick."

"We'll take my wagon. I'll drop you off at your place, then I'll go home for Clara."

As Nick rose with Summer in his arms, the schoolhouse let out a groan and collapsed, spraying the night sky with fiery embers.

Nicholas had been denounced as insane many times in his life. Never had he felt so close to insanity as he did that night.

Ben poured him a fresh cup of coffee and set it on the table before him. His hands buried in his hair, Nick stared down into the black liquid and blinked the steam from his eyes.

"Perhaps you should try and get some rest," Ben said. "Maybe lie down on the settee and sleep a while. It may be a long night."

"What the hell is taking so long?" Nick left his chair, moved to the parlor, and poured himself a drink. Ben walked up behind him. "That's not going to help, Nick."

"It sure as hell won't hurt." He tossed back the liquor and poured another.

Ben placed a compassionate hand on his shoulder. "She isn't going to die."

"You don't know that."

"I'm no doctor, but the injuries didn't seem to be internal."

Nick briefly, wearily, closed his eyes.

Ben regarded Nick sternly. "If you're thinking about blaming yourself for this, don't."

"If I hadn't ridden out to Windwhistle Bluff—"

"Your going about your business in a normal fashion had nothing to do with what happened."

Turning his dark eyes on Ben, Nick said in a cold, hard voice, "Don't stand there and preach patience and tolerance to me. They beat her and they left her there to die, to burn right along with that school-house. They hurt my wife, and possibly my child. They're going to pay dearly for this, Ben."

"Nicholas?" It was Clara, standing at the door, her hands clasped against her stomach. "Summer's awake. She's asking for you."

He stared down into her pale face. "Did they rape her?" His throat felt tight with dread.

"No."

Relief left him breathless, but as he turned for the bedroom door, Clara stopped him with a hand on his arm.

"I fear she's losing the baby, Nicky. It's only a matter of time, I think. There's been a great deal of bleeding."

His knees grew weak. The ability to speak seemed a monumental effort. "Does she know?"

"She suspects. The contractions are becoming stronger."

"Oh, God."

Ben moved up beside him but said nothing, just slid his arm around Nick's shoulders, offering him support as Nick sank against the wall. "Would you like another drink?" Ben asked.

Nick shook his head.

They stood there for a moment longer, until Nick found the strength to stand upright. He shrugged away Ben's help, then ran one hand through his hair.

Moving to the bedroom door, he paused, forcing a composure he didn't feel. He'd just been informed that his child might be dying.

Summer's head turned and she regarded him with glassy eyes. The dim yellow light from the lantern on the bedside table made her look jaundiced.

Nick moved to the bed and took the hand she

extended to him. He kissed it, turned his face into it, and nuzzled it with his mouth.

Summer smiled weakly. "I s'pose I look a fright."

He shook his head and swallowed hard. "A little bumped and bruised is all. Do you know who did this to you?"

"They wore hoods." Pain washed over her features, and she grabbed his hand. "I . . . meant t' tell y' this mornin' . . . I felt the babe move. He was like a butterfly inside me all day. I don't feel anythin' now, Nicholas. I—" Her eyes closed and her hand squeezed his with a fierceness that made him flinch. "The contractions are stronger. It's only a matter o' time before . . ." She began to weep. "Our baby is dead, Nicholas."

"Don't—"

"It's dead. I helped enough women through miscarriages when I lived with Martha to know what's happenin'."

Suddenly overwhelmed with pain, Summer groaned loudly. Clara ran to the bed and tried to get Nick to leave.

He shoved her away. "Get your goddamn hands off me and do something to help her!"

"Please, Nicky, there's nothing that can be done to save the child—"

He turned on Clara viciously, took hold of her shoulders in a punishing grip and shook her. "You do something to help them, Clara, or—"

"Nick!" Ben and Frank grabbed his arms. "Let her go, boy," Frank demanded.

"Please, Nick," Ben said. "You're hurting her . . . Please."

Gradually, he released his grip on Clara. But as his friends attempted to nudge him toward the door, he refused, pushing them aside and returning to the bed as Summer cried out again. This time Ben locked his arms around Nick, and both he and Frank struggled to remove Nick from the room as he fought and swore and threatened to kill them if they allowed Summer to die.

Finally, Clara managed to close the bedroom door and locked it. He slammed his fist against it, lacerating his knuckles. He didn't notice, just hit it again and still again until the pain obliterated his anger and he sank against the door. He slid to the floor and buried his face in his bloody hands.

Hours ticked by, Summer's occasional weeping the only sound to interrupt the silence. His back against the door, Nick stared up at the ceiling, thinking: *Please, God, please. I'm asking you to save my wife and baby. Don't take them away from me. Don't use them to make me pay for the sins of my past, I beg you.*

At last, he managed to force himself to his feet. His head pounded and his hands throbbed. He tried to flex his fingers, but the pain in his knuckles wouldn't allow it. He walked to the kitchen, where Ben looked up expectantly at him from his seat at the table. Frank's face was like old parchment as he smoked his pipe and stared off into space. Nick moved out the back door and into the bracingly cold night air, stood with his head thrown back and his face turned toward the stars as he continued to pray.

Betsy entered the halo of light and lay down at his feet, placed her muzzle on his foot and thumped the ground with her tail. Eternal minutes ticked by, the air growing colder and the sky darker, as the wind scattered clouds across the stars.

Nick sensed rather than heard Clara move up behind him. He held his breath as she said in a tight voice, "It's over. I'm sorry, Nicky. There was simply nothing we could do to save the baby."

He closed his eyes and rocked on his heels, the

pain in his chest too fierce. "Wh-what about Summer?"

"She'll be weak for a while, and it's imperative that she remain in bed. But she'll be fine in a few weeks. She'll need all the support you can give her, Nicky, so whatever you do, don't turn away from her now. She needs you too badly."

Then she left Nick alone. His body shaking in rage, he turned his face to the sky again, and said through clenched teeth, "Damn you."

Chapter 19

The hell-bent-for-leather ride across the misty paddocks did little to clear Nick's inebriated head . . . or calm the fury he'd tried to contain since finding his wife beaten and left for dead near the burning schoolhouse just hours before. By the time he reined up his panting, sweating mount at Sean O'Connell's house, the brandy and anger had become a fire inside him.

With the gun in his hand, he kicked open Sean's door. Sitting before a blazing fire in the hearth, a bottle in one hand, a glass in the other, the Irishman looked up, his face only briefly registering surprise as Nick filled up the threshold.

Nick covered the distance between them in three long strides. He grabbed hold of Sean's shirt collar and yanked him to his feet, drove him back, and slammed him against the wall hard enough to send glass knickknacks tumbling onto the floor. With his forearm thrust against Sean's throat, Nick shoved the gun barrel hard into his cheek and said through gritted teeth:

"Were you involved with the attack on the school-house?"

Sean tried to swallow. "Y' never struck me as a particularly stupid man, Sabre."

"Answer me, damn it!" He slammed Sean against the wall again.

"Detestable perhaps, but not stupid. Y' ignorant ass, o' course I didn't do it. I would never hurt Summer."

"But I wager you know who did."

Sean's green eyes bore into his, but he didn't respond.

"Who did Tennyson send down to that school-house to beat up my wife? Tell me or I'll blow your brains out." He cocked the gun hammer and pressed the barrel harder into Sean's cheek. "They beat her, O'Connell, and they murdered our baby," he said in a soft, pain-filled voice. "I intend to get even."

Sean's face drained of color. He briefly closed his eyes. "They didn't go there with the intention of hurtin' anyone. They went there t' burn the school." Sean laughed, a dry sound that fell short of humor. "Go ahead and kill me, because if y' don't they will, if I give y' their names. Tennyson has already made m' life hell. I owe him money and he's demandin' payment... in full because I helped Ben stop Ormsbee from pummelin' y' black and blue in Christchurch."

"Just why *did* you help?"

"I did it for Summer. She doesn't deserve the likes o' you, but she doesn't deserve bein' a widow either. Which is what she'll become if y' think y' can take on Tennyson alone."

"That's my decision to make."

"If y' want to die that badly, why don't y' just go on and put the damned gun t' yer own head?"

They stood there face to face without speaking. Finally, Nick backed away, releasing the pressure on the gun hammer as he relaxed. Sean straightened his collar with a shrug of his broad shoulders, then he poured whisky into the glass he still gripped in one hand. He walked to his chair before the hearth and dropped into it.

"It's amazin' what a woman can do t' our lives, isn't it, Sabre?" Sean tossed back the drink and poured another. "Men have conquered continents since the beginnin' o' time. We've constructed coliseums that stand for hundreds o' years. We've invented cures for diseases and built machines that can move across the countryside propelled by steam instead of horses. Hell, we'll probably fly through the air someday. Perhaps even travel t' the moon. Yet we're continually driven t' our goddamn knees by a pretty face and an innocent smile. 'Course, it's been that way since the beginnin', hasn't it? I often wonder where Adam might've ended up had Eve not tempted him with that bloody piece of fruit. If she'd just learned to mind her own damned business, we'd all be livin' in paradise by now. Would y' like a drink, yer lordship? Come on, come on, by the smell o' yer breath I wager y' already popped a wee bit before workin' yerself into enough of a froth t' come beatin' in m' door."

Sean walked a bit unsteadily into the kitchen and returned with another glass, which he proceeded to fill with whisky as he dropped back into his chair. He held the glass out to Nick.

Nick stared down at him without moving.

Sean returned his stare without blinking. Finally, he said, "I'm offerin' y' a drink. I ain't offerin' y' m' hand in friendship. And if y' don't drink it, I will."

At last, Nick reluctantly accepted it.

Sean settled back in his chair and ran his finger

around and around the rim of his glass as he gazed into the fire. "I'm sorry about the babe," he said. "I can understand yer anger. Now, can y' understand mine?" Without looking at Nick, Sean shook his head. "Y' love someone and then some outside force comes in and strips them from y'—"

"I had nothing to do with Colleen—"

"I know that." Sean's voice was husky. He drank his liquor, squeezed closed his eyes, and shuddered. "I know that," he repeated more quietly. "That's what made her feelins for y' all the more difficult to accept. I couldn't believe that a woman could fall for someone who had not in some way returned her affections. But I'm beginnin' t' understand, I think. Y' see somethin' y' admire in someone. Y' fall in love with 'em. They don't love y' back . . . Merciful Mary, it's enough t' make a man or woman a ravin' lunatic." He drew in a soft breath and recited,

"I told m' love, I told m' love, I told her all m' heart,
Tremblin', cold, in ghastly fears,
Ah! she did depart.
Soon after she was gone from me,
A traveler came by,
Silently, invisibly: He took her with a sigh."

Turning his gaze up to Nick, he said, "Percy Bysshe Shelley, I think."

Nick shook his head. "'*Love's Secret*' by William Blake."

"Whoever. The poor bugger got the royal shaft. There should be a club for people like us. The lovers and losers club. No women allowed unless they're ugly enough t' stop an eight-day clock." Motioning toward a nearby chair, he offered, "Why don't y' sit down and we'll discuss the problem o' Roy Tennyson like two slightly irrational drunks? Besides, it's too damn cold out there t' be ridin' all over creation killin' people."

"Are you going to tell me who beat up my wife?"

"I might eventually get drunk enough t' do just that."

"I might get drunk enough to shoot you if you don't."

Slouching in his chair, Sean poured himself another drink. "Sabre, there are names for men like you. I'm too much of a gentleman to repeat 'em, though."

"I've never met an Irishman yet who was a gentleman."

Sean drank his whisky. "I'm truly sorry about Summer and the babe," he repeated. "Had I the means to help—"

"Just give me the names of the bastards who did it, Sean."

"So y' can go and get yerself killed? I wouldn't be doin' Summer any favors, now would I? Besides . . ." He put aside his glass and looked Nick in the eye. "Y' can't do it alone. First y' have t' get yerself some vigilantes and hit the Clan one by one." Elbows on his knees, Sean offered Nick a drunken smile. "The trick is t' destroy 'em without killin' 'em. Y' hit 'em when they least expect it, just like they did the Cockatoos."

"Who are they?"

"Ormsbee. McIlhenny. A couple o' new hands Tennyson has recently hired. Names are Ralph Gilstrap and Howard Goetz."

Nick moved toward the door. Sean rose quickly and blocked his path. "Think about what yer doin', Sabre. Y' killed a man once and y've lived t' regret it ever' day since. Y've lost the babe, but y've still got Summer; there will be other children . . . but not if yer dead or put away in prison."

Sean was right and Nick knew it. Little by little, as his intense anger and grief drained from him and he was able to think coherently, he realized that, once again, he had come very close to losing control.

"Go home to yer wife," Sean said. "We'll deal with this problem once we've had some sleep."

"We?" Nick asked.

"Aye." Sean smiled and offered his hand. "We."

For the third evening in a row, Summer slid from the bed and walked to the back door where she looked out over the paddocks and up the hill. The mist almost obscured the small white cross where Nicholas had buried the babe a week ago. She could just make out Nick's tall form standing near it. She hadn't yet made the walk up to the grave. Nicholas wouldn't allow it until she was stronger. So he went himself every day, sometimes for a few minutes, occasionally to linger much longer.

She was losing him again. He was slipping farther away every day, becoming remote, withdrawn, uncommunicative.

And he frightened her sometimes.

He drank more. Late in the night, when he thought she was asleep, he would leave their bed and pace the floor. She would hear the quiet clink of his whisky bottle against the glass, and hours later, usually just before dawn, he would fall back into bed, stinking of liquor.

There was a mounting anger inside him, a fever of fury that was evident in the tautness of his body and the maddened flash of his black eyes. Her disquietude was heightened by the offhand comments he made about revenge, of making the bastards who'd beaten her and murdered their child pay for their crimes. But what troubled her most was that his feelings were shared by many of the other Cockatoo husbands and fathers.

Several times during the last days Dan and Arnie and others had met with Nicholas down by the wool shed. Then Nicholas had taken to leaving the house well after dark and not returning until nearly daylight. Dora and Nan had come to Summer with the same story about their own husbands, and they were growing worried. Summer sensed trouble. It charged the air like lightning.

Summer awoke deep in the night, her body shaking with the nightmares that had haunted her sleep since the attack. Her face was wet; she'd been crying again as she relived the moment the hooded brute had set upon her with his fists. Almost every minute of every day since then she'd been burdened with the question: What if she hadn't fought them? Then perhaps they wouldn't have retaliated with such violence. But the dominant thought in her weary mind was: *Had I only stayed home like Nicholas had wanted me t', I'd be pregnant still and we'd be happy. He'd be buildin' the nursery instead of allowin' those half-constructed walls t' remain as a stark, ugly reminder that our dreams have been incinerated along with the schoolhouse.*

Were the same thoughts plaguing Nicholas? Was he blaming her for their loss? Oh, God, would he ever forgive her for destroying the only thing that had brought him happiness during these last miserable years of his life?

Swept with a dizzying desperation, she reached out for Nicholas—the first time she had done so since the miscarriage. His side of the bed was empty.

Struggling to sit up, she focused on the light spilling from under the closed door. Leaving the bed, she tiptoed toward the door, opening it a fraction

of an inch and peeking out into the hallway to discover Nicholas dragging on his coat.

She was struck by the shocking change in his appearance. How could she have been so blind to it?
His hair appeared abnormally shaggy, as if he
hadn't taken a brush to it in days. The jet-black beard
stubble on his unshaven face accentuated the gaunt-
ness of his features. The clothes he wore, normally
so fastidiously neat and clean, looked as if he had
slept in them.

He must have sensed her there, or perhaps she
made some noise. Suddenly his dark eyes found
her, pinned her with an emotionless stare that made
Summer's gaze blur and the pain wash over her
again, the wrenching grief of what might have been
. . . and would now never be.

"What are y' doin'?" she asked, trying to keep
the desperation from her voice.

"Going out."

"Where? It's after midnight."

"I need some air."

Without another word, he turned for the door.
That was when she noticed the gun tucked into the
waistband of his breeches. She ran after him and
threw herself against him. "Don't," she pleaded.
"I'm beggin' y', Nicholas, don't start trouble. It
won't accomplish anythin', and it won't bring our
baby back!"

His black eyes burned her with anger. "I had
dreams, Summer. For the first time in years I allowed myself to look forward to the future. I allowed
myself to hope, to imagine the bleak despair of my
life obliterated by sunlight. I felt like a man con-
demned to the dank guts of a dark prison who had
suddenly been given his freedom. But just as I was
about to take that step into the light, the steel door

was slammed in my face again. I want to crush the bastards who did that."

"They didn't know I was pregnant."

The sudden tautness of his jaw revealed his anger. Astonishment flickered in his eyes. Obviously, he could neither believe nor accept her ability to forgive their enemy's transgression. He turned on his heel and started toward the door. Desperately, she cried, "Nicholas! Please, don't do this."

"I'm going to drive Tennyson to his knees. I'm going to make every man who participated in the raid live to regret his idiocy."

Fear washed over her in waves. "Until I'm forced t' walk up that hill and visit two graves? What about *our* future? Yers and mine?" She grabbed his arm. "Please!"

"Get out of my way."

"I won't. I can't allow—" His fingers closed around her arms so tightly, the pain robbed her of breath. Then he shoved her away. Not hard, but with enough force that in her weakened condition she sprawled heavily on the floor. Stunned, she watched shock and self-disgust sweep his features; he made a tentative move toward her, then stopped, waged some internal war with himself that was apparently lost. Turning, he stormed from the house.

She thought of running after him, but what good would it do? Instead, Summer stared at the space he had occupied and felt the emptiness and disappointment swell like a tide all around her.

Roel "Squealer" Ormsbee had settled in the Malvern Hills in the mid-fifties. He'd chosen a prime section of land out near Hunter's Glen. He was close enough to the forest so that he could partake in his biweekly shooting spree of wild pigs . . . that is, he *had* been close enough until that damned Cockatoo family squatted on the run separating his property line and the forest. That was bad enough, but the frigging squatters had erected stone fences so he was unable to trespass, forcing him to ride ten miles out of his way when he wanted to kill a pig.

He scratched his crotch and spat a wad of tobacco on the kitchen floor. Heaving himself to his feet, he let go a fart and yelled, "Winifred, keep them damn young'uns quiet! Their caterwaulin' is enough to give a man indigestion!"

"I'm doin' all I can!" came his wife's reply.

"Well, that ain't enough. Shit," he mumbled. "Kids ain't nothin' but a pain in the butt. If it was all left up to me, I'd strap their behinds three times a day just on principle."

He hauled his immense girth to the back door and gazed out into the dark. The distant lights from the outbuildings twinkled intermittently behind the swirling mists. He could just make out the shadowed forms of the barn, shearing shed, and the workmen's huts, all badly in need of repair. With winter pressing down on them, the complaints would start soon: The huts are too damp. The huts are too cold. The huts are too dirty. The huts are too crowded. The workmen threatened to quit every winter. He'd forestall their desertion with promises of a raise, then not bother to come through. Especially not this year. The price his wool had brought at auction was pitifully low. The buyers had complained about the poor grade and sorry condition of the fleeces. Scabby, weak, filthy, thistle-ridden was what the buyers had called his wool. He hadn't made enough to break even, much less tide the station over for the next year.

It was the damned Cockatoos' fault . . .

Imagine pampering the stupid, woolly beasts like they were a lot of house cats. That hoity-toity jailbird

Sabre had spent one entire season clearing the matagouri thornbush from his paddocks because they nicked his sheep's hides, inviting infection. Imagine a man breaking his back for such a butt-dumb reason. Well, nobody was going to catch Roel Ormsbee going to those lengths. And if he had any say-so about it, Sabre and his lot of ignorant Cockatoo friends wouldn't either. No doubt about it, the time had come to put an end to the interlopers once and for all.

Smirking, he recalled the weeks the Clan had bided their time while the foolish Cockatoos went about rebuilding the schoolhouse. They'd purposefully allowed the squatters to become complacent in their belief that the Clan would allow their attempts to educate their snot-nosed young'uns. The Clan had intended on burning the hovel down long after everyone had gone home, not anticipating that Sabre's wife would still be there.

Roel scratched his belly, his face screwing into a frown as he recalled Virgil McIllhenny dragging the spitting, clawing Irish termagant out of the burning building and shoving her to the ground. How were they supposed to know she was carrying a brat inside her? If she got a little roughed-up, it was her own damned fault. She shouldn't have gone flying at Virgil like a horde of mad hornets.

Besides, it was probably just coincidence that she lost the baby soon after.

Tennyson hadn't been pleased when word had reached him of the debacle. His wife Blannie had overheard Tennyson's foreman telling him about the incident and had gotten pretty prickly over it. The biggest blowup came when word reached Roy and Blannie about the miscarriage.

Roy had anticipated some sort of retribution. None had come, of course. It never did. The Cockatoos were nothing but a lot of yellow-bellied milk-sops who continued to roll over and play dead when there was trouble. Followers of the faith, they called themselves. Peacemakers. God-fearing folk who'd rather turn the other cheek than strike a blow against their enemy.

What a bunch of bunk, he thought as he stifled a yawn and slammed the door against the night. He'd no more than made his way out of the kitchen, however, when a sudden explosion reverberated against the walls of the house and stopped him in his tracks. Winifred let out a scream and tore up the hallway, her nightgown flapping around thighs that looked like a bandy rooster's. Six bug-eyed children followed, all screeching loud enough to wake the dead.

Roel stumbled to the door and threw it open. His jaw dropped. The pork he'd eaten for supper rose halfway up his throat and smothered him soundless.

Flames licked up from the wool shed and danced against the night sky. If that wasn't enough, all ten of his station hands were grouped together, buck naked, just outside the shearing pens, shivering and gawking at the fire and doing absolutely nothing to put it out.

Woodenly, Roel staggered out into the night toward the roaring conflagration. "Water!" he yelled, growing more frantic as the men gaped dumbly at him. "Don't just stand there like a bunch of idiot sheep! My wool shed is burning! My—"

The words died. His feet froze so suddenly he almost fell.

The riders streamed out of the darkness, the firelight casting their hooded and black-robed figures in long, menacing shadows over the ground. They formed a circle around him, drove their nervous, high-stepping horses around and around him, coming closer and closer until Roel could feel the ground tremble under his feet and the light from their torches grew bright enough to hurt his eyes.

"What the devil are you doing?" he shouted. "If this is a joke, it ain't funny! Virgil, is that you? Howard? Ralph? Jesus H. Christ, what the hell are you doing burning my wool shed? Answer me, damn you!" Then his eyes widened.

"Oh, Lord! It's Roy, ain't it? I done gone and pissed him off about something. What'd I do? Somebody tell me what I did! Don't just ride around me looking like a bunch of demons from hell! It's enough to give a man a heart atta—"

A rider broke free of the circle. Roel stumbled back, clutching at air as the devil with fire for eyes lunged his horse toward him, brushing by him so closely that the tail of the man's cloak swept his face. The man's torch hissed and sputtered, and as he thrust the fire toward Roel, he let loose a squeal and dove toward the ground.

"Ormsbee," the hooded rider called in a menacing voice. "Get up and face your judgment like a man."

Peering out from under one armpit, he quailed. "Judgment for what?"

"Murder."

"Murder!" he shrieked. "I ain't ever killed nobody!"

"You're a murderer of dreams," someone else shouted.

"And of hope," another yelled.

"And of unborn children," a third voice joined in.

His eyes growing even larger in his fat face, his jaw going slack, he slowly turned his gaze up to the solitary figure looming like a black mountain above him. Realization slammed into him. "Oh, shit," he muttered. "I'm a dead man."

Suddenly several men broke free of the ring and rode toward the barn, whooping and waving their torches around their heads. "Not my barn!" Roel screamed. "Lord, don't burn my gosh-dang barn!"

Two more riders broke away and headed for the workmen's huts. Rolling to his knees, gripping his hands as if in prayer, Roel stared up at his persecutor. "Mr. Sabre, I didn't harm a hair on your pretty little wife's head. I swear it. I told them others they ought to be ashamed and—"

"Who beat her?"

"It—it was Virgil. I swear it on my dead mama's grave. None of the rest of us touched her."

With a roar, fire leapt high into the night sky, and the roof of the huts incinerated like old parchment. Covering his face with his hands, Roel howled in despair. "I ain't got no money to rebuild them sheds!"

"Y' might try raisin' pigs since y' have such an affinity for 'em," a familiar voice called out, and Roel spun around. He was about to yell *Sean O'Connell, you traitor, you're gonna regret the day you was born,* but the sight of more horsemen, and what they had roped and tied and were dragging behind them, made his mouth snap shut.

The maddened screeching of the wild pigs turned pandemonium to chaos. They kicked and bucked and wrestled against the ropes around their necks. Their sharp little hooves sprayed dirt clods into the air and their stench turned the air rancid.

A rider rode up to the house and wrenched open the door. Winifred Ormsbee, in her billowing white nightgown, shrilled at the top of her lungs, grabbed for her huddled children, and rushed them from the house while the men left their horses and proceeded to drag the grunting, squealing porkers inside, where they released them. Then four men slid from their mounts. Two grabbed hold of Roel's arms; two latched on to his legs. He gyrated and jerked and screeched as they hauled him to the house and, swinging him like a pendulum, heaved him over the threshold and into the midst of the frantic pigs, which were running amuck over the rooms, shattering glassware and carving up the floor with their hooves.

A hooded figure filled up the doorway and looked down on Roel, where he had slipped in a pool of pig urine.

"If you raise a hand against another Cockatoo family," the hooded man said, "we'll come back and burn down your house." Then he disappeared from the entryway.

Roel struggled to his hands and knees and crawled to the door just as the walls of his barn collapsed in on themselves, sending up a shower of blazing embers.

The riders, however, were gone.

Virgil McIlhenny had named his station Mesopotamia, or The Land Between Two Rivers, because he liked the sound of it. He thought it was aristocratic and exotic. It was good land, close enough to the forest so that he didn't have to pay that bloody pirate Billy Malone for hauling wood up to the station. He was near to the lignite pit, so fetching coal was no effort at all. With his hut perched atop the highest hill, he wasn't even forced to leave his house to gander at his sheep unless he wanted to. All he had to do was climb atop the corrugated roof and look out over his paddocks and watch his work hands and dogs do all the labor.

It made him feel like a king. And that was how men ought to feel: respected and revered by their underlings. A man like him shouldn't be forced to sit on his roof throughout the night, waiting and watching for a bunch of hooded marauders to come sweeping down on to him like devil-bats out of hell.

They'd hit Ormsbee two weeks ago. Howard Goetz's and Ralph Gilstrap's wool sheds and barns had been burned to the ground last week.

Rumor was that the lot of idiot Cockatoos were being led by Nicholas Sabre. Still other stories put Sean O'Connell in charge. Tennyson had about hit the roof when he heard. He'd sent his foreman over to O'Connell's to *discuss* the situation, to explain that Sean better come to his senses fast or live to regret it. But Roy's messenger had gotten only so far as Sean's property line when he'd been met by two dozen rifles and a threat of bodily harm if he ever returned.

No doubt about it, things were getting out of hand.

Who would have ever believed that the lot of lily-livered squatters would suddenly develop back-bones? All because the Clan had burned down that stupid school and roughed up Sabre's wife. Hell, what was a man supposed to do? She'd come flying at him like a banshee, kicking and clawing. Besides, a woman ought to learn her place.

Teeth chattering, Virgil rubbed his eyes and thought longingly of his bed, such as it was. It consisted of little more than a flimsy wooden frame and a tattered mattress. Shoot, he'd made do with a lot worse; when he'd first arrived in Malvern Hills, he and his wife had slept on a pile of rotting fleeces. Eventually Anabel had gotten fed up and demanded a bed. He'd dragged one home that he'd found in some deserted squatter's shack. Anabel had taken one look at it and left him.

There just wasn't no pleasing women.

Damn, but he was tired. He'd not spent a peaceful

night since the Ormsbee raid. He'd tried to talk Roy into launching a full-scale retaliation against the Cockatoos before they hit his station—wipe them from the face of the map once and for all. The problem was, there had been too many converts to the squatters' side of the fence. And since Ben Beaconsfield had taken a public stand against Tennyson's so-called tyranny, the Christchurch officials were more and more reluctant to look the other way.

Yawning, Virgil stretched out his legs and leaned back against the tin roof, blinked sleepily, and briefly considering climbing down and fetching his bottle of blackberry wine. He'd made it himself, and it sure could go a long way toward warming a man up when he was forced to sit outside all night and—

What was that noise?

Sitting up, grabbing his rifle, he strained hard to see into the dark.

Was that smoke he smelled?

Damn, but he was becoming a nervous wreck. Where there was smoke, there would have to be fire, and so far the night remained black as pitch.

Maybe if he was real lucky they would forget about him. Or maybe they'd gotten all that revenge out of their systems.

Besides, Sabre didn't know it was him who'd shoved his wife around.

Did he?

Surely the others wouldn't have been so dim-witted as to snitch on him.

Would they?

What the hell had that man been convicted of in England, anyway?

The rumor was . . . murder.

Oh, hell.

The house quivered beneath him. Virgil caught his breath and sweat rose to his brow. "It's the wind," he said aloud, staring off into the windless night. "Nobody would be crazy enough to—"

The timbers moaned and the tin shrieked, and suddenly the house was being pulled from under him. Virgil McIlhenny plummeted downward into the bowels of darkness.

Chapter 20

Dora and Nan stood side by side in Summer's kitchen, each craning her neck to peer out the window over the dry sink. Dressed in their Sunday best, their hair swept up and confined with combs to the tops of their heads, they looked as pretty as proverbial pictures. But they were spitting mad.

"Something has to be done to stop them," Dora said. "The violence has gotten out of hand."

"I've tried," Nan replied. "I've never seen Arnie so obsessed."

"Look at them. Here we are meeting for church services and they're out there huddled together like an army."

"Someone is going to get killed. If it's Arnie, I'll never speak to him again."

Dora and Nan turned in unison and looked at Summer where she sat at the table. "Well?" Dora asked. "Have you spoken with Nicholas?"

"He won't listen," Summer said wearily.

Frowning, Dora took the chair next to Summer's. "You poor dear. You've been through so much the last weeks; now here we are fretting over trouble that may or may not come to pass. We don't mean to burden you, but there seems to be no end to this new upheaval, and it only promises to get worse."

"Rumor is that Tennyson knows about the church services being held here today," Nan joined in.

"Lines are being drawn, Summer. These hills are being ripped down the middle, with Roy's followers on one side and ours on the other. It's no longer a matter of just the Cockatoos versus a few of the farmers. It's army against army, and your husband and Sean O'Connell are at the center of it."

"Ma!" Wayne Johnson shouted from the front door. "The preacher's comin'!"

"Perhaps Reverend Martin can talk some sense into them," Nan said.

"I suppose it won't hurt to try," Dora replied. Patting Summer's hand, she rose and hurried from the room, Nan in her wake.

Alone, Summer closed her eyes and listened to the hubbub of activity outside. The day had dawned crisp but clear and without the blustery winter winds that often howled over the Alps. The squeals and laughter of children rang like bells in the crystalline air. A woman's occasional laugh told Summer that despite the portent of doom that hung over them all, the friends who were spreading blankets and food over the ground were determined to make this day special. Makeshift tables had been placed around the garden, their white lace cloths laden with cold pies made of mutton and pigeon. Bowls piled high with hot potatoes had been placed alongside the pies, and buckets of milk stood ready to be dipped into by thirsty children.

The back door opened and Frank stepped in. His face brightened when he saw her.

"Now, ain't ya lookin' fit to meet Jesus on this Sunday mornin'?"

Summer glanced down at herself. She had on the blouse and mended skirt she'd worn the day she first showed up on Nick's doorstep. Ah, but that seemed a thousand lifetimes ago. She'd been a different person then, full up with hope and ambition, with spunk and fire.

"Yer a bloody awful liar," she told him.

"Looks like we're gonna have a nice turnout fer Reverend Martin. Or ain't ya had a look yet?"

She shook her head.

"Ya plan on sittin' there in that chair fer the remainder of the day or are ya gonna do some socializin'?'

"Anyone ever told y' that y' ask too many questions?"

His eyebrows shot up. "Well now. That's about the most life I've heard outta you in a long time. Sounds like music to my hairy ol' ears. Is it too much to hope that yore gonna rejoin the world of the livin' today?"

"I wasn't aware that I'd left it."

"Darlin'," he said, smiling, "you and me is too good friends to start lyin' to each other now."

"If we were good friends, y'd do somethin' t' stop Nicholas from gettin' himself killed."

"I got no control over the man. I never did. Only one person can help him, and that's you."

"I've tried."

"Well, it might do a hell of a lot of good if'n you two would start talkin' to one another agin. That's all I'm gonna say on the matter." With that, he plunked down his cup and left the room. Summer stared after him.

Frank was right, and she knew it. It was again time to try to make Nicholas see reason.

She confronted Nicholas as he was returning to the house with Dan and Arnold. Pausing to watch him stride up the pathway, she was struck anew by the picture of British gentility he made in his formal suit. A cream silk shirt gleamed beneath the black lapels of his coat. His boots were highly polished and his cravat impeccably tied. She could easily imagine him posed within some elegant drawing room, sipping sherry and sharing polite, civilized conversation with his peers.

His step slowed as he looked up and saw her, and the idea occurred to her that many days had passed since she'd last confronted him, be it in anger or joy. In that instant, one look into those smoldering black eyes was enough to breathe life into the gasping embers of hope and desire in her heart. Her lips melted into a smile.

"Nicholas," she ventured bravely, "I'd like t' speak t' y'."

Dan and Arnold moved past her, into the house.

Stopping at the foot of the steps, Nicholas stared up at her. She watched his curious appraisal take in her freshly brushed hair and the color she had pinched into her cheeks. "We have guests," he replied simply.

"They can wait. Revered Martin won't begin the service for another twenty minutes."

He took a step back. His hands slid into his pockets as she watched a curtain of caution draw over his features. Carefully descending the steps and taking hold of his arm, she turned him toward the pathway.

They didn't speak again until they had reached the tiny grave atop the hill. This was Summer's first visit here. Finding the moment more difficult than she had anticipated, she stood for a time with her back to her husband, her gaze sweeping the pan-

orama stretching endlessly before her. The golden
tussock reflected the winter light like softly undulating waves of pale butter. Sheep filed in their cus-
tomary manner in long, zigzagging lines across the
hills. It struck her in that instant just how much this
beautiful country had come to mean to her.

"Nicholas," she said without facing him, "I want
y' t' take a long hard look at that grave. Go on. Look
at it."

At last, she turned. His head was down; his ebony
hair fluttered over his suited shoulders. "Now look
at me," she demanded quietly.

His gaze came up.

"*I* didn't die," she told him.

The words appeared to jar him.

Searching his face, she asked, "Has it occurred t'
y' that there can be more children?" She moved to
him and hesitantly placed her hand on his chest. "I
love y' and I want t' spend the rest o' my life with
y'. I love y'," she repeated softly. "I love y'."

He touched her face briefly, gently, his emotions
showing at last on his face—the grief, the pain, the
disappointment, and . . . dare she believe it was
love?

She slid her arms around him. They stood there
on the top of the hill with the wind whipping around
them, and pressed their bodies together for the first
time in weeks.

"I'm sorry," he whispered in her ear.

By the time they returned to the house, they
found their guests in turmoil. The grounds were
scattered with families in an escalating state of
unease because it appeared that not only the Cockatoos had chosen to participate in Reverend Martin's
church services and baptisms. So had a dozen farm

families . . . many of whom had sided with Tennyson in the past.

Jeff Mead stood confronting a farmer named Jack
Simpson. "You got no right to be here," Jeff declared
in a raised voice.

"Right!" several Cockatoo men echoed.

"We got as much right as you!" the farmers cried.

"Strange words comin' from the men who've tried
their damnedest to run us out of these hills," Arnie
joined in.

"I had no part in all that," Jack proclaimed.

Dan calmly took a stance at Arnie's side. "You
might not have lit the match that burned one of our
barns, Simpson, but you turned a blind eye to it and
that makes you partly responsible."

Jack looked back at the others, his face uneasy.
He lowered his voice and admitted somewhat
sheepishly, "I never reckoned on things getting so
out of hand. Neither did them others." He pointed
a thumb over his shoulder at the group of watchful
farmers, and for the first time Summer saw the
women and children who huddled together in their
wagons, their features full of fear, hope . . .

Like many of the Cockatoo women, several farmer's wives clutched babies in their arms. The small
infants were wearing the flowing, frilly frocks that
were their christening gowns. Their round, pudgy-
cheeked faces were flushed by the sun. Wedged
beside them on the wagon seats were covered baskets of food. But it was the cargo piled high in the
rear that caught and held Summer's attention. There
was lumber and saws and hammers. Dear God, had
they come with the intent of helping to rebuild the
school?

Summer glanced around in search of Nicholas.
Unable to locate him in the press of people, she
hurried back into the house in time to discover him

removing his rifle from behind the kitchen door.

"And just what the blazes are y' gonna be doin' with that?" she cried.

"Stay out of this," he told her.

"If y' think I'm gonna allow y' out the door—"

"I think you have little say-so about it."

Planting her feet firmly apart, Summer raised her chin and grabbed hold of the door frame, blocking his way. "Over m' dead body. If y' go out that door and start shootin', yer goin' to ruin any chance o' rightin' the wrongs Tennyson has inflicted on us all. Perpetratin' war on another person is not the way t' make peace."

"Summer!" Nan's frantic voice called out behind her. "There's trouble coming over the hill."

A dozen panicked squeals filled the air. Nick's face turned dark, his eyes violent. Flinging herself at him, her heart racing with fear, Summer grabbed hold of the gun.

"Don't make me pay for m' mistake for the rest of m' life," she pleaded, and for an instant he appeared both stunned and confused.

"What the hell are you talking about?"

"If I hadn't pressed the Cockatoos into rebuildin' the school, this entire escalation of hostilities would never have happened. Their dreams wouldn't have been smashed again and I wouldn't have lost the baby. If one life is lost due to this insanity, how d'y' think I'll feel, Nicholas? I'll hold m'self to blame. Think o' the guilt y've experienced the last years because o' the mistake y' made in killin' that man in a duel. Would y' have me burdened with the same hell for the rest o' m' life?"

A crescendo of shouts rang out, punctuating the silence between Summer and Nick. Gripping the gun more tightly, she said firmly, "Give it t' me." She tugged on it again. "Please."

Slowly, he released it. Without speaking again, he pushed past her toward the door just as the first crash sounded from the yard. Summer ran after him.

From the porch, she watched bedlam unfold as a dozen Clansmen on horseback kicked the tables aside and drove their horses through the crowd. The cacophony of shrieks and screams tore at Summer's ears until she was forced to cover them with her hands. Again and again the Clansmen swarmed into the crowd, intent on destruction. The Cockatoo men, grabbing up anything that could be used as a weapon, did their best to defend the women and children, while the farmer families who had ventured to Sabre's station in hopes of offering peace and compromise scattered like frightened rabbits as they were besieged by both the irate Cockatoos and the Clan.

Reverend Martin stood amid the melee with his arms thrown wide. "For the love of God," he shouted. "This isn't right! Stop this! In the name of Jesus Christ, end this violence now . . ."

His voice was drowned out by Rebecca Sharkey's screams. On her hands and knees, she wailed for her mother as a horse reared and slashed the air, its hooves just above her head. Nicholas ran down the porch steps and swept her up into his arms just as Nan dashed from behind a wagon to meet him.

"Stop this!" Summer shouted, her despair mounting as the violence escalated.

It was then that a rider veered his horse away from the confusion and spurred the animal toward Summer.

She didn't notice him until it was too late. Having run down the steps with the intention of grabbing Wayne Johnson out of harm's way, she glanced up just as the hooded rider bore down on her, leaned low in the saddle, and snatched her from the steps. He hauled her up and threw her across the saddle, driving the wind from her lungs. The racket around them suddenly blurred into a distant drone, and darkness flirted with her consciousness. A confused moment passed before she realized what was happening. She was being kidnapped! As she struggled to look up, she saw the other horsemen break away from the stunned and frightened crowd and turn their animals toward the road. Then there was Nicholas, his face white and terrified, running behind them and shouting her name.

Chapter 21

Summer stared down the barrel of Roy Tennyson's rifle. Her knees felt like water. Her ribs were bruised from being hauled like a sack of grain all the way to Roy's house. A thousand reasons for her abduction had flown through her mind as her captor, Virgil McIlhenny, had driven his horse like a madman over the paddocks. She could think of only two reasons: revenge or ransom. Since Nicholas had no money, she assumed it was revenge. Feeling her heart roll over in fear, she met Tennyson's hard gaze and lifted her chin in a show of bravery she didn't feel.

"Well," she managed in a dry voice, "if yer goin' t' kill me, then get it over with."

He frowned, and the gun barrel wavered. She watched his finger play over the trigger. "I have no intention of killing you yet," he said finally.

"Then what the blazes—"

"My wife," he interrupted. He motioned toward the closed bedroom door. "In there," he instructed.

Making her legs move was a supreme effort. She

walked to the door, and with a cautious glance at the gun aimed at the back of her head, shoved the door open. She noted first the trembling maid hovering near the foot of the bed. Then she saw Blannie. The woman lay with her hands twisting the sheet beneath her; her face was red and sweating. She looked at Summer with intense pain and desperation.

For an instant Summer forgot Roy. "Saints!" she whispered. "What—"

"It's the baby," Roy said. "It won't come."

Summer hurried to the bed. Blannie, her eyes glazed and her body bowed with the excruciating pain, made a desperate grab for her hand. "Help me, Mrs. Sabre," Blannie said, then whimpered. "Please."

Summer's gaze went back to Roy as the sobering realization began to set in.

"I heard you have midwifery experience," he said. "So help her."

"I lived with a midwife," she replied, attempting to keep the panic from her voice. "I assisted Martha on many occasions, but I've never delivered a babe by m'self."

His thumb yanked back the hammer on the rifle.

Blannie cried out again, and her hold on Summer's hand became excruciating. Forgetting her hesitancy, Summer bent over the panting woman and smoothed the hair back from her hot brow.

"Please," Blannie beseeched Summer. "Don't let this baby die."

The words washed over Summer in an icy rush, the irony of the situation hitting her with full force. She had lost her own baby because of Roy's cruel vindictiveness; now she was expected to save his.

Her thoughts must have shown on her face; as she turned back to Roy, she watched his features go white, his jaw slacken. The gun barrel began to shake.

Summer took a long breath. "Make no mistake, Mr. Tennyson. I'm not helpin' y'. If y' were bogged up t' yer damn neck in quicksand, I wouldn't throw in a rod t' spare y'. But I'm a firm believer that women and children shouldn't be sacrificed t' men's moronic obsessions t' make war with one another, t' manipulate through power and greed."

She began rolling up the sleeves of her dress. "See if y' can find me some permanganate o' potash. Nicholas keeps his down at the sheep shed. Mix it five grains t' a pint of water. If y' can locate tincture of iodine, all the better."

Summer motioned at the frightened maid and ordered as calmly as possible, "I'll need a basin of hot water for washin' m' hands. Another for rinsin' m' hands. Another for receivin' the soiled swabs and another t' catch the placenta when it's expelled. Bring me as many clean towels as y' can find. Sterilize the sharpest needle y' have, as well as scissors and a knife. I need silk thread. And gauze. Scorch it by the fire so it's sterile. When that's done, I want y' t' clear away all the knick-knacks, ornaments, and bric-a-brac from the room. They're harbingers o' dust." She swept the room with a glance. "This carpet should've been taken up long ago, the pictures taken down, the floor scrubbed and the walls and ceilin' washed."

"We would've done," the maid said weakly, weeping, "but the babe is a month early."

"Right then." Summer moved again toward the bed, her eyes taking in Blannie's pain-contorted features. "Get the hot water, soap, and a nailbrush. Well, what are y' standin' there gapin' at? Hurry!" The girl scrambled. "And while yer at it, tell ever'-one that no one is t' come and go from this room without wearin' gauze over their nose and mouth."

Roy said in a husky voice: "If she dies, I'll destroy you and everything you hold dear, Mrs. Sabre."

Meeting his damning words with a tight smile, she replied, "Y' already have, Mr. Tennyson."

It didn't take Summer long to ascertain the reason for Blannie's trouble.

"It's a shoulder presentation," she told Roy quietly.

Still gripping the rifle, he demanded, "What does that mean?"

"It's comin' shoulder first."

He glanced toward the bed where Blannie lay panting and writhing. "It means she and the baby are goin' t' die if somethin' isn't done t' rectify the situation."

"What can be done?"

Summer shook her head. "I can try shiftin' the baby. Blannie is still holdin' her water, so it might be possible."

"Can you do it?"

"I watched Martha do it once. The trick is t' turn the babe t' a breech lie and deliver it feet first."

"Can she stand up to it?"

"What choice do we have? She's gonna die otherwise."

Roy stared at her with protuberant eyes.

"The babe's lodged," Summer explained. "The only way it can be born in that position is if y' take a knife and cut Blannie open."

His face turned ashen.

There came a racket from outside. Summer ran to the window just as a train of wagons topped the hill. The Johnsons came first, then the Sharkeys and the Thorndikes. A horseman appeared then, leaning low over the galloping animal's neck. *Nicholas!* Gripping the windowsill with trembling fingers, Summer struggled to calm her pounding heart.

Roy moved up behind her. They watched Tennyson's men hurry to surround the house, their rifles raised and prepared to shoot. Without turning, Summer said in as steady a voice as she could manage, "If one shot is fired, I'll let her die."

It seemed an eternal minute passed as Roy stood there with the gun barrel pressed to her back. She watched her husband rein in his sweating, frothing mount. With his hair flying and his white lawn shirt partially open down his chest, he resembled a fierce savage.

At last, Roy reached around her and shoved open the window. "Hold your fire!" he shouted.

Nick jumped from the horse and started for the house. Virgil and Roel blocked his way, but Nick shoved them aside; several other men ran to offer assistance.

"I'll shoot her, Sabre!" Roy yelled, and jabbed Summer with the rifle barrel for emphasis. Two men grabbed Nick's arms as he again attempted to approach the house. Then he saw Summer at the window, and fought all the harder.

Dan and Arnie leapt from their wagons. Fearing more trouble, Summer cried, "I'm deliverin' Blannie's baby! Ever'one stay calm. Please! Roy hasn't hurt me and he doesn't intend t'. He just wants me t' help his wife."

Roy slammed the window shut, muffling Nick's curses. Summer turned back to the bed.

Two hours later, Summer felt fairly certain that she had managed to move the baby into a breech position. The effort, however, had taken a severe toll on Blannie's energy. Weakened, she thrashed helplessly each time her body tensed. She babbled nonsensically, only occasionally coming out of her stupor enough to recognize Summer.

"I'm sorry," Blannie had whispered earlier, before she lost her strength, as Summer had mopped her hot brow with a cool cloth. "I'm sorry for what my husband has done to you, Mrs. Sabre."

"Hush now. Y' need t' save yer strength." The words were slightly muffled as Summer spoke through the gauze mask she had tied over her nose and mouth.

"I tried to talk to him. But men . . . they don't listen. They hear what they want to hear."

Summer smiled and nodded.

Blannie gripped her hand. "If you must make the choice between me and the baby, please, whatever you do, save the child. The baby is most important to Roy." Smiling weakly, she closed her eyes. "He doesn't love me, you see. Ours was an arranged marriage agreed to between him and my parents. All he cared about was having a son to pass on his wealth and power."

"Oh, I don't know," Summer replied. "He seems very concerned about yer welfare t' me."

Blannie's eyes opened. "Do you think so? No, no. You must be mistaken. " 'Tis the well-being of the baby that so concerns him. I'm sure of it." Her eyebrows drawing together in a frown, she looked at Summer and confessed breathlessly, "He's never once said he loves me. If I only believed that he held one spark of true affection for me, then perhaps . . ."

Holding Blannie's hand tightly in hers, Summer leaned closer. "Listen t' me, Blannie. For some reason, men have a hard time admittin' their feelins, even t' themselves. So they find other ways o' conveyin' their love. It might be by buyin' a rare gem, or sellin' one so he can buy y' a pretty dress. Or maybe he dances with y' when he hates t' dance. Or maybe he simply holds yer head and strokes yer hair when yer sick."

"Do you think so?" she asked hopefully.

"Aye," she had replied. "A friend once told me: actions speak louder than words. I was just too blazin' stubborn t' believe it. But I do now. And so should you."

Now, Blannie's eyes drifted closed, and Summer called for the maid, then stood aside as the girl hurried in with fresh hot water. Summer caught glimpses of Nicholas where he paced among the Cockatoos outside, occasionally stopping to stare at the house and speak to Dan and Arnie and Frank, who perched on the porch steps. There were others as well. Many of the faces belonged to the farmers who had attempted to join the Cockatoos' church service. Still others were strangers who stood with Tennyson's men. Summer realized then that if anything happened to either Blannie or herself, a confrontation between the two factions would be inevitable. And it would be bloody.

Taking a deep breath, she turned her attention back to Blannie.

The labor progressed.

With the maid's help, Summer shifted Blannie so that she lay crossways over the bed, her buttocks at the edge of the mattress and her feet supported by chairs on the side of the bed. Having placed a footstool on the floor between Blannie's knees, Summer sat on it and waited nervously, not sure what to expect next. She could remember Martha's maneuvering the baby this way and that as it was pressed out through the birth canal. There had been talk of trouble if the arms became extended over the head. The baby couldn't be delivered in such a way, and the time it took to maneuver the arms into place might well mean the child could asphyxiate if the head pressed for too long on the umbilical cord, cutting off its supply of blood.

An hour dragged by. Then another. Twilight set in, then darkness. Servants came with lanterns and then food, little of which Summer ate.

Occasionally shouts of discontent rose up from the crowd outside, and Summer's disquietude increased. Louder and louder, the protesters yelled.

Wilder and wilder, Blannie screamed.

Still sitting on the footstool between Blannie's spread knees, Summer put her face in her hands and rocked forward and back. She wasn't up to this. Just that morning she had been grieving for her own loss and the apparent ruination of her marriage. She felt weak. She wanted to climb into the bed with Roy Tennyson's wife and let someone comfort her as well.

Midnight. Summer spooned tepid tea through Blannie's dry lips, then she stared into the lantern flame and imagined that it was she with a baby trapped and unwilling to be born inside her.

At three o'clock in the morning, Blannie lost consciousness just before her membranes broke and spilled greenish fluid into the bowl on the floor. Blinking sleep from her eyes, Summer bathed Blannie's face in cold water long enough to drag her back to consciousness. Blannie's pain seemed to rouse her as the contractions grew more intense.

When the buttocks of the babe appeared, Summer thought hard what to do. She'd only been sixteen when she'd assisted Martha at the one breech birth at which she'd participated, and she distinctly recalled thinking she would much rather be skipping stones on Mill Pond than standing there watching some poor woman go through such excruciating pain.

Swallowing, her hands shaking, Summer gently disengaged the baby's feet. With the action, memory tumbled in on her, and she remembered Martha had refused to assist the birth by pulling on the child's feet. "It's got to come natural," Martha had explained, "or you risk displacing the arms."

Think, Summer told herself.

The umbilicus appeared. Summer grasped it and felt its pulsation. The throbbing was steady, thank the saints, which meant the baby's blood flow and oxygen had not yet been cut off.

Blannie was weeping with pain and exhaustion, but Summer talked to her quietly, calmly, instructing her each time the contractions started to bear down. "Push," she chanted. "Yer almost there. Almost finished."

"I can't! Please, please . . ." Blannie cried.

"Once more," Summer beseeched her.

"Go away and leave me alone. Do something, for God's sake!"

The shoulders slid out. Grasping the baby's feet with her right hand, Summer slipped her left up the child's back and hooked her first and second fingers over the shoulders, and gently pulled as Blannie bore down one last time. The baby, tense and wrinkled, was delivered into Summer's hands.

She quickly went about the process of clearing the child's nose and mouth, as she had helped Martha do scores of times. She held the baby up by the feet and lightly slapped its back. Once. Twice. *Please*, she prayed silently. *Please breathe. I pray t' Mary and all the lovin' saints in heaven and ever' fairy who ever thought t' dance on m' shoulder and bring me good luck, make this baby breathe!* ·

The baby wailed.

Blannie struggled to lift her head, and although her eyes were circled with the dark shadows of pain and fatigue, her face lit with relief. "We did it?" she asked weakly, hopefully.

"Aye." Summer smiled. "We did it."

Dawn light was just creeping through the windows when Summer opened the bedroom door and stepped into the hallway. Roy Tennyson stood in the shadows, shoulders slumped, looking disheveled and bone-weary. His gaze went directly to Summer's, then down, slowly, to the blanketed bundle in her arms.

Silence stretched between them.

Summer walked over to Roy and peeled down a corner of the blanket to expose the baby's face. "It's a boy," she informed him.

His body shuddered. "My wife?" he managed to gasp.

"Exhausted, but with great care I think she'll be fine." Gently, she shifted the baby into Roy's hesitant arms. "I think yer wife would like t' see y'," she told him.

He nodded, and with a cautious step, like one cradling a barrel of explosive powder in his arms, moved toward the bedroom door. There he stopped and faced her again. His face a mottled red and streaked with tears, he said in a tight voice, "I'm sorry for . . . everything."

Summer shrugged. "Then maybe y'll leave us all alone."

He lowered his eyes and turned from her again. Standing alone in the hallway, her body trembling with exhaustion and relief, Summer closed her burning eyes.

The maid stepped to the door. "Mrs. Tennyson wants to see you," she told Summer.

Mustering her energy, Summer returned to Blannie's room. Roy stood near the foot of the bed, cooing and clucking at the sleeping infant, while the maid busily collected the soiled towels and bowls into a corner of the overheated chamber.

Blannie raised her hand and offered it to Summer. "Shall I call you friend?" she asked.

"I hope so."

"How nice. I haven't had any true friends since I came to New Zealand. At least none near my own age." A tired smile touched her lips. "How can I thank you?"

"I—"

"I know," Blannie interrupted. "Margaret," she called to the maid. "Bring me my jewelry box."

The maid swiftly took up the ornately carved mahogany box and hurried to the bed. As Blannie eased open the lid, tinkling music filled the room.

Blannie lifted a ruby stickpin—Nicholas's ruby stickpin—and held it out to Summer. "Please take it. It belongs to you anyway. I should never have bought it that day, knowing how dear it was to you. I felt so guilty afterwards, I couldn't bring myself to wear it."

Smiling, Summer closed her fingers around the stone. "Nicholas will be so grateful," she said.

"No more grateful than I am to you, my friend."

After making certain Blannie's needs had been taken care of, Summer walked down the hallway and stepped through the front door.

The waiting crowd was huddled together for warmth, the farmers on one side, the Cockatoos on the other. They roused as she walked onto the porch steps and paused, her eyes searching each tense, weary face.

Nicholas appeared out of the shadows, his face a portrait of immense anguish and relief as he saw her. Slowly, she descended the steps and then ran into his arms.

"Take me home," she pleaded softly.

No one spoke as Nick helped her up onto the wagon seat. Then Frank ambled out of the crowd. "I reckon I'll be home in a while," he informed them as he puffed on his pipe. "I'm told Roy has been havin' some problems with his baler. Thought I'd have a look at it, if'n that's all right with ya."

"Fine," Nick replied, heaving himself up beside Summer. "I'll see you later." As he directed the wagon toward the horizon, Summer glanced back and saw the farmers and Cockatoos milling together and talking, as if testing the tenuous thread of common concern for a mother and unborn child that had linked them together throughout the long night. Then she saw Roy, with babe in arms, leave the house and offer the spectators a first glimpse of his son.

The ride home was long and cold. Summer huddled close to Nicholas and fought to stay awake. At last he convinced her to lay her head in his lap, and she immediately fell asleep for what felt like only a moment before he was shaking her.

Betsy barked from the front porch steps as Nicholas carried Summer to the house. Kicking open the door, he went directly to the bedroom and nestled her down in the sheets and pillows without removing her clothes. Then he climbed in beside her. Hugging her against him, he said:

"When you're feeling better, and you're rested, do you know what I want?"

She shook her head.

"To make another baby. I want to have a baby with you."

Summer raised her head. His eyes were warm and arousing, his mouth supple with desire.

"What's wrong with now?" she whispered.

Burying his fingers in her hair, he lowered his head over hers, and with his lips but a breath's touch away from hers, replied in a low voice, "I thought you'd never ask."

Chapter 22

Six months later

Nicholas was late again. The Johnsons had left. So had the Sharkeys. Jeff Mead had come and gone, claiming he would return to the schoolhouse first thing in the morning and finish the roof before the spring rains set in. That left Summer and Sean to collect the hammers and nails and sweep up the sawdust that had accumulated in little piles over the floor.

When Nicholas still hadn't shown up at half past four, Sean offered her a ride home on the rump of his horse. "If he's on his way, we'll meet him," he told her.

She nodded and glanced one last time at the horizon. Sean, having mounted his horse, offered her his hand and hefted her up behind him.

Summer couldn't think of a reason for Nicholas's tardiness. It wasn't like him. These last weeks he'd been particularly punctual about retrieving her from the school, although most of the time he accompanied her to the building and stayed to lend a hand in its construction. Even if he couldn't ride out himself to pick her up, he sent Frank.

Maybe a wagon wheel had broken. Or perhaps he had gotten involved with a difficult lambing. The saints only knew how often that was happening these days, since the lambing season was heavily upon them.

As they topped the hill and looked down on the paddock, Summer was swept back to the moment nearly a year ago, when Sean had escorted her to the front door of Mr. Sabre, Esquire. Who would've thought then that he and Nicholas would become such close friends. Or that she would find such happiness in the hovel she had once regarded with such disappointment.

But there it sat, surrounded by beds of bright flowers and lush fern baskets, its stovepipes puffing blue-gray smoke into the crisp air. Frank was cooking again.

"Looks like y've got company," Sean said, drawing Summer's attention to the wagon outside the house. It wasn't one she recognized.

"I wonder who it could be?"

"I s'pose we'll find out soon enough," Sean replied.

Within five minutes Summer was sliding off Sean's horse and bounding up the porch steps, calling back for Sean to come in and take a drink before he began the ride home. The front door stood open, as it often did to allow a cooling current of air to whip through the house. "Nicholas!" Summer called. "Frank?"

She rounded the threshold of the parlor and halted. A stranger stood on the opposite side of the petticoat-slippered crate. There was a look of curiosity, and some concern, reflected in his eyes as he regarded her. Then her gaze swung to Nicholas, who turned from the window and fixed her with a stare so full of icy fury that she felt frozen to the marrow of her bones.

His face was white. Never, even at the death of their baby, had she seen such shock and pain and outright loathing on his face.

She watched his lips move. The words were dry and sounded nothing like his voice.

"There is someone I want you to meet," he said.

His trembling hand motioned to a third figure across the room that she had somehow missed upon entering. Her eyes focused slowly on the woman— slowly, because her mind refused to acknowledge and accept what her eyes told her must be some cruel trick of her imagination.

"Hello, luv," Sophie Fairburn greeted her with a nervous smile.

"Summer. May I introduce you to my *wife*," came Nicholas's voice.

"I reckon this is a real surprise," her old friend said.

Oh, God. *Sophie!*

"But yer dead," Summer whispered, her thoughts spinning. She backed away. "I saw y' die." She shook her head. "I don't believe it. I . . ." She swallowed and forced her gaze back to Nicholas, who still stood with his back to the window, his fists shoved deeply into his pants pockets, as if by hiding them there he could bury his need to wrap his fingers around her throat.

Sophie droned on in a voice that sounded abnormally high-pitched. ". . . got me to hospital . . . touch and go for a while . . ."

Sabre's eyes glinted with madness.

"You ran off for nothing, luv. Pimbersham survived. He was bloody mad, of course, once he woke up three days later and remembered what happened. He even talked of havin' you arrested. But we made a deal. I told him I wouldn't press charges against him for tryin' to murder me if he forgot you pushed him down the stairs.

"Anyway, you can imagine Mr. MacFarland's surprise when he saw me at hospital—him recoverin' from a couple o' broken legs and me from my great bump on the head. After all, I was supposed to be on his ship bound for New Zealand. But we got to know each other and became friendly-like. Well, the truth of the matter is, we fell in love . . . He asked me to marry him . . . But then we remembered that legally I was married to Mr. Sabre. So we sailed here with the intention of gettin' an annulment so me and Jamie can marry . . ."

Nick moved so closely beside Summer she could feel the heat radiating from him, could detect the tremor of anger in his voice as he spoke near her ear.

"Lies. All lies. *Everything*. You built our relationship on a deliberate falsehood. And me, the world's biggest cynic, fell for all of it." His eyes were burning black pools of anger. "I trusted you and you betrayed me."

"I didn't—"

"I once gave you the opportunity to confess—"

"I was afraid o' losin' y'!"

He laughed sharply. "You didn't give a damn about me, Irish. You were desperate, is all. Afraid I'd send you back to London—*to jail*."

"Perhaps at first—"

"You're just like all the rest, Summer—a scheming little bitch who lies her way into a man's heart to get what she wants—"

"Stop it!" She covered her ears with her hands.

". . . all you wanted was a name and a house—"

"House?" she cried, turning on him in fury. "What woman in her right mind would want this bloody hovel? What woman would want t' spend her life wastin' away on some stinkin' sheep farm out in the middle o' nowhere?"

He looked as if she had slapped him. His face drained of color; his eyes—oh, his eyes—appeared glazed with shock and disbelief. She wanted to take the words back, to throw her arms around him as she had done in the past and assure him of her love and her desire to stay with him forever. He was angry and hurt, but if he would only give her a chance—

"Get out," he said. "Get out of my house, and get out of my life, Summer Whatever-your-name-is."

She attempted to right her shoulders and lift her chin. She tried to will away the sting in her eyes. But nothing worked. All she managed was to turn and walk out of the house without stumbling, paying little attention to Sean who had remained on the porch watching the horrible debacle as it unfolded. Sean spoke in a clipped undertone to Nicholas, who replied:

"She's yours if you want her. I certainly have no legal claim on her."

Then the door slammed shut.

Summer stood next to Sean's horse with her hands gripping the stirrup. She couldn't quite work up the strength to heft herself up into the saddle.

So Sean did it for her, as easily as Nicholas once had. Strange that only now did she realize the absolute pleasure she had obtained from so simple an action. The realization that he would never do it again drove through her like nails.

She had come full circle. Sean had brought her here on a sunny afternoon nearly a year ago. She'd been confronted by a belligerent, angry husband who wasn't her husband, and in a fury he had kicked her out on her backside and told her to get lost. She'd walked to the top of the hill and stood there, bewildered, in a cloud of wind-whipped dust, and looked down on his house, praying he would reconsider and beckon her back.

He hadn't.

He wouldn't this time, either.

Nicholas stood at the parlor window and gazed, unseeing, into the dark. Too much whisky. Too many memories. A lifetime of regret.

Coward.

Fool.

Idiot.

Imbecile.

Just a few of the names he'd been calling himself recently.

Closing his eyes, leaning his forehead against the window glass, Nicholas massaged the back of his tense neck. Once, the very idea of marriage had sent him into an apoplectic fit of rage. Now he was unmarried and felt set adrift on a sea without a rudder. His house was empty. His mind was empty. His heart was empty.

No. His heart *wasn't* empty. It was filled to bursting with anguish. The kind that ripped thin threads of fire down the insides of your throat. That took hold of your lungs and squeezed the air out and wouldn't allow it back in. That settled inside your stomach and had a grand old time heaving back anything you dared try to feed it.

He'd decided to ask Summer to come back. But then Dora had shown up with the news that Summer had moved to Christchurch. Jamie MacFarland had offered her a free berth on the *Tasmanian Devil* if she wished to return to London, and she had accepted. Just like that.

Well, why the hell not?

She wouldn't have come to New Zealand in the first place if she hadn't been running away from trouble. She certainly wouldn't have taken on another woman's identity and sold herself to some faceless sheep farmer who didn't love her.

Ah, God. Desperation could turn a person crazy.

It could make a boy in need of his father's love strike out and make the very object of his adulation look at him as if he were a monster. It could drive rational thought from an infatuated young man's head and make him murder in the name of honor.

It could force a frightened and homeless young girl to become something, or some*one*, she wasn't.

He understood now.

He'd understood then, too. Even as he'd sent Summer O'Neile out the door for a second time, he'd understood why she'd lied. But he'd been fighting with his own devils. The old confusions, angers, disappointments, fear.

Oh, yes, the fear. Like some great fanged mouth, it had opened up under his feet and he'd tumbled deeply, deeply, down into its rank black throat. She would leave him. She was not really his wife, therefore she could walk away from him at any time. And once she had learned that Pimbersham wasn't dead, there had been no reason for her to remain married to a man who could never offer her more than a hovel in the hills and a few thousand mangy sheep. As she'd reminded him—who wanted to spend the rest of his life 'wasting away on some stinking sheep farm out in the middle of nowhere'?

Had she meant it?

Come on, Sabre. You know she didn't mean it. You're still trying to deny that you fell in love with the girl. And

God forbid that Nicholas Sabre should admit that he's capable of loving.

Besides, if you confronted her now, you'd have to admit your feelings for her.

And she might reject you.

After all, she didn't even bother to try and see you again before she moved to Christchurch.

He checked his watch. The *Tasmanian Devil* was scheduled to sail at noon tomorrow. The timepiece reflected eleven-thirty at night. It normally took fifteen hours to make the journey from his station to Lyttleton. But that was in a wagon. On a horse the time would be considerably less . . . besides, Frank had taken the wagon . . .

Leaving the room at a run, he hurried to the barn and saddled the horse. Turning the horse toward the barn door, he spurred the animal out into the night.

Ten miles out of Lyttleton, Nick's horse came up lame. Thrush again. Nick stared down at the inflamed hoof and swore aloud. Then he tied the animal to a low tree limb and began to run.

The sun had risen hours ago. It beat hot on his shoulders. Sweat poured from his scalp and his armpits as he ran along the path, occasionally glancing hopefully over his shoulder for any sign of an approaching wagon.

He tripped once. Sprawled heavily over the ground, ripping a hole in the knee of his breeches and smearing dirt into the front of his shirt. He removed his suit coat and discarded it. He tried not to think about the blisters his boots were rubbing on his heels, but eventually the pain grew so intense he found himself hobbling.

His lungs hurt.

His legs ached.

His back felt as if someone had driven a steel rod up his spine.

Two miles out of town he came upon a field of vibrant, sweet-smelling pink flowers. He waded into them with the intention of collecting a bouquet for Summer, only to discover they were attached to briers with sharp thorns that gouged his hands and made them bleed. He plucked them anyway and took off down the track again, glancing at his watch with growing panic.

Almost noon.

Gritting his teeth, he picked up his pace until he was running flat-out. At last, he saw the ocean, then the docks. The wagons were all clustered near the wharf . . . There was the Johnsons' dray, as well as the Sharkeys'. The Meads'. O'Connell's . . . the traitor who had allowed Summer to ride off with him when he should have reasoned with her and explained that eventually her moronic husband—or whatever Nick was—would come to his senses and realize what an ass he'd made of himself . . . *again*. There was Nick's own wagon. Of course Frank would be here. His old heart had been broken by the idea of Summer's returning to England. The codger hadn't spoken two words to Nick since he'd sent Summer on her way a week ago. Certainly Frank would be here to see her off. He loved her like a father. Just as he loved Nick . . . *better* than a father.

The *Devil*'s full sails were just visible over the customhouse. They appeared to creep along the roofline at a snail's pace.

Oh, God. He was too late. The ship had set sail!

His heart slamming against the wall of his chest, Nick plowed through the crowd who stood elbow to elbow speaking in low voices, taking little notice as they turned startled faces toward him and exclaimed in surprise. Running down the pier beyond the customhouse, he watched the ship grow more distant as it cut through the lapping waves toward the open sea. Passengers lined the ship rails and peered back at him from hazy faces. Someone, a woman, raised her hand and waved a hanky in the air.

Was it Summer?

Perhaps he could swim for it!

Fool. *Idiot.* With the wind in her sails the *Devil* would outdistance him in a wink. Hopping up and down on one foot, he yanked his boot from the other and surveyed the distance from the pier to the water. With a long running jump, he just might—

"Wait!" someone shouted.

"Stop!" cried another.

Looking over his shoulder, he saw the crowd pressing closer, expressions of anxiety on their stunned faces. Then a slender, red-haired figure materialized from behind Arnold Sharkey and headed toward him down the pier, one hand gripping her valise, the other holding a porkpie hat with a fluttering feather on her head. Summer.

He couldn't breathe. He stood there slightly lopsided with one boot off, the other clasping the flowers hard in his hand. Sweat ran down his dusty face. A gust of sea-smelling wind made his eyes burn.

She stopped before him and put down the valise. High color burned in her cheeks. Her eyes were like purple pansies. She looked, he thought, just like she had the first day she'd shown up on his doorstep and blown his worthless existence totally to hell with her heart-melting smile.

"I thought you'd gone," he said.

Up went her chin. "I thought I'd give y' one more chance t' come t' yer senses," she told him.

He glanced down at his boot, feeling a glow begin in his heart, a fever heat that spiraled out to every point on his body. Then he remembered the flowers he was still clutching in one hand. The stems were crushed. The blooms were limp. He thrust them at her anyway.

Summer regarded them with pleasure as she eased them from his scratched and dirty fingers. For a moment she buried her nose in them, then turned twinkling eyes on him again. She stepped toward him, and offered her hand. "M' name is Summer Shannon O'Neile, sir. I'm most pleased to make yer acquaintance."

Dropping the boot, he took her hand in his, closed his fingers around it, and held it tightly. "Hello," he said. "Will you marry me?"

Her brows drew together in serious consideration. "Well, I don't know. This is fairly sudden. Perhaps I should get t' know y' better."

"My name is Nicholas Winston Sabre, Esquire, and . . . I'm very lonely up there without you, and . . ." He grinned. "I love you."

"Oh." Her face, lit by a smile, beamed up at him. "Oh, well . . . in that case."

Epilogue

One year later

The new house had been completed just in time. There were, however, a few remaining details to take care of. Like paint. Shutters for the windows. And a front door. Nick had splurged and bought a ready-made door that had been shipped all the way from America; it was far sturdier than those constructed from New Zealand timber. Frank, and that pirate Billy Malone, were supposedly delivering it up from Christchurch today, along with a four-poster bed—a surprise for Summer—which Nick had purchased at an auction. He was determined that their child would be born in the most comfortable bed money could buy.

Only the baby was coming *now*.

Clara came to the bedroom door and looked out. "Why don't you get a breath of fresh air?" she suggested. "It's going to be a while yet."

"How is she?"

"Doing very well. She's more worried about you than she is about herself."

Ben moved up to the doorless front threshold. "Frank and Malone have arrived," he said.

Clara smiled. "Go on. There's absolutely nothing you can do to help us, Nicky. We'll call if we need you."

With some reluctance, Nick left the house, paying little attention to the dray burdened by lumber and furniture crawling down the track. His eyes were fixed upon the squealing children dashing here and there over his garden, and the parents who were trying their absolute best to keep them in line. As usual, tables had been set up in the green grass and were laden with food. Groups of men stood with their heads together as they discussed plans for constructing the porch that would run around three sides of Nick's house.

Then Nick found Rebecca Sharkey, on her hands and knees and buried up to her frilly-petticoated bottom in a thatch of blazing red foxglove near the end of the path that led to the house. Sliding his hands into his pockets, Nick walked over to her and stood there for a long time while the plants swayed this way and that as the little girl buried herself deeper into the flowers. She burrowed right into his boots.

"Ooops," came her little voice. Then her head, topped with lush brown curls, tipped back and she stared, round-eyed, up the length of him.

Bending down on one knee, Nicholas plucked a weed from her hair. "What are you doing in here, Rebecca?"

"Looking for fairies, of course. Summer told me they live here."

"Did she?"

She nodded. "She says she comes out here every

morning, and they invite her to drink tea made out of dew." Thrusting her little face up to his, she said, "It's magic dew. One taste and all yer dreams come true. Want a lick?"

"Don't tell me you have a pot already brewed down there."

The little girl snapped a foxglove stalk in two and handed the flower to him. The silken red petal was beaded with moisture. "Go on," she told him. "Make a wish and drink the dew."

Smiling, Nick turned the blossom this way and that, watching the sun reflect from the rich liquid drops like miniature rainbows. "What should I wish for?" he wondered aloud, his eyebrows drawing together. "I have everything I want. A beautiful wife. A child on the way. A successful station. A great many very nice friends..." He tweaked the giggling girl on the nose.

"But surely there's something," she said.

"Well..." He didn't dare wish it. It was futile, really. He'd buried the need to make peace with his father, and all the pain that came with it, a very long time ago. No point in resurrecting it now...

"Go on," her small voice encouraged him.

Gently, he took the shimmering bead of water on his fingertip, closed his eyes, and touched it to his tongue.

Giving Rebecca a wink, Nick tucked the stem of the foxglove through the slit in his coat lapel and turned toward Billy Malone's dray just as he brought it to a halt.

Frank leapt to the ground and ambled his way. He regarded Nick for a long moment before handing him a letter.

Nick stared down at his father's handwriting.

His trembling hands clumsily tore the letter open, and his stinging eyes focused on the salutation:

Nicholas, my dear son . . .

The pains were steady and intense. Summer panted and stared at the ceiling, not paying much mind to Clara and Dora's attempts to comfort and encourage her. In fact, she was becoming quite irritated by them. She would be sure to remind herself what a blazing pain in the butt such encouragement was the next time she helped deliver a baby.

Turning her head, she discovered Nicholas standing at the door. Saints, he looked as bad, if not worse, than she did.

"May I see my wife alone, please?" came his heavy voice.

"But—"

"A moment. Please."

Blinking sweat from her eyes, Summer watched her two friends exit the room in a hurry. "Saints!" she cried. "Don't y' be goin' far!"

Nick stepped into the room and closed the door behind him. His eyes were like black glass. Pushing up on her elbows, she stared at him hard. "What have I done now?" she asked snappishly. "Y' don't look at me that way unless I've piqued y' about somethin'."

He moved toward her.

"I didn't do it," she told him. "Whatever it is, I didn't do it."

Stopping at the edge of the bed, his hands in his pockets, he searched her face. "I thought we weren't going to have any more secrets between us," he said, his voice sounding odd.

Gripping the sheets in her hands, she panted through her clenched teeth.

Nick pulled a chair up by the bed and eased into it. He reached into his coat pocket, withdrew an envelope, and pressed it into her hand. He clasped it hard. "That's a letter from my father," he said.

"Oh?" she replied, momentarily forgetting her pain.

"He says that you wrote him and told him about the baby, and about what a fine man I'd become. You suggested that such a distinguished gentleman as the Earl of Chesterfield could surely look into his heart one last time and forgive his son for his mistakes."

"Oh."

She studied her husband's face, and saw a smile begin, first in his eyes that had gone blurry with the force of his emotion, then in the slight curving of his wonderful mouth. Bending near, he said:

"Thank you."

"Yer not mad?"

"No." He shook his head. "How could I be angry?"

She smiled back. Or tried to. The result was a little weak, considering she was in the throes of another contraction.

Tenderly brushing a tendril of hair from her sweat-moistened brow, he kissed her cheek. "He wants me—us—to go home, Summer."

"T' England?" He nodded, and she began, "But—"

"He beseeched the courts on my behalf. They pardoned me. I'm a free man."

"A free man," she repeated, never taking her eyes from his. "And we can leave New Zealand and go back t' England . . ."

"If that's what you want."

She glanced about the room, redolent with the smell of freshly cut kauri pine from the North Island.

"It ain't exactly a castle," Nick said, throwing open the doors of her mind, allowing the memories of their stormy beginning to tumble in. "If we go back to England, I can give you a castle. Would you like that, do you think?"

Summer turned her face back to his. "Anywhere I live with y' is a castle, m' lord. I . . . think I kinda like it here."

"I hoped you'd say that. I think our children will grow up strong and happy and healthy here."

Sinking back against the pillow, Summer laughed. "And speakin' o' children . . . I think y'd better get Clara. Our son is about t' be born."

"Son?"

"Aye. The babe is gonna be a boy, and he's gonna look just like his handsome father."

"How do you know that?"

With a sly smile, Summer touched her husband's cheek. "Why, a little fairy told me, that's how."

"I love you, Summer."

Closing her eyes, basking in the music of the words, Summer sighed. "Tell me again," she said.

"I love you."

"Again."

"I love you. I love you . . . I love you."

And he meant it.